HER DYING MIND

A British Murder Mystery

THE WILD FENS MURDER MYSTERIES

JACK CARTWRIGHT

HER DYING MIND

JACK CARTWRIGHT

The creaky floorboard had been on the list of things to fix before the new carpet had been put down – the list she had written, which Alex hadn't even looked at. Instead, he'd stuffed it into his gilet pocket. It was probably still there in the wardrobe. She remembered enough of the slip of paper to see it in her mind's eye. At the very top was the creaky floorboard. The one that, yet again, groaned above her head like the bones of an old man.

But Alex had been gone for years now. He still showed up, of course, when Alice needed him the most. But Alice put those fleeting visits down to her mind, or her heart, or both. Something she couldn't explain. It was just one of those things that happened. One of those things the mind does of its own accord.

One of those things Alice wished she could switch off.

One day, she would think of Alex and be certain he was gone. She supposed that would be the day she could call herself healed.

But not today. Tomorrow, she would remember today as the time she had thought of him last, which would incite one of those wonderful memories, such as the day he had proposed. And so, the cycle of denial would continue.

Grief was irrepressible, much like the creaking floorboard

above her. The one that caused her heart to hammer inside her chest.

Frozen to the spot, she clung to the front door, unsure if she should run out into the lane. Perhaps George was awake; he was an early riser. He'd known Alex, too. He wouldn't judge her for being silly.

The floor above creaked in response.

She wasn't being silly though. Was she? Floorboards don't creak of their own accord. She opened her mouth to call out but found her throat dry, and the idea of coughing to clear it absolutely terrified her.

But she couldn't very well just wait there. What if whoever it was, found her? She'd heard about people who disturbed intruders and burglars – those who would do anything not to work for a living. Those who would do anything not to be caught by the police. Not that the police would do much.

She wished she carried her telephone with her. Alex used to tell her to keep it in her bag. To keep it switched on in case he ever needed to call her. But of course, that was one of those things she hadn't done simply because he'd told her to do it. Oh, the joys of marriage and the foibles that make them unique, rememberable, for a number of reasons – some good, some not so much.

A thump from above was loud and clear. Not a groan or a creak. Not the noise of that board at the end of her bed, the bed they had shared for more than four decades, gently taking the weight of a person. It had been a thump. She was sure.

Alex would have gone upstairs. He wouldn't have frozen to the spot like a coward. That was half his problem. He never knew when to back down. Never knew when to just shut up and walk away.

She waited. The next time she heard the floorboard creak, she would go up. Or just call out? If somebody came down the stairs, she could get out through the front door.

Maybe it was time to get the floorboard fixed. Maybe there was nobody even up there. Maybe Alex was trying to send her a message from the other side.

She'd never believed in all that, but others did. Others swore they'd seen or heard, even felt, a presence. And not just one or two. Mary from Kirby Road had told them all once, she remembered now. They had been at Leslie McMillan's wake, which Alex had found to be in poor taste. But Mary had told them nonetheless, about how she'd been sitting on the edge of her bed, pulling on her slippers, when she'd felt a cool breath of air wash over her, despite the heating being on. Alex had said she was talking rubbish, of course. Mary never had the heating on.

"This is ridiculous," she whispered to herself, finding moisture in her throat where only moments before there had been none. Had it been moments? How long had she been standing there?

She peered up the stairs, not knowing what she might see. But she peered, nonetheless.

"Hello?" she said, her heard pounding in her chest. "Is anybody there?"

It was then that she felt the cool breath of air Mary had spoken of. It breezed down the stairs, seeming to caress the fine down on her nape, not hard like a gust of wind, but gentle like somebody had passed close by her.

But nobody had.

The temperature had dropped too. Of that she was certain. So much so that goosebumps rose on her arm and the tiny hairs rose like a summer breeze through wild grass. Suddenly, Mary from Kirkby Road's whimsical anecdote came to light. She peered up the stairs once more.

"Alex? Alex, is that you, dear?"

No answer came, and that breath of air had gone, leaving the stuffy summer heat to take its place.

"I'm coming up," she said, albeit far quieter than before.

She took a single, tentative step onto the first stair, gripping

the banister with her right hand and clutching her blouse buttons with her left. Gone were the days when she could bound up the stairs. That joy was a distant memory. Rarely could she even walk up them these days. Instead, she took them one at a time, as if each step was an individual challenge. There were thirteen individual challenges, and by the time she had accomplished seven of them, her heart pounded with fear and trepidation. It reminded her of that man on the television – the rugby player who ran seven marathons in seven days for his friend with motor neurones. He was a kind soul, selfless and unique. Not many people could run like that. And even fewer would choose to.

Once the eleventh of her challenges was complete, she gripped the banister and leaned to see into the front bedroom. The door was ajar. It was never ajar. It was either open or closed but never ajar. That had been one of Alex's bugbears – one of many, but one it was – and if she put her mind to it, she could recall the hundreds, no thousands, of times she had been to spend a penny during the advertisements and not closed the lounge door fully on her return.

"Door," he would say, without looking away from the television or his crossword.

She stared at the door now, adamant that she hadn't left it like that. Closing doors had been ingrained into her.

"Alex, dear?" she said, and that rush of cold washed over her once more, stronger now. "Alex? Alex, are you there?"

Twelve and thirteen were accomplished in much the same manner she imagined that kind soul had run his last marathon. She was on her hands and knees, trembling now, not from the cold, but from sheer terror.

She was breathless too. Not from the exertion, but something else. It was as if somebody was crushing her chest so hard that tiny lights danced in her eyes.

The landing was small. There was just enough space for the tall vase of dried pampas grass Henry had bought her for Moth-

er's Day many moons ago. She crawled past it, thinking not of that day but of the door. The door that should have been fully closed. And if not fully closed then fully open.

Not ajar. She never left it ajar, even if it was just a few inches.

She stopped outside the door, her eyes closed, imagining that Alex was inside – or hoping, she couldn't tell which. That was one of the things they said would happen. The doctor had said so, the Asian chap. Alex hadn't liked him, but she had. He'd had a good bedside manner and he was thorough. Not like the English ones who couldn't be bothered to get out of bed in the mornings.

Doctor Samson. That had been his name.

He had said that her imagination would run wild. And he'd been right. It *was* running wild. She could see Alex now, sitting on the edge of the bed pulling his socks on the way he used to. It was a far better image than the other one, the one where a burglar saw her crawl into the room and went for her. Probably a druggie. They were all druggies, weren't they? Alex had said so. He said they robbed people on their own, like her. They stole whatever they could get their hands on, then sold it to pay for drugs.

Well, they were welcome to it. She had no use for anything anymore, nothing material anyway.

"Is anybody there?" she said. "I'm going to open the door. You can have whatever it is you want."

Nobody replied.

She reached out for the door. How many times had Alex painted it? A dozen or so in the thirty years they had lived there?

"I'm coming in now," she said and took a deep breath.

If it was a burglar, and if he did go for her, then maybe it would be a blessing. Maybe then she could be with Alex again?

Maybe that was it. Maybe that was what she had felt that cool breath. Maybe that was Alex calling her upstairs so they could be together.

She gave the door a shove, expecting to see...someone. A man, probably, wearing a tracksuit like the kids do these days. They

wore suits back in her day, but these days, they all walked around with their hands in their underpants.

The door hit something and then shuddered back to where it had been.

Ajar.

She stared at the door, trying hard to remember what could be behind it. But the room was tidy. She always left it tidy. Rarely a day passed that she even ventured downstairs without making the bed, washing and dressing, and leaving the upstairs in a presentable state. And since they'd had the downstairs loo, there were days when she didn't go up at all, except for bedtime.

She gave the door another shove. Again, it bounced back.

"Is somebody there?" she said, this time finding the strength to climb to her feet, using the door handle for support.

Maybe she should call for help? Maybe George would be awake by now?

But if it was Alex calling for her, then he wouldn't want her to go back. She had come too far. She leaned on the wood, placing her face against the twelve layers of paint and listening for a sign. Gently, she pushed the door until it met with resistance.

"Is that you, dear?" she said softly.

But nobody replied.

Then she shoved hard, as hard as she could, as hard as her little frame allowed, until those varicose veins on her hands seemed to bulge with the effort.

The temperature dropped once more. It was colder now. Cold like she had opened the refrigerator.

Slowly, she turned and put her back against the door, not to go and fetch George but to catch her breath. She slid down the door until she was sitting on the carpet, blinking away those tiny, dancing lights and feeling the crush on her chest.

And that was where she stayed, hugging her knees to her chest like she was fifteen years old again. Fifteen years old, she thought. Alex had been twenty. They had courted for three long

years, as her father had been adamant that she should be eighteen before they wed.

It was a lifetime ago. Yet she could still smell him, that undeniable scent of Imperial Leather soap after he'd spent the day working under the sun and scrubbed himself clean before calling on her, cap in hand.

Those were the days, she thought, before speaking aloud for the last time.

"It is you, isn't it?" she said quietly, not expecting a reply. She smiled to herself and let her head rest on the wood. "It is you. I know it is."

CHAPTER ONE

It was the first Monday morning that Freya Bloom had woken up in her own house since making the move to rural Lincolnshire. From the familiar yet confined space of the motorhome she had once adored to a rented cottage on a friend's farm, she had finally made it. The journey symbolised the life she had created, and the one she had left behind in London. It was the final stepping stone towards independence, security, and all those nice-to-haves depicted in Maslow's Theory of Human Motivation.

Sure, the nice furniture she had bought was still at least ten weeks away from being delivered and was likely in a metal container on a ship bound from the darkest depths of Asia to somewhere in Europe. But it was coming. In the meantime, she could make do with the few items she had purchased second-hand as a means to get by. At least the expensive mattress, which she had bought new, had been delivered in under a week.

Regardless of the house being less than perfect just yet, it *was* her place, and to open her eyes in the morning to stare at her own ceiling felt tremendous. A crack in the plaster ran in a straight line from the window to the opposite wall. But it was her crack,

just like the cobwebs that seemed to have appeared almost overnight were hers.

She hadn't skimped on bedsheets either. The thin summer duvet slid from her body when she stretched, and the four plush, goose-down pillows almost swallowed her head.

She couldn't help but smile. Things were finally going her way.

Habitually, Freya reached for her phone, which was charging on the floor beside the mattress. There were no missed calls or messages, meaning there was no real urgency. She could saunter downstairs, savour a nice coffee, and have a slow morning.

Finding satin pyjamas cooler in the sticky summer months, she slid from the sheets as if she had been coated in olive oil, and then peered through the curtains to the little village green opposite the cottage. A mother duck ambled across the little road followed by half a dozen or so clumsy ducklings. But aside from that, there was no movement at all.

The view was terrific. It wasn't a dramatic landscape nor was it of rolling hills. All she could see through her bedroom window was the village green with the beck running through it, and beyond that, the village hall and the church. It was her view, just like the crack in the ceiling, and she adored it.

Remaining barefoot, she grabbed her phone, checked her reflection in the little mirror on the wall, and then reached for the door handle, which came away in her hand, leaving the door well and truly closed.

It took a moment for her to work out what had happened. She found herself staring at the door, and then the brass handle in her grip.

"Bugger," she said aloud.

A small, square rod was left protruding from the wood, and on closer inspection of the handle, she found an accommodating square slot on the reverse side. Carefully, she placed the handle onto the square rod, aligning it with care until she felt it click into place, and then she shoved it hard.

On the far side of the door, in her empty hallway, she heard the dull thud of the other door handle hitting the carpet, followed shortly by a metallic sound as the square rod followed.

"Bugger," she said again.

Not one to be defeated, Freya peered into the hole in the wood and spied the square slot in which the rod would have fitted. Presumably, all she had to do was find a way to turn the square slot. She dropped to her knees, finding that if she pressed her face into the carpet, she could just make out the rod and the other handle on the other side of the door. But the space beneath the door was too narrow even for her slender fingers.

She looked around the room and even contemplated ripping the window latch from the wood. But she thought better of it when her handbag caught her eye.

In the little makeup bag that she kept in her purse, she remembered the pack of nail files she had bought on a whim. They had been on offer at the checkout when she had been in town two days ago. She snatched them from her makeup bag, tossed the bag onto her mattress, and studied the little pack with wonder. They were lollipop-sized and although individually weren't strong enough for the job, together they formed a similar shape to the rod she had pushed through the door.

They slotted into the door almost perfectly, which meant that the brass handle also slotted onto them. This time, she did so with care, and this time, the door opened with ease.

"Ha," Freya said with a smile, as she strode from the room. She leaned into the second bedroom, which she had designated as her dressing room, and tossed them onto the little makeshift dressing table.

Enthused by her own ingenuity, she descended the stairs into her lounge. But she didn't see the old and worn, second-hand furniture; she saw her new furniture in her mind's eye. She stepped into the kitchen and pulled the jar of fresh coffee beans

from the cupboard. It took a few moments to fill the bean grinder, and then, once she'd replaced the jar, she hit the button for the grinder to do its thing. There was absolutely nothing like freshly-ground beans in the morning, and this particular batch, which she adored, was an Ethiopian bean she'd found on the internet.

The grinder was silent, so she depressed the button once more, harder this time.

Still nothing.

"Bugger," she said.

She shook the device a few times, thinking that a wire may have been loose. But still nothing. It was the first time she had used it in her new house, so she changed the plug to a different outlet.

Still nothing.

She shook the device again, this time with a little more vigour, which caused the lid to pop off and her precious beans to scatter across the terracotta-tiled floor.

"Oh please," she said, leaning on the kitchen counter, closing her eyes, and taking a deep breath. But, determined not to let the coffee disaster break her spirit, she strode back up the stairs and into the bathroom. She leaned into the shower, turned the dial on to hot, and let the water run while she undressed.

Her dressing room was a luxury Freya never thought she would have. With her clothes, makeup, and shoes all in one place, her bedroom could remain clutter-free. She slipped from her pyjamas, folding them neatly on an old, pine chair, then grabbed one of the new towels she had bought. It was large, soft, and luxurious, exactly how a towel should be.

Before showering, she checked her phone again to make sure nobody had called or messaged. But when she picked it up she noticed that, not only had nobody called or messaged, but that the damn thing hadn't charged.

She plugged it back into the charger, then stepped through to

the bathroom and into the shower, only to be doused in ice-cold water.

The shock took her breath away, and it took a few moments for Freya to gather her senses enough to turn the shower head away. Shivering, she turned the dial, testing the water with her free hand. But whichever way she turned it, the water remained the same temperature – Baltic.

It was a test. That's what it was. A test of her resolve. And she wouldn't give in. No way would she let a few minor setbacks ruin the day she'd been waiting for.

She could shower at work. They had showers there. It wasn't ideal, but she could suffer it for one day. In a few minutes, she had pulled on a comfy jogging suit and packed a bag with her clothes and makeup, slightly annoyed at having to disarray the dressing table she had spent so long arranging. On her way downstairs, she stopped to grab her phone, which still hadn't charged. It had only one bar of power remaining. So she stuffed the charger into her bag, then made her way downstairs with the weight of every mishap nudging her patience to its limit.

She found her keys hanging beside the front door, a spot she knew, more than anyone, not to leave them – as burglars could use the letterbox for a quick grab – then pulled open the front door, only to be greeted by two uniformed police officers walking up her garden path.

"Yes?" she snapped at them.

"Good morning," one of them said, a constable who Freya didn't recognise. He pointed at her Range Rover, which aside from her little cottage was her pride and joy. "Are you the owner of that car?"

"Yes," she said. "Why?"

"I'm afraid you're going to need to come with us," he replied. "That vehicle has reportedly been involved in an accident."

"Oh, for God's sake. Is this some kind of joke?"

"I'm afraid not, ma'am."

"An accident?" she said, folding her arms. "There must be a mistake. When was this accident supposed to have occurred?"

"This morning. Early hours," he replied and gestured for Freya to lock her front door. He was average and non-descript in almost every way, with clipped hair, a clean-shaven face, and no visible identifiers of any kind, not that Freya could see anyway, besides his large, brown eyes. "I'm afraid you're going to need to come with us. Can we just confirm your name please, to make sure you are indeed the owner?"

"My name?"

"Yes, miss," he replied. "I'm afraid so."

He was polite enough, but there was a pious air about him that Freya was beginning to dislike.

"Freya Bloom," she replied, which his partner, far younger, red-haired, and pale-skinned, made note of. "Detective Chief Inspector Freya Bloom."

CHAPTER TWO

For a rural town, Navenby offered everything Tammy Plant needed. Anything it lacked could be found either in the surrounding villages or in the city of Lincoln only a fifteen-minute drive away. But city life wasn't for her. She'd tried it once during her university years and hated the noise, the lack of privacy, and the anonymity. Her walk along Navenby High Street from her small house to her small salon usually gave Tammy ample opportunity to bump into a few locals, most of whom knew her by name, and that usually brightened her morning.

There were few amenities a city could offer that Navenby couldn't. One of them was a good cup of coffee in the morning – a proper latte or cappuccino. Instead, she had to make do with a home brew which she carried to work in a thermos mug.

After checking the back door was locked, she grabbed her bag from the kitchen worktop, collected her mug, and then left by the front door, pulling it closed behind her and taking a moment to give it a shove to double-check.

The end of summer was still warm, but cloud cover provided a much-needed cool breeze. It seemed like the world was taking a

breath after the relentless heat and humidity. She passed lawns that had been browned by the sun and lack of rain and hanging baskets displayed proudly beside her neighbours' front doors, where they spilled over in oranges, blues, violets, and reds. At least two of them still dripped from their morning drink, yet the lawns they hung over were withered and parched.

She'd heard a man on the TV say once that watering a lawn in a drought was fruitless. Better to keep plants and flowers alive as grass would usually be revived by the eventual and inevitable rain, whilst plants would die and be gone forever.

It all seemed a little callous, in Tammy's opinion. She was glad that all she had to take care of was a few pots in her tiny rear garden, which she usually kept alive with the waste water from washing up. Grey water, the man on the TV had called it, and she felt good to be doing something positively sustainable.

At the end of the road, she turned into the high street, which was also the main road from Lincoln to Sleaford. On a Monday morning, it tended to be quite busy with through traffic. Nonetheless, there were always familiar faces to smile at, wave to, and even greet when they were close enough.

One of the regular faces she saw on her journey belonged to a man in a white van, who wore shorts whatever the weather. He pulled up on the far side of the road, as usual, and when he saw her gave a mock salute by way of a greeting. She smiled back and watched him as he opened the rear doors of his van, rummaged through a pile of boxes, and selected the one he was looking for – a long, oblong box, light enough for him to carry in one hand. He must have felt her gaze, as he gave another glance as he closed his doors. Then, just as he turned to walk towards the florist shop, he narrowly avoided bumping into a man coming the other way. The other man barely broke step, rushing towards the bus stop a hundred yards away, and the driver looked back at Tammy wearing a sheepish expression that made her laugh out loud.

On Tammy's side of the road, coming her way, was an elderly gentleman who she saw at least three times every single day. He would walk the length of the high street all the way to the pub, then turn around and walk back the way he came. Having never said anything to him other than a polite, "Good morning," Tammy assumed it was part of his exercise routine. Good luck to him. Some days he looked as if he was in a serious amount of pain, but never did he stop before he reached the pub.

Behind him, a woman pushed a pram while guiding a toddler on a little pushbike. She wore the blue RAF uniform, which was quite common, and seemed unfazed as she corrected the wayward toddler's poor steering. Tammy had watched the young lad grow. She remembered when that same lady had pushed him along that same road in that same pram. When he'd learned to walk, his mother would escort him to the nursery at the far end of the village. Now he had a younger brother or sister, maybe Tammy would see him or her riding a little bike, one day, while the young boy, who would be much older then, might wear a little school uniform.

The lady smiled politely as they passed. Tammy overheard the boy ask if Daddy was coming home today.

"No," the mother said. "Daddy will be home this weekend. So, we need to make it extra special."

"Why?" the boy asked, more like a question of habit than inquisitiveness.

"Because he has to work," Tammy heard his mother say, just as they slipped out of earshot.

Tammy's salon was the last shop on the high street. It was half the width of most of the others but held ample space for two hairdressing chairs, two seats for people waiting, and a small reception, behind which was a tiny kitchenette and a washroom.

She was fumbling for her keys in her bag, careful not to spill her coffee, when somebody called out from behind.

"Hey up, Tammy," they said.

She turned to catch the local locksmith, Peter Talbot, riding past on his bike.

"Morning, Pete," she called out, as she found her keys.

"It's much cooler today," he called back.

"Yes," she said, as he rode out of earshot, leaving her to speak to herself. "Yes, it is."

Inside her salon, Tammy hung her bag on the kitchen door's hook, filled the kettle for her clients, and then set about making sure everything was shipshape.

It was nine-fifteen when she'd finished wiping down the chairs and the surfaces, and still nobody had arrived. She put the radio on, just as she did every day. She used to spend hours making playlists, but seeing as her clientele were predominantly mature women, her choice of music never really struck a chord. So she reverted to BBC Radio Lincolnshire, which offered her the chance to start conversations. In her experience, nobody had more to say on the state of current affairs than the elderly, and she enjoyed listening to their opinions.

She checked her diary, noting that the first appointment was Alice, an elderly lady from the village who came like clockwork every single month.

But Alice was never late.

She sat down in one of the waiting chairs and picked at the Tupperware box of grapes she had brought to see her through until lunch. But one grape became two, then three, and she could see herself demolishing them all. So, she stood, set them down on the counter, and stepped through the front door, slipping the latch on to avoid locking herself out.

She walked the few steps to the next shop, a small antiques owned by Harry Doughty. A bell sang out when she opened the door, and he looked up from his desk, removing his glasses and offering her a welcome smile.

"Now then, Tammy," he said, a typical Lincolnshire greeting. "What do you need? Milk?"

He was a kind man, small in stature but big in personality. They had bonded over the years, keeping an eye on each other's shops while one or the other walked down to the Co-op for some milk.

"No," she said. "No, nothing like that. I was wondering if you'd seen Alice this morning."

"Alice?" he said. "Alice who?"

Tammy realised that while her business served the local community, people would come for miles to peruse his wares, so he wouldn't be as familiar with the locals.

"Sorry," she said. "A local woman. Lovely lady. I don't suppose anybody was waiting outside my shop when you opened up, were they?"

"I didn't see anybody," he replied. "But it's twenty past nine on a Monday morning. I expect she'll be here soon."

"Yes," Tammy replied. "Yes, you're probably right. I've got a ten o'clock though and I was hoping not to run over. It's so hard to get back on schedule when somebody is late."

"Sorry, duck," he said, offering her a sympathetic smile. He donned his glasses again and prepared to carry on with his work.

"No bother," she replied and turned to leave. She opened the door, feeling a sense of unease in the pit of her stomach. "I don't suppose you could keep an eye out for a few minutes, could you?"

"So, you do need milk?" he said, removing his glasses again.

"No, I thought I'd just pop round to her house. She's only in North Lane, so I'd be quick."

"Offering home visits now, are you?"

"No, but she's never late. I've been doing her hair for three years and she's never missed an appointment."

He set his pen down and appraised her as a father might while considering some pearl of wisdom to impart.

"Go on, love," he said and raised his index finger at her. "But see to it she tips you well for going out of your way. Here, it isn't that mad one, is it? You know, the one they all talk about? The

one who walks up the high street having a full-blown conversation with herself?"

"She's not mad," Tammy replied with a gentle laugh, sensing she was convincing nobody. "And even if she is, I think she's lovely."

CHAPTER THREE

From his desk at the back of the incident room, newly promoted Detective Inspector Ben Savage sat at his desk appraising the team who, for a Monday morning, were in high spirits. He watched as they taunted each other, made fun of DC Cruz, and lobbed balled-up pieces of paper across the room, before at last the topic of conversation became a little more serious.

"So?" Gillespie said conspiratorially. He leaned forward in his seat, checking the door to make sure nobody was peering through the windows. "Where do you think she is?"

"The boss?" Nillson asked with a shrug. "I don't know. Maybe she hit traffic. Her new house is a bit further out now, isn't it?"

"It's in Dunston," Ben said quietly. "Another ten minutes, max."

"It's half past nine," Gillespie said. "She's over an hour late."

"I've never known her to be late," Cruz said. He was the youngest and smallest member of the team, the butt of most jokes, and yet, surprisingly, he was without doubt the most resilient. "You don't think she's had an accident, do you?"

"God help the man who crashes into her," Gillespie said,

letting his thick Glaswegian loose to add fervour to the statement. "Now that's a bad start to the week."

"Are we all up to date on paperwork?" Ben asked.

"Just finishing off," Chapman called out. She was old for her
years and rarely left her seat, save for when she had to make a tea
or 'spend a penny' as she put it. Despite it being the end of
summer, Denise Chapman still wore a knitted cardigan over a
pretty blouse and kept her broad glasses perched on the end of
her nose, chained to her neck by a lanyard of colourful beads.

"We're done," Nillson said.

"Aye," Gillespie added. "We're all caught up."

"No, we're not," Cruz said, appearing confused. "You haven't
even touched that report from last Friday."

Gillespie closed his eyes and looked as if he was doing his best
to refrain from letting loose more of his native tongue, and with
far more fervour than ever before. He sucked in a deep breath.

"Jim?" Ben said.

"Aye, well, we've a few wee bits and pieces to do. Crossing the
i's and dotting the t's and all that, you know?"

"Crossing the i's?" Cruz said. "You haven't even started it. And
you don't cross i's, you dot them, and cross the t's."

"Not when your handwriting is as bad as yours, Gabby," Gillespie told him. "It's like some clever sod gave a wee chimpanzee a
notepad and a crayon and told him to write his memoirs.
Honestly, I've seen better handwriting in the Red Lion toilets."

"The pub?"

"Aye. You know? The cubicle on the right. The one with a
crude wee picture of you being–"

"Okay, okay," Ben said. "Can we just get the paperwork done,
please? No doubt Freya will want us to start the week on the front
foot."

"Aye, Ben, no bother."

"The cubicle on the right?" Cruz said, screwing his face up to
recall the picture Gillespie had referred to.

"Aye, you do know your left from your right, don't you?"

"That's supposed to be me, is it?" Cruz said.

"Aye," Gillespie replied, seeming pleased to have annoyed the young DC. "Bloody good likeness if you ask me."

"With my trousers around my ankles?"

"Aye," Gillespie said again.

"Who would draw a picture of me on the wall of a public toilet?"

Gillespie puffed his cheeks out, feigning an effort to come up with an answer.

"Let's see. It could have been that PCSO downstairs. You know, the one whose car you backed into."

"That was an accident."

"Or it could have been the girl on the desk downstairs. The one you walked in on while she was—"

"Spending a penny?" Ben finished for him before the language became crude. There was a fine line between harmless banter and vulgarities, especially when everybody in the country seemed to be so easily offended.

"Aye," Gillespie said. "Spending a penny."

"The was an accident too," Cruz argued.

"An accident?" Nillson said, entering the conversation in a heartbeat. "Cruz, you were in the women's washrooms for ten minutes. The poor girl was trapped in the other cubicle listening to you humming the national anthem and laughing at videos on your phone."

"I didn't know it was the girls, did I?"

"Oh, aye," Gillespie said. "I mean, was the sign on the door with the stick person wearing a wee skirt not enough for you? Actually, come to think of it, I can see why you thought you could go in. I've heard the stories about you and your girlfriend's wardrobe, as has everybody in the station by the way."

"What stories?"

"Alright, alright," Ben said. "Let's keep it friendly."

"No, I want to know what stories people have heard about me," Cruz said, his voice rising in pitch. "If it's about that time I wore her underwear, that was because I had none clean. Besides, they were more like a unisex pair if you ask me."

Gillespie stared at him with his mouth hanging open and his eyes unblinking. The rest of the room fell into a silent state of shock.

"What?" Cruz said. "What are you all looking at?"

"How about that report then, Gillespie?" Ben said, quietly diffusing the situation as a bomb disposal expert might snip the red wire.

"Aye, Ben," he replied. "Aye, I'll get onto it."

The rest of the team all shared horrified expressions and, just as Ben expected, Nillson was about to trigger a secondary bomb when the doors burst open, and instead of an explosion of abuse heading for Cruz, Freya's perfume permeated every nook and cranny the way mustard gas filled the trenches in the Somme.

"Laptops closed, phones on silent," she said, striding towards her desk, where she set her bag down and began wiping the white-board. Without turning to look at anybody in particular, she addressed them all, "Will somebody tell me what's been going on in here, or will I have to torture one of you?"

Finally, she hung the cloth on its little hook and turned to stare at them in turn, her expression revealing a mood that none of them dared to tease into play.

"We were just discussing outstanding reports, boss," Cruz said finally.

"Outstanding reports?" she repeated. "Let me guess. Chapman, Gold, Nillson, and Anderson are up to date, while you pair have at least three to finish off. Am I right?"

"Aye, well," Gillespie said.

"Aye, well, nothing," she began and was just about to open her mouth to set the pair a deadline when Detective Superintendent Granger entered the room, stooping to avoid hitting his head.

He'd been the man who'd convinced Ben to ditch the uniform way back when he was green behind the ears, and Ben had always held respect for his calm disposition.

"Ah, DCI Bloom," he said, tapping his watch with a long, bony index finger. "I hope this isn't a sign of things to come now you've been officially promoted?"

"No, guv," she said. "Apologies. It's just been one of those mornings."

"I see," he replied. "Did I see you arrive in to work in one of the liveried vehicles this morning?"

All eyes fell on Freya as she did what she did best and sought a way to deflect attention.

"I've had some car trouble," she said. "I hitched a lift, that's all. Was there anything in particular you needed me for, guv?"

He smiled at her ability to maintain control of the situation yet Ben sensed a silent conversation taking place between the two of them, communicated through body language alone.

Granger stepped forward into the room without breaking her gaze.

"Are you busy?" he asked. "By which I mean your team?"

"Just a few outstanding reports," she replied. "I'd like to take the lull in investigations to wrap up any old business. It would be nice for us to start afresh. Of course, DCI Standing has left a rather fine mess, but it's nothing we can't handle. In fact, Gillespie and Cruz are already working on some reports he should have chased."

He nodded once.

"Come and see me at lunchtime to give me an update," he said, tapping a desk file with one of his great index fingers. "And please, for all of our sakes, don't be late, Bloom. There's no room for tardiness on this team. I don't care what rank you are."

The incident room doors swung closed in silence behind Granger, leaving the members of the team wondering how Freya

was going to react. But she had handled it well, and Ben hoped she could see Granger's offer of support.

"Well?" Ben said. "What will you have us do?"

"It feels like my first day all over," Gold said, always the one to see the positives in any situation. "It's exciting, isn't it?"

"Not exactly the word I was thinking of," Gillespie grumbled. "I mean, we've got reports to write and no doubt we'll be rummaging through bins or knocking on doors before the week is over."

"You're wrong," Freya said, snapping out of her trance. "Gold is right. It is exciting, and it is a new start for all of us, not just those of us who were promoted."

"Oh aye, and what will you have us do then, boss? What little gems do you have in store for us on this bright and sunny new day?"

She stared across the room at Ben, as if deliberating on an idea, before shoving herself off the desk and picking up her bag.

"I suggest you all use the washroom if you need to. Then meet Ben and me in the car park," she said.

"The car park?" Cruz replied, voicing his confusion. "Oh, we're not going to do any of that team-building stuff, are we? You know, where you have to fall backwards and pray someone will catch you?"

"You'd better pray you don't get paired with me then, Gabby," Gillespie said.

"I am praying," Cruz replied. "I don't want to have to catch you. It'd be like a bloody rhino sitting on me."

"Nobody is falling backwards and nobody is going to catch anybody," Freya said, raising her voice. "If you must know, we're going for coffee."

"Coffee?" Nillson said. "Where?"

"Anywhere but here," she replied, checking her watch. "Car park, five minutes, and don't be late. There's no room for tardiness, remember?"

CHAPTER FOUR

Leaving Harry to mind her salon, Tammy made her way along the lane that cut down the side of the building. She hadn't gone twenty steps when somebody touched her shoulder, catching her off guard. So she gasped as she spun to see who it was.

"Tammy?" It was Steven Greenwood, the postman. "Are you okay? I was calling out for you."

He was a familiar face and always keen for a little chat, be that about the weather, the traffic, or just to share some village gossip, which Tammy was always ready to listen to. Even if she rarely added to the headlines herself.

"Sorry, Steve," she said. "I was in a world of my own. I wasn't being rude."

"You look a little peaky. Good weekend, was it?"

"Eh?" she replied.

"Are you sure you're okay? I hope I haven't said anything to offend–"

"No, no, it's fine," she said. "Sorry, it's early and I'm a bit behind."

She smiled an apology and left him there with his post cart, turning to make her exit and walking straight into the path of an

elderly gentleman, who held on to the wall beside him to avoid falling.

"I'm so sorry," she said, reaching out to keep him on his feet, then she darted off.

"I sometimes forget the rest of the world doesn't have to get out of bed as early as I do," Steve called out.

All Tammy could do was wave a hand to dismiss any notion of him offending her. Then she turned a corner into the lane that ran behind the high street shops.

It hit her, then, the sickly feeling of being an imposter. Of overstepping her mark. But something was off. Something wasn't quite right. And if she heard later that something had happened to Alice, she wouldn't be able to live with herself.

She knew the cottage. It was at the end of a small terrace overlooking the fields. In fact, it was the type of house Tammy could see herself owning one day, if she could just make a success of her salon. As she approached, she caught sight of one of Alice's neighbours, a man she recognised and knew by name but had never spoken to. Her services were more aligned to the mature female and, as such, men found the salon a little uncomfortable.

He watched her approach and must have read something in her body language. He came out from his front garden to greet her, but stopped at the edge of his boundary, leaving the space of the middle house between them.

"Now then," he called out.

"Oh, hello," she said. "You must be George."

He cocked his head, intrigued as to how she knew his name, then took a few steps closer. Of the three houses that comprised the terrace, his was at the far end, sharing a mirrored layout to Alice's with a wrap-around garden on three sides, filled with neatly pruned, blush-pink roses.

"Sorry," she said, realising that all she'd done since leaving her salon was apologise. "Alice told me all about you. Good things, I mean."

"Alice?"

She gestured at the house to her right.

"She's one of my customers," Tammy said. "I do her hair. I own the little shop–"

"You're Tammy?" he said, his sharp eyes suddenly relaxing. "Well, why didn't you say? She's seeing you today, isn't she?"

"Seeing me? Oh, yes. Well, she's supposed to be. That's why I'm here. She had an appointment at nine, you see, and she's never late."

"So, you thought you'd come and fix her up at home, did you?" he asked.

"Not entirely. I was just a little worried–"

"Worried?"

He had a way about him that did little to ease the ugly sensation in the pit of her stomach.

"I'll just give her a knock," she called out, and to her surprise, he remained where he was, watching every step she made up Alice's front path. But the strange neighbour was soon out of her mind when she found the front door ajar. Tammy glanced back and found him leaning on the picket fence, taking the time to deadhead a rose bush.

Tammy knocked politely, letting her third knock push the door open a bit further so she could see inside the house.

"Alice?" she said softly. "Alice, it's me, Tammy. Are you in?"

She was greeted with a smell not unlike that of her own grandmother's house. It wasn't musty by any means, but it was the smell of age, of history. It was warm, despite the chill in the room.

The door creaked a little when she pushed it open wider, and she stepped inside.

"Alice, it's Tammy," she called out, louder this time. The hallway was empty, as was the little lounge. She stepped through into the galley kitchen, where she recognised Alice's handbag on the side, beside a wooden bread bin on top of which was a small stack of envelopes.

A gentle thud caught her attention and Tammy stepped back into the hallway.

"Alice? Alice, is that you?"

She took the stairs two at a time, pulling herself up with the banister and almost flinging herself onto the landing, where she stopped in her tracks, breathless at the sight before her.

"Oh, Alice," she said, dropping to her knees. "Oh, my dear, dear Alice."

CHAPTER FIVE

It had been exactly seven and half minutes since Freya had told them they had five minutes to get to the car park when Cruz ambled out of the fire exit doors. He jammed his little finger in his ear and shook it about as if scratching an itch. But then he removed his finger to see what had come out.

"Gross," Anderson said, turning away so she didn't have to watch. She looked up at Gillespie. "He's going in your car."

"Eh?" he said. "Ah come on. Gold, you'll ride with us, won't you?"

"No, she's with us," Nillson said. "We can talk about girls' stuff."

"What's this?" Cruz asked as he got closer. "Who's talking about girls' stuff?"

"We are," Nillson said. "You know, periods, babies, the menopause–"

"Oh, Christ, I'll ride with you, Jim," Cruz replied, blushing in an instant. He opened the passenger door to Gillespie's car and climbed inside.

"Woodhall Spa?" Ben said. "We could go to The Petwood Hotel."

"The Petwood?" Gillespie said. "Now we're talking. I quite fancy a slice of cake."

"The Petwood it is then," Freya said, and she nodded for Ben to unlock his car. But before she could climb in, a voice called out from the building. Custody Sergeant Priest was in the doorway waving at them.

"Ah, you've got to be kidding me," Gillespie said, voicing what everybody was thinking. Priest, a burly Yorkshireman who had famously worn the uniform longer than anybody he knew or remembered, strolled over to them.

"Inspector Bloom," he said as he neared.

"Michael, we're just going for coffee," she replied. "Can we get you something?"

He handed her a file, which she opened, and then, after reading the cover page, closed.

"Sorry," he said. "It's just come in."

"Not your fault," she replied. "If anything, you just saved me about thirty quid on cakes and coffee."

He turned and walked back to the station. Freya stared around at the disappointed faces.

"The Petwood will have to wait, I'm afraid," she began. "It looks like we're heading to Navenby."

"Navenby?" Gillespie said. "Bloody Navenby?"

"Must you always repeat everything I say, Gillespie?" she said. "It's like having a Scottish parrot on the team."

"We'll follow you," Nillson said, as the female members of the team climbed into her hatchback. Gillespie eventually climbed into his own car and slammed the door.

"Are you going to tell me about it?" Ben asked, as he started his car and pulled on his belt. "Or am I going to have to torture you to find out?"

She smiled at his reference to her earlier remark, but it was fleeting enough for Ben to see her mind was preoccupied.

"It's been a rough morning, Ben. I wouldn't try to understand my mood if I were you."

"I was talking about your car, Freya," he said. "Is it serious? I mean, if I'm going to be your designated driver again, I'll need to get this cleaned."

"You're much more than a designated driver," she remarked, then looked around the inside of the car. "But you're right, you should give it a once over. It looks like Gillespie has been sleeping rough in here."

Ben nosed the car out of the station car park and then turned onto the main road, checking his rear-view mirror to see Nillson's little hatchback and Gillespie's estate car following.

"What do we have then?" Ben said. "If I can't get inside your head, let's talk about the job at hand, eh?"

Freya flicked open the file on her lap, gave it a cursory glance, and then closed it again before staring out of the passenger window.

"It looks like somebody is covering their backside," she said. "Uniformed officers were called to attend the scene and they want us there to make sure it doesn't come back to bite them later."

"Does it look suspicious?"

"Not as far as I can tell," she said, sounding bored. "An elderly lady was found dead in her house."

"So why call us in?"

"According to the statement made by the girl who found her, the front door was wide open."

"Has the medical examiner been?"

"I don't know, Ben," she snapped. "All I've got is a file. I'm not bloody Mystic Meg."

"Alright, alright," he said. "Jesus, Freya."

"Sorry, I'm just..." she began. "I've got a lot on my plate, that's all."

"So let me help."

"You can't," she said, retrieving her phone from her jacket

pocket, which she instantly threw to the floor between her feet. She must have sensed Ben's expression, because she inhaled long and hard then gave in a little. "Sorry. I'm being a cow, aren't I?"

"Yes," he said, almost instantly.

"Wow. That bad?"

"Horrific."

She turned away from him for a moment and he thought he caught her wiping an eye.

"My phone didn't charge," she said finally.

"Oh my God," Ben replied, feigning a panic. "How long do we have? Should I go home to be with my dad?"

"Very funny."

"Oh, come on. It's not the end of the world. There's a charger in here somewhere."

"And my coffee grinder is broken," she added.

"Oh, now I see. You haven't had a coffee yet."

"And my shower doesn't work."

"Bloody hell, this is escalating," Ben said. "Why didn't you call me? You could have showered at my place or the station."

"Oh, really?" she said. "So, you're not avoiding me then?"

"Avoiding you?" he said, realising he'd just done exactly what she'd told Gillespie not to do. "Sorry. I haven't been avoiding you. What gives you that idea?"

"Oh, mainly because you haven't been to see me or called for two weeks."

"I've seen you at work."

"It's okay, Ben. You don't need to explain—"

"I know I don't need to explain because I've done nothing wrong. You're just being a little sensitive, that's all. If you needed help with something, you could call. I've just been a little busy with something."

"Like what?"

He paused, thinking for an answer that just might close her line of enquiry.

"My dad," he said. "It's a busy time of year on the farm. I've been helping out."

"Do you want to know the icing on the cake?" she said, ignoring his excuse.

"You don't believe me, do you?" he said.

"Icing? Cake?" she said, communicating that she no longer wished to pursue that particular conversation. And that she likely didn't believe a word he'd said.

"Go on."

"This morning, two uniformed officers turned up on my doorstep to arrest me."

"To what?"

"Yep," she said. "So, this morning, not only have I not had a decent coffee, but I have spent an hour sitting on the wrong side of the interview room table in Lincoln HQ. Apparently, the number plates on my car have been cloned and the other vehicle was involved in some sort of accident."

"Bloody hell," Ben said. Then he gave it some thought. "Hang on, if you were arrested, you shouldn't be here now. You should have been stood down."

"I am the *victim* of a crime, Ben," she said. "I'm not a criminal. But thanks for your support. It's nice to know you have my back."

"So, what happened?"

"Well, firstly my car does not have a single scratch on it, and secondly, the tech team can log into my car's computer to see when it was last driven. If my car was to have been involved in an accident in the early hours of this morning, then it would have a dented wing and scratched paintwork, of which it has neither."

"So, was there a witness or something? I mean, how did they arrive on your doorstep so quickly?"

"CCTV footage," she said. "Which they showed me. The cloned car had different wheels, but other than that it looked identical to mine. But unless I was able to leave the scene of the crime on the other side of Lincoln, have the bodywork repaired,

change the wheels, and get back home, it's unlikely to have been me, is it?"

"So, you got away with it?" Ben grinned.

"I got away with nothing," she replied. "Because I am guilty of nothing. But it bloody annoys me that I should have to do their jobs for them. If it had been anybody else, they would still be sitting in a cell in Lincoln HQ."

"That's a pretty crappy morning," Ben said. "Are you alright?"

"Not really. But what can I do about it?" she said. "I managed to convince the arresting officer to drive me to our station."

"Hence why Granger saw you in the back of a liveried car. Well, that was nice of him. Was it anybody we know?"

"Nice?" she said. "I had to fight for that lift. I told him if he made my morning any more challenging than it had already been I'd make sure every officer in the county knew about his mistake, and that the victim of the crime had to point out the evidence that was staring him in the face."

"Ah, blackmail. I bet he wasn't expecting that when he knocked on your door this morning," Ben said, as he slowed the car to enter the village of Navenby. "So, when do you get your car back?"

"Later today," she said. "I've told them that when they've finished gathering their evidence, they can wash it and deliver it to our station, free of charge."

"Wow, you know how to make friends, don't you?"

He turned into a side road, which led to a row of three pretty cottages behind the high street. A liveried police car was parked outside the end house and a uniformed officer was at the front door.

"It's not about making friends, Ben," she said. "It's about managing my misfortune and trying not to explode."

"How's that working out?"

"Have I exploded?"

"Not yet," he replied, as he drew up in front of the liveried car. "But who knows what's in store for us in here."

"A dead pensioner in her home?" she said. "I hardly think this will require a major crimes team to close off."

They flashed their warrant cards to the uniformed officer on the front door, who then called out to his colleague upstairs.

"Be prepared for the fastest investigation known to the force," the man on the door said, sounding like he was already bored.

But before they could reply, his colleague leaned into the stairwell from the upstairs landing.

"Up here. We haven't touched anything," he said. He was a smart-looking man, well-groomed with intelligent eyes, probably in his late thirties. "We just thought you should see this before she's moved."

"See what?" Freya said as she reached the top of the stairs.

He gestured at the far end of the upstairs hallway, where an elderly lady lay slumped against a bedroom door.

Freya glanced around the space and then peered down the stairs.

"See what?" she said. "What is it that we're supposed to be witnessing?"

"The body," he said.

"I'm sorry, am I missing something here?" Freya asked him. "She's an elderly lady and, as sad as it is, these things happen. Has control requested an ambulance?"

"Well, yeah–"

"And where is it?"

"Could be an hour or two, they said."

"And who found her?" Freya asked. "Or did you happen to be driving by and saw the open door?"

"A female. Hairdresser. We took a statement, but she said she had to get back to her shop."

"Her shop?"

"Hair by Tammy," he replied, referring to his notepad. "It's on the high street."

"You let her go?"

"She said her shop was unlocked," he replied. "I didn't think—"

"Contact details?" Freya asked. "Did you get a phone number? Did you see any ID?"

He looked sheepish but didn't make any excuses.

"Sorry, I didn't think to," he replied. "I don't see this every day."

"And in the meantime, are you expecting us to wait for the ambulance to take her away?"

"Freya, I think what the officer is trying to say is that he believes the scene to be suspicious," Ben said, looking at the uniformed officer for support. "Am I right?"

"Well, yeah. The front door was wide open and she's only got a nightie on. She's not even wearing slippers. It's a bit odd, isn't it?" he replied.

Freya studied the officer, clearly making the man feel a little uncomfortable. But he held his ground.

"How long have you been in uniform?" she asked, to which he shrugged.

"Five years or so."

"And where do you plan on going with your career?" she asked. "What is it you actually want to do?"

"What you do," he replied. "I want to work on bigger stuff. You know? Make a difference. Solve crimes. Not just take notes and issue crime numbers so somebody can have an insurance claim."

"And your name?"

"Sanderson," he said. "Jeff Sanderson."

"Why haven't I seen you before?"

"I'm based out of Lincoln HQ. We just got the call to attend."

"Okay, Sanderson," she replied, adopting a tone that Ben recognised as one she saved for giving lectures and gaining the

moral high ground. "You can't look for a serious crime. There's enough of them out there. I'm sure you're a good officer. I'm quite sure you're diligent, professional, and all those things. But honestly, this isn't a crime. This is just a sad fact of life, and one day it'll happen to you and me."

"But don't you think it's worth checking?" he asked. "Don't you think her story needs to be known? We can't just assume she keeled over and that was that. What about her family?"

"I tell you what," Freya said. "We have a forensic medical examiner on his way to us right now. When he gets here, he'll provide us a cause of death, if he can. If her death was caused by anything other than natural causes, then I'll apologise and put a good word in for you. How does that sound?"

"And if I'm wrong?"

"Then you can do me a favour, and we'll call it quits," she replied.

"A favour? What type of favour?"

"I'll think of something. In the meantime, I suggest you go downstairs and see if you can find details of a next of kin. Because you're right about one thing. Her family do need to know."

CHAPTER SIX

Tammy flopped down into one of the two hairdressing chairs, letting her head fall back momentarily before the reality of what she had just seen caught up with her. She pulled her knees to her chest as the burning rush of emotions swept up from her churning stomach. Then she fell forward, reaching for a waste bin to catch the hot bile.

She stayed like that for a moment, a string of acidic saliva hanging from her mouth, her eyes reddened by searing tears.

The door opened. "You're back then? Nice of you to let me..." Harry began, but he stopped almost immediately. "Tammy? Tammy, what's wrong, sweetheart?"

She spat and wiped her mouth with the back of her hand before he produced a clean tissue from his pocket and handed it to her. Although she couldn't meet his stare, she knew his expression would be sympathetic.

"Do you want to talk about it?" he asked, before he closed the door, put the latch on, and turned the little sign to *closed*.

She jumped from the chair, wiping her mouth with the tissue, then reached to put the sign back to *open*. But Harry held her by the wrist.

"Tammy, look at you. What's wrong?"

"Let go, Harry," she said quietly, feeling the thud of her heart in her chest. "I said, let go of me, Harry."

A moment passed, and the tone of her voice must have gotten the message through because his grip on her wrist relaxed.

"Talk to me, Tammy," he said, softly but with enough vigour for her to know he wouldn't let it go.

She reached for the sign again.

"You can't let people see you like this," he said.

"I can't afford to turn people away," she replied. "I have a ten o'clock, remember–"

"Tammy?"

She wiped away the first tear that had broken free but found no strength in her hand to turn the sign to *open*. It was as if her fingers refused to listen to the command.

"She's bloody dead, Harry," she said.

"Sorry, what?"

"Dead. Alice. I found her," she said, remembering the peaceful expression on the old lady's face. "She was just sitting there."

"Tammy–"

"How was I to know?" she asked. "She looked so happy. She was at the top of the stairs, leaning against a door. It was like she'd climbed up there and just sat down. And that was it."

"Oh, Christ. Have you told anybody?"

"I called the police," she said with a sniff. "I had to give a statement. That's why I was so long. But I told them my shop was unlocked, and they let me go."

"It sounds like you did the right thing," Harry said, and he glanced through the window to check on his shop door. "Come on. You can't stay here."

"I've got to work, Harry. I can't let people down."

"I'm sure they'll understand."

"No, you don't understand. I can't afford not to. I'm already behind on my lease."

"You have to look after your head, Tammy. Something like this can really take its toll. Just take a day, eh?"

"No," she said, and she forced herself to turn the sign. "No, I've got to work."

"Well, then at least let me help somehow."

"You? Help? What are you, a blue rinse specialist now?" she said, feeling the betrayal of a smile trying to break through.

"Let me make you a coffee," he said and walked through to the little kitchenette. From there, he called out, "How do you take it?"

But she didn't reply. She couldn't. In the mirror opposite, Tammy's reflection stared back at her, and she despised it. It didn't even look like her. The longer she stared, the more the image seemed to morph into somebody else. Somebody bad. Somebody she didn't like.

"Tammy?" Harry said, stepping out of the little room. "How do you like it?"

His voice snapped her out of it and she took a breath.

"I've got one," she said. "In the metal cup. I made it this morning. It should still be hot."

He removed his glasses to peer around the room, then emerged from the kitchenette holding the thermos. She took it from him and cradled it in both hands before he guided her onto one of the chairs for waiting customers.

"Is there someone who can help you out?" he asked. "Another hairdresser? Or a friend even?"

She shook her head.

"I don't want to leave you on your own, Tammy."

But she said nothing, and the silence that followed was filled with nothing but a numb sensation. He sat in the seat beside her and crossed his legs the way he always did.

"When I was fifteen," he began, "I found my grandad."

She turned her head a little, enough to see his expression. He

was staring dead ahead at his own reflection, and she wondered if he loathed what he saw, just as she had.

"He was on the kitchen floor in his pyjamas. I shouted and shouted, but he didn't respond," he explained. "I mean, I knew enough to check for a pulse and to check he was breathing, but I couldn't find anything, and I didn't have a clue if I'd even done it right."

"That's pretty awful," she said, and somehow his words had created something between them. She rested her head on his shoulder, and he continued.

"I know I called an ambulance, but I don't remember what I said, or even what they said. That part is a blur," he said. "But I do remember the guilt. I mean, I'd only popped round to drop his paper off, but I couldn't help thinking that if only I hadn't messed about in the newsagents, if only I hadn't read that magazine, I might have got there early. I might have been able to do something. I don't know what I could have done, mind, but I could've done something. I could've called for help sooner."

"You can't blame yourself for that," Tammy said. "How were you to know?"

"I know that now. But fifteen-year-old me didn't know it. I was miserable for weeks, I was. At the funeral, I thought everyone was looking at me. I was close to running out."

"But you stayed?" she asked, and he nodded.

"Aye. For him. He wouldn't have wanted me to leave," he replied. "I felt that he would be the only one who'd really understand. The only one who didn't judge me. And part of me felt lucky. It was me who found him. It was me who shared that last moment with him. I remember sitting there in the kitchen beside him, surrounded by all his worldly possessions. None of them mattered any more. They were special to him, but to everyone else, they were just things. Only he knew the stories behind them, where they came from, why he bought them. But all that was gone, and it was just me and my grandad. One last time."

"And the guilt?" she asked. "Did it pass?"

A gentle knock on the window in the door interrupted the moment. Harry was on his feet in a heartbeat.

"I'm sorry, can you just give us a few minutes?" he explained to the woman. "Tammy has had some bad news."

The woman had a kind face. It was like she already knew what Tammy had seen. She reached into her pocket and showed identification of some sort.

"I'm Detective Constable Gold," she said. Her voice was soft, like her eyes, with a tinge of Scottish somewhere which only added to her warmth. "I'm here to see Tammy Plant."

CHAPTER SEVEN

Talking to an individual who had just discovered a dead body required many of the skills Jackie Gold had developed in her role as the team's family liaison officer. She enjoyed the fact that people opened up to her and that, just by demonstrating empathy, she could make a difference. She didn't have to chase people or wrestle them to the ground, or even grill them across an interview room table. She could just be herself.

The burden of such a role, however, was as heavy as mud. During the twelve months she had been in the job, she'd been a shoulder to cry on, the target of both physical and verbal abuse, and a spy for her colleagues, as she sought facts that may have been omitted from formal interviews. The team looked to her to develop relationships and gain trust. The victims looked to her for everything, from being an emotional sponge to a guiding light through the often daunting police procedures.

Those first few seconds counted. The moment she raised her warrant card and introduced herself, that would be the deciding factor as to whether or not the individual would trust her.

Tammy Plant refused to make eye contact, and for a moment, Jackie thought she might make a run for the back door.

"It's okay, Tammy," she said. "I'm just here to make sure you're okay."

"She's had a hell of a shock," the man said, who then read Jackie's quizzical expressions and introduced himself. "Oh, apologies. I'm Harry. Harry Doughty. I own the shop next door. Tammy just asked me to keep an eye on things while she ran round to see Alice."

"And what time was this?" Jackie asked.

"Around a quarter past nine," he replied. "Nine-twenty at the latest. I hadn't finished my coffee yet, you see. But it couldn't have been any later."

"Thank you," Jackie said, and she looked towards the door. "I'll come and find you if I need you."

"Shouldn't I stay?" he asked, looking to Tammy for an answer.

"I'm sure she'll be fine. We know where you are if we need you," Jackie told him, and she held the door open. Tammy looked down, and eventually, she nodded that she would be okay.

"I'll be here in a heartbeat," Harry said. "Just call out."

"Thanks, Harry," she said, and Jackie closed the door, taking a moment to let the silence bring the tension down.

She took a few steps towards Tammy, who was now staring at the floor cradling a metal thermos cup, and then sat down in the chair beside her.

"Can I make you a fresh cup?" Jackie asked, to which Tammy raised the thermos and gave it a little shake to indicate there was still plenty of coffee left. "Well, you've stumped me there. That's my go-to icebreaker. I've got nothing left."

Tammy turned her head to see if she was being serious. Then the resilient facade cracked, revealing a warm smile.

"Did the ambulance come?" she asked eventually. "Did they..."

She paused, as if unsure of what to ask next.

"She's still there," Jackie told her. "Do you want to know what happens next?"

Tammy nodded. She sat back, letting Jackie into her world a little. It wasn't much, but it was progress.

"Well, a forensic medical examiner will have a look—"

"A what?"

"A doctor, of sorts. He'll record her body temperature, anything unusual he might find. Plus he'll often be able to hint at a cause of death. We can't officially do anything with that information. That has to come from the pathologist. But if the death is found to be suspicious, it allows us to get a head start in an investigation."

"Suspicious?" Tammy said. "But it's not, is it? I mean, she was just sitting there. She just died. Didn't she?"

"I don't know," Jackie said. "We try to keep the footfall to a minimum. My boss went inside to have a look. She just asked me to come and find you."

"But you don't think I—"

"No, no," Jackie said. "God no. I just came to make sure you were okay. It's not an easy thing to see, you know? Something like that can really affect you."

"I'm fine," she said.

"Really? Is that why your makeup is running down your face and that bin is covered in sick? Are you really that fine, Tammy?"

She bit her lower lip and squeezed her eyes together.

"No," she squeaked. It was the opening of the dam and something Jackie had been prepared for. The trick now was to let the emotion surge, and then only when the momentum was waning, encourage it to flow to get the last dribbles out into the open. "I'm really not. Oh, God. I should never have gone. I should have just stayed. It was none of my business. Do you know what they call her? The other women in the village?"

"Go on," Jackie said.

"Mad Alice. Mad? She wasn't mad. She was just lost and lonely."

Jackie opened her little notepad to jot down some key phrases

– statements that might jog her memory when she came to type her report.

"Why don't we start from the beginning?" Jackie said. "Tell me what happened. In your own words."

"I told you," Tammy said, scrunching her nose. "I told the other bloke. The one in the uniform. She was my first customer. She's normally on time. She's never late. And if she can't make an appointment, she tells me a few days before, you know? So, I can take another booking."

"So, you opened the shop this morning and Alice didn't show. Is that right?"

"Yes. That's what I've been trying to say."

"So, you decided to go round there, did you?"

"Yeah, just to check she was okay. She's an old lady," Tammy said. "I don't know why, but I just felt like...like I had some sort of obligation. You know?"

"You're caring and conscientious?"

"I don't know about that. But I know if it were my mum or my gran, I'd want somebody to check on them."

"So, what did you do?" Jackie asked. "You'd opened your shop and–"

Jackie was interrupted by a gentle knock on the door. She looked up to find a lady in her fifties peering through the glass.

"You-hoo," she said in a jolly singsong tone. "Only me, Tammy."

Before either Jackie or Tammy could stand, Harry Doughty appeared from his shop and politely led the lady towards his door.

"That's my ten o'clock," Tammy said.

"I'm sure she'll understand," Jackie replied. It was a risk to allow the shopkeeper to explain what was happening, but she was also keen not to break the flow of information. "He seems like a nice man."

"He is. I went to him. We help each other out, see? If we need to run out, we keep an eye on each other's doors."

"It's nice to have good neighbours."

"I know. I can't afford to lose customers or miss a booking. Most of the ladies I look after can't use the internet, and some of them don't like to phone to make a booking. They just turn up to talk to me face to face."

"So, Harry agreed, did he? He said he'd look after the shop?"

Tammy nodded.

"Yeah. She only lives around the corner. Alice, that is. So, I just popped round there–"

"Did you see anybody on your way?"

"No," she said, almost without thinking. "Oh wait. Yes, I did. Steve. He's the postman. He saw me. We spoke."

"And what did he say?"

She paused, staring at the wall by the door, seeming a little lost.

"I don't know. Sorry, I can't think straight. I know we spoke, I just can't remember what we said."

"That's okay. Was there anybody else?"

"Only an old man. I nearly knocked him over," she said. "I didn't speak to him. Only to say sorry, anyway."

"And then you walked to Alice's house, did you?"

"Yeah. It was weird, though. I knew something was up because the front door was open. She's normally so careful. She lost her husband a few years back."

"Was anybody there?" Jackie asked.

"No, not inside, anyway. One of her neighbours was in his garden. The old guy at the end. George, his name is. He was there deadheading roses."

"Deadheading roses?" Jackie said, making a note of the people she'd mentioned.

"You know what it's like when you're retired. What else are you going to do? I knew him from my times with Alice. She used to talk about him. She thought he had a crush on her. Saw himself

as a bit of a chaperone to her and the other lady, the one in the middle house."

"Do you know her at all?"

"The middle one?" Tammy replied, shaking her head. She leaned forward to peer through the window at her customer. "I think her name is Ethel, but I can't be sure. She doesn't come to me."

"Okay," Jackie said, seeing that she was keen to finish the chat. "This is the last part. Are you sure you're ready for this?"

"I am," she said, taking a deep breath. "So, I knocked on the front doors a few times, then pushed it open, and went in. I wasn't intruding or anything. I was calling out for her."

"I understand," Jackie said. "There's no law against being a kind soul."

"It's only a little house. I checked downstairs then went upstairs. That's when I found her."

She finished and stared at Jackie to put an end to her account. Jackie made a few notes, then closed her notebook and pocketed it.

"Alright," she said, reaching for one of her contact cards from her inside pocket. "I think I've got enough. But if you think of anything else, you call me, okay? Even if it's just to talk about what you saw. I can help you. I can also recommend some good therapy sessions to help you cope."

"I'm fine," she said. "Thank you, but I won't need it."

Jackie smiled politely.

"Will you need to talk to me again?" Tammy asked, as Jackie stood and made her way to the door.

"I shouldn't think so," she replied. "Unless, of course, the medical examiner finds something suspicious. Then we may need to."

"Why?" Tammy asked, to which Jackie shrugged.

"It's standard practice. If there is reason to believe foul play, then we'll need the fingerprints and DNA of everyone who

entered the house. It's just so we can eliminate them from the investigation. Nothing to worry about."

"But you don't think it is, do you?" Tammy said. "Foul play, I mean."

Jackie unlatched the door and offered her warmest smile. "Why don't you take the day off? Contact your customers and explain, then get some rest. Okay?"

Tammy nodded.

"I'll be seeing you," Jackie said.

She stepped through the door and pulled it closed behind her.

"She alright?" Harry said from his doorway.

Jackie didn't even look his way. She was still processing the information.

"She'll be fine," she said and then turned to face him. "Keep an eye on her, will you? She could do with a friend right now."

CHAPTER EIGHT

In Freya's experience, when a body is discovered, the world around the corpse bears a constant hum of chatter – questions back and forth, hypotheses, the clicking of camera shutters, and of course, in many instances, emotional outbursts. The only lull in this cacophony is when the detectives, the family, the photographers, and the crime scene investigators all step back to allow the medical examiner to do his or her work.

The silence was insufferable.

Doctor Saint, whom Freya had known now for nearly a year, was the type of man anybody might hope for in a friendly uncle or grandpa. He huffed as he pushed up from where he had been crouched before the body, made a note in his leather-bound binder, and then removed his glasses. He turned his back on the deceased and inhaled, a silent gesture that he was ready to divulge his professional opinion.

"Myocardial infarction," he said, peering down his nose at Freya as if he was waiting for her to comment.

"Myo...what?" Ben said.

"It's the medical term for–" Saint began.

"What Doctor Saint is trying to say is that our friend here

died from nothing more than a heart attack," Freya said, loud enough that Sanderson, whom Freya could hear shuffling about in the hallway downstairs, could hear. "A good, old-fashioned heart attack."

"Of course, an autopsy would confirm my suspicions," Saint continued. "Sadly, there are few visible signs that single out a heart attack as being the most likely cause."

"Well, I'm content with that if you are, Doctor Saint," Freya said. "I'll stand my team down."

"Can I just ask?" Saint said, clearly a little bemused. "It's just that I drove all the way from Horncastle this morning, and I must admit, when I'm on my way to meet you two, I'm usually preparing myself for the worst."

"But in this instance?" Freya said.

"Let's just say I'm more than a little surprised to have been called out for..." He waved his hand at the body. "Well, for this."

"And I can only apologise, Doctor Saint–"

"Peter, please."

"I can only apologise, Peter. If Ben and I had been first to arrive, we may have been able to offer the poor, old girl a little more dignity. But sometimes these things are beyond our control, and there are those who, despite being well-intentioned, often muddy the waters. But we mustn't strive to suppress good intentions, Peter."

"Of course not."

"However misguided they are," Freya finished, as she heard Sanderson leaving the house by the front door, mumbling something to his colleague as he did.

"I can't help but get the feeling you're quite pleased, Inspector."

"It's Chief Inspector now," Freya replied. "And you're right. I am pleased. Not for her, of course, or her family, but natural causes is natural causes. It does mean there is one less criminal in the world. I find that restores a little faith, don't you?"

Saint seemed quite intrigued by Freya's statement. He cocked his head to one side, to contemplate her opinion.

"If only that were true," he replied. "But given the odds, I expect that next time we meet, we won't be so fortunate."

"Until next time," she said, holding her hand out for him to shake.

"Until next time," he replied, unable to hide his amusement as he shook her hand, then Ben's. "Sergeant Savage."

"It's Detective Inspector now, Peter," Ben replied, to which the doctor again cocked his head.

"Two promotions? Am I to assume that DCI Standing has gone on to bigger and better things?"

Saint stepped onto the top stair, indicating that he wasn't looking to enter into a full conversation but was open to mild gossip.

"Steven Standing is currently in HMP Lincoln," Freya told him. "I expect you'll be reading about it in the papers before long. His trial is only a few weeks away."

"He's on remand?"

"I won't tempt fate by going into details," Freya said. "But rest assured, he won't be darkening our crime scenes ever again."

"Well," Saint said, "I suppose congratulations are in order, to you both, I mean."

"Thank you, Peter," Ben said.

"I expect I'll be seeing you before long."

"We'll try to make it worth your while," Ben replied, which raised a brief smile, and then Saint descended the stairs, leaving Freya and Ben alone with the corpse.

"Can't help yourself, can you?" Ben said.

"What do you mean?"

"You can't help yourself. Sanderson. He was only trying to do the right thing."

"Yes, well, in this instance, he got it wrong, didn't he? It's no good arguing that somebody tried to do the right thing if they

end up making a hash of it. I mean, how many times have you seen somebody try to do the right thing and unwittingly commit a crime as a result?"

"Well, I don't think we can take it that far—"

"It's a shame, though, isn't it?" Freya said, leaning into the bathroom for a quick peek. "It's a beautiful cottage."

"We're not here to appraise the property, Freya," Ben said. "Come on. We'd better hand the scene back to Sanderson so he can wait for the ambulance to arrive."

"Hold on," she said, as she stepped into the front bedroom. "I just want to have a look."

"You mean, you want to compare the place to your new house?"

"Inspiration, Ben. I'm still settling in."

"You don't even own any furniture," he said.

"Actually, I do own some rather expensive furniture. I just don't have it in my possession."

"No, it's on a ship somewhere, probably rounding the Cape of Good Hope as we speak," he replied. "Besides, I'm not sure if poor, old Alice's taste is quite up to yours."

"And what is that supposed to mean?" she said from inside the spare room. "I'm not looking to replicate the decor, but you have to hand it to the older generation, they don't go for cheap furniture. They built stuff to last back then, not like the toot in many of the shops these days."

She stepped out of the room and caught Ben yawning, which he stifled then feigned interest.

Freya continued, "You don't hear about one's grandparents sitting cross-legged on the floor in the middle of the night still trying to fathom how to assemble a chest of drawers, do you?"

"I suppose not," Ben said. "They don't know what they were missing, do they? I mean, some people enjoy building flatpack furniture."

"Some people also enjoy imitation cheese, plastic shoes, and

artificial grass, but that doesn't make them stylish or high quality."

He said nothing in reply, either because he knew he had been beaten, or because he couldn't be bothered with the argument. It didn't matter which.

"Help me, will you?" she said.

"Do what?" he replied. "Are we going to peel the wallpaper off?"

"Certainly not," she said. "I want to look in here."

She gestured at the back bedroom, which, due to the layout of the house, was the master.

"You can't move her."

"I don't need to move her," Freya said. "I just need to open the door a bit to see inside."

"Freya?"

"Just hold her, will you? Stop her falling forward," Freya said, as she gently pulled on the door handle.

"Freya, she's bloody dead. Show some respect."

"I am showing some respect, Ben. Well, I would be at least if you could just stop her rolling forward. Come on. I just want to have a peek."

"Freya?"

"It's not a crime scene, Ben," she said. "It's not like we need to preserve anything, is it? Come on."

"Oh, for God's sake," he replied, dropping to a crouch, holding his hands up so as not to touch her, but should she fall forward, he would be on hand to stop any further loss of dignity. "Right, go on."

Carefully, Freya pulled the handle. Despite what Ben thought, she didn't actually want to disturb the deceased. The door opened an inch, not enough for her to see inside.

"Can you just shift her a bit?" she said.

"What?"

"Oh, Ben, please don't make this any harder than it has to be."

"Alright, alright," he said, searching for somewhere to grip whilst maintaining some level of decency. He took hold of the lady's right ankle and her right shoulder, pulling one side of her away from the door. "Go. Quickly, Freya."

The extra space allowed her to open the door a further three inches, enough for her to see an immaculately made bed, a bedroom window, which was open, and something far more sinister on the plush carpet.

She gasped and let go of the door, stepping back in fright.

"What?" Ben said. "What is it?"

He pushed the body back up against the door, and made sure she stayed upright, before standing and placing a hand on Freya's shoulder.

"Freya, talk to me. You look like you've seen a ghost."

"Get Doctor Saint," she said finally. "We may have a use for him yet."

CHAPTER NINE

"I'm sorry," Tammy said. "But like I said, Mrs Drew, I've had some bad news. I wouldn't normally do this, but–"

"Tammy, you told me I could rely on you, especially after I was let down by my last hairdresser."

"I know, but if you'd only–"

"No," she said, her tone as sharp as a razor even over the line. "No, I'm sorry. This is how it all began before with my last hairdresser. She let me down once then promised it wouldn't happen again. But it did, didn't it? It did happen. Six weeks, I had to go. Six weeks without my hair being done, I ask you. I barely dared to leave the house without a hat. No. I shan't let it happen again. I'm sorry, Tammy. I like what you do, in fact, I love what you do. You're the best hairdresser I've had for a long time, but I won't be messed about. Not again. I'm afraid you leave me no option but to find somebody else. Margaret tells me she uses a girl in Boothby Grafoe. I suppose I shall have to give her a call."

"I'm sorry, Mrs Drew. I really am," Tammy said softly. "I'm sure if you let me explain that you would understand, but I see you've made your mind up already."

"I have. I'm sorry, but I have. One needs to maintain a good grasp of their scruples these days."

"Well, then I wish you the best of luck," Tammy said, doing her best to hold back the tears that threatened to fall. "Goodbye, Mrs Drew."

She ended the call before Mrs Drew had a chance to reply and dropped her phone into her handbag, catching sight of a flash of white paper from its depths, which only teased her conscience from its lair. But in her anger, all she could do was snatch her phone from her bag again and dial the number she dialled the most.

The call rang for three rings before it was answered with a chirpy, "Tammy, dear, is everything okay?"

"Oh, Mum," she said. "Oh, Mum, I'm having the most awful day."

"Why, dear? Whatever's happened?"

She heard her mother set her china cup down on the kitchen work surface. It was a sound Tammy would recognise anywhere.

"It's Mrs Glass," Tammy said. "You know the one I told you about? Alice Glass."

"The mad one?"

"She's not mad," Tammy replied. She almost couldn't believe she was about to say what was in her head. "Not anymore, at least."

"What do you mean? You don't mean she's died, do you?"

"I found her, Mum."

"You did what?"

"I found her. She was just sitting there. On her landing. All still and..."

"And what, dear?" her mother coaxed.

"Peaceful, Mum," she said. "She looked peaceful."

The few moments of silence that followed should have ended in some kind of sympathy. But her mother was far more intuitive than most people gave her credit for.

"Why do I get the feeling that the reason you're upset isn't necessarily because this Alice lady died, Tammy?"

"Mum, come on. Give me some credit. She was all on her own."

"I know you better than anyone, Tammy, remember?" said her mother. "When was the last time you cried for anybody but yourself?"

'That's not fair–"

"Don't get mad at me," her mother said. "I'm on your side, remember? I'm afraid it's a trait you inherited from me. So come on, what is it?"

Tammy let her head fall back onto the couch, hating the fact her mother was right. She was always right. Even though it wasn't a video call, Tammy knew that she'd be sitting in her nice, fancy kitchen, probably dressed for yoga, planning a coffee afternoon with her friends. Her father, meanwhile, would either be at the golf club or at work. There was barely any discernible difference between them both and one huge similarity – he was away from his wife.

"I had to shut the shop," she said.

"I see," her mother replied, and the image of her Tammy had in her mind developed a knowing grin. "Go on."

"I couldn't cope, Mum," Tammy said. "I kept breaking down. All I could think about was Alice and–"

"Da-da-da-da," her mother said, her very unique method of cutting in. It was what she deemed a polite way of saying, 'Stop right there, I don't believe a word of it.'

"It's true," Tammy said. "I might be a cold-hearted bitch, Mum, but I do at least have a heart."

"The old lady dying is not the reason you're upset though, is it?"

"Mum! How dare you?"

"In fact, I'd gamble that seeing her dead body had barely any effect on you–"

"Mum?"

The sound of her mother sipping her coffee came loudly across the line. It was a sound Tammy had always hated. She might be middle-class now, but she still carried a few habits of her life before she'd met Tammy's father.

"So, you saw a valid reason to seek sympathy, closed your shop, and now you're calling me for another bailout?" her mother said. "It's hardly a surprise, if I'm honest. It was never going to be a huge success, was it? I mean, you don't see adverts on the TV for blue rinses, do you? No, you don't. You see plenty of adverts for salons catering for the younger generation. My generation, even. But not old people, Tammy. I don't know why your father loaned you the money in the first place."

Tammy hit the red button to end the call and found her grip tightening on the phone. She stayed there, curled up on the couch for a few moments with her legs tucked beneath her. The urge to toss her phone across the room was overwhelming. She nearly did, but saw sense at the last minute.

She found the number again and hit dial, putting the call onto loudspeaker. While the call connected, she pushed herself off the couch to grab her shoes.

"I knew you'd call back," her mother said. She would still be sitting at her kitchen counter, her smug grin broader than before.

"I haven't called back to ask for money, Mum," Tammy said, somehow managing to keep her voice low and her emotions in check. "I called back to tell you where to stick your money. You don't believe in me—"

"And you wonder why—"

"You don't believe in me, Mum," she said. "But I'm going to prove you wrong. I called you because I needed you. I called you because you're my mum. I needed some support, not a bloody lecture. Not to be put down again. But thanks anyway, Mum. Thanks for nothing."

"If it's money you need, Tammy, you're going the wrong way about it."

"I don't need your money," Tammy said, losing the grip on her tone fast. She swallowed hard and wiped the burning tears from her eyes. "I don't need you for anything."

She hit the red button again, and this time, she let the phone fly.

Before she spiralled into self-pity, Tammy managed to get a grip on herself, a plan developing with every passing second. She'd show them. She'd make a success of herself one way or another. But if she was to do it, then it had to be right.

She snatched her bag from the couch and burst out of the front door in more of a run than a walk, crossing the high street at the far end. Then she slipped into the side road that eventually led behind the shops. She had to go there. She had to make amends. There was no way on this earth she could hold her head up high otherwise. And her mother would know. Tammy didn't know how she would know, but she would know that she hadn't earned her success.

But when Tammy rounded the last corner near the cottage that belonged to the old man, instead of being greeted by a few sombre neighbours, she saw three police cars. There was also an ambulance parked outside Alice's house, and two little, white vans marked with *Lincolnshire Crime Scene Investigation*. She stopped in her tracks, clutching her bag to her side.

"...help you?" a voice said.

She looked up to find a large man in a cheap suit wearing at least three days' stubble on his face. He looked as if he hadn't washed for a week, and with the palm of his hand, he flattened his hair back across his head. The man beside him was far smaller and had the wide-open eyes of a child. But despite his immature appearance, he was at least clean and well-presented.

"I said, can I help you?" the larger man said, his tone aggressive.

Tammy could have sworn he was Scottish, although his words seemed to be muffled, or blurred, if sound could be blurred.

"Are you alright?" the smaller man said, as they both approached her.

"Yes," she said. "Yes, sorry, I'm fine."

"What are you doing here, love?" the Scotsman said, flashing his identification, even though it was too far away for Tammy to read.

"I was coming to see Alice."

"Alice?"

"I found her," she said. "It was me who found her this morning. I spoke to one of your colleagues. Somebody Gold."

"Oh, aye," the big man said. "That'll be Jackie. She said she came to see you. Said you were a bit upset. How are you doing?"

"I'm fine," Tammy lied. "I just…"

"Aye?" he said.

"I just needed to be here, that's all."

"Right," he said, sounding doubtful. "Do you want to come and have a wee sit down? We've got some water somewhere."

"No," she said. "No, it's fine, thank you. I'm sorry, I didn't expect to see all this."

"Ah, the circus, you mean?" he replied. "Aye, and that's not even all of it."

"Why, though? I mean, why do you need all this? She just died, didn't she? I know that sounds callous, but I saw her. She looked so peaceful."

"Aye, she died," the man said, and he eyed her with practised suspicion. "Are you sure you don't want that water?"

"No, thank—"

"Gaby, run and get her a bottle of water, will you?"

"Me?"

"Just get it, will you?"

The smaller of the two men marched off in search of water, and the larger one took a few strides closer.

"I'm Detective Sergeant Gillespie," he explained. "I think you should come and have a wee sit down, love."

"No," she replied, backing away from him, shaking her head. "Sorry, I've made a mistake. I can't be here. I'm sorry."

CHAPTER TEN

For the second time that morning, Doctor Saint heaved himself from a crouch, this time accompanied by a loud click of his knee, which caused him to wince.

Before him, leaning against the bedroom door, much like Alice Glass had been leaning on the other side, was the body of a man who looked to be in his thirties. He had thick, dark hair, and tanned skin, with a large mole on his upper lip. It was only when Doctor Saint had raised one of the man's eyelids that Freya had noted the deep, brown eyes.

The cause of death seemed obvious, but Freya knew better than to jump to conclusions. It was always better to rely on facts rather than what was apparent.

"It would have been fast," Doctor Saint said at last. "It looks to me like a single blow to the head."

"Blunt force trauma?" Freya asked, to which the doctor nodded with a grave expression.

"I'm afraid so," he said, glancing around the room. "I expect the crime scene investigators will tear this place apart. But I very much doubt the weapon is still here."

"What makes you say that?" Ben asked.

"The shape of the wound. It's unmistakable," he said with an intake of breath. Then he held Freya's stare. "A hammer, or something round and coin-sized."

"A hammer?" she said, reminding herself of Gillespie. "Can you be certain?"

"Nothing is certain, I'm afraid," he said. "But no doubt Doctor Bell will confirm my thoughts. I can find no other injury on him, and given the haemorrhages in his eyes, well, need I say more?"

"Time of death?" Freya asked.

"Five hours at the most, but not less than three."

Freya checked her watch.

"So sometime between five and seven this morning?" she said. "We'll need to narrow that window."

The bedroom was large enough for Ben and Freya to stand side by side at the foot of the bed. It was as Freya would have expected to find an elderly lady's bedroom – immaculate, bed made, and nothing on show that shouldn't be. The only stains on the picture of perfection were the corpse, the bloodied carpet, and the spatter up the wall. Even that seemed to partially blend with the floral wallpaper – tiny dots of red like distant carnations on red stems.

"Now," Doctor Saint said, "I really think we ought to hand the room over to our friends in white suits. There's nothing more I can do here. Unless, of course, you're hiding another body in the attic?"

"No such luck, I'm afraid," Freya told him with a smile. "You'll send your findings on to pathology, I assume?"

"As soon as I'm back in the office," he replied.

"Well, of course," Freya said. "I was having quite the day from hell before this, and now I find I have reason to see Doctor Pippa Bell. At least nothing else can go wrong for me."

"The icing on the cake?" Doctor Saint asked.

"Sadly, it's not the type of cake I was hoping for," she replied

and then sighed. "Right then. Let's hand the room over. Ben, anything else to say?"

She seemed to have disturbed him mid-thought, as he seemed irritated for a moment.

"Sorry, I just want to stay here a minute. I need to get my thoughts in order."

"I'll leave you to it," Doctor Saint said. "Good day."

Carefully, he stepped around the body and through the door, careful to touch nothing, not even the door on his way out.

"Come on then, Sherlock," Freya said. "Let's hear it."

He shook his head, again irritated.

"Doesn't this seem odd to you?" he asked, then waved his hand at the immaculate room.

"Not really," she replied. "In fact, it could be the closest thing we've had to an open and shut case for a long time."

"I think you're wrong."

"I think *you're* wrong," she countered. "Man breaks into the house, comes upstairs, scares the bejesus out of Alice Glass, enough to give her a heart attack, but she won't go down without a fight and she clobbers him."

"What with?" he said. "Are we assuming the old lady carries a hammer around with her? Or maybe she was in the middle of knocking a wall down when the burglar disturbed her?"

"That's the lowest form of humour, Ben," she said, but he wasn't finished.

"And I suppose, in your world, anyone and everyone is capable of bludgeoning a man to death? I mean, did the thought even cross your mind that not all of us have that in us? We just can't bring ourselves to deliver a fatal blow."

The mood had shifted with some haste from verbalising embryonic theories to banter, and now it was bordering anger, rage even.

She stared hard at him, trying to discern the meaning behind his outburst, behind his intrusive stare.

"You'd be surprised what one is capable of, Ben," she said sharply. "When one finds themselves fighting for their life. Or protecting everything they hold dear."

She watched him try to decipher that statement for a moment. Then he shook himself out of his little tantrum with what she could only describe as embarrassment.

"Sorry," he said. "I shouldn't have—"

"Don't apologise for what you believe is right, Ben," she said. "There's nothing more unsightly than a man disguising his thoughts to suit his audience. Rather, I'd be keen to hear your own theory. If you have one, that is."

"Not as such," he said, turning away from Freya to stand beside the window. "But I don't buy the whole burglar thing. How many burglars have you known that, first of all, don't wear gloves, and secondly, close drawers and cupboards after they've rifled through them?"

She had to agree. It was a valid point. Small-minded, but valid.

"Unless he was targeting some other place in the house," she said. "For example, our man on the floor might have known about some little nest egg Alice had squirrelled away. Or something of value, for example."

"And how would he have learned of such a thing?" Ben asked.

"Ah, that's where we come in."

"Speaking of coming in," Ben said, pointing to the window. "The window is open, and so was the front door. Alice Glass was found leaning against the door on *that* side, and he was found leaning against the door on *this* side. Explain that."

"I can't," she said. "Not yet at least. Not before I've had a decent cup of coffee."

She stepped around the body and held the door open with a gloved hand.

"Shall we assemble the troops?" she asked, then left the room.

Ben followed with obvious reluctance.

At the foot of the stairs, Freya was met with two individuals in

white suits, masks, hoods, and protective footwear, one of which she recognised as Pat, but the other must have been new. "It's all yours."

A muffled response followed, of which she understood not a single word.

"Oh, Pat," she said, catching the attention of the familiar investigator. "You know me. I'll be chasing for a fast track on this one, so let's skip the game-playing and just assume this is a priority."

The two investigators looked at each other, then back at Freya, and Pat nodded.

"One of my team will be in touch later this afternoon," Freya called out, as Ben joined her by the front door, where Sanderson, the uniformed officer she had spoken to earlier, was standing with his chest puffed out, clearly looking for some kind of apology. "Ah, Sanderson, still here, are you?"

He was a handsome man with a strong jaw, keen, dark eyes, and neatly groomed facial hair, or at least he could have been handsome if only he worked on developing some kind of sincerity in his smile.

"I thought I'd wait to see what you had to say, Inspector Bloom."

"Chief Inspector Bloom," she corrected him. "And if you must know, it is I who should be waiting for some kind of apology from you."

"How do you work that out?" he asked. "SOCO is here, the whole place is being cordoned off, and you've two dead bodies. An old lady and some bloke."

"Ah, but your assumption was made on the circumstances of the former," she replied. "Had you applied the same argument to the latter, then I might have conceded. Sadly, you were wrong. She died of a heart attack. Whatever the trigger, Alice Glass was not murdered."

"He was right about you," Sanderson muttered.

"Who was?"

"Standing," he said. "Steve Standing. Told us all about you, he did. We worked with him at Lincoln HQ. Had plenty to say too, he did."

"Did he now? Ah, well, if you must insist on relying on the verbal pus of a corrupt police officer who is right now awaiting a rape and murder charge, then I'm afraid you should prepare yourself to lose time and time again," Freya told him, leaning in closer. "You owe me a favour."

"Is that right?"

"Unless you want me to include a short paragraph about the lack of experienced officers and the mishandling of a crime scene in my report, then I suggest you listen very carefully," she said, and he relented. He didn't reply or offer any visible retort, but his body language said all she needed to know. "I'll be in touch."

The two uniformed officers took their leave and made their way to the liveried cars parked along the street, where more of their colleagues had gathered.

"Look at them," Freya said, nodding at the other party of officers outside. "You'd think they'd be all over this by now, wouldn't you?"

"I believe they're waiting for your command, Herr Bloom," he replied, sounding like an extra from the old sitcom *'Allo 'Allo!*

"Herr means mister, Ben," she said. "And if that was your German accent, I'd stick to police work if I were you."

"*Achtung.*"

"Wrong again," she said, but this time, he did actually raise a smile on her face. "Come on. Let's get this going so I can get some coffee."

CHAPTER ELEVEN

"Aye, she just buggered off," Gillespie explained. "She's a bag of nerves, that one. Seeing the old girl on the floor must have really hit her, poor kid."

"Maybe I should go and see her," Gold suggested.

The team were in a circle near their cars, close enough for Gillespie to sit on his bonnet despite the metal denting under his weight. Anna Nillson positioned herself on the footpath beside Jenny Anderson, making an effort to stay with the team but where she would be the first to meet Ben and Freya when they finally emerged from the house.

The crime scene investigators were back and forth from their vans to the house, and the terrace of three cottages was being cordoned off by uniformed officers. She watched them for a moment, remembering the days when she performed the same tasks while wishing she could play a bigger role. It was while she was watching that Cruz rounded the corner of the street, nodded to the uniform fixing the perimeter, and ducked beneath the tape.

"I've got that water, Jim. Where is she?" he asked, as he joined them, slightly breathless. "I had to go all the way to the shop.

You'd think there would be some water in one of the marked cars, wouldn't you?"

"I'll take it," Gillespie said casually, and Cruz naively handed it to him without question, only for Gillespie to unscrew the lid, down half the bottle in a single swig, then burp loudly.

"You're a pig," Anderson told him. But the insult slid off him like pork grease on a Teflon pan.

"Aye," he said. "But even pigs need a drink now and then."

"That was for her," Cruz said.

"For who?"

Cruz looked about the scene and then to the far end of the terraces, where they'd spoken to the woman.

"Where is she?"

"The wee lass? Ah, she's gone, mate. You took too long," Gillespie said. "She said something about dying of thirst, and how, as the person who discovered the body, she should have been treated better. I tend to agree if I'm honest."

"But–"

"Then she said she was going to make a complaint about some short-arse detective or something," Gillespie continued. "I don't know. I wasn't really listening."

It was then that Cruz caught on and realised he was the target of a wind-up.

"Very funny," he said. "You owe me one pound thirty."

"One pound thirty? You were robbed, Gabby. There's barely two mouthfuls in here," Gillespie told him and then proceeded to finish the bottle in one long swig. "See? Look. That's fifty-five pence a mouthful. You should have got some beer. It would've been cheaper."

He put the lid back on the bottle then rested it on one of his window wipers.

"Actually, it's sixty-five pence per mouthful, you halfwit," Cruz said under his breath.

"Eh?"

"Right, listen up," Freya called out. She and Ben emerged from the house and strode up the garden path towards them. She waited until she was close to say anything else so that she could lower her voice, and the reason soon became clear. "As of fifteen minutes ago, we are dealing with a murder enquiry."

"A murder?" Gillespie said. "And here's me thinking we were heading out for some tea and cake."

"Gillespie, I'll say this once and I do hope that you'll pay attention. Whilst your rhetoric is often charming and has its part to play in the team dynamic, for the rest of the day, at least, please try to keep your mouth closed unless you have something useful to say. Do I make myself clear?"

"Aye, boss," he said, as a schoolboy might pay lip service to a teacher's warning.

"Alice Glass was eighty-three years old according to the girl who found her. Cause of death, according to Doctor Saint's preliminary examination, was a heart attack."

Gillespie opened his mouth to say something but then caught Freya's glare in time to shut up.

"But?" Anna said, and Freya turned to look at her.

"But we've discovered the body of a male. Mid-thirties, Caucasian, average build, no ID, no tattoos. Death occurred sometime between five and seven this morning."

"Hair?"

"Dark, as his skin."

"How dark?"

"I don't want to assume, but he could be Eastern European."

"He could be a labourer or a farm worker," Ben added. "My dad employs plenty of Eastern Europeans. He swears by them, and without sounding like a racist bigot, our man certainly looks like one of my dad's helping hands."

"He employs them?" Gold said. "I thought your dad preferred locals?"

"Well, he employs an agency," Ben replied. "But let's face it, you're not going to convince the great British public to go out and pick vegetables these days, are you?"

"Precisely," Freya said. "Gold, talk to Chapman back at the station. Have her go through the usual procedures, missing persons, et cetera. Also, ask her to look into any recent burglaries in the area. The bedroom window was open. So our initial thoughts are that Alice caught him in the act."

"That's enough to give anybody a heart attack," Gillespie said, to which Freya stared at him.

"Quite right," she said finally. "I don't like to cast aspersions, but he wouldn't be the first guest in this country to seek additional income immorally. And before anybody says anything, that isn't a racist comment. It is a fact based on statistics."

"It's okay, boss," Anna said, hoping she was speaking for the team. "I think we've all experienced enough nice migrant workers to know that it's only a handful who let the side down."

"Good," Freya replied. "Sadly, that handful is just that. A handful. More than a handful, in fact. I just hope to God this doesn't start an immigration war."

"Do you think we should keep his identity quiet?" Ben asked.

"Considering we don't know who he is, I don't think that will be a problem, do you?" she replied, then turned to face Gillespie and Cruz. "Which leads me to you two."

"Aye," Gillespie said, who by now was lying on his bonnet, resting his head on one arm. "What do you have for us? Do you want us to have a wee sniff around the local farms?"

"Gillespie, what on earth do you think you look like?" Freya asked, her expression one of utter disappointment.

"Eh?"

"Draw me like one of your French girls, Jack," Cruz said in a mock feminine tone, which raised a few laughs amongst the team. Gillespie slid off the car with an audible huff, then straightened his unironed shirt.

"Sorry, boss," he mumbled, but Gillespie, being Gillespie, never stayed down for long. "So, what do you think about me and Gabby hitting the local farms?"

"I think it's a terrible idea," Freya said. "But I do have a job for you both."

"Oh aye?"

"In fact, it's perfect for your skillset."

Gillespie said nothing at first, visibly trying to read her expression.

"Oh no," he said, to which Freya nodded.

"Yes."

"Ah, come on."

"Gillespie, it has to be the shortest street in Lincolnshire. There are literally three houses and one of them is the crime scene. That leaves two doors to knock on."

"Sorry, boss. But I'm going to have to refuse. Gabby and I have landed the door-to-door gig in pretty much every investigation we've had for the past year."

"You're refusing to follow an order?" Freya said.

"Aye, boss. Reluctantly, but yes."

"You'll be done in thirty minutes."

"I'm sorry, boss. It's a matter of principle. I hope you understand? It's unfair is what it is."

"That is a shame," she said. "A crying shame, if I'm honest."

"Aye, I know," he said, his tone and disposition both glum.

"I mean, I was looking forward to it," she said, turning to Anna with a little wink. "How about you, Nillson? Were you looking forward to it?"

"Looking forward to it?" she replied, catching on with what Freya was doing. "Oh, yes. I mean, who wouldn't?"

"Ben?" Freya said. "How about you?"

"It would have been the highlight of my day," he replied.

"I don't get it," Cruz said. "Sorry, have I missed something? What are we supposed to be looking forward to?"

"Well, I was just going to suggest we go for that slice of cake when we're done here," Freya said. "I mean, it looks like it's going to be a long week after all."

"Cake?" Gillespie said.

"From The Petwood Hotel?" Cruz added, and the two of them stood upright like puppies seeking a treat, which did little but raise a smile on Freya's face.

"We can be done in ten minutes," Gillespie said, shoving Cruz towards the houses. "Can't we, Gabby?"

"Quicker than that," Cruz replied.

"Well, like I said, it's a shame," Freya said.

"Eh? Is there cake or no cake?" Gillespie asked.

"I'm sorry," she said. "It's a matter of principle. I do hope you'll understand."

He stared at her, his face a picture of disappointment.

"Aye," he said eventually. "I get it."

"Good," Freya replied, and she slowly made her way towards Ben's car. "And while you're here, organise a search of the fields, will you?"

She pointed to the open land in front of the houses.

"Eh?" he said. "All of that?"

She nodded, somehow maintaining a straight face.

"You're looking for a murder weapon, Sergeant Gillespie. How is that for responsibility?" she said. "Most likely a hammer, but we can't be sure yet."

"A hammer?"

"A hammer," she said, then clapped her hands. "Well, we'll meet you two back at the station for a debrief."

She opened the passenger door and waited for Ben to reach the driver's door.

"I don't suppose..." she began, staring directly at Ben. The whole team paused, waiting for her to finish.

"You don't suppose what?" Ben asked.

"Oh, I was just going to ask if The Petwood does good

coffee?" she said, with a furtive glance in Gillespie's direction, who shook his head in disbelief. "It would be a terrible shame to miss out, wouldn't it?"

CHAPTER TWELVE

It was nearing eleven o'clock in the morning when Gillespie put the phone down on Sergeant Priest back at the station and then stared at the middle cottage while Cruz did his best to stay calm. It was clear from the look on Gillespie's face he was annoyed about having to stay and miss out on cake.

Cruz, however, was simply annoyed at being partnered with a man who seemed to be magnetically attracted to bad fortune, and who simply couldn't keep his mouth shut.

"Right," Gillespie said. "Sergeant Priest said the reinforcements will be here in twenty minutes. That gives us fifteen minutes to talk to the owner of this place, and that one." He pointed at the end cottage for clarity, despite there being no other houses on the street.

"Why fifteen minutes?" Cruz asked. "Surely if they'll be here in twenty minutes, we have twenty minutes. Ten minutes per house. That's enough for an initial chat, don't you think?"

"Fifteen minutes, Gabby," Gillespie said. "That's six and a half minutes per house, leaving five minutes for you to run up to the high street to grab us some coffee."

"What? First of all, it's seven and a half minutes. Your maths is appalling. Secondly, I am not your bloody gopher."

"My what?"

"Your gopher. I'm a bloody detective, and unless you start treating me like one–"

"What's a gopher? Isn't it some kind of squirrel?"

Cruz shook his head in disbelief, feeling a headache starting to build.

"A gopher, Jim. As in go-for this, go-for that."

"A gopher?" Gillespie replied. "What are you trying to say?"

"I'm just saying..." Cruz began, but words failed him. "Ah, forget it."

"No, if you've something to say, Gabby, come out and say it."

"It's not important," Cruz said, exasperated.

"Aye, so if it's not important, what the bloody hell are you going on about?" Gillespie said. "We'll talk to the neighbours and then you can run off and grab some coffees before we start the search."

"Right," Cruz replied, feeling the big man staring down at him. "Alright, alright, I'll get the bloody coffees. Anything just to shut you up."

"Aye, that's the ticket," Gillespie said, straightening his collar. "Now then, off you pop."

"Off I pop?"

"Aye," he said, gesturing for Cruz to lead the way. "Off you pop."

"You want me to lead the interview?"

"Aye, I think you're ready, don't you?"

Cruz stayed where he was, staring up at Gillespie in utter incredulity.

"Can you actually hear yourself speak?" he asked. "Do you know how patronising you can be sometimes?"

"Aye, I do. You should thank your lucky stars you're with me, Gabby, and not Nillson. Imagine that? All that talk about babies,

shopping, and makeup, and God knows what else. Stick with me, Gabby. I'll see you alright."

Cruz had to check himself, to stop from reacting to such a misogynistic statement. It was the type of thing he would expect Gillespie to have said, and also the exact attitude that severed them from the rest of the team when they were going for cake and coffee.

"Do you ever wonder why people don't like you?" he said.

"Eh? What do you mean?"

Shaking his head, Cruz rang the doorbell, doing his best to find his game face, and felt Gillespie looming behind him.

The front door opened a fraction and a young woman peered through the crack.

"Oh, hello," Cruz said, holding his warrant card up for her to see. "I'm Detective Constable Cruz. I wonder if we could have a quick word?"

"Is it her next door?" she said. "Is that what all this is about?"

"Sorry?" Cruz said.

"Her?" she said, jabbing a thumb out of the door. "What's Mad Alice done now, run naked down the high street?"

"Well, I'm, afraid there's been an incident," he said. "Are you able to tell me if you were up and about sometime between five and seven this morning?"

"Between five and even this morning? Yes, I was up at five-thirty. Why?"

"We were wondering if you happened to see anybody in the area? Or if you saw anything unusual?"

"Unusual? No," she said. "No, not this morning."

"You didn't see Alice Glass walking around or talking to anybody?"

"How would I have seen her walking around? I live three miles away."

"Three miles..." Cruz started. "Sorry, have I missed something? You are the owner of this house, aren't you?"

"No," she said. "No, this is my mum's house. I just popped in to get her up and dressed, just as I do every morning."

"I see," Cruz said, becoming increasingly agitated. "Well, perhaps your mother saw something? Might we have a word with her?"

"You're welcome to try. But I don't think she'll be able to help," the woman said.

"Even so," Cruz replied. "It's always good to ask the question."

The woman smiled as if to say, 'have it your way', and then let the door swing open. She walked a few steps to the living room and leaned in, raising her voice. "Mum? Mum, there's two men here to see you."

Cruz and Gillespie entered the hallway, which had just two doors leading off it, the kitchen at the far end and the living room, out of which the woman poked her head and waved them in.

"Mum, these two gentlemen are with the police," she said, still raising her voice.

"The police?"

"That's right," Cruz said, and he flashed his warrant card. But she paid no notice. He raised his voice, too, and spoke clearly, mirroring the younger woman. "We were wondering if you saw anything unusual this morning."

"Outside?" she said, looking confused. She wore her hair short and had long since given up on concealing the grey hairs which, if anything, accentuated her pale eyes. "I haven't been outside."

"No, I meant through the window."

"Sorry, dear, you'll have to speak up. I'm a bit mutton these days."

Cruz dropped to a crouch before her, moving his head into her line of sight.

"I asked if you happened to look out the window this morning and saw anything going on?"

"Anything going on?" she said. "What's going on?"

Exasperated, Cruz looked up at the elderly lady's daughter.

"A bit of help?" he said.

"Mum, can you tell these two men exactly what you saw this morning? Something has happened to Alice and they're hoping that you saw something."

"This morning?" the lady said with a little laugh. "My dears, I haven't seen anything since nineteen ninety-one."

"Sorry?" Cruz said, and he saw Gillespie turn away, heading back to the hallway, biting down on his knuckle. "What do you mean?"

"What my mother is trying to tell you, officer, is that she's as blind as a bat."

"Blind as a bat?" Cruz repeated, to which the younger woman nodded with an expression that said, 'I told you so'.

"What's that, dear?" the older lady said.

"And she's hard of hearing, too?" Cruz said.

"Hence why I come every morning to help her dress and get settled in for the day."

Gillespie appeared in the doorway looking irritated and impatient.

"Well," Cruz said, "I think we've wasted quite enough of your time."

He stood and made his way to the door and the younger lady followed. At the front door, Gillespie let himself out, but Cruz had a final question on his mind.

"May I ask what time you reached here this morning?" he asked.

The daughter held her hands before her, interlocking her fingers.

"I get here at six forty-five most mornings," she said. "I have to be at work at nine, and as you can imagine, getting Mum dressed isn't a five-minute job."

Cruz checked his watch.

"Aren't you working today?" he asked.

"I was supposed to," she replied. "But with all the commotion out there, I didn't want to leave Mum on her own. If she'd managed to hear anything, she would have called me anyway. So, I phoned in sick. My boss is okay, but I'll have to make up the time."

"I thought you said she was hard of hearing," Cruz said.

"I get the feeling it's selective," the woman said. "She'll hear what she wants to hear. She hears The Archers on Radio Four just fine. Next door's dog barking and strange noises in the house don't seem to be a problem either. But the telephone or the doorbell, no chance."

"I see," Cruz said, understanding what she was getting at. "Well, Mrs..."

"Blake," she said. "And it's *Miss* Deborah Blake."

"Thanks," he said. "Well, if we need anything else—"

"If you need anything else, I'd appreciate it if you could call me." She leaned behind the front door and scribbled her phone number on a little notepad, then tore off the slip of paper and handed it to him. "If two strange men knock on the door while she's on her own, she'll have a heart attack."

"No problem," Cruz said, and he glanced up the garden path to find Gillespie on the footpath, eager to move on to the next house.

"I think you'll have better luck with next door," she said, following his stare and seeing Gillespie.

"I hope so," Cruz replied. "Who lives there?"

"Oh, that's George. He's an old boy, but he thinks he's in his thirties. If there's anything you need to know about Alice, he'll know."

"Oh, really?" Cruz said. "Bit of a busy body, is he?"

Miss Blake lowered her voice, presumably in case her mother's selective hearing came into action. "He's Alice's brother-in-law," she said. "I sometimes get the feeling he thinks Mum and Alice are his harem. Like they're his responsibility. He does their

gardens, signs for parcels, and all that stuff. If anybody saw Alice this morning, it'll be him."

"That's really helpful, thank you," Cruz said. "We're usually met with a barrage of abuse and questions when we do this. That's if people actually answer the door in the first place."

"No problem. I feel like a bit of a letdown if I'm honest. One more thing," Miss Blake said, stopping Cruz in his tracks. "Can I ask how it happened? Alice, I mean. She was a kind soul, really. A little lost in life, maybe, but she was nice enough."

"How what happened?"

"Well," she said, almost hesitant to speak the words out loud, "she's dead, isn't she? I mean, you wouldn't have all these cars and people otherwise, would you?"

"I'm afraid I can't really go into details," Cruz said.

"Well, I'm no expert, but three police cars, an ambulance, and all the other vehicles, it's a little concerning. I'm glad Mum can't see what's going on."

Cruz checked Gillespie was out of earshot, then leaned into the house and lowered his voice.

"It was a heart attack," Cruz replied, and her expression changed to one of guilt. "Maybe two strange men knocked on her door?"

CHAPTER THIRTEEN

"Right then," Freya said, as the team filed into the incident room.

Ben took his seat and watched as Nillson, Anderson, and Gold took theirs. Chapman, meanwhile, barely even looked up from her computer, her fingers tapping away on the keyboard as if she was just trying to finish her work before the briefing began. Freya noticed her frantic typing, too, and waited a few moments, until the plain but efficient Chapman finally hit enter with a flourish, took a breath, and laid her hands on her desk.

"Sorry about that," she said. "I just wanted to get all that down before we began."

"That's quite alright," Freya told her. "In fact, I'm rather looking forward to hearing what you've managed to dig up while we were out."

"Well, if I were you, I'd set aside any preconceptions you may have had," Chapman replied, teasing them all into intrigue. "Alice Glass was quite something. And as for the second victim, there are no missing person reports matching his description."

Freya sat back on the edge of her desk, thoughtful in her expression, and then addressed the room.

"If that hasn't whetted your appetites, then perhaps this will,"

she said. From where she was perched, Freya dragged the white-board closer and selected a black pen with which she wrote the name *Alice Glass* in the centre of the board to the left. Beside the name, she drew a straight horizontal line and a question mark. "Two deaths. One more natural than the other, but still there is a link, and I mean to find it."

"We don't have much to go on," Nillson said. "What's the plan?"

"Well, as it happens, I do have a plan," Freya told her. "But first, let's recap. According to Doctor Saint, Alice Glass suffered a heart attack. So, until that fact is either proven or an alternative is placed in our midst, this is all we have to go on. We have no time of death and no eye witnesses."

"Unless Gillespie uncovers something," Ben added.

"Oh, God," Anderson said. "That's not a picture I need to imagine."

"Agreed," Freya said with a smile. "But moving on to our mystery man, we can confirm he received a blow to the head with a round object, something like a hammer if not one. Time of death was between five and seven this morning, and from his appearance, he could be Eastern European, South American, maybe even Middle Eastern."

"Given his tan lines and the rough skin on his hands. I'd say he worked outside. My money is on him being a farm worker, especially out in Navenby where farming is the predominant industry. But we won't know for sure until we know his identity," Ben said.

"Quite right," Freya replied. "But given the scant facts we have to work with, I'm happy to ponder a possibility than wonder the whys, whos, and what fors."

"Sorry, you lost me," Gold said, looking around the room to see if anybody else was confused.

"What she means is that it wouldn't hurt to use an educated guess as a basis for a theory until he is formally identified," Ben told her.

"So, you want to look into the farm workers?" Gold asked. "Is that right?"

"No, I want Chapman to look into them," Freya replied. "Ben, you said your father uses an agency. Is that a common approach?"

"It saves him a fortune on payroll, sick pay, and holiday cover. Not to mention the translation issues, visas, and God knows what."

"That's what I thought," she said, turning to Chapman. "Can you please develop a list of agencies in the area? I imagine it'll be short. Nillson and Anderson can follow up."

"You want us to call them?" Nillson said.

"No, I want you to pay them a visit."

"Can I add," Ben began. "That you should do so with caution."

"Why?"

"If you managed an agency that hired migrant workers, how would you feel if the law walked through your door and started asking questions? I can only imagine how many hoops those businesses have to jump through to keep their operations legal."

"And you think that talking to the actual workers might prove more fruitful?" Nillson asked.

"Focus on the foreman," Ben said. "Quite often you'll find that the workers' English is less fluent than the foreman's."

"Ah, *comme tu as raison*," Freya said, to which Ben could do little but feign his understanding, which only served to fuel Freya's knowing smile. She turned to Nillson. "Don't do anything yet. Just do the spadework. Nobody is to move on anything until A, Gillespie is back with some news, or not, whichever be the case, and B, we've attended the autopsy. With any luck, we'll have his DNA on file. If not, you two girls are in for a rough ride."

Anderson and Nillson shared a worried expression.

"Never before have I prayed Gillespie does his job well and comes back with some good news," Nillson muttered.

"Well, until then, all we can do is gather facts," Freya said,

finally letting her eyes fall on Chapman. "And now, I believe the floor is yours, Detective Constable Chapman."

Chapman gathered her notes then struck her keyboard. The printer whirred into life, and with complete poise, she strolled across the room to collect her printouts.

"Right then," Chapman said, looking around at them all to make sure she had their attention. "Mrs Alice Glass was eighty-three years old. She bought the cottage with her husband in nineteen fifty-nine, where she lived with him until three years ago."

"God bless singledom," Nillson added. "At least I won't have to go through the heartache of seeing my husband die, or vice versa."

"I'm sure the pros outweigh the cons, Anna. Although, in my experience, marriage isn't for everyone," Freya said. "How did he die, Chapman?"

"He was attacked," she replied, which raised a few eyebrows. "According to my sources, he was out walking one morning and didn't come home. He's buried in Navenby."

"Poor old girl," Nillson said. "I remember when my granddad died, my nan didn't have a clue what to do. It's not like he left a manual describing how to pay the bills, where all the paperwork was or anything. It took my brothers weeks to understand it, and they're still trying to explain how things work now."

"One of the pros of singledom," Freya said. "It means you know exactly how much money you don't have."

"Sadly, Alice's story doesn't end there," Chapman said, regaining their attention. "In the past three years, she's developed a rather impressive form."

"Form?" Ben said. "As in, she's been arrested?"

"Six times," Chapman said with a nod. "All resulting in cautions and slaps on the wrist."

"My God," Anderson added. "That poor old lady was a bank robber?"

"Or a stalker?" Nillson said.

"Actually, it's not what you think," Chapman said, once more taking control. "Indecent exposure."

There was silence as each of them processed that thought.

"That's rather the cliff hanger," Freya said. "I do hope you managed to get a little more detail on the matter."

"Not really, ma'am," she replied. "But there is a statement from one of her neighbours. A Mr Benson. Apparently, he lives two doors away."

"The end cottage," Ben said, remembering the terrace of three. "What did he have to say?"

"From his statement, he says that Alice has been experiencing mental difficulties since the death of her husband. It looks to me like he's been managing to smooth things over."

"Sorry, what?" Nillson said. "Her husband dies and her way of dealing with it is by flashing people?"

"Not flashing exactly," Chapman said. "Just not dressed appropriately for certain places, including the fields surrounding Navenby."

It was as if nobody dared speak ill of the dead, but the looks on their faces suggested that each of them was harbouring a quip or two.

"Tell us more about this George Benson chap," Freya said. "Why would he stick his neck out for her?"

"Brother-in-law, ma'am," Chapman replied. "He's the husband of Alice's late sister."

"Well, I can't wait to hear what Gillespie and Cruz uncover when they speak to him," Freya said, as Chapman's desk phone began to ring. "If you can all get past that image."

Leaning over her desk, Chapman regained everybody's attention again.

"Ma'am," she said. "It's Pippa Bell, the pathologist."

"Oh, God," Ben muttered to himself.

"She's ready for you," Chapman added. "She said you should attend as soon as you possibly can."

CHAPTER FOURTEEN

"I thought you were never coming out of there, Gabby," Gillespie said. "What were you doing? Giving her your number?"

"Eh?"

"The lass, what was all that about?"

"She was just telling me about Mr Benson," Cruz said.

"So, you didn't give her your number?"

"What? No. I'm with Hermione, remember?"

"Oh, come on. I know the look she gave you. Seen it many a time, I have," he said. "You're forgetting who you're talking to."

"Why do you always have to make everything sound so smutty?" Cruz said. "I'm perfectly happy with Hermione, so whether or not Miss Blake took a shine to me is irrelevant. Besides, what happened to you the last time you spent the night with a witness? It's hardly a great goal to aim for, is it?"

"Aye well, that was just misfortune."

"For her or for you?" Cruz said as they stepped onto Mr Benson's property.

"Anyway, who's Mr Benson?"

"George," Cruz said, and he nodded at the house in front of them. "The man who owns this house."

"So, you're on first-name terms, are you?"

"Well, no, but she just told me—"

"I suppose you want to take the lead on this as well, do you? Seeing as you made such a cracking job of the last one."

"What's that supposed to mean?"

"Oh nothing," Gillespie said. "Except for asking a blind woman if she saw anything this morning."

"I didn't know she was blind, did I?" he said. "Besides, it's not like you stepped in at any point. No, you just loomed there in the background like a bloody great, big, hairy—"

"Can I help you?" a voice said, and Gillespie watched as Cruz turned on his heels, his face reddening. "Are you going to tell me what's going on here?"

"Ah, you must be Mr Benson," Cruz said, scrambling for his warrant card, which he eventually found in his inside pocket and presented for Mr Benson to inspect. "I'm Detective—"

"Constable Cruz," the older man finished for him, peering down his nose through his glasses to read the little card. He looked up at Gillespie. "And you are?"

"Detective Sergeant Gillespie," Gillespie replied, holding his own warrant card up for inspection.

"So, you outrank your friend here?"

"Aye, I do," Gillespie said.

"So, will one of you tell me what's going on?" Mr Benson said. "I've seen you all traipsing in and out of Alice's house all morning, but when I asked one of the men up there, they wouldn't tell me anything."

"I'm sure they were just following protocol, Mr Benson," Gillespie said. "At a time like this, we prefer to manage the spread of local news."

"Local news is one thing, but what about Alice?" he said. "Something's happened, hasn't it? Is she okay? She's not answering the phone."

"Perhaps we can go inside, Mr Benson," Cruz said.

"No," he said, rather abruptly. "No, she's my sister-in-law. If something has happened to her, then I need to know, and I need to know *now*."

Cruz glanced up at Gillespie to make a decision, and he nodded in return, letting the younger officer's reins loose a little.

"I'm sorry to say, Mr Benson, but Alice passed away this morning," Cruz said, and to his credit, he spoke clearly and with empathy, without wasting words – all the tips the force recommended under such circumstances. The trick now was to wait and read the reaction of Mr Benson, which Cruz seemed to be doing well.

"How?" Benson said, his eyes softening. He leaned on the gate post and stared at Alice's house as one of the white-suited investigators emerged through the front door carrying a flight case. "How did she go? Did she suffer?"

The more questions he asked, the greater weight he put on the post, as if he was loading a burden with every word.

"It was a heart attack," Cruz said. "We can't say if she suffered, but suffice to say, her ordeal is over now."

"A heart attack?" he said, straightening. "A heart attack, you say? So why the circus? You don't do this for a heart attack, do you?"

"I'm afraid it's a little more complex than that," Cruz explained, and he took a breath, clearly searching for the right way to phrase the next part. "You see, while we were dealing with Alice, one of our team discovered another."

"Another what?"

"Another body," Cruz said. "A man. Mid-thirties. Possibly Eastern European. We wondered if you saw anybody hanging around this morning? Or if you saw anything unusual? Say, between five and seven o'clock?"

Mr Benson stared at the ground in disbelief.

"A man, you say?" he said. "In Alice's house?"

"That's right," Cruz said. "He was in her bedroom."

Benson looked Gillespie in the eye, perhaps seeking the perspective of a man closer in years and with a more mature disposition.

"Am I to presume this man did *not* die from a heart attack?" he asked. "And he was in the house uninvited?"

"The answers to those questions will become clear in time," Gillespie said. "And when the time comes for us to share them, we will. But it's important right now that we understand if anybody saw anything usual this morning."

Benson shook his head sadly.

"Nothing unusual," he said. "No. Between five and seven, you say?"

"That's right," Cruz replied. "Why? Is there something you want to say?"

"No," he said, again abruptly. He glanced back at his own house, and Gillespie followed his gaze.

"Mr Benson?" he said, drawing the old man's attention from the upstairs window. "Are you sure?"

"No," he said. "I mean, yes, I'm sure. It's just... Well, there's something you should probably know. About Alice, I mean."

"Should we go inside?" Gillespie asked. "You look like you could do with a sit-down."

"I'm fine. I just need to stretch my legs. Maybe we can walk," he said. "It might be a good distraction, if you know what I mean."

"Aye," Gillespie said, looking left and right along the little lane. But then another place caught his eye. "How about through there?"

"The fields?" Benson said, a little taken back.

"Why not?" Gillespie replied. "It's quiet, it's away from the circus, and–"

"No, it's perfect," George said, leading the way off the lane onto a little footpath marked by a traditional, wooden sign. He

stopped at the edge of the field and turned back to them. "You'll understand why in a minute."

Cruz followed him and Gillespie fell in behind. But they didn't just take a few steps into the field; they had walked for more than a minute before Gillespie finally thought to say something.

"You had something to tell us, Mr Benson," he called out.

But the old man soldiered on, heading for a spot ahead where two footpaths met beside an old tree. A bench had been placed there, with a red bin for dog walkers to use.

It was at the bench that Benson stopped to take the weight off his feet, and Gillespie manoeuvred himself to sit beside him, leaving Cruz, the youngest of the three, to stand before them.

"It's a cracking view, Mr Benson," Gillespie said, ushering Cruz out of the way with a wave of his hand. It was late summer and the fields had been harvested, leaving them with a view of Navenby, the three cottages in the foreground. "Aye, I could get used to looking at that, I could."

"Pretty, isn't it?" Benson said, his voice belying his years. He leaned back in the seat and placed his arm on the wooden backrest. It was then that Gillespie saw the little plaque. He leaned forward to read it.

"Margaret Benson," Gillespie said. "Your wife?"

The old man nodded and smiled the smile of a man who fondly remembered better times.

"She loved it here," he said. "It was her favourite spot."

"Hence why you had a bench installed?" Cruz said.

"That's right," Benson replied, then turned in his seat to point at the large oak tree. "That was where we did it. Right there."

Gillespie felt himself blush a little, and Cruz turned away, feigning interest in something on the ground.

"I remember it like it was yesterday," Benson continued.

"I'm sure it was—"

"The sun was high in the sky and we lay there on my little blanket with a picnic lunch and a bottle of beer between us."

"That sounds lovely," Gillespie said, looking to move the topic on.

"It wasn't just us either," Benson said. "Alice and Alex did it there too."

Cruz, who had only just rejoined then, turned away again with considerable haste, his face as red as a baboon's backside.

"Oh, yes," Benson continued. "And you can see why too, can't you? It's a fabulous spot, and you can be quite sure of all the privacy you need to do the deed. If you know what I mean?"

"Aye, I do," Gillespie said, a little startled at the man's frank discussion. "I've done the deed, as you put it, beneath more than a few old oak trees in my time."

Mr Benson stared at him, slightly horrified.

"More than a few times?" he said.

"Aye," Gillespie said, as if the two had met at a bar and were discussing days of old. "None with a view quite like this though. To be honest, most of them were in the old playing field, so we had to be quick."

"I'm sorry, but I'm not sure I understand," Mr Benson said. "Exactly how many times have you been engaged?"

"Engaged?" Gillespie said, seeing Cruz's head jerk upright in the corner of his eye. Gillespie shook his head. "None. Marriage is not really for me, if I'm honest."

"Oh, well, I must say that is a callus thing to do," Mr Benson said. "You proposed to multiple women but never married one of them?"

"Proposed?" Gillespie said, suddenly understanding what Mr Benson meant by 'doing the deed'.

"Yes. You proposed to all those young girls and then let them down?" he said. "I do hope you didn't jilt them at the altar. Now that I find unforgivable."

"Aye," Gillespie said, moving the conversation on. "I couldn't agree more. Unforgivable. So, Alice and her husband *did the deed* here too, then, did they?"

"They did," Mr Benson said, smiling that smile again. "We lost him a few years ago, but she still comes here – sorry, came here – to speak to him. Every morning at five a.m."

"Every morning?" Cruz said. "It's a bit of a hike in the wind and rain, I'll bet. You'd need your head examined to traipse all the way out here in the pouring rain at five a.m."

"That's the point," Mr Benson said. "In fact, that's exactly the point I was hoping to make."

"Hold on," Gillespie said. "Why did she come out here at five a.m.? Why so specific?"

Mr Benson's smile faded and his eyes shone with a memory.

"Because this is where Alex died," he said.

"At five o'clock in the morning?" Cruz asked. "Right here?"

"By the bench," Benson said. "The police found signs of the front door being forced open. Alex was a twitcher. He'd often go out before sunrise to indulge in his hobby. The theory is that he came home, saw the front door open, and then chased them into the field where they turned on him."

"They beat him to death?" Gillespie asked, to which Benson nodded sadly.

"It was awful," he replied. "And do you want to know the worst part? They never found the culprit."

"He was murdered?" Cruz said.

"That's what sent her round the bend," Benson said, his voice soft and distant. "And that's why she came out here at five o'clock every morning. She hoped that one day she'd find him here. And the whole thing might have been a dream."

CHAPTER FIFTEEN

It was gone midday by the time Ben reversed into a parking spot in the hospital car park. Freya sat in the passenger seat with her hands on her thighs like a public schoolgirl awaiting a reprimand from the headmaster.

It didn't matter how many times she adjusted her posture, she couldn't help but feel guilt, and it didn't matter how many times she considered the reason for it, she could fathom nothing.

"I wish you'd tell me what's on your mind," she said, as Ben turned off the engine. He removed the key from the ignition and stared ahead. "It's okay. You don't have to be totally honest with me, but at least now I know I'm right."

"Why?" he asked. "What is it that you're right about?"

"That something is on your mind."

"And how did you come to that?" he asked.

"Because if there was nothing wrong, then you would have denied it," she told him, to which he had no response. "There. I've said my part. Now all you need to do is buck your ideas up and get whatever it is off your chest."

She pushed open her door and climbed out, before waiting for

him to do the same. And when he did, he locked the car and spoke to her from across the bonnet, as they always used to.

"Have you ever considered that I might have a problem, or something on my mind, that doesn't involve you?" he asked.

"Yes, actually," she replied. "But then I remembered that you and Michaela split up last month, and for the life of me, I can't think of anything else that puts you in a mood."

"I am not in a mood," he said.

"There," she said. "That's more like it. When you're ready to talk, just let me know. Now come along. We don't want to keep Pip waiting, or you will have something to be down in the dumps about."

She turned her back on him and headed towards the main entrance before he could contest, and heard him run a few steps to catch up.

"My dad might be ill," he said, taking long strides to keep pace with her. "Have you considered that? Or my brothers. One of them could be sick."

"Your father is in good health," she replied. "And so are your brothers. And now you have exhausted your list of people you care for, meaning the only person left to have either offended or upset you is me."

"I could be sick," he said. "Have you considered that?"

She stopped and appraised him from his shoes to his hair, then lowered her eyes to his.

"You're a picture of health, Ben," she said. "Aside from the bags beneath your eyes and the fact that you haven't shaved, which suggests a lack of sleep, which then leads me to believe something is keeping you awake at night."

His mouth opened as if he might say something, but nothing came out.

"There it is again," she said, restarting her march towards the hospital. Ben followed, of course, but said nothing in reply. "You,

of all people, should know, Ben, that silence is just as much a sign of guilt as a man who cannot keep his mouth shut."

They walked through the main entrance doors, past the reception, and into the main corridor, where a series of painted lines on the floor marked the path to various departments. Each of them knew the lines like the veins on the backs of their hands, and they walked quite habitually along the long corridors.

"What about a woman whose main mode of defence is to question the lives and dispositions of others?" he said. "Surely there are things you aren't telling me."

"We're not married, Ben. I don't have to tell you everything."

"But I have to tell you?" he asked, holding the door to the morgue open for her.

She breezed through and let him catch her up again.

"Yes, actually," she said. "You see, if you were able to somehow disguise whatever it is that burdens you, then I wouldn't feel it necessary to push. But you aren't, are you? So therefore, as a friend, I'm obliged to ask."

They reached the double doors and Ben reached up to push the buzzer.

"And I suppose you're able to disguise your moods, are you?" he said. "I wonder what the rest of the team would have to say about that."

"I am actually," she replied. "If, for some reason, I wear my heart on my sleeve, then it's not because I have emotional intelligence issues. It's for a purpose. Sometimes one needs to put on a display to keep the questions at bay."

He pushed the buzzer and stared at her.

"There is a seriously messed-up girl inside that head of yours, Freya," he said, just as the door opened. They were greeted by Doctor Pippa Bell, a stout young woman with piercings in her nose, lip, tongue, and God knows where else, and a tattoo of a Welsh dragon reaching up from her ample bosom.

"Oh, it's you," she said, her Welsh accent somehow making the phrase sound even more disappointed.

"Well, I must admit, Pip," Freya said, "I've had nicer greetings in the past, even from you."

"Were you expecting somebody else?" Ben asked.

"My lunch," she replied, stepping aside for them to enter the little reception room. "Ordered a pizza two hours ago. You'd think it would be here by now, wouldn't you?"

"You ordered a pizza at ten o'clock in the morning?" Freya said.

"Yes. They don't open until twelve, but I was hoping my pizza would be the first one they made," she replied, pushing her hair from her face. "I've got a long day ahead of me, and you'd be surprised how hungry my work makes you."

"You cut up bodies and examine human organs," Ben said, looking more than a little shocked. "And that makes you hungry?"

"Do you know how many steps I do in a day?" Pip said, to which Ben shrugged.

"I haven't got a clue," he said.

"Go on. Have a guess."

"No, really. I wouldn't know–"

"Eight thousand," she said. "Eight thousand steps, Ben. We don't all sit around on our backsides."

"Neither do–"

"How have you been anyway, Pip?" Freya said. "You're looking well. Have you done something with your hair?"

Pip turned her inquisitive glare onto Freya.

"Why? Don't you like it?"

"I was just being polite," Freya said.

"You want to know if I've discovered anything?" she said. "Should I tell you about my hair, or do you want to get down to business?"

"You know me, Pip. All work and no play."

"Well then, we'd better get to it," Pip said, pushing her way

through the heavy doors into the mortuary. "You know where everything is by now, don't you?"

The doors closed with a swish and Ben leaned against the wall.

"Honestly, I hate her," he said.

"No, you don't. If you had a problem with her, you'd be silent and sullen like you are with me."

He said nothing, and she smiled to herself as they donned their gowns, masks, and gloves.

"Tie me up, will you?" he said, turning around to proffer the strings.

She did as he asked, then slapped him on the backside when she was done, and he tensed at her touch.

"There really is something wrong, isn't there?" she said.

"Freya, can we just get on?" he replied, moving away to stand beside the door.

She watched him, noting his body language. Gone was the relaxed, confident man she had once admired, and in his wake was a man who seemed withdrawn and tired. She saw it now; something was truly troubling him.

"Ben, you do know you can talk to me, don't you? You can tell me anything."

He nodded but didn't smile.

"I know," he replied. "And if you must know, Freya, yes, there is something on my mind. Is it something I want to talk about? No. No, it isn't. Will I share my thoughts with you? One day maybe. But for the time being, I'd like to get on with my job. It's the only thing that seems to work as a distraction right now."

Freya softened. It wasn't like him to open up, and she felt a pang of guilt that he had felt under pressure because of her.

"Just so you know," she said. "I'm here."

They shared a brief moment during which nobody spoke but volumes were conveyed. It soon was broken, not by an enraged Pip growing tired of waiting, but by footsteps in the corridor outside.

Freya peered through the little window, then looked back at Ben, unable to hide the glee in her expression.

"This should cheer you up," she said, as she opened the door to the corridor. A man in a motorcycle jacket, heavy trousers, and boots approached carrying a fast food delivery bag.

"I was hoping it would be you," Freya said to the man. "Is that for Pippa Bell?"

"Yep," he replied, as he tore open the bag and produced a pizza box, which he then handed to Freya without question. "Have a nice day."

He turned and left without waiting for a tip, and Freya closed the door behind him. She set the pizza down on the little table near the couch and opened the lid.

"Pepperoni?" she said.

"Freya, no. You can't."

But it was too late. She had torn off a slice and taken a large bite, letting a string of cheese hang from her mouth.

"God, it's good," she said, covering her mouth with her free hand as she spoke.

Just as she knew he would, Ben checked the mortuary door, then eyed the pizza.

"We can't eat it all," he said.

"Just enough to put a smile on your face," she said, and he did smile as he reached for a slice. Then he grinned broadly at the idea of Pip finding half her pizza missing when they'd left.

And the sight of him smiling was beautiful.

"I've missed that smile," she told him. "I've missed that a lot."

CHAPTER SIXTEEN

Standing beside a stainless steel bench on the far side of the examination room, the Welsh dragon's beady eyes followed Ben and Freya as they stepped cautiously towards her.

"Now then," she grumbled, and Ben took a breath as they came to a stop at the bench, strangely glad of the corpse between them. The thin, blue sheet that lay over it disguised any features, leaving only the size and shape of the body. By comparing it to the one on the next bench, Ben could ascertain that this was Alice Glass's body they were standing beside. "What's up with you two?"

"What do you mean?" Ben said, and she eyed them both with obvious suspicion. Ben and Freya exchanged nervous glances, then both shrugged.

"How are you getting you on, then?" Freya asked, always the one to distract, divert, and direct a conversation towards a destination more suited to her own requirements. "I presume this is Alice Glass?"

"You're up to something," Pip said.

"I can assure you, Pip," Freya said, "the only thing Ben and I

are up to is developing an understanding of how Alice Glass and our mystery man died."

Pip's eyes narrowed and she gave them both a disbelieving stare before carefully peeling back the corner of the blue sheet.

"Heart attack," she said finally. "Doctor Saint was right."

"Time of death?" Ben asked.

Pip did that thing she often did when the answer should have been a simple statement. She puffed out her cheeks and stared at the old lady on the bench.

"Heart attacks are not as sudden as you might think," she began. "Her heart would have been under severe stress for several hours before the event, and she may have even suffered minor heart attacks before the main event. Judging by the damage to the arteries surrounding it, I'd say there were at least two."

"And could these attacks have been caused by anything?" Freya asked.

"Caused by something?" Pip said. "Of course they were caused by something. The heart is a wonderful thing, Freya Bloom. It doesn't just give up at a moment's notice."

"I was referring to third-party intervention, Pip," Freya said. "Drugs maybe?"

"I know where your head is at, don't you worry. But we won't know the answer until the bloods come back. I've sent them already, along with notes of what they might be looking for."

"Very pragmatic," Freya said with a sigh. "So poor old Alice Glass died from a simple heart attack at the top of her stairs."

"All alone," Pip said.

"Not entirely," Ben added, and he gestured at the only other bench with a lump beneath a thin, blue sheet.

"Ah," Pip said. "Our mystery man."

She said it with a roll of her Rs and a flourish that only she could accomplish in such a setting.

Pip covered Alice and they all moved to the next bench,

where she once more took her position on the far side of the corpse.

"I'm sure you both have questions just popping out of your ears, but if you don't mind, I prefer to give my assessment before I have to listen to you two work on whatever theories you may or may not have."

"The floor is yours, Pip," Freya said.

"Thank you," she replied. "Before we start, I read in the notes somewhere that he's assumed to be foreign, is that right?"

"It is," Freya said. "I think he might be Eastern European, but I could be wrong."

"What makes you think that?" Pip asked.

"I don't wish to sound like a racist bigot, Pip," Freya replied. "He just has the look. The dark features, the skin tone, and his attire."

"His attire?" Pip asked, pulling Freya into an awkward corner with ease. "Do Eastern Europeans wear a uniform?"

"Don't make this harder than it already is," Freya replied. "I just mean that it's not uncommon to find Eastern Europeans wearing the type of tracksuit our man was wearing. It's not a uniform, but if he was wearing a tweed suit, I'd have no difficulty in assuming he was English, or British at least."

Pip smiled.

"Nicely swerved," she said. "In fact, you're right. I think so anyway. I've called in a favour for you and sent scans of his teeth and jaws to a friend of mine."

"His teeth?" Ben said.

"He's definitely not British," Pip said. "The dentistry work is different. I'm not an expert, but I've seen enough teeth to recognise when something isn't quite right. Let's see what my friend comes back with."

"How long until we know?" Freya asked.

"A day, two at the most," Pip replied. "And anyway, before we get into the theories you may or may not have—"

"May not, at this stage," Ben added.

"I disagree," Freya said. "I think we're about to have my suspicions confirmed."

"And what are your suspicions?" Pip asked.

"That our man here was in the process of burgling Alice's house when she heard him, went to investigate, and although the rest of the event was a bit of a blur, the long and short of it is that the shock caused the heart attack."

"So, what caused this?" Pip asked, and she withdrew the thin, blue sheet enough to reveal the man's head wound.

"A hammer," Freya said,

"Right," Pip said, and she looked for some support from Ben, who shook his head, not willing to enter the battle. "And who, pray tell, was holding the hammer? Or did it simply jump up off the carpet and whack him? Maybe she'd left it on top of the wardrobe while she was doing some DIY and it happened to fall off at the exact moment he walked beneath it?"

"I think Pip is referring to the fact that Alice has no blood spatter on her hands or arms," Ben said.

"I'm astute enough to follow the thread, Ben," Freya said. "Even if it has been wrapped in sarcasm. But what I was saying was that the details are unclear as to how this man came by his injuries."

"It's also unclear who died first," Ben said. "Which leads me to an idea I had."

"Go on then," Freya said.

"Well," he began, suddenly feeling quite uncomfortable under the scrutinous eyes of the two strongest women he'd ever known. "What if he was already dead?"

The two women stared at him expectantly.

"And?" Pip said.

"Then what?" Freya added. "Or is that it? Is that the sum total of the idea you had?"

"It makes more sense than your idea," Ben said.

"Uh oh, sensing a wager coming, I am," Pip said.

"There won't be any wagers," Ben said. "But the fact remains that we need to know who died first, and we need to know who this man is if we're to have any chance of making progress."

"When can we expect the lab results, Pip?" Freya asked, and Pip puffed her cheeks once more. "I need it to be hours, not days."

"It will be hours," Pip said. "But it'll be double digits. They have their hands full over there at the minute."

"So, we have nothing to go on," Ben said. Then he muttered, "Why is this sounding familiar?"

"I wouldn't say nothing," Pip said. "And if you'd actually let me provide my analysis before you rambled on about your theories—"

"It wasn't me who—"

"Do you want to know why I called you here?" Pip said, cutting him off. "Or are you going to talk over me every time I try to explain?"

"But I—"

"There's more to this man than a simple wound to his head," Pip continued. "In fact, I'd say the injury is of very little significance compared to what I'm going to show you."

She pulled back the sheet slowly, revealing the man's chest and torso, where a thick scar ran across his stomach. Pip let the sheet drop to protect the man's modesty, and the three of them studied the scar, pale against his tanned skin.

"An operation, maybe?" Ben suggested, to which Pip shook her head. "Unless, of course, he had a caesarean. But I doubt that."

"I'm guessing everything is intact," he replied and nodded towards the man's groin. But she was less than amused and glared at him. "You never know these days."

"This is a prison scar," Freya said, ignoring their back and forth. "See here. It's actually two scars. An old prison trick to seri-

ously injure somebody. Although you'd usually find this type of scar on the face."

"What do you mean it's two scars?" Ben asked.

"Exactly what I said, Ben. Two razor blades, separated by a matchstick or something of similar size. A wound like this is almost impossible to stitch–"

"Hence why it's usually found on somebody's face," Ben said, nodding. "Permanently disfigured."

"Typically, this type of wound is inflicted on somebody the assailant wouldn't want dead. Rather, they'd prefer them to see their handiwork for the rest of their sentence. But there's no reason why the weapon shouldn't be used anywhere else on a body."

"So, our man has been to prison. That narrows it down," Ben said.

"Not necessarily," Freya replied. "The wound is similar, that's all."

"I'm impressed," Pip said. "I thought I'd blow your minds with this little find."

"Well, I'm sorry to steal your thunder," Freya said. "What else can you tell us? Can we determine the type of hammer used?"

Pip shook her head and, with a gloved hand, moved the man's hair so they could view the wound.

"There's no guarantee it's even a hammer," she replied. "The weapon was very obviously round as is noted by the shape. I can also tell you that the face of the weapon was flat, which we can determine by the debris. Had it been convex or pointed, the debris would have suffered fractures. But as you can see, aside from a few imperfections, it's almost coin-shaped."

"That sounds like a hammer to me," Ben said.

"It does," she replied. "We could be looking at a claw hammer or a ball hammer. The type that most people have in their sheds or toolboxes."

"I can't see dear old Alice there wielding a hammer. She looks

like she could barely climb the stairs," Freya said, and she looked up at Ben. "Thoughts?"

"I think at this stage it doesn't matter which theory is right. I think a third party was involved," he replied. "She had no blood spatter on her hands or arms, she couldn't have wielded a hammer, and let's not forget that they were both found propped against the same door."

"I agree," Freya said, and she nodded for Pip to cover the body. "Let's have another chat with Tammy Plant."

"The girl who found her?" Ben said and looked at her quizzically. "She's given a statement already."

"Ah, yes," Freya said. She gestured for Pip to return to the first of the benches and pull the blue sheet down again. "What do you see?"

"We've already looked at her, Freya," Ben said. "Nothing has changed in the past ten minutes."

"Who found her?" she replied, to which Ben stared hard at Freya, looking for a sign that she had finally lost the plot.

"The hairdresser," Ben said. "Tammy Plant. We've just spoken about her."

"And what do you notice about Alice?" Freya said.

It was Pip who caught on to the point Freya was trying to make, and she shook her head at Ben, disappointed.

"What?" Ben said, hearing the frustration in his own voice. "What am I missing here? She has suffered a heart attack, or several, or whatever. I can't see what the point is."

"Her hair," Pip said, and Freya nodded.

"I don't know much about the style, but I do know something," Freya said, waving her hand over the dead lady's head. "This lady is not in need of a haircut."

CHAPTER SEVENTEEN

It was mid-afternoon by the time Tammy had built up the courage to leave the house again. After having done all she could to deliver the bad news to her clients, she switched her phone off, resigning to revenue being down for a day and for at least one or two of the ladies to punish her by finding an alternative hairdresser.

She tossed her work clothes onto her bed, slipped into a pair of leggings and a loose t-shirt, and then packed everything she needed in her little rucksack. Outside the house, she felt like curtains were twitching. They weren't, of course. Why would they have been? But she felt it, nonetheless. The scrutinising eyes of her neighbours, reading the guilt on her face as if it were a neon sign.

Her pushbike was her saving grace. Limited funds meant limited purchases, but the bike had been a must-have, keeping her fit and saving money. It was a step-through with a little, wicker basket on the front and a pannier on the back. She dumped her rucksack in the basket and, after a few steps, she was off down the hill, building speed away from the village.

Cars overtook her slowly, and every time she heard the rumble

of an engine behind her, she expected to see a police car nudging into view with its bright stripes. She imagined the police officer would switch on the blue lights briefly, long enough to tell her to pull over, and then the whole village would see her. And those scrutinising glares would become knowing nods.

But no police car came, and she was glad when she turned off into the lane, where she could free-wheel down the long escarpment that ran from north to south away from Lincoln. Usually, she adored that part of the ride and it was the return journey that she dreaded. But not today. Today she just wanted to get to where she was going, and any thoughts of the return journey were so far away they paled in insignificance.

The descent tailed off into a long, flat road and the momentum she had gained petered out, forcing her to pedal the last few hundred yards to the farm turn-off denoted by a hanging, white sign with the words *Locks Wood Farm* marked in thick, black letters. The tarmac gave way to gravel, and for the first time since leaving the house, she felt safe.

Hares frolicked in the fields on either side of the track. Then, one by one, they froze as her presence was somehow communicated through the ranks. A few darted off, sprinting through the late crops, while others remained as still as they could, their black eyes following her every move.

Aside from the hares, a few pheasants bobbed back and forth, scratching the soil for grubs – or whatever it is they eat. None of them fled. They merely watched Tammy for a few seconds before returning to their task.

And so, the ride went. The track seemed to go on forever, and it was only when she saw a great cloud of dust coming from the field ahead that she knew the end was in sight. Again, her progress was observed, but this time, it wasn't from the nervous hares or arrogant pheasants; the eyes belonged to a beast far more dangerous and carefree than those.

A tractor drove slowly through the fields, dragging behind it

some kind of machinery that unearthed potatoes and placed them onto a conveyor. The spuds were then sorted by a dozen or more men who discarded the rejects and sent the approved potatoes onward to a waiting trailer.

It was a process that had changed little for hundreds of years, made easier by technology but yet to become fully automated. The human touch was a requirement to ensure quality.

She rode as close as she could to the field, then dumped her treasured bike on the track and ran across to where they worked, all the while studying their faces, and not finding the one she sought.

"Ah, look what we have here," a voice said in a thick Eastern European accent that she couldn't quite place. "Boss man has sent us a bonus."

He was a large-framed man with tanned skin and thick, dark stubble covering most of his face, even the tops of his cheeks. He eyed her with a curious smile, his hands never stopping from sorting the potatoes as he did.

"Where's Max?" she said. "I'm looking for Max."

"Max?" he said, and feigned ignorance by sending a questioning expression around the team. He was the alpha. Of that Tammy was certain. Thankfully, most of the men ignored him, and her, and continued with their work, their practised hands feeling, judging, and sorting. "Who is this Max?"

"Maxim?" she said. "Maxim Baftiroski. He works here. I know you know him. You're Vlad, aren't you? He told me about you."

"Ah Maxim," he replied and nodded for one of the men to cover his position. He wiped his hands on a rag that he stuffed into one of the pockets of his tracksuit bottoms, and then took a few steps towards her. But despite his confidence and arrogance, he took the opportunity to glance up at the tractor to make sure the farmer wasn't watching. "He's not here."

"He's not here? He's supposed to be working."

"I know he's supposed to be working," he said, making a

regretful clicking noise with his tongue. "This is what you get with Moldovans – weakness. Not like Albanian man. Moldovan doesn't show up, Albanian man has to work twice as hard."

"No, he's meant to be here. Where could he be?"

He tapped his temple with a strong index finger.

"Crying somewhere. I don't know," he replied. "Maybe he has a blister? Maybe he go for band-aid? Maybe he run away? He's Moldovan. He's not one of us. He's not Albanian."

"You haven't seen him? Not today?"

He swept his hand through the air as if presenting his team.

"Does it look like he was here today? No. No, Max doesn't show and we have to work more. Longer hours. Why? Because Moldovan man is weak man. Moldovan man all the same. Always run away."

"You share a house with him," she said. "I know you do. He told me. You must have seen him."

"Breakfast five a.m. No Max. No breakfast, no work," he said, and Tammy's heart was crushed. "Why you like Max anyway? What you see in him? He's small man. No spirit."

"He has spirit," she told him. "He has more spirit than any of you."

He gave a laugh and looked back to see if any of the others had heard, which they hadn't. But he cared little for the remark; it washed off him with ease.

"Max doesn't belong," he said. "Max buys his place here. But he work too hard. He leave like the others. Me and my friends here, we work for our place. English man doesn't pick potatoes. English man too proud. Moldovan man too weak to stand all day. Moldovan man too much girl."

"That's not true," she muttered quietly.

He tapped his head again, leaning towards her.

"What you see in Moldovan Max anyway?"

"He's a friend," she replied, taking a step back, which he then closed with a step of his own. "He's a good man."

"I can be a friend," he said, inhaling to swell his chest. "I can be good friend. All of us can be good friend."

"I just want to speak to Max," she said.

"Talk to me. You want friend, I'm friend. You want fun, I'm fun."

"No, no," she said, holding her hands in the air. "You don't understand."

"What is there to understand? You want a man. I'm man."

"I want Max," she said. "I just need to speak to him. It's urgent."

She had done little to convey any strength, but something she had said, or her body language, must have delivered the message. Vlad backed down with a sneer.

"Can you tell him?" she asked. "Can you tell him I was here? Can you tell him I need to see him?"

"I don't see Max," he said, his voice lower in pitch than before. "If I see him, I tell him."

She stared into his eyes, finding a glimmer of something gentle.

"Thank you," she said, then turned to walk back to her bike.

"I tell him pretty English girl comes looking for him," he called out. "But if he doesn't come, I call you. Okay?"

She ignored him, not daring to re-enter the conversation.

"You hear me? I call you, okay?" he called out again. "Vlad show you real man. Vlad not run away."

"Just tell him," she found herself calling back, despite her efforts to ignore him. "Just tell him, will you?"

"You didn't tell me your name," he replied, shouting to be heard over the revving machinery. "How can I tell him if I don't have your name?"

She picked her bike up from the dirt and brushed the dust from the grip before looking back at Vlad.

"Tell him Tammy came," she said. "Tell him I'm in trouble. A lot of trouble."

CHAPTER EIGHTEEN

It wasn't often that Freya was afforded the time to sit back in her chair and appraise her team. How long had it been since she had enjoyed a view such as this? Nillson and Anderson sat beside each other both poring over a laptop and notes. Chapman's fingers were a blur. Yet she hadn't even looked at the computer screen for more than a minute, referring to her notebook, which was laid out beside her. Ben, who was clearly avoiding eye contact, was back to his usual routine of resting his head on his hand silently cursing his laptop, which Freya could hear from the far side of the room, its fan whirring away like a jumbo jet preparing for take-off. He stabbed at a button repeatedly, yet nothing changed, and he grew more tense by the minute.

Gold was the only one not fully occupied, yet she did a damn fine job of masking it. She flicked through her notes, acting out a thoughtful charade, despite Freya knowing full well that the only task she'd had to complete was to type up her report on her visit to Tammy Plant's salon.

The sight of the team working was fine. It had taken months of hard work for Freya to earn her new rank, which was in no uncer-

tain terms helped by Ben's friendship and loyalty. Sadly, now that she had finally reached the pinnacle of her career, she felt her grip on that bond slipping. And there seemed so little she could do about it. He was friendly and courteous, of course, but that was just his nature. He seemed to grasp the charm and etiquette of a gentleman easier than some of her father's peers who had been born into wealth, those who held esteemed positions and wouldn't know how to even hold a spade, let alone rely on one for their sustenance.

She found herself staring at Ben from afar. He had it all – the boyish grin, which was rarely directed at her these days, the charm and good grace, and the strength and pride of a man who wasn't afraid to dirty his hands.

He is a bridge, she thought to herself. A bridge between classes, to whom she owed so much, yet found herself unable to tread near.

"Ma'am?" a voice said, rousing Freya from her thoughts. She exhaled loudly and found Chapman peering around her computer monitor waiting for a response.

"Chapman," she said. "Sorry, I was miles away. How can I help?"

"I was just wondering if you wanted me to email you my findings," Chapman replied, using the break in her typing as an opportunity to fasten the top button of her cardigan.

"Yes," Freya said. "But not yet. We'll debrief as soon as Gillespie and Cruz get back."

"If they get back," Gold added. "If I know Jim Gillespie, they'll be in the pub by now while uniform scour the fields on their hands and knees."

"Yeah, and if they find anything, Gillespie won't be shy in taking the credit," Nillson said.

"I can handle Sergeant Gillespie," Freya said, her tone sharper than the smirk she shared. "Besides, Cruz isn't shy in calling him out whenever he stretches the truth."

"He's coming on leaps and bounds, he is. I..." Gold said, then shied as if she'd overstepped the mark.

"Go on," Freya said.

"Sorry, ma'am, I was just thinking aloud."

"That's fine," Freya told her. "What were you going to say?"

Gold seemed loathed to speak, but Freya allowed her no room to manoeuvre.

"Just that Gabby, DC Cruz that is, he's really developed since you've been here. He's coming out of his shell."

"Agreed," Nillson said, before returning her attention to the laptop and muttering under her breath. "We'll have to watch out though."

"What out for what?" Gold asked.

"He'll hit puberty soon," Nillson said with an evil-sounding chuckle. "Then it'll be all dirty magazines and squeaky voices—"

"Alright, alright," Freya said. "No need for vulgarities. But as it happens, I agree. Cruz is developing. He's not afraid to say what he thinks and, in this game, sometimes you have to air your thoughts, even if it's to be told you're wrong by everybody else."

"Like Alice Glass discovering a burglar in her home and suffering a heart attack, you mean?" Ben said, closing the lid on his useless laptop.

"Something like that," Freya replied, pleased to see him entering into a conversation without having his arm twisted behind his back. He even looked like he was about to add something, but the doors burst open in a flurry of hair and overcoats as Gillespie entered the room with Cruz on his heels.

"Fear not, ladies and gentlemen," Gillespie said, his Glaswegian accent saturating the words with colour and flow. "The hero has returned."

"The what?" Cruz said, as he pulled out his chair and hung his jacket on the back. He stared at Gillespie like he had spoken in another tongue. "Hero?"

"Don't spoil the effect, Gabby," Gillespie said, as he sat in his

own seat, leaned back, and folded his hands on his lap. He stared up at Freya. "Now then, what's the plan, boss?"

"The plan?" Freya replied, quickly checking her watch. She shoved herself out of her seat and made her way to where she preferred to address the team – the edge of her desk. "It's three o'clock. We'll debrief and make a plan on the back of our findings, and seeing as you're in such high spirits, Gillespie, you can start."

"Me? Start?" Gillespie said. "Shouldn't we get some coffee or something?"

"No, we're all coffeed out I'm afraid. We had a rather fine cup from The Petwood earlier."

"Cake too," Nillson added. "Blooming lovely it was."

"Coffee and cake?" Gillespie said disbelievingly. "From The Petwood?"

"You are ready, I presume?" Freya asked. "Given that you've been gone all day."

"Aye, well, I mean, I could have done with a few minutes to gather–"

"But?" Freya said.

Gillespie paused to stare around the room. "But I'll wing it. It's all up here anyway." He tapped his forehead with a long, bony index finger.

Freya peered down at her own notes, recalling the tasks she had set the pair.

"Shall we start with the door-to-door?" she said. "What did you learn? I mean, there were only two doors to knock on, but I would expect even you, Gillespie, could have come away with some kind of direction."

"Door-to-door, aye," he began, stalling for time. "Well, we knocked on the middle house first."

"The middle house?"

"Aye, but there wasn't really much to learn."

"Who did you speak to?" Freya asked, snapping the lid off her marker and preparing to make a note on the whiteboard.

"Who did we speak to?" Gillespie said, to which Freya sighed.

"Are you repeating me, Gillespie? I thought I'd asked you not to do that."

"Well, not repeating as such–"

"The names?" Freya said.

"Blake, boss," Cruz said, his voice light and airy in contrast to Gillespie's gruff tones. He flicked through a few pages of his notepad for reference. "Miss Blake. It's her mother's house, but the old lady's been blind since ninety-one and her hearing isn't great."

"Thank you, Cruz," Freya said. "Did you learn anything of significance? Presumably, the mother wasn't aware of the goings on outside, but did the daughter see anything?"

"Not really, boss," Cruz said. "She's only there for a couple of hours each morning and then again at night. But she did tell us something interesting about Mr Benson."

"Mr Benson?"

"The man next door," Gillespie said, trying to recover.

"It's okay, Gillespie, DC Cruz seems to have a handle on your day," she said, turning to Cruz. "Why don't you give us an account, Cruz?"

"Me, boss?"

"Yes, Cruz."

"But I..." he began, then saw the encouraging look on Freya's face and faltered, jutting his chin out with pride. "Alright. Alright, I will."

Freya finished writing the name on the board and then sat back to listen to the rest of his account, while Gillespie muttered something illegible under his breath and put his feet up on the chair opposite.

"Well, it seems Mr Benson is Alice's brother-in-law," Cruz said. "*Was* her brother-in-law, anyway. According to Miss Blake, George Benson acts like her mother and Alice are his harem. She

said it was almost as if he felt responsible for them both, doing their gardens, signing for packages, and whatnot."

"It sounds like we need to speak to Mr Benson, then," Freya said.

"Oh, we did," Cruz replied, not recognising the playful jibe. "We spoke to him after. Interesting bloke, actually. He took us for a walk over the fields."

"Well, that sounds lovely," Nillson said. "While we've been working here, you've been going on a little jaunt with an old man."

"You've been having bloody coffee and cake," Gillespie said. "We had to listen to an old man drone on and on about the past. Honestly, if he'd given me a Werther's Original, I'd have felt like I was eight years old again."

"What did he tell you?" Freya said, finding Gillespie's remark mildly amusing but choosing not to let him know it by maintaining a straight face. "Why did he take you out to the field?"

"It was Alice, you see," Cruz said, and he took a breath as if deciding where to start. "According to George—"

"Mr Benson," Gillespie added.

"Right, according to Mr Benson, Alice's husband died a few years back. He was found by a bench out in the field, and Alice used to walk there every morning at five a.m., rain or shine."

"Hence the indecent exposure episodes?" Chapman suggested.

"The what?" Gillespie said.

"Our innocent Alice has form," Ben added from the back of the room. "Turns out she was a serial flasher."

"A serial what?"

"Not a flasher," Freya explained. "But it's beginning to make sense now."

"What makes sense, boss?" Cruz said, but Freya was lost in thought.

"Tell me," she said. "Was there any mention of Alice suffering from some kind of mental illness?"

"She was mad as a bat from what I can tell," Gillespie said, but before Freya could silence him, Cruz spoke up.

"Actually, Miss Blake referred to her as Mad Alice," Cruz said. "I didn't think anything of it at the time."

"Mad Alice?" Gold said. "That's what Tammy mentioned, too."

Freya smiled at the room, to nobody in particular.

"It seems we might just have found a thread to pull on," she said. "Tell me everything, Cruz, and leave nothing out."

CHAPTER NINETEEN

The world was closing in on her and she felt as if whichever way she ran, she'd hit a wall. The few people she had passed as she returned from the farm seemed to scrutinise her. Max's work-mates had very little to say of any use, and now, as she came to the end of the shortcut through the fields, she saw a line of uniformed policemen, scouring the land, searching for God knows what – or who.

From the line of hedges that marked the edge of the field, Tammy watched in fear. She felt like one of those escaped prisoners of war in the old films her dad used to watch, with the nazis hunting her down. Only, the dogs here were not barking. They weren't even German Shepherds, more like Working Cocker Spaniels, and the uniforms the men wore were not the grey tunics of Hitler's forces; they were bright yellow.

Still, the feeling of being hunted down was strong enough to send her back behind the hedge, searching for a place to ditch her bike while she watched. In the end, she wheeled it behind the hedge, out of sight, then scampered down the dyke at the edge of the field, and climbed up the other side to watch the police from beneath.

She peered out through the long grass and wildflowers, unsure of what she might see, but even more uncertain about her options. Was it her they were looking for? If so, should she go home?

But the question at the forefront of it all was what the hell were they doing? There were at least a dozen police officers in the field, and those were only the ones she could see. The whole thing looked like something from the six o'clock news when somebody had been killed or kidnapped or something. It hadn't been a murder, had it? Alice had looked so peaceful and there hadn't been any blood.

The line of officers moved through the field heading towards her. They were about three hundred yards away, with a dog handler at each end of the line. The spaniels sniffed the ground and the air, and although everything Tammy knew about police dogs could be written on one side of a cigarette paper, they didn't look like they were onto a trail of any sort. They looked like they were going for a Sunday walk after dinner rather than to hunt down a killer or find a dead body.

The whole day had gone from bad to worse and showed no signs of relenting. It was times like this when she wished she had a mother she could call who would actually help her, rather than offer unwanted advice, rebuke her for her life choices, and no doubt tell her to go to the police station and hand herself in. The worst part was that her mother had barely even worked a day in her life. She'd always had Tammy's father to pay for everything. Her advice had no weight behind it. Anyway, it was rarely advice, just her own bitter opinions spewed down her nose at the insufferable world in yet another effort to turn Tammy into a younger version of herself. And the world just wasn't ready for two Marjorie Plants.

Her thoughts, no matter how negative they had been, had at least served as a terrific distraction from the scene in front of her.

The scene seemed to spark a thousand thoughts into play at once, like tiny clouds in the wake of a passing tornado.

And as those thoughts rose once more, a cacophony of doubts, worries, and dreadful imaginings, she heard voices. Men, two of them approaching from the left. They must've been walking the perimeter of the field. Whatever they were doing, they were in no rush and they clearly weren't too happy to be there.

"I don't know why we're bothering," one of them said with a local accent, heavy and gruff in tone. "Bloody foreigners. It's not enough to come over here and get all the bloody handouts they want, they have to nick everything in sight as well. It's our taxes that pay for them to stay in hotels. Our taxes that feed them. And whatever money we have left over has to be spent on either nailing everything down so they can't nick it, or replacing it once it's been stolen. I tell you, this bloody country is going down the drain."

"That's a bit of a sweeping statement, Jeff," the other one said, lighter in tone and with more of a southern accent. "I wouldn't let the guv hear you talk like that."

"I'm just saying what we're all thinking, Steve. That's all. Except we can't say it out loud because we'd be classed as racist or something. Makes me bloody sick, I tell you."

"I get what you're saying, mate," the second one said. "But you can't tar them all with the same brush. Some of them are here to work. My missus works with a few and they're bloody hard workers. You can't knock somebody for working hard."

"Oh yeah, and what about the rest of them? What about the ones that come over in little boats, get given a cushy little room in a hotel, and then join the first criminal gang they can find? Eh? What about them?"

"Well, then that's where we come in. But there's a big difference between the ones who come over here illegally and the ones

that arrive by plane in search of a better life as a reward for hard work."

"And I suppose the bloke they found in the house was one of the good ones, was he?" the gruff man said. Their voices were growing louder, and it sounded as if they were swishing through the long grass as they walked. "Somebody caught him in the old lady's house and gave him what he deserved. If I had my way, I'd close the file, archive it, and move on to something important."

Fearing she would be caught, Tammy slipped back down beneath the hedge, into the dyke, and up into the adjacent field. She stayed low and moved slowly, hoping they wouldn't see her through the hedge. She crawled towards her bike, untangling their discussion as she went with a sense of looming dread, blurring her peripheral vision, so the world around her became dream-like.

"First of all, we don't know that he was an immigrant," the southerner said. "Second, we don't know that he was robbing the place. She could have invited him in. He might be a relative or something."

"Invited him in? You mean he could have been her lover?" the gruff man scoffed. "Behave, Steve. He was robbing the place and you know it. He's no better than the rest of them. The problem is, if you suggest sending them home, you get labelled a bigot. I'm not racist. I've got loads of foreign friends. I just happen to love my country and don't want to see it going down the pan."

"Bloody hell, I'm glad you're not running the country."

"You've gone soft, you have. What's happened to you? You going for promotion or something?"

"No," Steve said. "I just think there's a middle ground between barricading ourselves and letting any Tom, Dick, or Harry come in. I think there's a place for compassion for genuine immigrants, for people who come here wanting to contribute. I don't think labelling a dead man as a no-good criminal just because he looks Eastern European is the way forward. At least not until major crimes find out who he is."

"Major crimes?" Jeff said. "They won't find anything. They've all scarpered. You would have thought that big Scottish bloke would have helped out, wouldn't you? He's probably sitting in a cafe somewhere waiting for the guv to call him. He looked like he wasn't afraid of a bacon sandwich or two..."

His words trailed off and Tammy stared at the two men's shapes as they walked on the far side of the hedge.

"Dead man?" she whispered to herself. "Eastern European?"

The tornado in her mind died down, letting the random thoughts fall like dust, leaving only one in her mind. And it was a terrible, terrible thought.

"Hold on," Steve said, raising his voice above his colleague's racist rant. "What's this?"

There was urgency in his voice, and the sound of the long grass being trodden grew louder.

"Probably a badger or something," Jeff said.

"Someone's been lying here," he said, as Tammy pushed her bike away slowly, hoping they wouldn't catch sight of her through the hedge.

"It was probably the Eastern European," Jeff said. "Casing the joint before he robbed it. Look, he could have been watching the place for days for all we know."

"Call it in," Steve said. "This could be important."

That was the last thing Tammy heard, as she deemed herself far away enough to jump back on her bike and pedal as fast as she could towards the road, the southerner's words taunting her on repeat.

I don't think labelling a dead man as a no-good criminal just because he looks Eastern European is the way forward. At least not until major crimes find out who he is.

It was one of those times when her legs felt like they belonged to somebody else. She couldn't pedal hard enough over the bumps on the narrow footpath trodden by decades of dog walkers and farm workers.

She didn't dare look back, not until she had reached the road, where she did her best to look like she was just a girl out for a bike ride.

But it was useless. She couldn't hide the fear in her face, no matter how hard she tried. She couldn't mask the tears that flooded across her skin, blinding her. She rolled to a stop in the middle of the lane, dumping her bike on the tarmac and falling to her knees.

Not until major crimes find out who he is...

"Major crimes," she said aloud to herself. "He saw me. The Scottish bloke. He saw me."

A terrible thought struck her.

The blast of a loud horn startled her. Tammy turned in time to see the truck bearing down on her in a cloud of tyre smoke.

CHAPTER TWENTY

"So, let me get this straight," Freya said slowly. "This bench. It was a special place to Alice and…"

"Alex, boss," Cruz said. "That's right. George and Ivy, too."

"Mr and Mrs Benson?" Freya said, again slowly, as if she was leaving no room for error in her understanding. "It's where both men proposed, and I'm assuming both women said yes?"

"That's correct, boss," Cruz said.

"And then, three years ago, Alex's body was found there."

"At five a.m., yes, boss."

"Which is why Alice traipsed across the fields every morning, hoping it all might have been a dream," Freya said, to which Cruz nodded. "And hence why the locals thought she might have been suffering from–"

"Madness, boss," Cruz said.

"Dementia," she said. "I was going to say dementia. For God's sake, if we're going to deal with this investigation, we're going to need to talk to her family, and the last word I want to hear coming from any of your mouths is madness, or mad, or any variation."

"Dementia," Cruz said. "Yes, boss."

"And how did Alex Glass die? Did Mr Benson give a cause of death?"

"He just said that he was attacked," Cruz replied. "He often used to go out early in the mornings. George said something about him being a twitcher, whatever that is."

"You don't know what a twitcher is?" Nillson said. "Seriously?"

"Should I?" Cruz replied. "I thought it was some kind of dance. You know, like when girls shake their..."

"Shake their what, Cruz?" Freya said.

"Bums, boss. When they shake their bums. You see it on social media all the time."

"Is Hermione a twitcher?" Gillespie asked. "I could see her as a twitcher, eh, Ben?"

"Don't bring me into this," he said. "That is one conversation I'm staying well and truly clear of."

It was as Ben finished speaking that he heard what he thought was somebody crying. He looked around the room at everyone and found Gold with her hands covering her face, shaking uncontrollably.

"You alright, Jackie?" he said, and she lowered her hands slowly, wiping tears from her red eyes.

She nodded, taking deep breaths, then fanned herself with her hand.

"Oh, Gabby," she said, in that soft, lullaby-like Scottish accent of hers. "Oh, Gabby, you're going to kill me one of these days."

"What?" he said. "What have I done?"

"Twitching? You mean twitching, surely?" she said. "He was a bird watcher."

"A what?" Cruz said. "A bird watcher?"

"You're thinking of twerking. Twerking is when you shake your backside like all those ridiculous girls on social media."

Cruz's face reddened.

"Yeah, well... It explains why he had to get up early," he said defensively.

"Hang on a wee minute there," Gillespie said, jamming his index finger down on his desk. "You thought that Alex Glass got up at five a.m. to go into a field just to shake his backside?"

"I said it didn't make sense," Gabby said.

"Have you lost your mind?"

"Oh, well, sorry if I'm not up to date on the definition of twerping–"

"Twerking," Gold corrected him.

"Whatever. All I know is that he came home, heard a burglar, chased him into the field, for whatever reason, and was attacked."

"Did they catch whoever did it?" Freya asked, clearly amused by the back and forth but wanting to push on.

"Apparently not," Cruz said, hoping to regain some semblance of credibility. "Apparently it was quite bad though. Bad enough that George had to go and identify the body. He said he couldn't let Alice see him like that."

"That doesn't make sense," Ben said. "Why would somebody attack an old man who they could easily outrun? Did they mug him?"

"Nope, his wallet was in his pocket. Nothing taken," Cruz replied. "It was just one of those things."

"Just one of those things? I'll tell you that when your father passes away, which I hope will be far less terrifying than it was for Alex Glass. People don't get attacked for no reason," Freya said, then turned to the rest of the team. "Nillson, Anderson, talk to me."

"Not a lot to say, boss," Nillson said. "We've got one farm within a three-mile radius that uses an agency, plus three more farms within a five-mile radius."

"Good. Focus on the closest one first. I don't wish to cast aspersions, but if we are dealing with a farm labourer looking to bring in some extra cash, then the chances are he would have been on foot, which means homes and businesses closest to where he's staying are more likely to be a target," Freya replied. "Pay the

foreman a visit. See what he has to say. See if any of his workers are missing."

"Will do," Nillson replied, then immediately huddled with Anderson for a few seconds before looking back up. "That would be Locks Wood Farm, boss."

Freya checked her watch briefly.

"Let's have an update first thing in the morning," she said, then turned to Gillespie and Cruz. "You two, head back to the search. Take it wider if you need to. I trust you to use your common sense."

Making no attempt to hide his displeasure, Gillespie let his head fall back with a loud groan. But he did at least recognise that any attempts to fight for another task were futile.

"Aye, boss," he said. "I'll debrief you in the morning. That's if I haven't strung myself up in the meantime."

"Well, then I suggest you arm DC Cruz with the facts just in case," Freya said, dismissing his insensitive comment with an obvious lack of sympathy. Then she turned to Chapman, who, as ever, was sitting quietly. "Chapman, you've been patient enough. Let's hear what you've found."

The young detective constable shuffled her notes, spreading three sheets of A4 paper out in front of her before taking a sip of water from a metal bottle adorned with flowers and a buzzing bee – the type a mother might buy for her daughter to take to school.

"I'll start with the burglaries," she began. "Although, if you want details of every reported breaking and entering incident in the area, we'll be claiming overtime."

"Are there really that many?" Freya asked. Chapman replied with a grim expression. "I don't believe for a moment you haven't done your due diligence on the list. Am I right, Chapman?"

Chapman nodded, glancing down at her notes to memorise the key facts.

"A total of ninety reported burglaries in the immediate area during the last five years," she said. "Although I have managed to

go through the MO of each incident where I can. The reason being that criminals who undertake these types of crimes usually have a preferred method of access and steal the same types of possessions – window entry, small items – which suggests somebody acting alone. Door entries usually result in larger goods being stolen and require a larger number of individuals. In this instance, I was looking for smaller items."

"Why small items?" Cruz asked, and the team all stared at him.

"Isn't it obvious?" Gillespie said. "Alice Glass's house wasn't exactly cleared out, was it? There was no van parked up ready to load up. They were clearly on foot."

"Quite right," Freya said. "But that doesn't mean we're excluding any incidents where larger items were taken. It just means we have a smaller list to work with. We can expand if necessary."

"Right," Cruz said. "I would have thought it better to analyse the demographics, that's all."

"The demographics?" Gillespie said with a scoff. "What the bloody hell are you talking about?"

"Age," Cruz replied, as if he was trying to convince the team of his idea. "Alice Plant was an elderly lady. How many of the other victims were of a similar demographic?"

"That's a very good point," Freya told him and turned her hopeful expression towards Chapman.

"That's the interesting part," Chapman added. "If we take out the larger robberies, which I've assumed the suspects would have needed some kind of vehicle for, we're left with nineteen burglaries in the last five years."

"Nineteen burglaries?" Nillson said. "That's not a lot."

"It's a safe area," Freya said. "A quiet and remote village with a strong community. There are areas in London where you'd see that number on a daily basis, but not here."

"And then I identified window entries," Chapman said and

waited for all eyes to fall on her to give the number. She smiled at them. "Nine."

"Nine?" Gillespie said, clearly shocked.

"Nine," she repeated. "Then, as Gabby pointed out, I applied the demographic."

Again, she waited for the team, seeming to enjoy the limelight, which was rare for the quiet, mild-mannered woman.

"Don't say it was just one," Nillson said, at which Chapman smiled broadly.

"One," she said, then summarised her findings. "Of all the burglaries in the area in the past five years, only one did not require a vehicle, was accessed via a window, and had an elderly victim, and that was Alice Glass."

"There are no matching incidents?" Freya said. "None at all?"

"Not reported," Chapman replied. "All it tells us is that if our man was responsible for other offences, then he either wasn't particular about his victims or was confident in various entry methods."

"That was an extremely detailed analysis, Chapman," Freya said. "I was hoping to have at least one other incident with which to compare DNA and fingerprints. But if that's all we have to work with, then so be it."

"I did find something else," Chapman said, making use of the floor while she had it. "Alice Glass had a son. A Henry Glass. I'll forward the address to the team."

"How did I know that was coming?" Freya said, nodding her thanks to Chapman then turning her attention to Ben. "We'll take that. There's nothing quite like delivering bad news to relatives to round off an already challenging day."

"What about me, ma'am?" Gold asked, raising her hand with trepidation. "Did you want me to come with you and sit with Henry when you're done?"

"No," Freya replied. "No, I want you to find Tammy Plant."

"The lass who found the body?" Gillespie asked rhetorically. "She came to the crime scene."

"When?" Freya asked.

"While you and Ben were inside the house. Acting a bit odd, she was. A wee bit twitchy."

"She had just found a dead body," Gold said.

"Aye, it was more than that, though. It was like she wasn't expecting to see the circus."

"Did you talk to her?"

"I tried, boss," he said. "But she made her excuses."

The room was silent as Freya took in the news, digested it, and then spat out the solution.

"Chapman, do some digging on her, will you? George Benson, too," she said. "We don't have many names on our board, but I want to know everything about all of them by midday tomorrow. Is that clear?"

"Ma'am," she replied.

"Gillespie, while you're at the crime scene, take George Benson into Alice's house. See if he can spot if anything is missing. I'd like to rule out the possibility that our man had accomplices."

"Aye, boss," Gillespie said, seeming pleased to be tasked with something other than the search.

"Right, get to it," Freya said, finding Ben's watchful gaze. She collected her bag from her desk. "Shall we go and deliver the bad news?"

"Gillespie," Chapman said from her corner of the room. She held her desk phone handset up for him to see. "I've got a Sergeant Jeff Sanderson on the phone. He says he's found something you might be interested in."

CHAPTER TWENTY-ONE

With her hands against the glass to shield the sunlight, Jackie Gold peered into the salon to see if Tammy was in there, but there was no movement. She tried the door again, hoping that she might have missed a latch or a handle or something, but there was nothing. It was firmly locked, and the lights had been turned off.

She found the email Chapman had sent to the team and searched for Tammy's home address. Then, using the maps app on her phone, Jackie made her way along the high street, admiring the abundance of amenities Navenby had to offer. Considering it was such a small village, residents would hardly have to leave it, except to go to big shops, supermarkets, or into town. But for Jackie, part of the beauty of living in a small village was supporting the local businesses. There was a double-fronted bakery shop, a chemist, and she had even seen a large butcher's shop on the drive in. For people in the later stages of life, it was ideal, and for the young families, there was ample opportunity for parents to demonstrate classic values, such as telling a stranger in the street good morning without fear of offending them, or worse, or picking litter from the ground, even if it wasn't you who dropped it.

So lost in her thoughts was she that she nearly crossed the side road at the far end of the high street before she realised it was the turning she had meant to take. According to Chapman's email, Tammy Plant's house was just up it and on the left. She found it easily. A small hatchback was parked outside. Nothing flash, but it certainly wasn't an old banger. It was the type of car a parent buys for a son or a daughter, something safe, reliable, and cost-effective.

She rang the doorbell and stepped back, peering up at the windows for any sign of movement − the flicker of a curtain, or the shape of Tammy looking down at her through the nets.

But she saw nothing, and enough time passed to warrant a second ring of the bell. This time, she didn't wait. A little alley ran down the side of the house. It was a place to store all four bins out of sight − the black general waste bin, the green recycling bin, the purple paper and cardboard bin, and the brown bin for garden waste. She'd heard somebody say once that the council required residents to have so many different bins a portion of their council tax should be deducted for their storage.

Beside the waste storage was a small shed which had been left unlocked. The door was ajar. There wasn't much inside, except for a few old boxes against one wall and a bike lock that had been fixed to the opposite wall.

She moved on along the alleyway, coming to a small back garden. It wasn't much, but Tammy had clearly made efforts to create a relaxing space. A small, white, steel bistro set had been placed directly outside the French doors at the back of the house, and for greater comfort, a rather plush-looking, rattan, L-shaped sofa. The small amount of lawn that was left was cared for, and despite the recent heat the county had seen, the grass was still green, unlike Jackie's, which, thanks to the lack of rainfall and her young boy's passion for football, now resembled one of the locust-damaged African fields she had seen in awareness campaigns during her younger days.

She tried the French doors, not expecting them to be open. And she was right. They were firmly locked. Through the glass, she could see the open-plan kitchen and lounge. It was clear just from looking at the tidy space that Tammy loved her home. It was also clear that no children lived there.

With no idea of where Tammy might be, Jackie made her way back to her car. She opened the door but hesitated before climbing in. Instead, she leaned on the car roof staring up at the house, hoping that, just by staring at Tammy's property, she might somehow gain insight into where she might be.

She hadn't mentioned any friends during her chat, and there was no mention of family. But that didn't mean she lacked either. In fact, if Jackie had discovered a body, as Tammy had, the first person she would go to would be her mother.

Chapman was one of her most frequently called contacts, and Jackie found her number in her recently dialled. Jackie phoned her so often, in fact, that she couldn't recall a time when her name hadn't been either at the top of the list or at least in the top five. She hit the button to make the call, then turned to lean on her car while she waited for the ringtone.

"DC Chapman, Major Crimes," Chapman said, as she answered her desk phone. Her voice was so light and tender that Jackie might have been dialling her son's school to talk to the receptionist.

"Denise, it's Jackie," she said. "Sorry to bother you."

"Oh, hey, Jackie. No bother. I was just about to visit the little girl's room. I haven't torn my eyes from this computer all day."

"Well, hopefully, this is an easy one for you," Jackie said. "I'm looking for a contact. Tammy Plant's mother."

"Her mother?"

"Or somebody close by. A family member. I've hit a wall," Jackie explained. "She's not at her shop and she's not at home. If I'm honest, I'm a little worried about her. She was in a right old state earlier."

"I'm not surprised," Chapman said. "Let me see what I can do."

"I'll wait," Jackie replied. "If that's okay? I'd like to make one last effort before close of business. I've got to get Charlie from my mum's before she goes out, and the last thing I need is a phone call this evening. I'm quite sure the boss won't appreciate me attending a call with my boy in tow."

"Hold on," Chapman said, her smile evident in her tone. "It might take some digging, but I'll find something."

Jackie relaxed, hearing Chapman's fingers typing away as she looked in all the usual places. The radio she kept on her desk burst into life, then quietened as Jackie imagined her turning the volume down.

"Sorry about that," Chapman said. "I had it on so I could listen out for Gillespie and Cruz."

"Was that it?" Jackie asked. "What did they find?"

"Oh no, that was a road traffic collision," Chapman replied. "I can usually filter all that background stuff out, especially when Jim Gillespie gets on the radio."

"I know what you mean," Jackie said, listening as the sound of distant sirens approached the village. "He's like a foghorn."

She watched as two liveried police cars sped along the high street, shooting past Tammy's road in two bright flashes, followed by a lumbering ambulance a few moments later.

"Nearly there, Jackie," Chapman said. "Bear with me. It's always tough when they don't have previous. Thank God for social media, that's what I say."

"Was it near me?" Jackie asked, listening to the fading sirens.

"Was what near you?"

"The RTC. Was it near Navenby?"

"Oh, that, yeah, I think so. Out near Wellingore, I think the controller said," Chapman replied. "Some poor girl on a bike went head to head with a truck. I tell you, Jackie, the speed some of those truck drivers go down the lanes is terrifying."

"On a bike?" Jackie said.

"Yes, that's right. Why?"

Jackie stared at the house again, her eyes falling on the little shed down the side alley with the open door and vacant bike lock.

"Send me the details, will you, Denise?" she replied. "I've got an awful feeling I know who it is."

CHAPTER TWENTY-TWO

A port-a-cabin placed at the edge of a potholed hardstanding served as the office for Lincs Agricultural Labour Ltd. In the distance, three huge barns with cat slide roofs dominated the skyline, whilst the farmhouse, which was older than the rest of the buildings and possibly the original, was nestled into a neat copse of trees, presumably to protect the home from the terrific south-westerly winds that tore across the fens against very little in the way of natural barriers.

The port-a-cabin, however, was exposed to the elements, and Nillson was silently grateful that the late summer evening was calm, with only a welcome gentle breeze to tease the Ragwort and Mallow into a slow dance.

"Don't expect to be met with a cup of tea and a welcoming smile," she said to Anderson, who was quietly taking in the scene. "I've been to one of these places before and they don't like people interfering in their business."

"I'm not surprised," Anderson replied. "I can't imagine how difficult it is to employ foreigners. I'll bet most of them are on minimum wage. No doubt there are a dozen or more groups hitting them with petitions and abuse. And that's not to mention

the red tape they most likely have to jump over just to get the home office to leave them alone."

"That's very astute of you, Jenny," Nillson said. "You haven't even lived in Lincolnshire for a year and you managed to pick all that up?"

Anderson laughed the comment off.

"I might be from London, Anna," she said, "but if there's one thing I know, it's that employees will always moan about wages, protesters will always find a cause to bear their signs, and government departments will always wrap processes in red tape. Immigration, welfare, social housing, it's all the same. The differences are semantic."

They climbed from the car and Anna scanned the few windows to see if anybody was looking out. Nobody was.

"Well, let's see if you feel the same in thirty minutes," she said.

Three iron steps led up to a door that pushed open and then slammed closed behind them like it was some sort of rodent trap. The space was divided into four desk spaces, the farthest occupied by a balding man who looked as if he could do with a good meal and a handful of vitamin tablets. He didn't look up, but there was no way he wasn't aware of them. Instead, he chose to continue with his work, squinting at his laptop and then checking his fingers the way people do when they aren't quite familiar with using a computer.

Anna cleared her throat with a gentle cough. "I'm looking for Mr Venables."

He said nothing. He didn't even acknowledge her. She looked back at Anderson, who simply shrugged and pulled a face as if to say, 'He wants it the hard way'.

"I'm from Lincolnshire Police," Nillson said, raising her voice just a little but staying on the side of polite for the time being. Again, he was unmoved by the announcement. "Major Crimes Team."

This caught his attention.

But not enough for him to look her way. Instead, he glanced through the window closest to his desk, as if he was checking to see if any reinforcements were waiting outside, and then finally sat back in his seat, linking his fingers across his chest.

Anna held her warrant card up for him to see, then stepped close enough for him to read the details.

"Detective Sergeant Nillson," she said.

"I can see that."

"And you are?" she said, cocking her head to prompt him for an introduction.

"Mr Venables," he replied. "Stuart Venables."

Anna pulled out the visitor seat in front of his desk and sat down, crossing her legs to signify that she wouldn't be leaving anytime soon.

"I was hoping you could help us with our enquiries," she said.

"It wasn't me," he said, and for the first time, he flashed a smug smile, revealing a missing front tooth and a stained, brown canine.

"What wasn't?"

"Whatever it is you're going to ask."

"Mr Venables, there was an incident in the early hours of this morning—"

"Ah, I was with the wife. She can vouch for me."

"During which a man died."

"Do you want her number?" he said. "You can call her if you want."

"We're having some difficulty identifying him and we're wondering if any of your employees are missing. Or haven't turned up for work?"

He looked perplexed, switching his gaze between Anderson and Nillson.

"Why come to me?" he asked finally.

"Because we believe him to be Eastern European and there are

no obvious signs of transport," Nillson explained. "Therefore, there's a good chance he travelled on foot."

"He could have used a taxi."

"He had no money on his person, and no wallet," Nillson countered, to which he gave some thought, then shook his head.

"Nobody has reported anything," he replied. "My foreman would have notified me."

"Are you able to ask them for us, please? Just to eliminate this line of enquiry."

"I am busy, you know."

"So are we, Mr Venables. So the sooner you help us, the sooner we can be on our way," she replied. "I'd hate to have to call in the home office for a passport check."

He scoffed at the threat but saw there was weight behind it and sighed heavily before checking his watch.

"They'll be on a break," he said. "Is there a number I can call you on?"

"There is, but I don't mind waiting. Why don't we pay them a quick visit? I presume you can locate them."

"I can," he said with obvious suspicion.

Nillson turned in her seat to address Anderson. "How many visas did you say are operational?"

"Fourteen seasonal visas," Anderson replied. "Plus a few more still being processed. No doubt they're being lined up for the late harvest."

Nillson looked back at Venables, who was clearly deliberating his options.

"Fourteen," she said. "I hope you can account for these individuals."

He nodded slowly.

"I can," he replied. "Although we do sometimes move them from site to site—"

"And I imagine you have some sort of paperwork that can demonstrate that?"

Again, he fell silent, then took a deep breath, snatched up the keys to his truck, and shoved himself out of his seat.

"Right, come on then. I can see I'm not going to get anything done while you're here."

He was of average height but slender enough for his jeans to hang on his hips, despite his belt being fastened on the smallest hole, and for his tan work boots to give him the appearance of a golf club.

"We'll have to be quick," he said. "They'll be heading back to the accommodation soon."

"I thought you said they were on a break?" Nillson said.

At this, he paused at the door, looked down and to his left, and grumbled as he descended the iron steps, "How the bloody hell do I know what they're doing?"

Nillson and Anderson followed, closing the door behind them.

"Is it far?" she called out, and Venables looked across to Nillson's little hatchback with obvious disdain.

"You'd better ride with me," he said.

The inside of the truck was as Nillson had imagined it might be – basic, barely functional, and filthy. Half-empty water bottles were scattered across the floor, no doubt left there due to the door pockets being stuffed full of paperwork, crisp packets, and empty sandwich cartons, the type someone might buy from a petrol station.

He drove as if the loose gravel track had been tarmacked and rolled flat, forcing the suspension to work overtime. It felt as if each corner they took would be their last, and twice Nillson felt the front end slide on the loose surface. But he held it well and then gunned the engine. In the distance, they saw a tractor, farm machinery, and a handful of men working.

He caught her glancing down at the speedometer, which flicked up and down loosely, providing the driver with the vague knowledge that they were doing somewhere in the region of forty to fifty miles per hour. Anna felt him look sideways at her, daring

her to comment on the speed. But it was private land, and even if it wasn't, there was little to be gained from lecturing him about a traffic offence.

The truck slid to a halt, waking a cloud of dust that the breeze carried off before they'd even opened their doors.

"Thirteen," Anderson said quietly and offered a questioning look which Nillson acknowledged with a nod.

"Vlad," Venables called out, and the largest of the workers looked up to see him wave him over. "I need a minute."

The large man wiped his hands on his tracksuit bottoms and walked their way, saying something in another language to his colleagues, presumably something along the lines of, *'Keep working, I'll be back in a minute,'* or, *'What does this bloody idiot want now?'*

"Mr Venables," Vlad said, as he drew nearer. He eyed Nillson and Anderson, making no attempt to hide his appraisal of Anderson's legs. "What is it?"

"You're a man down," Venables said. "Who is it?"

"A man down?" he replied, and looked back at his team, making a show of counting them. "Ah, you are right. I didn't even notice."

"You didn't notice?" Nillson said. "It's five o'clock in the afternoon."

"Must be the Moldovan," he said with a grin. "If it was anybody else, we would have had to work harder than usual."

The man's carefree demeanour did little to help with Venables' irritation, but there was clearly a power play in action. The slender agency manager could do little to intimidate the broad-shouldered farm labourer yet cared little for being shown up in front of Nillson and Anderson.

"Where is he, Vlad?" Venables asked.

"Maxim?" Vlad replied with a shrug. "How would I know? Maybe he's with the pretty English girl."

"Was he in the accommodation this morning?"

Again, his question was met with a shrug.

"I don't remember."

"Vlad, these women are with the police," he said, which only served to broaden the man's grin. "If Maxim is missing, then now would be a good time to say so."

"How do I know?" Vlad replied. "I'm not mother. I'm foreman. Here, at work, I am boss, but not in the house."

"Sorry, Vlad, is it?" Nillson said, cutting into the conversation. "It's important we locate Max. We believe he could have been involved in an accident. You mentioned an English girl. Do you know her name?"

"She was here," he replied. "Earlier. She was here looking for him."

"Her name?" Nillson said, and he made a show of trying to remember.

"Ah, that's it. Very pretty girl," he said. "Tammy. She come on pushbike."

Nillson looked across at Venables, whose confidence had waned. He now wore the expression of a man whose day was about to get longer.

"What's his full name?" she said. "The missing man?"

"Maxim," he replied. "Maxim Baftiroski."

"Do you have a photo of him? A passport or something?"

Venables spoke up. "We don't keep passports—"

"Don't give me that, Mr Venables. We all know you have his passport."

"Of course he has," Vlad said. "He has all passports. Every one of us. In case we run, or do something stupid. It's protection. It's illegal. We all know. Of course we do. But what can we do?"

Nillson nodded her thanks and turned back to Venables, who failed to meet her eye to eye.

Eventually, he nodded.

"I think it's time to stop playing games, Mr Venables," she told him. "I need to see that passport and I need to see it now."

CHAPTER TWENTY-THREE

The address that Chapman had provided led Freya and Ben through the town of Ruskington, along a lane, and to a pretty, little cottage that boasted a fantastic view across open fields, much like Henry Glass's mother's house. The house itself was quite similar, in fact, save for the fact that the Ruskington cottage was detached with a Volvo Estate on the driveway.

Ben pulled onto the drive, something he wouldn't have done had the lane been a few feet wider. The car shuddered to a stop, and he couldn't help but smile to himself at the contrast between his old Ford and Freya's Range Rover.

"Nothing like arriving in style," he told her.

"At least we arrived," she replied. "And besides, you never how these people are going to take the news. At least in this, we might come across as a little humbler."

"More on their level, you mean?"

"Something like that," she said. "You'd be amazed at the perception we have following the first few seconds of meeting somebody."

"You'd be amazed at the perceptions we have following the

first year of knowing somebody," Ben countered, to which she peered across at him in question.

"What is that supposed to mean?"

He shook his head and reached for the door handle.

"Nothing. Come on–"

"No," she said and grabbed him by the shirt sleeve. "You've been off with me for a while now, and if I'm honest, I don't know how much longer I can play the sorry friend. At least not until I can be sure of what I'm sorry about."

He looked down at her hand as if she might remove it and apologise. But she didn't. She held him there to assert her position.

"If there's something wrong, Ben–"

"There's nothing wrong."

"Something I can help with then?" she said, softening her tone. "I know we've been through a lot, and I know our relationship hasn't exactly been orthodox."

"Freya–"

"But I need you to know that if I've done something, said something, or, bloody hell, even touched you wrong somehow, then just say," she said. "I was married before, you know that. I know what the cold shoulder feels like. I know what lip service feels like. And I know what men are like when they're brooding over something."

"You make us sound like we're all cut from a template, Freya," he said, and then gave a laugh she knew to be fake.

She let go of his shirt and made a mock attempt to smooth the crease out before looking up as he finally looked her in the eye.

"Aren't you?" she said and winked. She shoved open her door, got out, and waited for him to join her.

"Freya, listen," he said, and this time it was Ben who grabbed Freya by the arm. She stared at his hand, eyebrows raised, and he

released his grip. "Look, I'm sorry," he said. "I've just got a few things to deal with."

"Michaela?" she asked.

"No," he replied, almost irritated at the thought.

"Well, it's too fast for you to have met anybody else, Ben," she told him. "Christ, it took you nearly a year to hit on me—"

"I think you'll find it was you who hit on me."

"Only because I'd exhausted my list of positive signals," she said. "I just wanted you to know that you can talk to me. It doesn't matter what happened before. If anything, the fact that we've been intimate should make it easier."

He looked back at his car, which she guessed was for no other reason than to avoid eye contact with her.

"She gave you something," Freya said, which caught his attention enough at least to grace her with the courtesy of looking at her.

"Who?"

"Michaela. She gave you something in the station car park right after you had loaded DI Standing into the transporter."

"You were watching us?"

"I was looking out of the window at my friend. I didn't think that was a crime."

The car once more became the focus of his attention.

"Well, if you don't want to tell me..." she said.

"It was nothing," he replied, with a little more aggression than she had expected. He must have recognised his tone, and he softened. "It was just a few things, papers and stuff. You know what it's like when you break up."

"I do," she replied. "But I tend to avoid the awkward exchange of belongings."

"Oh yeah. You just take the family motorhome and leave, don't you?"

"Worked for me," she said and was about to leave him to it

when she caught sight of a man beside the Volvo, not ten yards from where they were.

"Help you?" he said, clearly confused as to why they were parked on his drive.

"Oh sorry, we're looking for a Mr Henry Glass," Freya told him, and she reached into her pocket for her warrant card.

"That's me," he replied, opening his car door and dropping a bag on the passenger seat before taking a few steps forward to examine her warrant card.

"Detective Chief Inspector Bloom," she said. "And this is Detective Inspector Savage. We're sorry to disturb you, but might we come inside?"

"Inside? What for? What is it? Has something happened?"

"Perhaps it's best if we—"

"Just say it. Is it Mum? It is, isn't it? It's Mum."

Freya hated these moments. She hated the build-up, the pretence, and the formality. Most often, she just wanted to be human and tell them. There had even been times when she had wanted to give them a hug. Not this time though. That sentiment was reserved for the parents who had lost children.

"It's best if we sit down, Mr Glass," she said.

He stared between them in disbelief then turned to lean on his car, which groaned under his weight. He raised his hands to cover his face, then pulled off his wire-framed glasses to rub his eyes.

Freya gestured for Ben to step in, who reached back into his own car, retrieved a box of tissues from the glove box, and set then set them down on the Volvo's bonnet.

"Shall we go inside," he said softly, and in the absence of anything to add, Freya took a moment to admire his ability to be so gentle despite his six-foot-something frame.

Glass pulled his hands from his face, sniffed loudly, and then allowed Ben to lead him towards the house. Such was Ben's manner that he had empathy enough to take the man's keys from

him, unlock the door, and then lead him to the lounge. Typically, those terrible discussions were eased with tea, prolonging the inevitable suffering. But much like her relationship with Ben, this episode was far from orthodox.

"How?" was all Glass said between sniffs. He looked up at Ben as if Freya wasn't even there.

"It was a heart attack," Ben replied, taking a seat on the sofa opposite him. "Her hairdresser found her this morning."

During those painful moments of silence, Freya took in the room. The walls were almost bare, save for a few pieces of artwork, prints mostly in cheap frames, but at least they matched.

There was a distinct lack of clutter on the surfaces. No family photos, no little mementoes, and not a single houseplant.

"Her hairdresser?" he said, then looked up and to the right, recalling the girl. "Tammy, isn't it?"

Ben nodded but said nothing.

"Poor girl. Is she okay?" Glass asked. "Must have been awful for her."

"She's holding up, as far as we know," Ben replied and looked at Freya.

"We have one of our family liaison officers looking after her," Freya added. "It's not usual, but given the circumstances, I wanted to be sure she was handling it."

Glass nodded his thanks but refused to look at her. That was okay. His relationship and trust was with Ben.

"Was she..." Glass began, then faltered, sucking in a breath. "I mean, did she suffer?"

Ben adjusted his position and leaned forward to catch his eye.

"I saw her," he said. "She looked peaceful."

"And was she..." he began again, seeming unable to complete a sentence.

"In bed?" Ben prompted. "No. She was on her landing. We think she climbed the stairs and..."

It was Ben's turn to falter.

.

"And she didn't make it?" Glass said knowingly. "No doubt she'd been for one of her walks."

The statement roused Ben enough for him to look up at Freya.

"What makes you say that?" Freya asked, jumping on the thread while it hung in the air.

"That's what she did, isn't it?" he replied. "I've told her a hundred times to stop. Anything could bloody well happen, especially after what happened to Dad."

"Mr Glass–" Ben began.

"Henry, please," he said as if the formality irritated him.

"Henry, can you tell me if your mum suffered from any mental illness?"

The reaction that followed was not what Freya had expected. Glass gave a laugh that died as fast as it had come.

"Nothing formally diagnosed," he said. "But she hasn't been the same since Dad died. There are the walks, for one thing. But mainly it's just a confidence thing. It's like she's afraid to do anything. If it wasn't for Uncle George, she wouldn't have made it this far."

"Helps, does he?" Ben asked, at which Glass nodded.

"He sees her more than I can," he replied. "Same old story, right? The son who neglects his elderly mother."

"We all have lives, Henry."

"Yeah," he said. "Yeah, I suppose. Can I see her? I mean, that's what happens, isn't it?"

"It can be arranged," Ben told him. "If that's what you want."

"It is," he said. "The term horse bolting and closing the stable door springs to mind."

"It helps sometimes," Ben said, his voice calm and reassuring, which seemed to ease Glass's anxiety.

"I always hated myself for not seeing Dad," he said finally, then gave his words some thought. "I want to. This time, I mean. I want to. I want to say goodbye without the entire family pitying me."

"I'll make the call first thing in the morning," Ben told him.

"Thank you," he replied, then seemed to shake himself out of his thoughts. "My God, I'm so sorry. I should offer tea or something."

He stood and made for the door, which was more of a means to hide his emotions than anything else.

"Henry, there's something else I need to ask you," Ben said, stopping Henry in his tracks. "Your mother wasn't alone. There was a man in the house."

"A man?" he said. "Uncle George?"

"We're as yet unsure of his identity," Freya added, and for the first time, Glass looked at her with something more than casual indifference. Sadly, her moment of triumph was cut short by her phone, which vibrated in her hand. She glanced down at the caller ID displayed on the screen, then continued with her reply. "But unless your Uncle George is an Eastern European man in his mid-twenties, then I think it fair to assume it is somebody else," she said. "Please excuse me, I have to take this."

CHAPTER TWENTY-FOUR

"Ma'am, it's Gold," Jackie said, as the driver rounded a corner as fast as he dared.

"Gold, is everything okay?"

"No, ma'am," she replied. "There's been a road traffic accident. It's Tammy. Tammy Plant. She's been hit by a truck."

"Oh, good Lord," Freya replied, and Jackie got the sense she was moving into a more private space. "Is it serious?"

"It's hard to say, ma'am," she said, tucking herself into the seat as tightly as she could to allow the paramedic to tend to Tammy's broken body without hindrance. She set the call to loudspeaker to make holding on while maintaining the call easier. "We're on our way to the hospital now. I'm in the ambulance with her."

"What are we talking about here, Gold?" Freya said. "Is she conscious?"

Jackie ran her eyes across Tammy's twisted body on the gurney opposite. The paramedic must have sensed her; he paused briefly to convey the seriousness of the injuries. Tammy's eyes were closed and her mouth was ajar, while her consciousness roamed some better place.

The paramedic shook his head.

"No, ma'am," she replied. "The injuries appear to be extensive."

"Has she mentioned a next of kin?" Freya asked. "I tasked Chapman with looking into her, but can you see if she has any details to hand?"

"Details?"

"A phone number. Her parents or a sibling or somebody."

"You mean, I'm to go in her bag, ma'am?"

"Oh, for heaven's sake, Gold. I'm not asking you to break any laws," Freya said. "The fact is that somebody's daughter or sister has been seriously injured. I can't see that she would mind."

Jackie reached for the little rucksack that the paramedic had cut from Tammy's back.

"I've got her bag," she said, tugging open the zip.

"Can you find her phone?"

"Hold on," Jackie said.

"Or a purse or something," Freya said.

"I'm looking now," Jackie said, removing a little cardigan and a stack of envelopes to search the bottom of the bag. "There's a phone."

She stuffed the belongings back into the bag and tapped on the phone.

"It's locked, ma'am," she said.

"Well, unlock it then."

"How?" she said. "I don't know the passcode."

A heavy breath came over the phone as if the boss was growing impatient.

"Try her fingerprint or something," Freya said. "Or hold it up to her face."

"I can't do that—"

"Gold, listen to me," Freya said. "Is there a chance the girl won't make it?"

Again, the paramedic looked at her gravely, then nodded sadly.

"Yes, ma'am," Jackie said.

"Well, then it is imperative that we inform her family," Freya said. "Now unlock that phone."

Jackie stared down at the phone and then leaned forward to hold it up to Tammy's face. The device took a moment and a little circle whirled around on the screen as it processed, comparing what the camera saw to the image stored on its database. Then it unlocked and Jackie was presented with the home screen.

"I'm in," Jackie said, navigating to the contacts. "There's a number for her mother."

"Well then," Freya replied, "that wasn't so hard, was it? I'd suggest sending me the number, but if I'm honest, Gold, I think you're far more suited to the task than I. Are you up to it?"

Jackie took a breath and smiled gratefully at the compassionate expression the paramedic offered.

"It's okay," she said. "I'll call her. I'll keep you updated."

"Good, see that you do," Freya said. "Are you okay to stay with her?"

"Well, I have to collect Charlie," she said, then sensed the disappointment in Freya's silence. "I'll make some arrangements."

"Thank you, Gold. If there's anything you need, just call."

"Will do," she replied and then ended the call.

"You've got your work cut out," the paramedic said.

She appraised him and the task he was burdened with and smiled sadly.

"Said the kettle to the pot," she replied and then hit the button to initiate the next call. "Wish me luck."

The call connected, rang a few times, and was then answered with a heavy breath followed by what sounded like a tired and weary greeting.

"I wondered how long it would be before you came grovelling," the voice said.

"Is that Mrs Plant?" Jackie said.

"Tammy?"

"No, it's Detective Constable Gold," Jackie said. "I'm with Lincolnshire Police."

"The police? Whatever's happened?"

"I'm sorry to say, Mrs Plant, that Tammy has been involved in an accident. I'm with her now."

"An accident? Can I speak to her? Is she okay?"

"I'm afraid that won't be possible," Jackie explained. "The paramedic is dealing with her now, but as yet, the extent of her injuries is unknown."

"What?" she replied, and there was a scraping of a chair or a stool across a tiled floor. "Is she awake? How bad is it?"

"I was wondering if you could meet us at Lincoln County Hospital, Mrs Plant. I'm sorry, I didn't know who else to call."

"No, no, you did the right thing," the girl's mother said. "I'll come now. Sorry, who am I speaking to again?"

"Detective Constable Gold, ma'am," she said, which, under the circumstances, sounded far too cold and formal. "Jackie Gold. I'll keep Tammy's phone with me. You can call her number when you arrive, and I'll meet you."

"I'll bring her some things," she said. "What will she need?"

Once more, Jackie looked across at Tammy on the gurney.

"She won't need much," she replied. "Pyjamas and the like. I think you should prepare yourself for her stay to be lengthy."

There was a pause, and the girl's mother swallowed.

"I understand," she said, and the call ended.

Jackie sighed a breath of relief and dropped the phone back into the rucksack. She zipped it up and sat it down by her feet as the driver braked heavily and rounded a bend, toppling her balance so that she had to lean on the paramedic for support.

"Sorry," she said, regaining her composure.

"It can be rough back here," he replied, as the driver called out from up front.

"Thirty-seconds," he said. "There's a crash team meeting us."

"She's ready," the paramedic replied and then seemed quite sad that the meeting was coming to an end.

He had nice eyes, hard but rich in hues of blue, and his dark hair bore small, carefree ringlets that hung over his ears and forehead.

Jackie grabbed the rucksack and placed it on her lap, more for something to do with her hands than anything else. But then an idea struck her. She delved into her pocket for one of her contact cards, which she held out for him.

He reached for it and, for a moment, the two of them held it between them.

"Just in case," Jackie said, and she gestured at Tammy. "For your report. That is if you need to write one up."

"My report," he replied with a smile. "You're not familiar with how we work, are you?"

"No, I'm not," she said with an embarrassed laugh. "But I'd be keen to learn."

The driver brought the ambulance to a stop, and almost immediately, the rear doors were opened by the crash team. It was one of those times when Jackie knew the best course of action was to let the professionals do their jobs, and they did so with practised calm.

It was only when the gurney had been offloaded, and Tammy was being rushed into the building, that the paramedic, who had communicated his findings, was able to take a breath.

"Well, I'd better get in there," she said and gestured at the door.

"I doubt you'll be able to do much for a while," he told her, as he closed the rear doors. "They're taking her straight to theatre."

"Do you think she'll be okay?" Jackie asked, realising almost instantly how absurd the question was. "I mean, do you have a hunch, or maybe you saw something?"

"You really don't know how this works, do you?" he said, as his colleague called for him, announcing another call for them to

attend. He started towards the passenger door, then stopped and turned to her. "I'll be writing my report later. You can expect a message from me."

"So, you do write reports?" she said, as he climbed into the front and reached for the door handle, looking back at her with that smile of his.

"No," he said. "But this time, I might want to go over some details."

He winked, closed the door, and the ambulance lurched forward, leaving Jackie standing in its wake.

Her thoughts were interrupted by a hand on her arm.

"DC Gold?" the voice said, and Jackie turned to find a young female nurse with an urgent look in her eyes.

"Yes?"

"I was wondering if you've managed to make contact with the next of kin," the nurse said. "She's taken a turn for the worse. The doctors can't say how long she has."

CHAPTER TWENTY-FIVE

"And this is it, is it?" Gillespie said, pointing at the flattened patch of grass beneath an old, ratty hedge at the back of a field. "This could have been a badger."

"Or some deer," Cruz said, inspecting the area with an untrained eye. "It's an ideal place for them."

"Deer?" Gillespie said. "What are you on about?"

"I mean it. This is a perfect place for them. It's a good vantage point, access to grass, water in the dyke, and it's just a quick sprint across the field to the trees over there," he replied, pointing at the trees with the bench in front.

Gillespie shook his head and exhaled loudly. Turning back to the uniformed officer, he closed his eyes for a moment to block out Cruz's incompetence.

"Ignore him," he said, gesturing at the flattened area. "What makes you so sure this is relevant to the investigation?"

Gillespie recognised the officer from the morning. He had been the one who had shown Ben and the boss inside the house where Alice Glass had been found.

"Nothing concrete," he replied. "At least, not until SOCO have been in and had a look around."

"And what is it you expect them to find, Sergeant..." Gillespie cocked his head, hoping the man would provide a name.

"Sanderson. Jeff Sanderson," he said, as he twisted the police tape around one of the steel poles he had driven into the ground to form a square around the site. "I would hope they might find some boot prints in the mud down there, not to mention any debris in the grass. I mean, God knows how long they were waiting there watching."

"Watching?"

"Yeah," he said, looking confused. "I thought the theory was that the old girl's house was burgled. I'd say this is a good place to watch it for a while. You know, to understand her movements."

"Aye, yeah," Gillespie said. "That's what I was thinking. And you say you've been in touch with the crime scene guys?"

Sanderson snapped the tape and pocketed the roll.

"All done and dusted," he replied. "They'll be over just as soon as they've finished in the house."

"Haven't they finished yet?" Gillespie said. "Bloody hell, they're going to town, aren't they?"

"By order of Her Majesty DCI Bloom," Sanderson said, which caused Cruz's head to snap to attention, although he said nothing. "She said they were to throw everything at the place. Something about there being no obvious link in the deaths."

"I suppose she wanted to see if the dead man had been in more than one room," Cruz said from where he was standing in the tall grass outside the cordon, peering into the dyke where the suspect may have been hiding.

"Aye," Gillespie said and then caught the uniformed officer's sneer. "Do I know you? Have we worked together before?"

"Not likely," Sanderson said. "I'm based out of Lincoln HQ. I was over in Newark for a few years, but you know how it is, more chance of promotion and all that."

"So, you're chasing the leadership positions, are you?" Gillespie said. "Risky game that, you know?"

"You must have met DCI Standing, then," Cruz said. "Stephen Standing?"

"He was detective inspector when I knew him," Sanderson said. "But yes, I knew him fairly well. He was never shy to shout a round of drinks."

"That sounds like him," Gillespie said. "And I suppose he managed to get you in his pocket fairly quickly, did he?"

"In his pocket?" Sanderson said.

"Aye," Gillespie said. "You see, I worked with Stephen Standing for many years. That is before he disgraced the uniform. If anyone knows what that man is truly capable of, it's me."

"We had drinks every now and then, that's all," Sanderson replied, looking uneasy.

The hour was late, and as the sun sank lower, so too did both the temperature and the mood.

"I think we're done here, Gabby," Gillespie said. "I think it's time to pay Mr Benson a visit. What do you think?"

"Yeah, we probably should. I can't be late tonight. I've got to go into town to get Hermione a present. It's her birthday on Saturday and I don't have a thing yet."

Once more, Gillespie closed his eyes, baulking at the volume of information the young detective constable was willing to share in front of a complete stranger.

"Tell the CSI team I'll be in touch," Gillespie told Sanderson. "Until then, I'd appreciate if you stayed here and kept an eye on the place. We wouldn't want any Tom, Dick, or Harry walking over it now, would we?"

Sanderson checked his watch, seeming a little put out. But he relented, realising it wasn't worth the argument, leaving Gillespie and Cruz to make their way across the field towards the three cottages.

"Bloody deer," Gillespie said, with a playful shove of Cruz's arm, which sent the wee scamp further away than he had intended.

"What? They love places like that," Cruz said, tramping his way through the field to catch up. "I saw it in a documentary."

"Aye, right," Gillespie scoffed. "This little documentary you saw, it didn't feature a wee baby deer whose mother was shot by hunters, did it?"

"Eh?"

"Nothing," Gillespie said, lacking the mental energy to pursue the topic. "What do you make of that Sanderson?"

"He seems alright," Cruz said. "You can tell he's Lincoln HQ and not one of our lot."

"What makes you say that?"

"Oh, I don't know. There's just something about him, isn't there? Like he's a cut above the rest of us."

"There's something about him, for sure," Gillespie said, as they reached the lane and the three cottages. "But I think it's something altogether different to what you're thinking."

"Eh?"

"Nothing," Gillespie said again, as he stepped onto the lane.

The scene had vastly altered since that morning. Only two liveried police cars remained, plus the two white CSI vans, which were being loaded by two white-suited individuals, one of whom had partially removed their paper overalls and tied the arms around their waist. The other, the taller of the two, had yet to remove their hood, mask, and goggles.

"Shall we see how they got on?" Cruz asked.

"No," Gillespie said. "No, Pat gives me the creeps."

"Pat? You mean the one with the hood?"

"Aye, scares the bejesus out of me if I'm honest."

"Why?" Cruz asked. "I thought they were always quiet and reserved."

"Aye, it's their quiet reserved nature that spooks me," Gillespie said, and he bent a little to whisper in Cruz's direction. "How long have we been working with Pat?"

Cruz shrugged. "I don't know. A few years."

"Aye, and in all that time, have you ever seen Pat without their hood or mask on?" Gillespie replied, over-emphasising the crime scene investigator's name and finishing with a questioning stare towards Cruz.

"Come to think of it, no," Cruz said, rubbing his chin. "Why haven't I ever noticed it before?"

"Because, Gabby, you are what your wee nature documentary might call asexual."

"A...what?"

"Asexual. You demonstrate no interest in either the opposite or the same sex."

"I like Hermione, and she has nothing to complain about in that department," Cruz said, defensively. "And anyway, what does that have to do with Pat?"

Gillespie laughed to himself.

"Tell me, Gabby," Gillespie said, unable to hide his smile. "What team does the mask-wearing Pat there play for?"

"Eh?"

Gillespie sighed.

"Which team does Pat play for?" he said again, flicking his eyes at the crime scene investigator and back to Cruz as discreetly as he could. "Are they a man or a woman?"

"Are they a—" Cruz began, far louder than Gillespie would have hoped for.

"Shhh," Gillespie said, holding both hands to quieten the buffoon. "Don't bloody shout it out. Just tell me if you think they're a man or a woman?"

Scrunching his nose up, Cruz peered across the lane at the two individuals, who by now were preparing the equipment to cart across the field to the flattened patch of grass. The young DC appeared totally transfixed.

Gillespie clicked his fingers in front of Cruz's face to grab his attention.

"Don't bloody stare," Gillespie hissed. "For God's sake.

Remind me never to send you in under cover."

But it was no use. Cruz's head was tilted to one side, his mouth ajar as he tried to find an answer to Gillespie's question.

"I wondered when you'd be back," somebody said from behind them, and Gillespie turned to find George Benson strolling towards them with one hand on the fence that belonged to the blind lady. "Have you found anything?"

"Ah, Mr Benson," Gillespie replied. "We're just gathering facts at the moment. These things take time, you know?"

"I see," he replied, coming to a stop and staring, slightly bemused, at Cruz, who was still awestruck with Pat. He glanced briefly and quizzically at Gillespie, jabbing an old, gnarled thumb at the young DC. "Is he all right?"

"Oh aye. He's just learned about the birds and the bees," Gillespie told him. "I'm glad I bumped into you though, Mr Benson. I was wondering if you could accompany us inside Alice's house?"

"Accompany you? Whatever for?"

Gillespie led the old gentlemen towards Alice's front gate.

"Well, things aren't exactly as we first thought," Gillespie said. "What we need is for somebody to tell if anything is missing or out of place. An experienced eye, as it were."

"An experienced eye?"

"Somebody who would know what the house looked like while Alice was alive," Gillespie said. "You did say that you were close, did you not?"

He seemed to hesitate, taking a moment to glance once more at Cruz, who, if anything, was far more intrigued by Pat's gender than before.

"Mr Benson?" Gillespie said.

"Yes, yes," he replied and held out his arm as if extending an invitation to Gillespie. "Shall we?"

CHAPTER TWENTY-SIX

"Can I offer you a drink?" Freya said from the passenger seat as Ben eased the car beside the kerb outside her cottage.

He looked up at the little house with fondness. It was the type of place that reminded him of the times his father used to speak about – days when his mother had been alive, and the world was clean, green, and innocent. Poppies dotted the herbaceous borders along with tall oxeye daisies and foxgloves, all of which were well-suited to Freya's hands-off approach to gardening. A sprawling Jasmine reached its tendrils up across the old stone, and the few roses still in bloom were in dire need of deadheading.

"Do you mind if I don't?" he replied. "It's been a bit of a day."

She paused, her hand on the door handle.

"What if I said that I did mind?" she said. "What if I told you that I missed our post-shift chats so much that I might just go inside and drown myself in wine?"

"Will the bottle have a little sailing boat on the label?" he asked, referring to an ongoing joke between them.

She smiled.

"No, it certainly will not," she replied. "In fact, I'd say the

bottle will have no pictures on it at all and will be entirely written in Italian."

He looked up at the house again, then back at her. And although her puppy dog eyes were quite obviously a rouse to delay her loneliness, there was something in those immovable features that he had always found irresistible.

"One," he said.

"One it is," she replied, shoving her door open, leaving him a moment's silence to gather his thoughts. She waited by the quaint, little garden gate and called out to him. "Well, are you coming in, or will we drink in the street like teenagers?"

He couldn't help but laugh out loud, yet the idea of sipping a glass of wine with her at the little table and chairs in her front garden seemed far more appealing than entering the lion's den, where guaranteed escape would in part rely on his cunning and timing, and also his ability to control his own desires.

He shoved open the door and climbed out, and just as she likely knew he would, he followed Freya up the garden path and into her new home. The furniture wasn't as coordinated as the items she had ordered, but she had made it a home in that way many women are able to.

"Make yourself at home," she said, as she hung her coat in the cupboard beneath the stairs and ventured into the kitchen – a habit he knew to be carried out on a daily basis. The next sounds he would hear would be the pop of a cork, the chink of glass on glass, and the sigh of satiation, in that order.

He didn't sit. Instead, he chose to browse her home, sparse as it may be. In true Freya style, there were no photos. The few photos she kept of her previous lives would be placed on her dressing table, with perhaps one of her father on the spare bedside table. That is if she had bedside tables yet. There were pictures on the walls, most of which she had picked up during her past year in Lincolnshire, and most of which he knew only

because he had taken her to collect them from the art shops dotted around the county.

"Here you are," she said, startling him from his thoughts. He spun and found her standing behind him, barefoot with one placed atop the other. "You're twitchy."

"I'm tired," he replied hastily, then sipped at the wine. It was a chianti, which he only knew on account of having demolished several dozen bottles with her during the past year. "Aren't you going to show me around?"

"I thought we could talk about the investigation," she said, dropping into an armchair. "Like old times."

"I suppose you want me to rub your feet too?"

"Maybe later," she replied. "Shall we eat?"

"No," he said, again hastily. "No, I really can only stay for one."

"That's a pity," she said, taking a long sip of her wine and relaxing back into the seat. "Well, I suppose we should get down to business then."

"Sorry?"

"The investigation, Ben," she said. "Get your mind out of the gutter for a minute, won't you? I want to go over what we know."

"That won't take long," Ben said. "Alice Glass died of a heart attack on her landing and the mystery man died from a head wound, most likely caused by several hammer blows to his temple."

"What about Alice's husband?" Freya said. "Doesn't it strike you as odd that he died from similar injuries to the man we found?"

"No," he replied. "In fact, I think we'd be adding complexity by trying to bring a crime that took place five years ago into this investigation."

"Is that what you think, or what you hope?"

"It's what I think," Ben replied.

"And Tammy Plant?"

Ben paced across the room, then turned on his heels.

"She found Alice."

"Who was in no way in need of a haircut," Freya said. "And who, coincidentally, has been hit by a truck less than a mile from Alice's house."

"George Benson," Ben said. "The only man we know of who had access to Alice's house, and aside from an estranged son, the only person who really knew her."

"Has Gold contacted you yet?" she asked.

"Not yet. But I imagine she'll call when she leaves the hospital," Ben replied. "How about Gillespie? Has he been in contact?"

"Do I have steam coming from my ears?"

"No," he said.

"Then you can presume he hasn't contacted me."

"In which case, we won't really know anything until the debrief tomorrow morning."

She took another sip of her wine and seemed defeated.

"I hate this part," she said. "It's like doing a jigsaw puzzle with somebody handing you bits piecemeal. I much prefer to arrange the parts in the right order."

"Edges first?" he asked, to which she laughed.

"That would be a dream," she said. "But I'll settle for working from the inside out rather than have nothing to go on."

Ben took a long sip, leaving himself just one more mouthful.

"So how about that tour, then?" he asked, and made his way towards the stairs, stopping at the foot of them for her to follow.

"You really are growing in complexity, Ben Savage," she said, as she pushed herself out of her chair. "You spend the day keeping me at arm's length, and then, after just a few minutes in my home, you beckon me to the bedroom."

He waved his arm, allowing her to go first, then followed slowly, fighting that primal part of him that gleaned pleasure from her gently swaying hips.

They stopped at the landing, which was much larger than Ben

imagined the cottage could be. She bit down on her lower lip, a wry smile teasing the corners of her mouth into play and she leaned on the doorframe of her bedroom.

"Just a tour, Freya," Ben said, trying hard not to sound cold or bitter.

"How disappointing."

"I just want to see that you're living with some semblance of comfort. I'm not a complete bastard," he replied and nudged open the door to one of the two spare rooms. "May I?"

She stared at him for a moment, as if searching for the tiniest strand of doubt in his conviction. But even Freya's tenaciousness had its limits, and she flicked her head at the door.

The room was large enough for a double bed but boasted only a wardrobe and dressing table, which had been laid out with much deliberation. A single photo frame had been set to one side of the dressing table, bearing an image of a couple, which, due to the unsaturated colouring, Ben presumed to have been taken in the seventies.

"It's a dressing room," he said. "What about your guests?"

"I have another. It's much smaller, but how often will I really have company?"

"And how many of your guests will require the use of a spare bed?" Ben said with a grin.

"Don't be vulgar, Ben," she said. "Have you finished inspecting my dressing room? I do hope it meets your satisfaction."

"To be honest, the decor surprises me. It's not really to your taste, is it?"

"I'll decorate in time," she said.

"Yes, more leather and chains," Ben said, and he rapped on the wall closest to him to the tune of a reassuring, solid thud. "Good wall for some shackles, that one."

"How very droll, Ben," she said, and left the room to wait for him on the landing. "Is there anything else you would like to see?"

She eased open her bedroom door, revealing an immaculate

space, sparse but well-presented, with none of the distractions that a lack of space might breed.

Her dressing table was bare, save for a glass for her water, whilst the other bedside table bore a framed photo of her father. It had taken the same place in the house she had rented from Ben's father, presumably set on the opposite side of her side of the bed, so she may remember him daily, whilst maintaining some kind of modesty and separation during moments of intimacy.

Realising he was staring at the photo, Ben stepped over to the window to admire the view across the little green and the beck that cut through it. A family of ducks were on the grassy bank, the ducklings all lined up in what appeared order of size.

"Excuse me for a moment," Freya said, leaving him to his thoughts. He heard the bathroom door close and lock, giving him the opportunity he'd hoped for. Using his phone camera, he took a quick snap of her father's image then left the room, calling out to Freya as he descended the stairs to give her some privacy.

"I'll see you downstairs," he called out, knowing that, in Freya's world, calling out whilst using the restroom was as vulgar as eating with dirty hands.

He stepped into the kitchen, only for something to crunch underfoot. He started, panicking that he had broken something of importance. But to his surprise, he found coffee beans scattered across the floor. It was only when he started to investigate that he realised the clocks on both the microwave and oven were off. The coffee grinder he recognised from her previous house had been placed on the sideboard, apparently in some haste, as she normally wrapped the cord around it and returned it to the cupboard.

Then he remembered that she had commented on having a difficult morning, and suddenly, he thought he might understand why.

It took a few moments for him to locate the electricity consumer unit in the cupboard beneath the stairs. As he had

suspected, he found the main breaker switch had tripped. He clicked it back on, then spent a moment adjusting the clock on the oven, which, if it was anything like his own, was far more difficult than using the thing to cook a three-course meal.

On the little table beside her armchair, he found the little CD radio she had brought with her to Lincolnshire. It had been the main source of entertainment in the motorhome she had called home for those first few days in the county.

He smiled when he saw the CD inside and, setting the volume on low, he hit the play button.

She descended the stairs much as the hostess of a great house might reveal her new dress to a party of admiring onlookers, except, in this instance, the house was a quaint, little cottage, and the admiration was only in Ben's eyes.

"I should go," he said, as the opening notes of Chopin's Moonlight Sonata began faintly in the background, so quiet that she perhaps hadn't registered the noise. Or perhaps she was so familiar with the piece that its effect had waned to insignificance over the years. He opened the front door, admiring the fact that she offered no argument and displayed no sign of regret that he was leaving, her pride banishing the thought of either. "Do you want me to pick you up in the morning?"

"I've arranged for my car to be returned tonight at some point," she said.

"Well, God help the driver when he comes," he said. "Thanks for the wine and the tour."

He started down the garden path and opened the little gate when he saw her in the doorway looking after him.

"Ben?" she called out, softly enough for him to pause as he closed the gate. Her serious stare softened to an appreciative smile, and she flicked her head back into the house. "Thank you. With any luck, tomorrow morning will go a little more smoothly."

"I hope so," he replied, climbing into his car and leaving her with one final thought. "For both of our sakes."

He started the engine, pleased with himself for both escaping her seductive clutches and for having the last word, which was a rare occurrence for anybody in Freya's company. He found first gear, checked the side mirror, and was about to set off when there was a gentle tap on the window.

Freya was standing beside the car, peering down at him expectantly. So, he opened the window just a crack to maintain some kind of control over the conversation and its duration.

"You're quite wrong, you know?" she began, leaning forward to speak with some discretion.

"Oh?" he replied.

"You mentioned that the two deaths are creating complexity," she said, thoughtfully. "But in fact, the two deaths are the key to the investigation."

"How so?" he said, pulling the gear stick into reverse and tugging the handbrake on once more.

"To understand this fully, we need to establish a link between Alice Glass and the dead man. If we do that, then we'll be one step closer to a motive more worthy of resources," she said.

"And if we fail to find a link?"

"*When* we fail to find a link, then we must deduce that he was simply burglarising the place while she was out for her morning jaunt in the fields," she replied, straightening and preparing to walk away. "In which case, my theory will stand. Goodnight, Ben, and thanks again."

CHAPTER TWENTY-SEVEN

When Freya had first entered the incident room on the first floor
of the station nearly a year ago, she'd been hit by what others had
called the aroma of fresh coffee but what she knew to be the
stench of cheap instant coffee. Her predecessor, the shamed
Stephen Standing, had at least elected to install a decent coffee
machine. However, in Freya's opinion, he was not graced with any
sense of refinement and had filled it with coffee beans far worse
than any she had encountered in a jar.

But today, the first morning that had gone according to plan,
the incident room smelled like a barista's paradise. She was sitting
at her desk when the first of the team arrived, who, of course, was
Chapman, wearing a knitted cardigan and a floral blouse, and
carrying her handbag in much the same manner as Queen Eliza-
beth II. She was young in years but old in soul – a trait Freya
admired. Along with old traditions came virtues and morals that
so often seem to have been waylaid.

"Good morning, ma'am," she said, only one of two who
insisted on calling Freya ma'am instead of boss.

"Morning, Chapman," Freya replied, as she sipped at her
espresso and continued to finish reading Gillespie's email.

"Today's the day, then," Chapman said, as she fired up her computer and arranged her desk to start the day right.

"For what?" Freya replied, without looking up.

"It's day two, ma'am. It's the day when things usually get a little heated."

"In what way?" Freya said, intrigued.

"I mean, if you think about all the investigations we've worked on, it usually takes a day for us to go over the basics, and then sleep on them before we come up with a solid plan. The first day is always a write-off, really. But day two, that's when things get real. Things become exciting. What I'm trying to say is that I'm expecting an interesting briefing this morning. No doubt, you have a plan in mind, that's all, ma'am."

Freya beamed inwardly at the young woman's intuition and keen insight, although she couldn't help but feel she was about to disappoint her. The fact was, until she heard the accounts in detail from Gillespie, Gold, and Nillson, she couldn't even think of making a plan.

"Well, let's see, shall we?" she said by way of avoidance. Thankfully, the double doors opened and in walked Nillson, Anderson, and Gold, the latter with her head hanging low and rings around her eyes like the tyres on Freya's Range Rover. "Good morning, ladies. I hope you're all as keen as Chapman and I?"

"Keen?" Nillson said, hanging her jacket over the back of her chair. "Keen for what, boss? A day free of men?"

She indicated the empty space where Gillespie, Cruz, and Ben usually sat, smiling like the cat who'd got the cream.

But before the idea of a fantastic day of feminine harmony could be enjoyed, the doors opened once more, and, in a rush of long coat tails and hair, Gillespie entered, bringing with him the odour of cheap aftershave.

He tossed his coat onto a spare chair and flopped down into his own, all arms and legs, before slapping his laptop bag onto his

desk. It took a few moments to realise that everybody was looking at him, and he froze with his fingers on his keyboard. His eyes travelled between each of them the way an antelope might assess an encircling pride of lionesses.

"What?" he said slowly. "What is it?"

The three women all looked towards Freya for a response, but she let him hang there for a few moments longer, prolonging the man's misery and anxiety.

"Nothing," she said eventually. "Nothing for you to worry about."

"Have you smelled that coffee?" Cruz said, as he too entered the room in a flurry, already removing his jacket and fighting to shake a sleeve from his arm. "It's like somebody took a load of mud from that dyke in the field, dried it out, and left it in the kitchen. What a stench."

He plopped down in his seat and then set his laptop up with a little more grace than Gillespie, though not much more.

Eventually, he must have sensed Freya's abhorrence. He looked up at her, naive in almost every way.

"What?" he said. "What is it?"

"It's nothing," Gillespie told him. "Apparently nobody is talking this morning. It's going to be one of those telepathic briefings, so I think you can handle this one. My psychic powers aren't as sharp as they used to be."

"Eh?" Cruz said, his face screwed into a look of absolute bemusement. And as if a stage manager was positioned outside the door leading the cast on with timely cues, Ben entered.

Freya downed the rest of her espresso and moved to sit on the edge of her desk where she could address them all and write on the whiteboard.

All eyes were on Ben as he opened his laptop, sighed at the idea of even attempting to turn it on, and then sat back in his seat with a trusty notepad and pen.

"Are we doing this?" he said, which pleased Freya by reminding

her of just one of those hundred differences between him and most other men.

"We are," she said, sensing a lull. "You have five minutes to get coffee and use the washroom."

"Coffee?" Cruz said. "Can we get some decent stuff? I'm not sure my stomach can handle that sewage some idiot has brought in. I tell you, it's like whoever got that stuff has no sense of taste."

"Unlike you?" Gillespie countered. "A man who wears his woolly sweater over his shoulders like a nineteen-thirties cad. And whose idea of date night with his girlfriend is a watching a pirate copy of the latest marvel movie and sharing a bag of chips."

"I'll have you know I do not watch pirate movies—"

"Alright, alright," Freya said, clapping her hands three times to regain control. She checked her watch. "Four minutes. If you want coffee or a comfort break, then I suggest you do it now. Something tells me this will be a lengthy briefing and I want you all on form."

Nillson and Anderson filed out, whispering shared jokes which Freya presumed were at Gillespie and Cruz's expense.

"Are you not getting a coffee?" Gillespie said to Cruz.

"No," Cruz replied. "Besides, if I stand up to get a coffee, no doubt you'll ask me to make you one and I'd prefer not to start my day bowing and scraping."

"I believe there's some of the coffee that Standing left behind," Freya said. "If I recall, I saw it in the cupboard at the back."

"Oooh, good shout, boss," Cruz said, and he eased himself out of his chair, eyeing Gillespie as if he might suddenly launch an attack.

"Are you not having any coffee this morning, Gillespie?" Freya asked.

"Me? No, boss. I'm all coffeed out. I've been up since half past seven."

"Half past seven, wow. You night owl, you."

"I know. That's why I sent you that email. I had to get it all down while the details were clear in my head."

"Well, in that case, would you mind doing me a favour and popping downstairs to see Sergeant Priest? Ask him when he plans on pulling resources from the crime scene for me, will you?"

"Aye, boss," Gillespie said. "I need to see if the expanded search came up trumps anyway."

He slipped from the room, leaving just Ben and Gold seated before Freya. Ben was drawing something, which, if Freya knew him as she thought she did, would be a tree of the contacts and the connections between them, which he could then annotate during the briefing.

Gold, however, was staring into space.

"Is there something you want to say, Gold?" Freya said. "Before the others come back?"

She blinked a few times and wiped her eyes with the corner of a tissue, and then seemed to sigh to herself as if the idea of revealing her deepest thoughts was the very last thing she wanted to do.

"It's Tammy Plant, ma'am. She's gone under again this morning," Gold said, a sadness in her eyes.

"I presume you managed to speak to the doctor?" Freya said. "Did they give any indication of an outcome?"

Gold nodded, using the tissue to dab at her nose.

"I'm sorry. It's just, I've been at the hospital all night with her mother. The family has been torn apart by this. It's absolutely heartbreaking to see. I'm running on adrenalin right now."

She took a few moments to compose herself and then closed her eyes for a second or two.

"She's undergoing a nine-hour procedure today, ma'am," Gold said. "If she pulls through, then her chances are good."

"But if she doesn't?" Ben asked, but that particular question needed no answer, which was just as well, as Cruz entered the room carrying a cup of Standing's foul coffee.

He dropped into his seat, taking a large mouthful, and finishing with an exasperated sigh.

"Is everything okay, Cruz?" Freya asked. "You look like you also had a night from hell."

"Also?" he said, with a laugh. "I doubt anybody had a night as rough as mine. I forgot to get Hermione a birthday present, so I was up all night looking for something on lingerie websites. I tell you; I wouldn't wish a night like that on anybody."

"No," Freya said, pleased to see Cruz's naivety had at least neutralised the downward curve of Gold's lips. "No, that really must have been awful for you."

CHAPTER TWENTY-EIGHT

"Right then," Freya said, as the girls and Gillespie filed back into the room. "In a moment, I'll be asking each of you to provide a brief account of your findings. Please do keep them brief and keep to the major points. I'm keen for us to get out there and make some real progress today. Once we've built a better picture of where we are, I'll be assigning tasks for the day, which will then feed into this afternoon's debrief. I'm not a fan of meeting for the sake of meeting, but as it stands, a man died more than twenty-four hours ago and we're still no closer to understanding who he is or why he was in Alice Glass's house."

"I think we can help there," Nillson said, and she glanced at each of them as if apologising for the interruption. "Mind if we go first?"

"Be my guest," Freya said, reaching for a pen, something Ben had noticed she always did, like an ex-smoker occupying their hands.

"Well, we did as you suggested, boss. Locks Wood Farm. It's about a mile south of Navenby by road," Nillson began. "To be honest, it was easy. They have fourteen temporary visas but only thirteen guys on site."

"So, they're a man down?"

"They are, yeah," Nillson said. "A guy called Maxim Baftiroski."

"Why didn't you message me last night?"

"The agency manager had his passport. He didn't send the copy through until this morning, and I didn't really want to be the one to raise false hopes," she replied. "It would only add to the confusion."

"Fair enough."

"But he fits the bill perfectly. Same height, same build, same approximate age. All we need to do is get him formally identified."

"Is the agency manager prepared to ID him?" Ben asked, seeing a need for his farming experience to play a role. "I'm guessing none of his family are here and we'll need somebody who can prove they knew Maxim well enough for his word to have any substance."

"That's something I hadn't considered," Freya said, an odd admission of an oversight on her behalf.

"Nillson, can you pass whatever you have to Chapman?" Freya said. "Chapman, before we venture down the path of having CPS throw the case out before we've even started, can you contact whoever it is you need to see if he had any relations here? I'm not familiar with the cultural habits of Eastern Europeans, but many cultures like to bring more of the family over."

"The home office, ma'am?" Chapman said. "I'll get onto them right after the briefing."

"Good, thank you," Freya replied. "Nillson. Good work. Anything else to report?"

"That's the big one, I'm afraid."

"Don't be afraid. You might not realise it, but you just found our corners. Now all we have to do is find the edges."

"Sorry?"

"Nothing," Freya said, realising the analogy she and Ben had

used hadn't yet been shared. "Chapman, when you've made contact with the home office, can you please run some background checks on this Maxim Baftiroski?"

"Ma'am," she replied.

"Gold, you should stay in the office today. Call round the local hospitals to make sure Baftiroski isn't simply lying in a hospital bed somewhere."

"Ma'am, I told Tammy's mother I'd be back."

"If you have another day like yesterday, Gold, you'll be no use to man nor beast. Arrange for the doctor to call with any updates."

"Ma'am, I'll be okay," she replied regretfully, but she'd committed. "I'd like to go if I can."

"Boss?" Cruz said, raising his hand like a schoolboy with a curveball question.

"What is it, Cruz?"

"I was just thinking, that's all," he began. "You see, I know you might think I'm being a bit over cautious–"

"For heaven's sake, Cruz, will you just come out with it?"

"Well, don't you think it's a bit funny that Tammy Plant, the woman who found Alice's body, was involved in an accident not far from the crime scene?"

The room held its breath, as seven minds processed what he had said in their own ways.

"What are you saying?" Freya said.

"Well, what if it wasn't an accident, boss? What if she saw something else?"

"She *was* acting oddly," Gold said. "I mean, she was a bit shaken up, but still."

"Aye, I told you she was a wee bit twitchy," Gillespie said. "She came to the crime scene. Nervous as hell, she was."

"Are you suggesting that somebody made an attempt on her life, Cruz?" Freya asked.

"It's possible, isn't it?"

"Aye, if this was nineteen-fifty and it was Michael Corleone driving the truck," Gillespie said.

"Michael Corleone was a fictional character, Jim," Nillson said. "You mean Al Capone."

"No, no, he has a point," Freya said, dismissing the inevitable argument that was about to erupt. "It might be prudent to put a uniformed officer in there."

"That'll be Lincoln HQ," Ben said.

"I could go," Gold said.

"No, I want you here. You've barely slept a wink. Find somewhere quiet and call the hospital, will you?" Freya told her. "I'll talk to Detective Superintended Granger and make the arrangements for a guard. Well done, Cruz."

"Eh?" Gillespie said, as Gold sipped from the room with her phone in her hand. "Well done for being paranoid?"

"Well done for being pragmatic," Freya replied. "You should try it sometime. In the meantime, I'd like to hear what you two discovered yesterday."

"Aye well," Gillespie began, sitting up in his seat. "We took the old man—"

"Mr Benson?" Freya said.

"Aye, him. Mr Benson. We took him around to Alice's house when CSI had finished up. You know, just to see if anything was out of place or missing."

"Don't say it like it was your idea, Gillespie," she said. "I told you to do it."

"Aye, I know, but everything was in order."

"Nothing was moved? No cupboards emptied, drawers rifled, furniture moved?"

"Nope," he said. "It's just your average, run-of-the-mill pensioner's home. Not a speck of dust to be seen and not a thing out of place."

"How disappointing," Freya said to herself, but loud enough

for the team to hear. "Perhaps Mr Benson wasn't as familiar with Alice as he let it be known?"

"He seemed it, boss. He knew what was in every cupboard, where she kept her photos, her money, her coffee and the like. Nothing creepy, like, but just as you would if you'd been in the house often enough."

"Her money? And I presume there was nothing missing?"

"All there," Gillespie said. "Only a wee bit of cash like. Kept it in an old coffee tin behind the soup. I mean, he did say it was odd that she hadn't got her bills ready—"

"Her bills?"

"Aye," Gillespie said. "Apparently, she didn't quite trust herself, so at the beginning of each month, she'd put money in wee envelopes to give to the window cleaner and house cleaner. That type of thing. She usually kept them on top of the microwave, but there was nothing there."

"My gran used to do that," Chapman said. "She didn't keep them on the microwave, but she'd organise her monthly payments like that so that she knew how much she had left."

"Aye, I mean, I don't know when pension day is, but maybe she just hadn't got around to organising them?"

"And I suppose one of those payments would have been for her hair appointment?" Freya said, and she stared at him, more than disappointed.

"Aye, I suppose so," he said with his usual nonchalance. And then it hit him. "Oh aye. It would have been."

"And I suppose we have no way of knowing how many envelopes there might have been?"

"I don't suppose we do," Gillespie replied.

"Alright then," she said. "What else? Why were you summoned to the search? Don't tell me, they found nothing except an old hammer with blood on the handle which you thought insignificant?"

"No, boss," Gillespie said. "No *items* were found, as such, so we

broadened the search area. You know, just to make sure nothing was missed–"

"Again, one of my requests," Freya said.

"Aye," he said, faltering in that clumsy fashion she found quite endearing. "But they did find something a wee bit odd. You see..."

He paused as if struggling with his words, which was unusual for Gillespie who typically managed to verbalise the minutest of detail, even if his tone and use of adjectives could portray an Akoya pearl as a pebble scraped from the bottom of a manhole.

He stood and walked over to where Freya was perched, then gestured to the whiteboard.

"Mind if I..." he said, nodding at it.

She relinquished the marker with visible intrigue and folded her arms as he set about drawing three adjoining squares. In the first square, he wrote the name *George Benson*. In the third square, he wrote the name *Alice Glass*.

Opposite the three squares, he drew a much larger square, giving the far edge a squiggly line, and adding an X to the left-hand edge.

"Is this a film, book, or play?" Gold asked, as she re-entered the room and took her seat. She nodded to Freya to confirm the call had been a success.

"It's a map, if you must know," he said, as he added a small circle on the squiggly line, and then snapped the lid back onto the pen. "This is Alice Glass's house."

"Oh," Freya said, "I did wonder."

He caught her sarcasm, and it seemed to amuse him that she'd sunk to his level of wit. He stabbed the pen at the board, indicating each of the other features he had drawn. "The bog square is the field. The X is the bench where–"

"They did the deed?" Freya suggested.

"Aye, and the wee circle here is a patch of flattened grass."

Freya's amusement dissipated like a snuffed candle.

"A patch of flattened grass?"

"Aye, and before you say it, I know it sounds like nothing, and it might be. But there is a chance it could be more. You see, boss, it's directly opposite Alice Glass's house."

"And you believe this could be where Maxim Baftiroski viewed her movements?"

"Aye, boss, I do," Gillespie said. "I was doubtful at first. Still am, if I'm honest. But I have instructed CSI to give the place a good going over."

"No, you didn't," Cruz said, from behind him, and Gillespie closed his eyes in dismay. "It was that other bloke, Sergeant What's-his-name. The one from Lincoln HQ."

"Sanderson?" Freya suggested.

"That's it, him," Cruz replied. "It was his idea. Jim thought it was just a badger or something."

"Aye, well you thought it was Bambi if I recall," Gillespie countered.

"Anyway," Freya said, raising her voice as a school mistress might gain control of a classroom full of excited children. "The fact remains that, until we hear from CSI, we won't know. So let's wait to see if this is of interest to us or David Attenborough, shall we?"

"Aye, boss," Gillespie said, handing her back the pen.

"It's good though," she said, sensing he needed some kind of pick-me-up. "It might prove useful, and the missing envelopes are particularly interesting."

"Missing envelopes?" Gold said. "What missing envelopes?"

"Alice's neighbour suggested there may be some missing envelopes with cash in," Freya told her. "Payments for the window cleaner and such."

A troubled frown grew on Gold's brow and she cast her eyes to the floor in thought.

"What is it, Gold?" Freya said, to which she shook her head, almost as if she was contesting her own thoughts. "Gold?"

"I saw them," she said. "The envelopes. I saw them when I was looking for her phone. They're in Tammy's bag."

Chapman ended her call and made a note on her pad, no doubt recording the date and time of the call.

"Sorry, ma'am," she said softly, which was enough, as you could have heard a pin drop after Gold's announcement.

"Yes?" Freya said.

"That was Doctor Bell," she replied. "She said she found something you might find interesting."

"Please don't tell me I have to go and see her."

"No, no, she told me over the phone," Chapman replied. "She said she was certain that the man in the bedroom died before Alice Glass. She said there wasn't much in it, an hour at the most. The lab will confirm her theory, but she's quite sure."

CHAPTER TWENTY-NINE

"That shines a new light on things," Ben said, watching as each of the team evaluated the information. "So, the man dies in Alice's bedroom and falls against the door. Alice comes home, has a heart attack on the stairs, and falls against the door on the other side."

"So, who killed the man?" Nillson asked. "Are we sure it wasn't Alice?"

"Quite," Freya said. "There is no blood spatter on her arms, but there is some on the walls. She couldn't have made those injuries and escaped without getting some blood on her. Nobody could."

"How about if Tammy did it?" Gold said. "She did steal the envelopes, after all."

"My window cleaner costs me around fifteen quid a month," Nillson said. "Hardly worth murdering an old lady over, is it?"

"Fair point," Freya said. "Chapman, I asked you to take a look into Tammy Plant and George Benson. What did you find?"

"Not much to write home about, if I'm honest," she replied. "No historical offences. Parents Jan and Mark Plant live in Boothby Grafoe, but then, Jackie has already made contact with the mother so it's not really newsworthy. The only thing of real

interest is her hairdressing business, which according to Companies House isn't turning over very much at all. Without her being an official suspect, and without a warrant, I can't officially access her financials. But if the business is her only source of income, then I think it's safe to say she could very well be in some kind of financial difficulty."

"Parents in Boothby Grafoe?" Ben asked. "Expensive area."

"Just because they live in an expensive area, it doesn't mean she's living on the bank of Mum and Dad, Ben," Freya replied.

"You're right, it doesn't," Ben agreed. "But it does make you wonder if she uses her position to aid certain people who might have a mutual interest in making money on the side, doesn't it?"

Ben had always enjoyed watching Freya's expression change when either he or somebody else raised an idea or perspective that she hadn't thought of. When they'd first met, the irritation in these moments had been clear on her face, and she would either resist the idea or somehow manoeuvre the theory to become her own. But those days were coming to an end. Freya was becoming one of them, and she enjoyed their successes as much as her own.

"I worked on an investigation in London," she said finally. "Two women would go door to door selling insurance for some tin-pot firm, but they weren't really interested in making any sales. They were eyeing up victims, identifying easy and worthwhile targets."

"That's a bit of a leap, boss," Gillespie said. "Even by our standards."

"It's plausible, Jim," Ben said. "Chapman, can you find out how much debt she's in, if any?"

"I just need a warrant," she replied. "Will Detective Superintendent Granger authorise it?"

"Tammy Plant is in possession of missing items from Alice Glass's house," Freya said. "She discovered the body, and, as weak as it sounds, there was no way on earth Alice Glass needed a haircut."

"CPS will love that one," Gillespie said with a grin. "I'll bet they've never had that listed as grounds for prosecution before."

"I don't doubt it," Freya replied. "And if I'm honest, I don't think I could bring myself to list it. But with any luck, we won't need to. It's just another corner to get us started."

"A what?"

"Nothing," she replied. "What we need is a link between her and Maxim Baftiroski."

"Hang on," Anderson said, and she whipped out her notepad. "Vlad said something about an English girl."

She thumbed through the pages, searching for the entry.

"Vlad?" Gillespie said. "As in, the impaler?"

"As in, Maxim Baftiroski's foreman," Nillson said.

"Here it is. I knew it. The foreman mentioned that maybe Maxim might have been off with the pretty English girl."

"Anything else?" Freya asked.

"We didn't think anything of it, boss. It didn't seem relevant, not compared to seeing a photo of him."

"Well, it's relevant now. Can you go back to the farm? If you need warrants, say so, but I don't think you'll have any trouble."

"You should find the agency helpful," Ben said. "And if you don't, you can always exploit the farm owners."

"Why's that?"

"Because the last thing they will want is for us lot to be giving them grief about migrant workers."

"We'll go straight after this," Nillson said. "Maybe we can convince one of them to ID him while we're tearing their accommodation apart."

"Good," Freya replied, ignoring the petulance. "Right, so where does that leave us?"

"One dead man, as yet unidentified," Cruz said, reading from his notes and using his hand to indicate Nillson and Anderson. He then moved it towards Chapman. "Tammy Plant's financial records."

"Thank you, Cruz," Chapman said. "I'll just throw away my pen, shall I?"

He ignored the comment and continued with his commentary by aiming his hand at Freya.

"Which leaves the lab results and anything CSI found," he said, completely missing the astonished glare on Freya's face. She was so dumbstruck by the fact that a young Detective Constable had just reminded her of her task that she laughed, to the surprise of Ben, who held his breath in anticipation of an explosion. "Did I miss anything?"

"Yes," Freya said. "What are you two going to do to?"

"Well..." he began, unsure of what to say but clearly feeling the need to make some kind of noise.

"I'll tell you what you're going to do," she said before he could enter into some kind of nonsensical waffle. "You're going to take the list of local burglaries that Anderson and Nillson kindly prepared, and you're going to compare it to Tammy Plant's list of customers to see if there is any crossover."

"Eh?" Gillespie said. "How are we going to get her customers?"

"I don't know, maybe by doing some police work? Maybe you could gain access to her shop. Maybe you could talk to the other shops nearby to see if this Maxim Baftiroski ever visited her there. And if he did, how close were they?"

"You should talk to Harry Doughty," Gold said. "He owns the little furniture place next door. He was with Tammy when I went to see her the first time, and they seemed pretty close."

"Thank you, Gold," Freya said.

Gillespie glared at Cruz for landing them the largest and most mundane of all the tasks, then shook his head and leaned back in his chair, which was a standard move for briefings.

"And if you need to get into Tammy's house, maybe I could have a word with her mother for you?" said Gold. "She's a bit of a dragon, but I'm sure she'd help. She has to go back and get some of her things anyway."

"Aye," Gillespie replied. "Aye, if you could, that would be a great help."

"Gold, when you talk to Tammy's mother, can you gently see if she knows about any boyfriends? You know the drill."

"Ma'am," she said. "I'll get another coffee and give her a call."

"I could do with another coffee," Gillespie said. "Maybe we could swing by The Petwood–"

"The only swinging you'll be doing, Gillespie, is from a nearby tree, and you can use your imagination if you want to know which part of your anatomy will be fixed to the rope if you don't come back with something useful," Freya told him, politely but with enough venom to drop a cow.

"Aye, boss," he said.

"Good. Thank you everyone," she said, checking her watch. "We'll meet back here at three. Get to it."

CHAPTER THIRTY

Freya flopped down into her seat, letting out an exasperated huff, which, under normal circumstances, she might have internalised, but being as only Chapman and Ben were left in the room, she felt little need.

"I honestly feel like a school teacher sometimes," she said, finding Ben staring at her silently. Chapman's fingers continued to tap away but she gave a knowing grin, despite not taking her eyes off her notes.

"Don't forget you've got to push for the lab results," Ben replied.

"And CSI," Chapman added, to which Freya gave a little laugh.

"Can you believe that little sh–"

"Bloom?" a voice said, and she found Detective Superintendent Granger leaning through the doors. "A moment, please."

He gestured towards his office and then slipped out, leaving Freya no room to contest or find a reason to delay the meeting.

"That's very ominous," she muttered quietly. "Something tells me I should take a good book with me."

That was when Chapman's typing stopped, and she looked to one side, clearly considering what Freya had said.

"I'll chase the lab and CSI while you're gone," Ben said, leaning back so he could put his feet on a nearby chair and thumb through his phone contacts.

"Well, wish me luck," she replied, gathering her notes and making her way through the room.

"Ma'am," Chapman said, and she delved into her handbag, eventually producing the latest Kevin Banner mystery novel. She held it out for Freya. "Did you want to borrow this?"

The idea was cute, Freya had to admit, but somehow Chapman had missed the mark on this particular occasion.

"You are lovely, Chapman," Freya said from the doorway. "But I was hoping for a hardback."

Again, Chapman didn't fall in.

"Oh, sorry. I only get paperbacks."

"She doesn't want to read it, Denise," Ben said, which seemed to blow Chapman's mind even more.

"I was hoping to tuck it into my trousers," Freya said with a smile. "To protect it from the inevitable spanking I'm about to get."

Blood filled Chapman's cheeks, turning them a rosy pink, and she looked away in a mixture of embarrassment and mild amusement. But there was no time to enjoy the joke. Freya left the room, walked the few paces to Granger's office, and knocked.

"Come in, Freya," he said, and she entered.

It was by no means the first time she had been called into his office, and it wasn't the first time she had been called in for a reprimand. But it was the first time she had been called in for a reprimand she hadn't been able to prepare for, and the sensation was far from joyous.

The trick was, as she had learned a long time ago, to say nothing. It was akin to a driver being pulled over by traffic police, who, as by way of introduction, typically ask if the driver knew how fast they were driving or why they were stopped, in the hope that an admission of guilt might come freely.

And so, Freya waited for him to finish what he was doing, and eventually, he closed his file, added it to his pile of three, and then removed his glasses.

"So," he began, "why don't you tell me how the investigation is going?" he said, then checked a note on his desk. "The Alice Glass murder. Where are we?"

"Making progress, guv," she replied. "It's early days, but—"

"Any suspects?" he said, cutting her off.

"One," she replied. "We're just dotting the i's and crossing the t's before we plan an arrest."

"Who is he? Does he have previous? Anything we can leverage? It would be nice to see interviews taking place."

"*She* doesn't have previous," Freya said. "And as for an interview, I'll be pushing for that just as soon as—"

"You're not sitting on this one, are you?" he said. "I don't think it will come as a surprise to learn that all eyes are on you right now. Eyes that are perched far higher up the food chain than mine."

"I'm not sitting on anything, guv," she replied. "It's just a complex investigation, that's all."

"Aren't they all?"

She showed her agreement with a slight shrug.

"We have two bodies. Alice Glass, a widowed pensioner, died from a heart attack. However, only once we had actually confirmed that could we move her, we discovered a second body. A male, late twenties to early thirties, Eastern European, who died from what we believe to be several hammer blows to the side of his head."

"Hammer blows?"

"His injuries are quite severe. Round fractures to his skull."

"How close are you to an identification? I don't want this to become a media-feeding frenzy, and I also do not want any light shone upon any kind of immigrant community. Not by us. The

locals will be out for blood if they get wind of something like that."

"We've managed to contain it so far, and I see no reason to go public, not yet at any rate," she replied. "And as for an ID, there's only one nearby farm that employs workers on temporary visas. We've made contact with the agency and highlighted one individual who has yet to be accounted for – a Maxim Baftiroski. The agency manager sent through a copy of his passport this morning, which I am yet to see, but Nillson has seen it and seems to believe he's our man."

"Formal ID?"

"Chapman is doing some research now, just to see if he had any family members in the UK before we approach the agency again."

"And his connection with Alice Glass?"

"None, guv, that we've uncovered yet anyway. The most likely reason for him being there is burglary, but that's going to be difficult to prove."

"Could he have been carrying out some work for her?"

"At five a.m., guv?" she replied. "The best hope we have is that he's somehow linked to Tammy Plant, the girl who discovered the body. Nillson and Anderson seem to think the foreman mentioned a pretty English girl."

"That could be anybody. She's not the only pretty English girl."

"I realise that, guv. But Gold has since discovered some items that belong to Alice Glass in Plant's bag, items that her neighbour thinks are missing."

"Such as?"

"Some money. Envelopes with cash in. You know, the type of thing somebody might do if they were careful with money and wanted to put some aside to pay for window cleaners, hair appointments, and the like."

Granger pondered the statement, and if he drew his own conclusion, then he did a fine job of retaining a poker face.

"And she discovered the bodies, you say?"

"She discovered Alice Glass, guv. We didn't discover the second body until after we could open the door she was propped up against."

"In which case, how could this Tammy girl have known he was inside?"

"I'm not suggesting she did. But there's a chance she was working with him."

"Identifying targets, you mean?" he said, and she nodded.

"We're seeing if a link exists between local burglaries and her client list. We should know more by this afternoon."

"Good," he replied. "And this business yesterday morning?"

She took the change of topic to be a positive sign that he had agreed with her but was loathe to say so.

"A mistake, guv," she replied. "I was the victim of a crime."

"You, Freya, are many things. But a victim you are not."

There was a compliment in there somewhere, or an admission of admiration at least, and she again shrugged to convey that the whole episode had been forgotten.

"I don't imagine for a minute that my unfortunate incident yesterday morning is the reason I'm sitting here now," she said. "Nor do I believe that you brought me in here to discuss the investigation."

"How intuitive you are," he said, leaning forward to rest his elbows on the desk. He adjusted the pile of files needlessly, then steepled his fingers. "I've had a complaint."

"A complaint?" she said. "Why, what have you done?"

He glared at her and she glared back. There was little use in cowering to him, better to meet him head-on.

"A Sergeant Sanderson," he continued. "He's suggesting that you publicly belittled him, made comments about his qualifica-

tion as a police officer, and then went on to strike some kind of deal based on the results of what I can only describe as a gamble."

She recalled the conversation with Sanderson, and although she would never have dressed the interaction as Granger had, she had little room in which to contest.

"What would you like me to do, apologise?" she asked. "Will an email suffice, or would you prefer I pay him a visit in person?"

"I would prefer it if, in future, you simply give a little thought to the individuals that support us, Freya," he replied. "No need to visit him or write an email. Just be mindful, that's all I ask. You're a good leader to the members of your team. Just expand on that a little where required."

"Expand on it?" she said, then prepared to stand by placing her hands on the arms of the chairs. "Okay. I'll bear that in mind. Will there be anything else, guv? We've got a busy day ahead."

"I mean it, Freya," he said. "I don't need to give you a lesson on how the force works. You've been around the block enough to know how rumours spread. One officer tells us another about an incident, he tells an embellished version to his mates, and so on. Before you know it, you're infamous and nobody trusts you."

"Do you speak from experience, guv?" she asked, making her way to the door.

"I've seen my fair share. That was enough for me," he said. "It's not weak to be kind. You'll do well to remember that."

"I'll do my best, guv," she said when a thought struck her. She paused with her hand on the door handle.

"Are you okay?" he asked, shaking Freya from her thoughts.

"Yes," she said, turning briefly with a weak reassuring smile. "It's just something you said. It resonated with me."

"Well," he replied, dragging the file back in front of him, "I'm glad I made an impression. Close the door on the way out, will you?"

CHAPTER THIRTY-ONE

Nillson parked her little hatchback beside Venables' truck and killed the engine, taking a moment to prepare herself for the task ahead.

"Do you think he'll let us in without a warrant?" Anderson asked.

"I think Ben was right," she replied. "The last thing the farm owner needs is us lot sniffing around, which means the last thing the agency manager needs is to be the cause of our sniffing."

"I'll take your lead," Anderson said and offered an honest but weak smile. "I'm still learning the ways of the yellow belly."

Nillson laughed.

"I haven't heard that name for years," she said. "I'm not even sure it's still relevant anymore, so don't go calling anybody that, especially not Venables."

They climbed from the car and took a moment to scan the fields in search of the labourers. But the land was vast and the team was small. They could have been anywhere.

"Why yellow belly anyway?" Anderson said. "Where does the name come from?"

"It's an army thing," a voice called out, and they were greeted by Venables filling the doorway at the top of the iron steps. He looked down at them as pleasantly as could be, which was far more welcoming than the previous day. "The Lincolnshire Regiment wore a yellow waistcoat and the name kind of spread to anybody from the county."

"Ah, there you go," Nillson said. "I was going to suggest it had something to do with the good weather. How are you, Mr Venables?"

"Busy," he replied. "Always busy."

"Not too busy to help with our enquiries, I hope?" Nillson said, as he stepped down to the ground and made his way toward his truck.

"You got my email, I presume?"

"I did," she replied. "And has he been seen?"

"Nope. No sign of him," he said. "Which doesn't bode well, does it?"

"I must say, you seem very cheerful for a man who has potentially lost an employee."

"Do I?" he said. "Must be something in the air."

He rummaged around in the back of the truck, dragging a few tool bags around as though searching for something.

"We'd like to see his accommodation, if we may?" Nillson said. "We're hoping it might give us an insight into who he was."

"Won't be nothing in there," Venables replied, sliding the tailgate closed and turning to face them. "But I'll show you if you like. I suppose you have a warrant?"

"No, but I can get one if necessary. All I'd have to do is make a call and it would be delivered, along with a van full of uniformed officers to help us search."

He said nothing at first, choosing to plunge his hands into the pockets of his cargo trousers.

"Been told to keep you happy, I have," he said finally. "We

don't want any trouble. If one of our boys has done something, then that's their business. The labourers' cottages are on the far side of that field. You'd better jump in. I'll run you over there."

"No, we'll follow you," she replied. "If you don't mind."

He eyed them both, then controlled his expression, forcing one that resembled pleasant.

"Have it your way," he said, climbing into the truck.

"Don't you need a key or something?" Anderson asked, and he leaned out of the open window to reply.

"No need. Vlad and the boys will be there. They can show you around.

He started the engine and the exhaust coughed out a great cloud of diesel smoke that the breeze carried off across the field.

By the time Nillson and Anderson had got back into Nillson's car, Venables was careering along the track leaving thick dust in his wake.

"Well, we won't have any trouble seeing which way he went," Anderson said. "The man's a maniac behind the wheel."

Nillson reversed out of the spot, finding first gear before the car had come to a stop, and she floored the accelerator.

"Oh, for God's sake. Just because he thinks he's Colin McRae doesn't mean to say you have to copy him," Anderson said.

"I'm not worried about losing him," Nillson replied. "But what I don't want is for him to give Vlad and the boys the heads up that we're coming. He might have taken a happy pill this morning, but that doesn't mean to say I trust the bastard. Not after yesterday's performance."

She followed the truck's dust cloud as fast as she dared push her car. Its smaller wheels struggled on the gravel and found the potholes with ease. Twice Anderson was bumped from her seat until she leaned forward and held onto the dashboard. But she said nothing, allowing Nillson to focus on the track, until, after a series of long straights and deadly ninety-degree bends, she

brought the hatchback within one hundred yards of the truck, just as a row of newish cottages came into view.

The truck slowed and then came to a stop beside the centre of what looked like five terraced houses, where a large porch had been erected with a pair of large double doors.

Nillson slewed the car in beside the truck before Venables had climbed from his seat, and stared at him through the glass.

He laughed to himself as if conceding that he was impressed, and then climbed out, appraising her car for damage.

"After you," Nillson said, and, as if he was internalising his reply, he made his way towards the building, grinning to himself.

"Vlad," he called out as they entered.

It was as if, Nillson thought, the ground floor of the middle house had been converted into a central leisure room with some old couches dotted about for the labourers to use. Spent drinks cans and the same sandwich wrappers Nillson had seen in his truck were dotted about various tables, and pairs of dirty boots were lined up against a wall. Two doors led off the space to the right and left, presumably to the various rooms in the cottages.

"Vlad, you about, mate?"

He nudged open the right-hand door and peered inside.

"Vlad?" he called out, as the large man appeared in the left-hand door.

"Are you checking on us now, Mr Venables?" he said, and the manager turned on his heels. "You don't come to our home. This is our place."

"I haven't come to check up on you. The detectives wanted to speak to you –"

"Then you should have called," he replied, and for the first time looked at Nillson and Anderson. "He hasn't returned. You have wasted your time."

"We've come to see his room," Nillson said. "Are you able to show us?"

"This isn't a good idea. His room is private."

"Not anymore it isn't," Nillson replied, and she gestured to both doors with each hand. "Left or right?"

He studied her, perhaps looking for the same kind of weakness Venables had displayed. But there was no weakness in Nillson's expression, and she held her ground, unwilling to be bullied.

"This way," he said finally, pointing at the left-hand door.

She walked through, holding it open for Anderson, and then waited for the two men to follow. Vlad pointed to the second door off the corridor and Nillson tried the handle, expecting it to be locked. But the door swung open to reveal a large room that reminded her of a studio flat one of her brothers had rented when he was at university.

It was a room like any other, with a TV, bed, and a pile of clothes on a chair. It was clean and tidy for the most part.

"Here," Anderson said, making a beeline for Maxim's mobile phone on the bedside table. She snapped on a blue, latex glove, and tapped the screen. Then, after a moment of what looked like sheer delight spreading across her face, she showed it to Nillson. The phone was locked, but the illuminated screen showed several missed calls, all from Tammy Plant.

"Bag it," Nillson said, then turned to the two men in the doorway. "Does Maxim have access to any other buildings? Grain stores or anything like that?"

Vlad shrugged, his huge shoulders rising and falling in time with a deep breath that seemed to stretch the fabric of his t-shirt to its limit.

"No," he said. "Maxim is just labourer, like me."

"What about the containers?" Venables said. "You all have access to those."

"What containers?" Anderson asked.

"The fertiliser stores," he replied. "There's a few of them around the farm, for ease of access, I suppose."

"Can I see them?"

"I will take you," Vlad said.

"No," Nillson replied, cutting him off. "No, I think, in this instance, it's better if you give Mr Venables your keys."

"You don't trust me?" Vlad said, his smile cruel and uncaring.

"No," Nillson replied flatly. "No, I don't trust you one little bit."

CHAPTER THIRTY-TWO

"Ah, Mrs Plant," Gillespie said, as the mature lady climbed down from a large BMW SUV. He held up his warrant card for her to see, which she made a point of scrutinising by peering down her nose at it, then giving a curt nod. "DC Gold mentioned you might be able to help."

"I don't have long," she replied, her face as taut as a snare drum. "I don't know what you could possibly want in my daughter's house, but whatever it is, you'll have to be quick."

"It's all part of our investigation, Mrs Plant," he replied, inviting her to walk up the driveway with a wave of his hand. Cruz fell in behind them, clearly a little intimidated by the lady's tone and demeanour.

"Never mind your investigation," she replied, as she unlocked the front door. "What about my Tammy, eh? What about the driver of the truck that hit her?"

"I'm afraid I can't comment on that, but I do believe they have someone in custody."

"He was probably drunk or on drugs or something," she muttered, begrudgingly letting them both inside. Then she raised

an index finger sternly. "You're not to go into her personal things now."

Gillespie held up three fingers.

"Scout's honour, ma'am," he replied, which failed to produce any hint of a smile.

"Right," she said, looking between them both disapprovingly. "I just need to pack her a few things. You've got two minutes."

She ventured up the stairs, leaving them to look around the lounge and kitchen downstairs. Gillespie strolled over to the back doors and peered out into the neat, little garden.

"Not a bad wee place this," he said.

"Please tell me you're going to help," Cruz said from a little desk in the corner of the room. Gillespie reluctantly strolled around the kitchen, nosing into a few cupboards to see what a girl like Tammy Plant kept in stock.

"Muesli?" he said. "Ah, can't stand muesli."

"I've found her laptop," Cruz replied. "I'll bag it, shall I?"

"Aye, you'd better," he said, opening the fridge only to be utterly disappointed again. "Yoghurt? What is it with yoghurt these days? And it's Greek yoghurt as well, not even the bloody flavoured stuff. Kale, tomatoes, carrots. God didn't give us teeth to chew on bloody leaves."

"God didn't give us teeth," Cruz replied, sounding bored of Gillespie's running commentary.

"You don't believe?" Gillespie asked. "I had you down as a God-fearing man, or boy, as may be the case."

"If you're asking if I believe God created man, then no I don't," Cruz replied. "But if you're asking if I believe in God, or if I believe there is a place for God in this world, then yes, I do."

"That doesn't make sense."

"Yes it does," Cruz said, closing a desk drawer. "God, or at least believing in God, creates hope, which gives people a common entity to believe in, defined morals to live by, and standards to which we hold ourselves accountable. Just because a

person believes in that, doesn't mean they have to subscribe to the whole Adam and Eve thing. That's the good thing about believing. It's not an all-or-nothing belief system."

Gillespie stared at the wee lad who rarely demonstrated any level of deep thought.

"Is that so?"

Cruz held up an iPad he found tucked between some books at the back of the desk.

"Might be useful," he said.

"Bag it then. With any luck, the tech guys can get into it," Gillespie said. "I'm not much of a believer myself."

"Now there's a surprise," Cruz muttered, as he strolled around the lounge. Gillespie leaned against the kitchen wall.

"All that jumping up and down, Hallelujah this and Hallelujah that."

"What?"

"You know, the praying thing."

"Nobody jumps up and down, Jim. At least they didn't when I last went to church."

"No?"

"No, the church has modernised quite a bit. They even have bands."

"Bands, eh?" he said. "Like Led Zeppelin, you mean? Do they bite off the heads of bats?"

"Of course they don't, and anyway, that was Ozzy Osborne," Cruz said. "No, the church band that I saw was pretty good. It was just like normal rock or pop music, and if I'm honest, it was better than some of the awful stuff you hear on the radio."

"Aye, well, that's one thing we can agree on, Gabby. Music seems to have lost its way a little, don't you think?"

"Jim, are you actually going to help?"

"I already helped," he replied.

"You looked in the fridge, Jim. That's hardly helping. We're

supposed to be looking for some sort of customer list so we can see if any of them tally with the list of burglaries."

"Burglaries?" a voice said, as Mrs Plant stepped into the room. "Did I just hear you say burglaries?"

Cruz winced silently.

"Aye," Gillespie said. "It's just a theory we're working on. Nothing to worry about at this stage."

"I don't suppose you know where she might keep a list of her customers, do you?" Cruz asked.

"In her journal," she replied. "It's a brown canvass thing. A5 sized. But I still don't see what local burglaries have to do with my Tammy?"

"Mrs Plant, I'm going to level with you," Gillespie said, trying to regain some kind of control of the conversation. "Did Tammy tell you about the old lady she found dead in her home?"

Mrs Plant's eyes narrowed and she adjusted her feet to a stronger posture.

"Yes, of course."

"Well, without going into too much detail, the old lady wasn't the only body we found in that house yesterday morning."

"I don't understand."

"Do you know if Tammy has a boyfriend, or a male friend, at least?"

"No, she doesn't," Mrs Plant said. "Tammy is focused on her business. She doesn't have time for that sort of thing."

"Then I'm sorry to be the one to tell you this, Mrs Plant, but we found the number of a man on Tammy's phone. They've been communicating with some regularity."

"That doesn't mean anything–"

"The same man we found lying on Alice Glass's bedroom floor," Gillespie continued.

She took a few steps towards Tammy's little desk and held onto the back of the chair while the picture formed in her mind.

"And you think that my Tammy has been providing information to this man," she said. "Am I right?"

"We'd like to rule it out," Gillespie said. "We're not accusing Tammy of anything, but our primary concerns are to identify the second body and understand why he was in an elderly lady's house."

"So, Tammy isn't in any trouble?" she said. "Should I ask my husband to alert our solicitor?"

"Not right now," Gillespie said. "Rest assured, we're not investigating the burglaries."

"So, what are you doing? What is all this about?"

"We're investigating a murder, Mrs Plant. The man we found suffered severe head injuries," Cruz explained. "His family deserve to know."

"Of course," she said softly, then sighed and sat down on the swivel chair. "There is a man. I told her it would come to nothing. He was only after a meal ticket."

"Do you know his name, Mrs Plant?" Gillespie asked.

"Yes. Yes, I do," she replied. "I met him once. He was at her little shop for one reason or another."

Gillespie sat down on the couch to meet her eye-to-eye.

"His name, Mrs Plant?" he said. "I'm sorry, I know this is difficult."

"Maxim," she said. "I don't know his last name. He told me, but I'm afraid it was one of those foreign ones."

Gillespie leaned back in the seat, letting his hands fall to his sides when his fingers touched something alien and hard tucked down the side of the couch.

He pulled it out and Cruz gasped, which caught Mrs Plant's attention.

"Is this Tammy's journal?" Gillespie asked, holding it up for her to see, and she nodded.

"That's it," she said, and she held out her hand. But Gillespie

held it out of reach. She glared at him. "That belongs to my daughter. Give it to me."

"I can't do that," he said and gestured to Cruz that they were leaving. She sat there on the swivel chair, her face a picture of panic and worry.

"If you find something—"

"Then you'll be the first to know," he said, cutting her off. "We'll be in touch, Mrs Plant."

He followed Cruz out to the hallway, but instead of leaving the house, he stopped by the front door.

"I'll just be a minute," he told the young detective constable and then re-entered the lounge where he found Mrs Plant still seated, sobbing into her hands. He dropped to a crouch beside her and took her by the hand. "She'll be okay. You'll see."

Tammy's mother shook her head and wiped away her tears with a tissue.

"I knew he would be trouble for her," she said. "I tried to tell her, but she's—"

"Young and impressionable," he finished, smiling up at her. "Why don't you go to see her? She needs you now more than ever."

"I know," she replied. "Do you have children?"

"No," he said. "No, that little journey has eluded me so far, for better or worse. I'm not sure if I'm really parent material if I'm honest."

"Oh, I don't know," Mrs Plant said. "My husband only agreed to have kids because I threatened to leave him otherwise. Wouldn't know what I'd do without her now. It's funny. The last thing I said to her was unkind. We had a row, you see."

"What about?"

"About money. What else?" she said. "But you don't know, do you? You never know when something like this will happen. Now I find myself wondering what life would be like without her."

"It can't be that bad. It was just a row."

"What do you know? You weren't there. You didn't hear her. I honestly think I've lost her," she said. "And I don't know if I'll ever have the chance to tell her how sorry I am."

Her voice trailed off and Gillespie imagined her mind wandering to a nicer memory – one that didn't involve arguments and bad feelings.

"You're right. What do I know? I didn't really have a mum or a dad," Gillespie started, and she looked down at him. "But if things had been different for me, if I'd had parents, then I'd like to think they'd have been like you. Nobody ever really fought my corner for me, not the way you fight for Tammy. She's a lucky girl."

Her eyes had softened and warmed, and she beamed for a moment.

"I'm sure you'll be a lovely father one day," she said. "But don't wish your life away, love. These things come in good time. You just need a little faith."

"In God," he said, wondering how on earth he was going to keep the conversation going after just telling Cruz he was an atheist.

"In yourself," she said, and instead of answering her, he prepared to stand.

"Go and see her. Tell her you love her," he said, straightening to look down at her and resting his hand on her shoulder. "All that matters is that you're there when she opens her eyes."

He left her there and was about to leave the room when she called out.

"Sergeant," she said, and she gazed at him hopefully. "If she is in any kind of trouble. It's my husband, you see. He won't understand–"

"I don't think she'll be in any trouble," he whispered. "You just tell her what I told you to say, and leave everything to me."

CHAPTER THIRTY-THREE

Venables fished a set of keys from his pocket, from which at least half a dozen coloured tags hung in addition to keys of all shapes and sizes.

The container was one of three that were situated side by side in a small, gravelled area between two fields and beside one of the farm tracks, making it accessible for anybody working on any of at least four adjacent fields.

"Maybe it's best if we did this," Nillson said, as she pulled on one of her latex gloves. Perhaps it was the sight of the glove or her tone that caused his helpful expression to wane, and he held the bunch of keys out for her. "Don't take it personally, Mr Venables. When were you last here?"

"I rarely come," he replied. "No need, if I'm honest. The labourers handle the fertiliser. All I do is make sure none of it grows legs and walks out of here of its own accord."

"And does it have a tendency to do that?" she asked, as she found the key to fit the padlock and slid it into the lock.

"In the past, it has," he replied. "But not since Vlad came. He's a good foreman, you know? A little rough around the edges, but then they all are. The trouble is that when something goes

missing, it's not them who get dragged into the farm office, it's me. I take full responsibility for them."

"That must be a burden," Anderson added, as Nillson occupied herself with the large container handles. "Taking full responsibility for men you don't know."

"All part of the job," he said. "I suppose it gives me a little incentive to do my due diligence on the men before they arrive."

"So, you do vet them, then?"

"Of course," he replied. "The truth is that contracts like this keep this firm going. If I were to let any old bloke loose, it would be given to a competitor before the end of the day, and where would that leave me? Not to mention the rest of them? No, these are good blokes. Hard workers, harder than most of the kids these days at any rate. No, you'll not find anything out of place here, mark my word."

Nillson yanked on the heavy container door and it swung open with an awesome squeal to reveal a dark space, filled on one side with blue two-hundred-litre barrels, each marked with a white label.

Venables adopted a knowing look but didn't dare smile, and after walking up and down the dark space, Nillson slammed the door closed.

"Next one?" she said, leaving him to faff with the lock.

It took him a few moments to snap the lock closed, and then he joined them at the next container along where Nillson was unlocking the padlock.

"So, what did you learn about Vlad?" Anderson asked, more to fill the void than anything else.

"Oh, not much. He did his time in the army and then got out, like most of them. He's a natural leader, that one. A bit brutish, but you can't take it personally. They're a proud people."

"You aren't tarring them all with the same brush, are you?" Anderson said with a smirk.

"I'll tar them all with the same brush if I see fit," he replied. "But I can assure you, those Albanians are bloody reliable."

"What about Moldavians?" Nillson asked as she pulled open the second container, only to be greeted with a similar view to the first.

"We don't see as many of them as we do Albanians," he replied, as Nillson moved on to the last container. "Maybe there are larger Moldovan communities elsewhere in the UK?"

"Maybe they have less reason to leave their country in the first place?" Nillson replied, tugging open the door now that she had got the knack of them. But this time, the sight that greeted her was not of two hundred litre barrels in rows along one side. It was of boxes and cables and paintings and electrical goods. It was, or appeared to be, at least, a treasure trove of stolen goods. "Or maybe not."

She stood to one side to allow both Anderson and Venables to look inside.

"Get CSI Down here," she said. "I want this stuff gone through before we touch it."

"But—" Venables began.

"Full responsibility, Mr Venables?" she said. "Do you still stand by that?"

"There must be some kind of mistake," he said. "It must be the farm's. I'll talk to the owner. I'll bet he's just using it as storage."

"You do that," Nillson said. "In the meantime, I'll have this lot compared to a list of stolen items. We'll see whose conversation is more fruitful, shall we?"

"You were talking about Moldovans," Anderson added. "What did you learn about Maxim Baftiroski?"

"Maxim?" he replied, still stunned by the sight before him. "Oh, not much. I knew his father so I knew he came from a good family."

"You knew his father? He was here? In the UK?"

"Yeah," he replied. "Yeah, he used to work for us. Good bloke, too. Viktor Baftiroski, his name was. He was probably the first Moldovan we had on the books."

"When was this?" Nillson asked, to which Venables shrugged.

"Five years, I suppose. It's funny really."

"Why's that?" Anderson said. "Why is that funny?"

"Because, young lady," he said, "like his boy, Maxim, Viktor Baftiroski upped and vanished without a trace about five years ago. He finished work one night, then the next morning he was gone."

He clicked his fingers as if to accentuate the point.

"And you didn't think this was important?" Nillson asked. "The fact that Maxim's father went missing. Did you call the police, at least?"

"I did," he said, holding his hands up in defence. "But they didn't do much. Filled out a few forms, asked a few questions, but not much else. Nobody seems to care about the immigrants, do they? It's like they don't matter to you lot."

"Oh, they matter," Nillson told him. "Especially when one of them is responsible for this lot, they matter. You can trust me on that one."

CHAPTER THIRTY-FOUR

It wasn't the first time Jackie had spent her day in the hospital waiting for somebody to regain consciousness. But it was the first time she'd ever had doubt as to whether or not that victim was a viable suspect. The girl had seemed so innocent, so shocked at what she'd seen, it was difficult to believe that she could ever be involved in such intrusive crimes.

But whether suspect or victim, Tammy had been afforded a private room just off the main ward in which nurses to-ed and fro-ed endlessly, and the sound of curtains being whipped along the metal rails, ringing telephones, and beeping machines added an incessant backdrop to what should have been a place of peace.

A machine did beep in Tammy's room, but it was low in volume, and Jackie had already become quite used to it, in the same way she had grown accustomed to the trains at her friend's house that backed onto the railway line. The noise was there, but distant and far from intrusive.

Tammy lay still, save for her rising and falling chest beneath the thin sheet. It was hard not to wonder just how involved the girl was, what part she had to play in the deaths, and how culpable would she be deemed if she *had* been feeding the dead man infor-

mation on vulnerable people. It was an appalling thing to do, yet she seemed so harmless lying there. Whether or not it was because she was unconscious, or if her beauty was truly skin deep, but there were no crow's feet, no deep lines across her brow, and no signs of age or stress at all around her eyes, where Jackie found it hardest to cover.

She leaned over to the spare chair, where Tammy's things had been stored, and after a quick check to make sure the door was closed, she stuck her hand inside the open zip compartment and felt around, finally retrieving the pile of envelopes. She felt them, one by one, all four of them. Two of them had coins inside – the ones marked *Window Cleaner* and *Debbie*. The other two contained only notes and were marked *Christmas* and *Heating Oil*.

The Christmas and heating oil envelopes were closed but not stuck down, as if Alice had added to the amount each week or month, building a little stockpile ready for when the time was needed to use them, and when Jackie peered inside, she found several hundred pounds in each. Each of the other envelopes had been stuck down, but the labels suggested the amounts would be low in comparison.

Jackie slipped them into her own handbag and wondered if Tammy had felt that same pang of guilt when she had taken them. Barely had she closed her bag and set it down by her feet when a slight rush of cold air licked the back of her neck, and she turned to find Mrs Plant standing in the doorway.

"Oh, hello," she said, standing and grabbing her bag. "I hope you don't mind. I just wanted to keep an eye on her."

"No, it's fine," Mrs Plant replied, smiling softly. She made her way over to her daughter, stroked her cheek, and then set a striped overnight bag down on the floor beside the bed. "How is she?"

"No news, I'm afraid," Jackie replied, standing up. "Perhaps I can ask a nurse to pop in and–"

"No," she said. "No, I'd like a minute to be with her."

She lowered herself gracefully into the seat Jackie had occupied and then took her daughter's hand in her own.

"I'll give you some time," Jackie said. "If you need anything–"

"Can you stay?" Mrs Plant said without looking away from Tammy. "I'd like you to."

"Well, if that's what you want," Jackie replied, and she made her way to the far side of the bed. "She looks so peaceful doesn't she?"

"Like butter wouldn't melt, you mean?" she said, to which Jackie smiled a little, as much as she dared to. "It's okay. I've just had a good chat with your colleague. Scottish chap."

"Jim? I mean, Sergeant Gillespie?"

"That's him," she said thoughtfully. "He was nice. Like he understood what I was going through. Of course, it's not about me, is it? It's about my Tammy. But as a mother, you still go through it."

"I can relate to that," Jackie said. "I can't tell you the amount of times I've had my Charlie in here. You feel so helpless, don't you?"

"You do," she agreed. "But he said he doesn't have kids."

"That's right."

"Well, he should. I mean, he seemed quite off with me at first, my own doing most likely. I wasn't exactly friendly when we met. But near the end, when his little mate had left, he seemed to warm to me. It was almost as if didn't want the other one to know he has a heart."

"That sounds about right," Jackie said, grinning as her mind conjured an image of the pair. "They'd never admit it, but those two are thick as thieves. Wouldn't surprise me if they grew old together, and if they did, neither of them would know the other one, not truly."

Mrs Plant stared at her daughter for a while, pushing a lock of her hair behind her ear.

"I can leave you if you want–"

"He told me why they wanted to get into Tammy's house," she said, dismissing the idea of Jackie escaping. "He said she might be suspected of somehow working with this man they found. Is that right?"

Jackie nodded slowly.

"I'm sorry," she said. "It's the last thing you need right now—"

"But why didn't you tell me?"

"Well, like I said, you've got enough on your plate."

"My dear, if there's one thing I have learned in this life, it is never to run away from hard times. If Tammy is guilty of anything, then we'll face it head-on, both of us."

"It could be serious, Mrs Plant," Jackie explained. "If Tammy had anything to do with that man being inside Alice Glass's house, then we'll need to take action."

"He found her journal," Mrs Plant said. "Where she writes down all of her appointments. He said he was going to see if any of her customers were on a list of burglary victims, or something."

"I think that for now, we should focus on getting her better," Jackie said.

"Don't mollycoddle me, please," she replied. "If she's done wrong, then she'll pay for it, and I'll be beside her, whatever that journey might look like."

Jackie sat back in her seat, letting the girl's health occupy the mother's mind. She checked her watch, then the door, where she noticed a uniformed officer was now standing guard, just as Freya had said they would be.

"I do have one more question," Jackie said. "Before I leave you to it."

"You want to know if I think Tammy would be capable of such abhorrent acts," she said and found Jackie's apologetic stare.

Jackie nodded but said nothing, and Mrs Plant was lost in her daughter's face for a moment.

"If I tell you something, will it stay between us?"

"I can't promise that," Jackie said. "There's a whole team

working on this. But I can keep information away from any press releases, if that makes a difference."

"And the members of this team?" she said. "Are they anything like your friend, the Scottish man?"

"Every one of them," Jackie replied. "I'd trust them with my life, all of them."

The statement seemed to have had an effect, and Mrs Plant took a few seconds to consider what she wanted to say.

"Tammy's business isn't doing well. Couple that with her stubbornness and her desire to succeed without help from the bank of Mum and Dad," she said, with noticeable pride, "and you have yourself a girl in serious financial trouble."

"What are you saying?" Jackie asked, sensing she had only skirted around the edge and the truth was hard to admit.

"I'm saying, my dear, that I do believe my Tammy would be capable of becoming involved with the wrong people to get what she wants," she said softly. "In fact, I'd go as far as to say that she is capable of almost anything if it means that she doesn't have to come running to me for help."

CHAPTER THIRTY-FIVE

The team returned to the incident room in their respective pairs, and whilst listening to the lab result being relayed over the phone, Ben watched with anticipation as, first of all, Nillson and Anderson entered, seeming fit to burst with excitement, then Gold, who bit down on her lip to keep herself from spilling her news prematurely. Finally, Gillespie and Cruz entered, both of whom seemed far more subdued than any of the women.

"And that's about all I can tell you," the forensic specialist finished. "I'm sure if Pat finds anything else, we'll be in touch."

Freya's eyes danced around the room as if she had had the same thoughts as Ben and was wondering what, if anything, Gillespie and Cruz had discovered during their day.

"Hello? Inspector Savage?" the voice said. "Are you there?"

"I am," he said eventually when Freya's eyes had rested on his, perhaps wondering what he was thinking. "Thank you for letting me know. Will you be sending the report across?"

"I'll do it before I leave," she said. "We've been called out to a farm in Navenby."

"Thank you," he replied. "Oh, can you please include Denise Chapman on that email? She'll be collating the information."

The girl made a note of Chapman's name, then inhaled loudly over the phone.

"Consider it done," she said and ended the call, leaving Ben to put his phone down and for the briefing to begin.

"I hope you all had productive days?" Freya said, peering at them all in turn, and then lingering on Gillespie, who had very little to say for himself.

She paused for a while, perhaps deciding where to start, and then stood to perch on her desk so she could refer to the whiteboard.

"Nillson, I wonder if you'd care to start?" she said.

"I'd be happy to," she said and cast her notes to one side. "Following another visit to Locks Wood Farm, we discovered three key facts. The first lies within Maxim Baftiroski's mobile phone, which, although we haven't been able to unlock it yet, did tell us that he was in contact with Tammy Plant. The notifications on the phone's home screen displayed several missed calls from Tammy. So, in respect to Tammy's guilt, all we need to do is link Tammy's clients to the list of local burglaries in the area and we have a pretty strong case to put forward for Maxim's reason for being there."

"Gillespie?" Freya said. "Have you managed to link Tammy's clients to the burglaries?"

"No, boss," he said. "Tammy's mother allowed us to access the house, in which we discovered an iPad, a laptop, and her journal where she noted down her appointments with her clients' names and phone numbers, none of which marry up to any of the reported burglaries."

"None? Are you sure about that?" Freya asked, looking as confused as ever.

"I've been through it twice, boss," Gillespie said, shaking his head. "I went all the way back to the beginning of the year. There's isn't a single match."

"Nothing unusual?"

"Not really," he replied. "Alice's appointments are in there, as were all her other appointments. Most of them are monthly but she sees a few customers every couple of weeks. She wrote a little P in a circle beside them, presumably they're her priority clients. You know? The biggest payers."

"Well, that's rather a blow, but not the end of the world. This is, after all, a murder enquiry and not an investigation into housebreaking. But the fact remains that Tammy was in contact with Maxim Baftiroski, who was, as far as we can tell, burglarising Alice Glass's house when he was killed."

"That's if it is Maxim Baftiroski," Ben said. "We still haven't got a positive ID."

"That's where our second piece of information comes in," Nillson said. "It seems that Maxim's father, Viktor Baftiroski, used to work for the same agency at the same farm."

"His father?" Freya said.

"I found him too," Chapman said. "Although, by name only. I couldn't find a link between him and Maxim. I've sent an email to the British Embassy in Chisinau to see if they can help, but they haven't got back to me yet."

"Well, we can take it as confirmed," Nillson said.

"And what happened to this Viktor Baftiroski? Are we able to contact him?" Freya asked.

"It's unlikely," Nillson said. "Viktor Baftiroski disappeared five years ago."

"If it's the same man I found records for, he had a POSB account, which migrant workers use for payments, but it hasn't been touched since two thousand and eighteen," Chapman said.

"It does sound like the same man," Freya said. "But it strikes me as odd that he should disappear. I mean, aside from sleeping on the streets, it's quite difficult to stay under the radar for five years in the UK."

"Maybe he is on the streets?" Gillespie said. "Sleeping in doorways and begging for food?"

"Why would a man migrate to the UK and then give it all up to live on the streets?" Nillson asked. "According to Mr Venables, the agency manager, he was a model worker. He had a home, a regular income, and everything he would need."

"He also sent money back to his family in Moldova," Chapman added. "If the embassy gets back to me, maybe I should ask them to see if he returned?"

"If he returned through legal means, then border force would have some kind of record," Ben said.

"You can try," Freya told her. "But I'll wager he's still in the country somewhere, perhaps under a new identity."

"I'll see if I can access witness protection," Chapman said. "You never know."

"It's worth a shot," Freya said, then turned back to Nillson. "You said you had three pieces of information?"

"Ah, yes," Nillson began. "We asked what areas Maxim Baftiroski had access to, barns and stores, and the like."

"And?"

"It turns out that, seeing as he was just a labourer, he only had access to the residential cottages and a few old containers dotted around the farm. They use them for fertiliser and anything the labourers need."

"It's a way of maximising the labourers' time," Ben said. "My dad does the same. You can't have a dozen or more paid hands standing around waiting for tools."

"Exactly," Nillson said. "Except one of the containers wasn't full of tools or fertiliser."

"Stolen goods?" Freya asked, and Nillson grinned.

"A treasure trove," she said. "TVs, cookers, paintings, jewellery, the works."

"The investigator I spoke to on the phone said they were heading to a farm," Ben said.

"Yeah, I called them on the way here. I hope that's okay?"

Nillson said. "We waited for uniform to arrive to make sure nobody touches anything."

"Good," Freya said. "If they can find Maxim Baftiroski's fingerprints or DNA from the haul, then at least we have a reason for him being in Alice Glass's house, which then gives us a motive for his death."

"Then all we need to do is find somebody with a hammer," Ben added. "Somebody who would have been upset at an intruder being inside Alice Glass's house."

"I think we need to start working on the assumption that Maxim Baftiroski was indeed burgling Alice Glass's house. With any luck, the evidence to support that will come in due course, but we can't sit on our backsides and wait for it," Freya said.

"There is one thing that is troubling me," Ben said, leaning back in his chair to ponder how he might phrase his concern.

"Technology?" Freya said.

"Women?" Gillespie added, which raised a few smiles but didn't hinder Ben's thought process.

"Nillson, you said there were TVs and paintings," he said. "Which reminds me of something you said, Freya. A man working alone couldn't have taken that kind of thing on foot. I mean, did Maxim Baftiroski even have a car or access to a farm truck?"

"He doesn't have a driving licence," Chapman said. "I checked that already."

"I think if a man embarks on a mission to rob houses, then he probably wouldn't be too concerned about driving without a licence," Ben said. "But that doesn't help us with the fact that, if he was involved, then he would need help."

"Maybe the other farm workers?" Freya said. "Was he close to any of them?"

"Quite the reverse, as far as I can tell," Nillson said. "He was the only Moldovan. The rest of them are Albanian, and judging by the foreman, a brutish man named Vlad, there was a clear distinc-

tion between them. In fact, I think it's fair to say that Maxim was ostracised and disliked by the rest of them."

"The rest of the team..." Freya said, and she stared into space while making sense of her thoughts.

"I also have some news," Ben said. "Fingerprints taken from the dead man, who we're assuming at this stage to be Maxim Baftiroski, were *not* found anywhere in Alice Glass's house, except for the window ledge in the bedroom where presumably he gained entry, and the cast iron drain pipe outside the window. However, there were a number of fingerprints found on the stairwell and around the house, none of which match any on the central database. Interestingly, one of these sets of prints was also found on the window ledge in Alice's bedroom."

"And presumably on the drain pipe outside?"

Ben shook his head slowly in confirmation of the conundrum.

"So, let's assume that our man gained access through the bedroom window, was heard by somebody, and was then stopped by that somebody who then left the house before Alice returned."

"There's more," Ben said. "According to the CSI team, footprints were found in the flattened patch of grass Gillespie discovered."

"Maxim's?" Freya said, and she pulled a face as if she dared not hear the answer.

"I'm afraid not," Ben replied. "Maxim Baftiroski wore size nine Nike trainers and the prints were a size six Reebok."

"Which might lead us to the individual helping him," Freya said after some thought. "Right, so if I can just recap. We have Maxim Baftiroski entering Alice Glass's house through the window—"

"We still need a positive ID, boss," Nillson said. "And if we can't locate the man's father—"

"If he hasn't shown his face for five years, then we can assume he isn't going to pop up now," Freya said. "Will the agency manager help? I can't see who else we could enlist."

"Will CPS allow that? I mean, he's not family or a friend," Gillespie said.

"They'll have to, I'm afraid," Freya replied. "Given the limited choices we have, I'm sure they would prefer him to ID the body than for us to simply leave a man unidentified and another murder investigation to go unsolved."

"Fair enough," Gillespie said.

"So based on Nillson and Anderson's discovery, let's assume that Maxim Baftiroski was working with somebody else. He entered the house through the window and was heard. Why would somebody hit him? And if I can just embellish that point, why would somebody hit him with a hammer, several times, hard enough to render him dead?"

"The first name that springs to mind is Henry Glass," Ben said. "A son protecting his elderly mother. Hears somebody in her house and sees red."

"He told us he hadn't been to visit for a while," Freya said. "But you're right. Let's see if we can eliminate him."

She leaned toward the whiteboard and circled Henry Glass's name.

"Anybody else?"

"George Benson?" Cruz said. "I mean, he isn't a blood relative, but he was close to her."

"Well done, Cruz," Freya said, circling the elderly gentleman's name. "Anybody else?"

"What about this?" Nillson began. "Vlad, the foreman. He would have had access to the container. He has access to a farm truck and men."

"You said they ostracised Maxim Baftiroski," Freya said.

"They did," she replied. "But what if Maxim knew of their plans and wasn't trying to rob the place, but instead was trying to stop them?"

A silence fell over the room which was broken by Freya snapping the lid of her marker back onto the pen.

"That's very good," she said thoughtfully. "That's very good indeed."

"I'll need the images of the prints found in Gillespie's patch of flattened grass," Nillson said. "I can check them against the rest of the labourers' trainers."

"I'll send them over to you," Chapman said.

"Take their fingerprints too," Ben said. "Maybe CSI can link them to the stolen goods in the container."

"In the meantime, Gillespie and Cruz, please arrange for George Benson's property to be searched," Freya said. "Ben and I will take Henry Glass."

Ben nodded at her by way of confirmation.

"I'll also ask the agency manager if he could spare a few hours to ID the body."

"That might not be necessary," Gold said, speaking up for the first time in a while. "Mrs Plant, that is Tammy's Mum, knew him or met him at least. She could ID the body for us."

"That's a big ask, Gold," Freya said. "Her daughter is in a coma."

"Which means she'll be at the hospital," Gold countered. "I've spoken to her and she's quite helpful."

"You do realise that by identifying the body as Maxim Baftiroski, she would be helping us build a case against her daughter? She was, after all, in contact with the man."

"She claims to have been aware of their relationship," Gold said. "She also stated that if her daughter has done wrong, then she must face the consequences."

"I wonder if Tammy herself would agree," Freya said, as Gold reached into her bag and retrieved a pile of envelopes. She walked across the room and handed them to Freya. "I took these from her bag."

"Very good," Freya said, as she felt each of the envelopes.

"There is one more thing," Gold said. "Although it's rather subjective."

"Go on," Freya said.

Gold took her seat and then inhaled.

"She said that Tammy was indeed in financial difficulty. But she's too proud to ask for help from her parents and fiercely driven to succeed."

"I don't get it," Cruz said. "Who does this help?"

"She said, in no uncertain terms," Gold said, "that she believes her daughter would go to any lengths not to go to her parents."

"Any lengths?" Freya said.

"Any," she said, and Freya pondered the sentiment.

But then she stopped and her head cocked to one side. She held a single envelope.

"This one is marked Debbie," she said. "Do we know who Debbie is?"

The room was silent for a moment as each of them looked to the others for an answer.

"Not Deborah Blake?" Cruz said, and all eyes fell on him. "She's the neighbour's daughter. Her mother is the blind woman we told you about. Why would an envelope be marked with her name?"

"I'll ask Henry Glass and let you know what he says. If it is the neighbour's daughter, then you can pay her a visit while you're nearby," Freya said, checking her watch. "Right, we all have jobs to do. Nillson, Anderson, you're back at the farm. Gillespie and Cruz, you'll be searching George Benson's house and looking into Deborah Blake. Gold, I'll let you handle Tammy Plant's mother. See if you can get her to add a little more weight to her statement."

"Yes, ma'am," she said.

"And Ben and I will be paying Henry Glass another visit, perhaps taking a look inside his tool shed. If you need a warrant, please go through Chapman, who will make the arrangements. If you need uniformed support, then please speak to Sergeant Priest

downstairs. We'll debrief in the morning, but call me if you find anything of significance. Any questions?"

"No, boss," Gillespie said, giving Cruz a dirty look for adding to their workload.

"Good. We now have several lines of enquiry," Freya said, pointing at the whiteboard. "One of those names belongs to a guilty person. The only way we're going to understand who it is is by eliminating the others. Now, let's get to it."

CHAPTER THIRTY-SIX

"I thought it might be you," Henry Glass said when he opened the door to Freya and Ben. His shoulders sagged under the weight of death and his eyes bore the scars of loss. Yet he had a strength to him that Freya admired, a dignity of sorts.

"I know this is a difficult time for you–" she began.

"But there are some formalities you must attend to?" he said, finishing her sentence on her behalf. "It's fine. I half expected it, to be honest."

He stepped to one side, allowing them to enter, and then, once he had closed the door, he led them through to a large lounge. The furniture was old and reminded Freya of the pieces she had bought to see her through until her new items were delivered.

"Please," he said, presenting a tatty, old couch. "I'll fetch some tea."

"Not for me, thank you," Ben said.

"Nor me," Freya added, and Glass saw that delaying the inevitable was going to be difficult.

"Well then," he said, finding his way to an armchair which

looked to be as old as the house. He sank down into the cushion, resting an arm on each side. "How can I help?"

"Before we start, may I ask how you are coping?" Freya said.

"Coping?" he replied, showing a mild amount of amusement. "Well, that I am. That's all we can do, isn't it?"

Despite his heavy local accent, he seemed to be practised in speaking clearly, annunciating his t's where another might have let them drop.

"The truth is, I've been expecting it for a long time," he continued. "You do, don't you? When they get to a certain age. You prepare yourself for it. You tell yourself it's coming, and you even picture the scene and how you might react. When Dad died, I didn't get that chance. He went long before his time, in my opinion. But Mum? Well, she's been going downhill ever since. It's still a shock though and any ideas of how I might have reacted fell by the wayside. We're all flesh and blood, aren't we?"

"We are," Freya said, then glanced at Ben before commencing with their true motive for being there. "Mr Glass—"

"Henry, please," he said, and she relented.

"Henry, do you remember the last time we were here we spoke of a man being found in your mother's house?"

"The dead man?" he said, again mildly amused. "How can I forget? Have you identified him?"

"We're making progress," she said. "But, and please understand—"

"You need to somehow eliminate me from your enquiries?" he said. "Sorry, I've been through this before with Dad. Plus, I read a lot of mysteries. Kevin Banner mostly. He's a local author—"

"We know of Kevin Banner," she said. "And in answer to your question, yes, we do need to eliminate you from our enquiries. You have to see it from our perspective, Henry."

"I do," he replied. "I get it. Who else would protect Mum from an intruder? Uncle George?"

"We are looking into him."

"The man can barely hold his knife and fork," Glass said, then sighed. "So, what do you want to do? Look around?"

"With your permission," Freya said.

"I have nothing to hide," he replied. "But if you don't mind, I'll wait here."

"Then I'll wait with you," Freya said. "And my colleague here can conduct a search."

"In that case, I think I'll make myself a cup of tea," Glass said when Ben had left the room. He stopped at the door. "Are you sure I can't tempt you?"

She smiled, still unable to fathom him.

"Milk, no sugar," she told him.

Then, after a few moments of waiting alone, she followed him into the kitchen where she found him leaning on the kitchen counter, watching Ben through the window.

"It is only a formality," she said, announcing her presence. "Just like you said."

"I know," he replied. "There's nothing to find."

"I'm sure," she said, then took one of the two wooden stools that served the breakfast bar. "I'm afraid we're rather in awe of you."

"You mean, you're wondering why I'm not hurling insults at you? Perhaps I should kick you out, tell you to come back with a warrant?"

"Perhaps," she said.

"But Mum wouldn't have wanted that. She was a kind soul, really," he said wistfully. "In a way, I'm glad. I know it sounds callous, but it's true. She wanted to be with him. No, sorry, it's more than that. She couldn't live without him. Maybe that's a better way of putting it. I suppose you've spoken to her neighbours?"

"My team has, yes," she said.

"Then you'll have heard the gossip."

"Gossip?"

"That she had some kind of mental illness," he said. "Mad Alice?"

Freya nodded that she had heard that name, but gave it little weight.

"I thought it true as well, you know?" he said. "At first, anyway. When Dad died, and she started on her little morning jaunts, I tried to bring her back. Even slept there for a few nights so I could stop her. She used to say how she wanted to see him, how she had to be with him. She spoke like he was still alive and, well, what was I to do? I couldn't very well lock her in her bedroom, could I? I had to let her go. All I could do was make sure she was suitably dressed. She'd go out in all weathers, sure as hell that she'd find him, or speak to him. I don't know. Who knows? Only her, I suppose. It was like she thought that somehow, by being there, she would be attacked, like he was, you know? It was like she wished it to happen."

The kettle boiled, and he set out two mugs, which Freya discreetly inspected from a distance. She'd experienced more than her fair share of dirty mugs from people who lived alone.

"Why don't you tell me about your father?" she said. "From what I hear, he was a nice man."

"Oh, he was," Glass said. "He was a good father, at least. As for being a good husband, I'm not really the best one to ask."

"How so?" she said, and he flicked the tea bags into the waste bin, then slid one of the mugs towards her, before resuming his position of leaning against the counter, this time facing Freya with a heavy intake of air.

"Dad wasn't always around," he said finally. "And to put it delicately, he might have been a little frivolous with his loving."

"He had an affair?" Freya said, which he simply absorbed with a neutral expression.

"Plural," he replied, then shook his head. "I don't know how many. I don't suppose anybody does, or did, him included. But he loved her. Mum, that is. He did love her. He loved us both. It was

just that, well, she wasn't always around when he had surplus love. Does that make sense?"

"It's taking shape," Freya said and watched him take a sip of tea while he watched Ben exit the garden shed.

"Dad worked in refrigeration. Industrial cooling, he called it. The rest of us just called it engineering. He could talk for hours about the benefits of recirculating systems or evaporative towers." Glass gave another little laugh as he remembered his father with some fondness. "Once he started, you couldn't stop him, especially after a glass or two, if you know what I mean?"

"I think we all know somebody like that," she said.

"Who did he work for? Was it a large company?"

"Oh, he started his own firm in the end. A.G Glass Cooling and Refrigeration."

"A.G?"

"Alice Gloria," he said. "He named the business after my mother. If that isn't a testament to how he felt about her, then I don't know what is."

"I'm a little astonished that in an industry that most of us might deem as a dull necessity, he found romance."

"That was Dad," he replied with a smile. "A lover, not a fighter."

"And what happened to the firm when he died?"

Henry inhaled a deep breath.

"I took over," he said like the burden of responsibility was a weight on his shoulders.

Ben re-entered the house through the back door, and without interrupting, he slipped past to have a look upstairs.

Glass watched him pass, and although he made no effort to stand in his way, his expression did convey disappointment.

"We'll need to take some of your clothes," Freya said, and Glass closed his eyes with a heavy sigh.

"I know," he said. "They're in a bag by the laundry basket upstairs, and don't worry, I've put everything I've worn since..."

He faltered for the first time.

"Thank you," Freya said.

"It's going to take some getting used to, I suppose," he said, talking through his emotions rather than letting them get the better of him. "You should know, I mean to finish the business as soon as I can."

"Are you saying you'd like to go ahead with the funeral?" she asked, to which he nodded.

"I've already been to see Stowes," he replied. "They're the funeral directors. They handled Dad's, and Mum trusted them."

"Did she want a cremation, or..."

"A burial," he replied. "She wanted to be buried with Dad. I've made arrangements for the headstone."

"So soon?"

"I need to," he replied, steeling himself. "I know it's going to hit me soon, and I'll be capable of nothing if I don't do it all while I can."

He took another sip of his tea and then turned to stare out of the window, hiding his face from Freya.

She gave him a moment to himself and felt a presence behind her. She turned to find Ben in the doorway, a black bag in his hand, with a sticky label marked with Henry Glass's name.

"If we need any more information—" Freya began.

"Then feel free to get in touch," he replied without turning, although his voice belied the strength of his posture.

"And I'll do what I can for your mother," she added, this time catching his attention. "For the funeral, I mean. I'll see about having her released for you."

"I'd appreciate that," he said, turning back to the window. "I wasn't the best son for her. But I'd like to do what I can now that she's gone."

Ben backed into the hallway and Freya made to follow, pausing at the door.

"I do have one more question," she said. "Your mother had prepared several envelopes with cash inside."

He smiled at the thought but didn't look her way.

"She did that," he said. "Dad didn't leave her an instruction manual, and that was the only way she knew how to keep track of her outgoings."

"The old ways are the best," she replied, then heard her tone harden. "One of them was marked with the name Debbie. Do you happen to know who that might be?"

"Debbie?" he said, as if everybody knew the answer. "Debbie Blake. She's next door's daughter. She did Mum's shopping for her sometimes."

"I see," Freya said, and she left one of her contact cards on the counter beside her cooling tea. "Well, if you need anything, just give me a call. Anything at all, okay?"

CHAPTER THIRTY-SEVEN

"Right, it's four p.m.," Gillespie said, as they pulled up outside George Benson's house. "We've got an hour to get inside George's house, have a wee looky-loo, then get out. I've got a date tonight, so the last thing I need is you and him jabbering on about the old days."

"You do know that looky-loo is not an actual word, don't you?" Cruz said.

"It is where I'm from," Gillespie replied, as he climbed from the car. But he was stopped by a rumbling in his pocket, and he sat back down again to answer his phone. "DS Gillespie," he said, routing the call to the phone's loudspeaker and setting it down on his knee.

"Gillespie, it's Ben," the voice said. "How's it going there?"

"We're just about to go in, mate. I've already given Cruz instructions to keep his mouth well and truly shut. Any more of his bright ideas and the boss'll have us picking through the old man's rubbish bins."

"That's not a bad idea," a second voice said, which was posher than Ben's and decidedly female. Gillespie closed his eyes and

cursed under his breath. "We're going to need any clothes he's worn since Monday morning, too. I presume you do have an evidence kit in that junk heap of yours?"

Cruz smiled at him from the passenger seat but said nothing.

"Aye, boss," Gillespie said. "Never leave home without it."

"Good," the boss said. "Oh, and I spoke to Henry Glass about that envelope. It seems that Cruz was right, the envelope was for the neighbour's daughter, Deborah. Apparently, she did Alice Glass's shopping every now and then, so you might as well pop in and arrange for her to make a formal statement."

Gillespie sneered at Cruz, who seemed to delight in his pain.

"Are you there, Gillespie?" the boss said.

"Aye, boss," he said. "Sorry, I was, erm, just making notes."

"Good. It should only take a couple of hours to go through Benson's cottage and his rubbish. If I remember rightly, Cruz said that Debbie Blake usually pops in to see her mum after work."

Again, Gillespie stared at Cruz, shaking his head at the young DC's big mouth.

"Gillespie?" the boss said. "Have I made myself clear?"

"Aye, boss. Loud and clear."

"Good. I'll see you both in the morning."

Aye, night night, boss," he said, then winced at what he had said. "I mean, I'll talk to you in the morning."

"Right," she replied and ended the call.

"Night, night?" Cruz said, making absolutely no effort at all to hide his amusement. "Sleep tight."

"Alright, alright," he replied, and once more shoved the car door open to climb out.

"I'm surprised you didn't tell her you love her," Cruz continued, as they made their way up Benson's garden path. Then he began to imitate both Gillespie and the boss. "You hang up. No, *you* hang up. You first. No, *you* first."

Gillespie turned on his heels and shoved his index finger under Cruz's chin.

"You're loving this, aren't you?" he said. "I suppose you're looking forward to flirting with the little madam next door?"

Although the young DC silenced, he continued to grin smugly. Gillespie knew he probably deserved to be made fun of, and had it been Cruz who had made the faux-pa, then there was no way on earth he would let him get away with it. "You heard what she said, eh?"

"Yep," Cruz said. "A couple of hours' work. You'll miss your date."

"No," he replied. "No, I won't be missing any date. You see, when we've been through Benson's shed and searched his house, I'll be going to meet my friend."

"Eh?" Cruz said. "You can't leave me here to do all that on my own. We're not supposed to work unaccompanied."

"I can," Gillespie replied. "I think that by the time my friend and I have had a wee drink and a chat, and she's let me give a wee kiss on the cheek, you'll be just finishing up going through Benson's rubbish, leaving just enough time to have a word with the wee lass next door before I come and pick you up."

"What?" Cruz said. "Have you heard yourself?"

"Aye," Gillespie said. "Aye, I have."

"And just what the bloody hell makes you think I'd agree to that?"

"I mean, we could always talk about the alternative."

"What alternative?"

"Oh, you know the one. It's where we both go into the house, search the shed, and the bins, and then we both go and talk to the lass next door."

"Right?" Cruz said.

"And I miss my date."

"Okay."

"And then Hermione learns about how you were flirting with Delicious Debbie."

"Delicious Debbie? I was not..." Cruz began, then stopped

himself when he saw Gillespie's serious expression. "You wouldn't."

"Oh, I don't know, Gabby. I mean, if push came to shove..."

"Jim, this isn't fair."

"And I suppose me missing my date because of your big mouth is fair, is it?"

"You bastard," Cruz hissed as Gillespie reached up and knocked on the door.

"Take it or leave it, Gabby. Take it or leave it."

The door opened and George Benson stared out at them wearing a smart-looking cardigan, loose trousers, and a pair of ratty, tartan slippers.

"Oh," he said. "Back so soon?"

"Good afternoon, Mr Benson," Gillespie said. "I was wondering if we could have a wee chat."

"A chat? But we spoke earlier."

"I know, but there's a few details we need to clear up, sir. May we come in?"

"Well, I suppose," he replied, leaning on the door to step to one side. "Does this mean you've found out who he was? The man you found, I mean?"

His face bore a sadness as if weights hung from his loose skin, but a glimmer of hope shone in his reddened eyes.

"Not yet, Mr Benson, but we do have some leads we're working on," Gillespie replied, as he stepped through into the hallway, then made his way towards the kitchen where there was more space. "How are you? It must have been a trying day for you."

"In here," Benson said, opening a door off of the hallway. "It's a little more comfortable than the kitchen."

He ushered them through into a neat and tidy lounge, which was as Gillespie had imagined it, with photos of family on nearly every surface, and random ornaments dotted between them.

"It's cozy," Gillespie said when Benson came into the room and held onto the arm of a chair to slowly lower himself onto it.

"It does me," Benson replied. "I can't keep it clean like my wife used to, but nothing much has changed. It's funny, the older you get, the fewer memories you make." He reached for a frame on the little table beside him and held it in both hands, caressing it with a gnarled and yellowed thumb. "You tend to cling to the memories you made when you were younger, when everyone you knew and loved was still alive."

Cruz perched on the arm of another chair and Gillespie took a few steps towards the old man. The photo was of four individuals, standing beside what Gillespie knew to be an old Ford Anglia.

"They don't make them like that anymore, do they?" he said, and reached for the photo. "May I?"

Benson took a moment more to savour the memory in his hands, then held it up graciously for Gillespie to take. But instead of looming over the little old man, Gillespie dropped into the seat closest to him and held the frame out for Benson to see.

"This one's you, isn't it?" he said, pointing to one of the two suited gentlemen.

"Time hasn't been kind," he replied. "To me anyway, not like Alex. No, Alex..." He paused to clear his throat and lick his lips. "Alex always had youth on his side. He was the youngest of us all and the first to go. Anyway..."

He took the photo from Gillespie's hand and replaced it on the little table.

"It's just me now," he said. "They've all gone."

Cruz turned away, allowing the man a little privacy while he regained control over his emotions, and Gillespie sat in silence. There was nothing to be gained from breaking a man who teetered on the edge of a breakdown.

"I'm sorry," he said eventually, doing his best to hide his face. "It's been quite a difficult day."

"I can imagine," Gillespie replied. "And there's nothing to be ashamed of."

Benson, like many men who experience loss, bottled his emotions, and pushed himself to his feet.

"Now then. You said you had some formalities."

"Ah, yes," Gillespie said. "You see, and please understand, Mr Benson, that there are processes we need to follow when a suspicious death occurs. There are things we need to do in order to not only find the culprit but bring him or her to justice."

"What are you saying?"

"I'm saying that in order to prove to a jury that a suspect is guilty, we need to demonstrate that all other parties are innocent."

"Other parties?" he said. "What do you mean, other parties?"

"I mean exactly that," Gillespie began. "That is, until we can prove that Alice's friends and family are innocent, there may be reasonable doubt surrounding a suspect's guilt, which may or may not hinder the prosecution's case."

"Are you saying that I'm a suspect?" he said, in a tone that was bordering a whine. "I was her brother-in-law."

"Which means that, in the eyes of a defence barrister, you would have had good reason to defend Alice."

"But I wasn't there. I was here, at home. Good God, it was five o'clock in the morning, man. What on earth would I be doing at Alice's?"

"We just need to be able to prove that you were here," Gillespie said. "Please, this isn't an accusation. God knows you've been through enough today."

"What my colleague is trying to say, Mr Benson," Cruz began, "is that we need your help to eliminate you from our enquiries. We just need to know what you were doing when the incident took place and if anybody can corroborate the fact. Once we've done that, we'll have a quick look around—"

"A quick look around?" he said. "What for? What could you possibly want to find?"

"It's just so we can verify that—" Gillespie began, but Cruz cut him off.

"We believe the man was killed with a hammer, Mr Benson," Cruz said. "We'll need to check your garden shed, or wherever it is you keep your tools, and then check your laundry and your rubbish bins."

"Good God," he said, almost falling back into his seat. "Is all that really necessary?"

"Here's the thing," Gillespie said. "Alice's death is linked to a murder enquiry."

"But she wasn't murdered."

"Aye, but that's just it," he said. "They won't release her body until the investigation has progressed."

"They won't release her body?" he said. "Why ever not?"

"It's a..." Gillespie began.

"Formality," Benson finished for him, clearly growing agitated with police procedure, but having the maturity to realise it was neither Gillespie nor Cruz that created it. "It's okay. I've been through all this before, remember? When Alex died, this place was torn apart."

"Well, we won't be tearing it apart," Gillespie said. "It's more of a box-ticking exercise."

"I see. Well, you might as well know, I was here yesterday. The only time I left the house was when I took you to the bench."

"Can anybody help us prove that?" Cruz asked.

"Not really," he said. "Mrs Blake keeps herself to herself, not that she'd see much."

"Aye, she's not really in a position to help in this instance," Gillespie said, trying to be as mindful as he could. "Well, I'll report back, but I can't guarantee you won't be questioned later on, I'm afraid. Our boss is keen to identify anybody without a corroborating alibi."

He sighed and deflated.

"I'm afraid this is all bringing back rather terrible memories."

"It's a tragic affair, Mr Benson," Gillespie said. "I'm sure it'll be over soon enough."

"I spoke to Henry earlier. Her son," he said. "He's already begun the funeral arrangements."

"I'm sorry, Mr Benson," Gillespie said, standing and straightening his trousers, before adopting a helpless expression.

"Very well," Benson said. "Then I'd better let you do your jobs, hadn't I?"

"We'll be as quick as we can," Gillespie told him, leading Cruz from the room. "Why don't you stay here? We'll give you a shout if we need you."

The old man sat back in his seat, closed his eyes, and seemed to purse his lips.

"I suppose that's it for you, is it?" Cruz whispered in the kitchen. "You're going to bugger off now, are you?"

But the very idea of leaving George Benson in his emotional state at the mercy of Cruz seemed too much to bear.

"Let's just get it done," he said. "It'll be quicker with two."

Cruz seemed shocked to hear it and made no effort to hide his glee.

"You're just a big softy, aren't you?" he said. "You feel sorry for him."

"Ah, shut it, Gabby, before I change my mind," he said. "Now then, I'll fetch the gloves and bags, you can search the shed."

"I don't suppose my doorbell could help, could it?" Mr Benson said, catching Gillespie off guard. He stood in the kitchen doorway holding onto the frame, peering hopefully at the two of them.

"Is it any good at searching through rubbish bags?" Gillespie said as a joke and immediately wished he hadn't.

"It's one of those new-fangled camera ones," Benson said. "Henry got it for me, so I could keep an eye on Alice's house."

"You have a camera doorbell?" Gillespie asked, speaking slowly and clearly.

Benson nodded and shrugged as if it was no big deal.

"Yes," he said. "Yes, do you think it'll help?"

CHAPTER THIRTY-EIGHT

It was five o'clock when Nillson brought her car to a stop outside the labourers' accommodation for the second time that day. She switched off the engine and sat back, savouring a brief moment of peace.

"And now we wait," she told Anderson.

"I thought we'd pay them a visit while they worked," Anderson said. "What are we doing here?"

"Catching them off-guard," she replied and then beamed at her. "Nothing gets a heart racing like a couple of nosey police officers waiting to ask questions." She checked the clock on the dashboard again. "We shouldn't have to wait long. They might be hard workers, but I very much doubt they'll be too keen on working overtime. Besides, I'd like to have a closer look at Maxim's bedroom. The whole business about his father doesn't sit right with me."

"I was thinking the same," Anderson replied. "It's a bit weird that his dad disappeared while working here and then Maxim is murdered."

"If only something being a bit weird was grounds for an arrest."

"Oh, yeah, who do you have in mind?"

"I'll give you a clue. He's big, arrogant, and Albanian," Nillson replied, leaning forward to look into her wing mirror. "And he's right behind us."

Anderson checked her mirror and Nillson climbed out, ready to greet the oncoming pickup that was heading their way. Being private land, there was no law against the handful of men sitting on the back, and the driver was either driving slowly as a precaution or because he had seen Nillson's car and was buying time.

Anderson came to stand beside her as the pickup made its way along the gravelled track.

"Do you think there's something going on with Ben and the boss?" she asked, which caught Nillson by surprise.

"In what way?"

"I don't know. I can't really put my finger on it," Anderson replied. "It's just that when I first joined the team, I'd have had money they were seeing each other. You know, outside of work."

"You're not alone in those thoughts, I can assure you," Nillson said.

"But ever since they got their promotion, there's a distance between them. They drive to work separately for one thing."

"She has bought a new house."

"I know. Oh, I don't know, and don't get me wrong, I know it's none of my business. Personally, I think they would make a great couple, but recently, they just seem at odds. Don't say anything, will you? I'd hate them to think I was prying."

"Oh, I wouldn't worry about that too much," Nillson said. "But if it's gossip you're after, then I'm the wrong person to be asking."

"Who should I ask, then?" she said. "Not Gillespie? I wouldn't trust him or Cruz with a secret."

Nillson gave a laugh as the pickup grew close.

"No, it sounds to me like you should have a quiet word with

Gold," Nillson said, offering her a sideways glance. "If there's a secret to be told, then she's your girl."

"Of course," Anderson said as if she should have thought of it herself. "I'll bet everyone tells her everything. She has that way about her, doesn't she?"

"Which is why she is perfectly positioned as a family liaison officer," Nillson replied. "Right, come on. Get your game face on."

She folded her arms as the foreman brought the pickup to a stop beside her car, and ignoring the men in the back, she waited for Vlad to climb out.

"Good afternoon, Vlad," she said. "I was hoping we'd catch you before you all disappeared."

"It's been a long day, Detective," he replied. "We have to cover the work of Maxim, you know?"

"Well, I'm afraid it just got a little longer," she said, as the men began to jump down from the back of the truck and climb out from the rear seats. "Can you ask your men to stand in a line for me?"

"A line?" he said. "What is this? They need shower. They need food."

"Well then, they'd better hurry up and form a line, Vlad," she said. "I'm afraid my Albanian isn't up to scratch. Now, are you going to help me, or do I need to call in support and have the whole building turned upside down?"

He stared at her as if wondering how sincere she was, or perhaps he was trying to break her resolve. But being the only sister of a group of unruly boys had given Nillson the ability to stand her ground, and he eventually gave in.

He held up a hand as a few of his men tried to pass, and they stopped, giving him equally questioning looks.

"*Rreshtoj*," he told them, his eyes never leaving Nillson's.

"Vlad?" a small man said as if he hadn't heard correctly.

"*Rreshtoj*," he said again, louder than before, and after exchanging nervous glances, the men formed a line, which seemed

to be practised from their years of national service. Nillson was doubtful most British men would fall in with such ease at the word of a single man.

"Thank you," Nillson said and then made her way towards them all.

Considering they were using heavy machinery, Nillson was surprised to see that only five of them were wearing boots, while the remaining seven wore trainers, sullied and torn from the unforgiving land.

She started at one end, offering no clue as to what she was looking for until she reached the fourth man in the line whose tattered Reeboks stood out like a sore thumb.

"I need to see this shoe," she said to Vlad, and his chest rose and fell heavily.

He clicked his fingers and pointed to the man's feet.

"*Këpucën,*" he said gruffly.

Reluctantly, the man slipped his shoe off, leaving it on the ground for Nillson to bend and collect. She pulled back the tongue to check the label, which thankfully was printed in English, only to find a clear and disappointing number eight.

She handed it back to him and moved along the line, finding nothing of interest until the last man, the small man who had questioned the foreman. He wasn't wearing Reebok trainers, but his feet were far smaller than the rest. This time, all Nillson had to do was glance in Vlad's direction, and once more, he clicked his fingers.

The small man took inspiration from the first and left his trainer for Nillson to bend and collect. And once more, disappointment came in droves in the form of the number five, which was revealed only when Nillson rubbed away the grime.

She held it out for him, then dropped it to the ground when he reached for it, before nodding for Vlad to let them go about their business.

His reply came in the form of a smug grin that seemed to

stretch from one of his undersized ears to the other.

"Do you want to check their rooms?" Anderson asked as she approached.

"No point," Nillson replied. "It's not theirs, and I very much doubt if the big bastard has feet that small." She was interrupted by her phone, which rang out loudly in the near-silent farmland.

"Nillson," she said, putting the call onto loudspeaker as she leaned on the roof of her car. She felt rather than saw Anderson come to stand beside her.

"Hello, this is Katy Southwell," the voice said in a light yet confident tone, oozing professionalism. "I'm with the Lincolnshire Crime Scene Investigation team. You asked us to check a container on Locks Wood Farm out in Navenby."

"That's right," Nillson said. "In fact, we're on the farm now. Have you had much luck?"

"We have," Katy said. "Fingerprints. Plenty of them, too. But there's no need to come. I just wanted to let you know that we're finishing up here and we'll do our best to get you the results by the morning."

"Finally, some good news," Nillson said. "Thank you. I'll look forward to your email."

She ended the call and clutched the phone in her hand, staring at Anderson in near disbelief.

"Well, that's a positive note to end the day on," she told her, as a shadow drew over them. They each turned and found Vlad looming over them, his arms hanging by his sides with clenched fists. "Can I help you, Vlad?"

There was a hatred in the way he stared at them, which he forced himself to overcome. He coughed once, as if unsure of what to say, his eyes never leaving the phone in her hand.

"Vlad?" she said. "Is everything okay?"

"For me, everything is fine," he replied, like anything else

would allude to his being less than masculine. "But there is something I think you should see. It is something regarding Maxim Baftiroski."

CHAPTER THIRTY-NINE

"Are you sure you're up to this, Mrs Plant?" Jackie asked the tall lady wearing what looked like an outfit from *Country Life* magazine. Her coat was from Barbour and her silk scarf probably cost more than Jackie's entire outfit. Her blue jeans hung neatly over her boots, leaving only the fat tongues of each poking out to knock her whole appearance just shy of perfect. "I'm sorry to have asked."

She looked about the little reception room, and then finally offered Doctor Bell a weak smile.

"Oh, sorry," Jackie said. "This is Doctor Bell. She'll be with you every step of the way."

"Won't you be coming with us?" Mrs Plant asked. "I thought that's how it worked."

"I can do, if it would make you feel more comfortable," Jackie replied. "But it's not like in the films, I'm afraid. It's not something you can forget easily."

"She's right," Doctor Bell said. "We can all go if it makes it easier for you. I just want to make sure you're prepared."

"I am," she said, then looked at Jackie. "I told you, if my

Tammy has done wrong, then we'll meet it head-on, as a family. I just want to help and somehow make things right."

"I'm afraid the people we deal with aren't always so accommodating," Jackie replied, then nodded at Doctor Bell. "Please, lead the way."

The doctor opened a door on the far side of the reception, which led into a room the size of a hospital booth, except a heavy, burgundy and quilted drape hung in the place of the thin, green curtains that were often found in an A&E department.

"After you," she said to Mrs Plant, who followed the doctor with obvious trepidation.

"Now then," the doctor said. "He's covered by a sheet, so when I pull back this curtain, don't worry. You just tell me when you're ready, and I'll do the rest."

"If you want to stop at any point, Mrs Plant–" Jackie said.

"It's fine," she replied abruptly. "I'm not sure how ready I am, but I'll do it if it helps Tammy."

Jackie nodded at Doctor Bell, then stepped to one side for the curtain to be drawn back. The scene was exactly as had been described, a lifeless mound beneath a thin sheet that revealed nothing but the human form it masked.

"Let me see him," Mrs Plant said, before either of them could offer any more words of advice and, as instructed, Doctor Bell pulled back the thin sheet to the man's shoulders. Little effort had been made to disguise the injuries, but at least the dried blood had been cleaned away. His eyes were closed and surrounded by dark rings. His skin was pale and scarred by acne. But his hair had been cropped short, in what Jackie could only describe as a military fashion.

Mrs Plant studied his features for a moment, then nodded gently.

"It's him," she said softly, then turned away to get out of the little booth, and she hurriedly pushed through the doors to the reception.

Jackie watched the doors close and felt the doctor's gaze.

"It's never easy, is it?" she said, her Welsh accent strong in the near silence. "The dead can have a strange effect on the living."

"I think she did well," Jackie replied. "I just hope her word is enough."

She left the doctor to finish up, then joined Mrs Plant in the little reception, feeling like an intruder as she entered the quiet space.

"Thank you," Jackie said. "I know how hard that must have been."

Mrs Plant dropped to perch on the edge of one of the seats, her movements purposeful and what her mother might have called ladylike. Jackie joined her, aware of her own lack of finesse and feeling quite cumbersome. She picked at the side of her nail, something her mother hated to see.

"How is she?" Jackie asked. "Have the doctors said anything?"

"What is there to say? She could wake up tomorrow or she could lie there like the living dead for another month," she said. "Given the circumstances, I'm not sure which is best for her."

"The doctor mentioned the results of her scan were due, that's all," Jackie said. "I was just wondering—"

"You were wondering what? Is she going to be fit enough to arrest when she does wake up?

"No, of course—"

"I know you took them," she said, with guilt in her eyes. "The envelopes that were in her bag. I know you took them."

It was Jackie's turn to display guilt, whatever her reasons.

"Mrs Plant—"

"It's okay," she said. "I understand why you did it. I suppose you had to, for your investigation, no doubt."

"I'm sorry, I should have told you."

"It would have been nice."

"But this is a murder investigation, and like it or not, Mrs Plant, your daughter is involved," Jackie said. "You see, not only

did she have items from Alice Glass's house in her bag, but she's been in direct communication with the man we found in the house. Now, I'm sure if Tammy was awake, then she could simply tell us how she's involved." She reached out for the woman's hand. "Nothing would please me more than to see Tammy pull through, not just for her health, but so she can clear her name and put things right. We're not trying to make Tammy's life harder, Mrs Plant. We're just trying to solve a murder enquiry."

It was as if the events of the past day had been put to one side until there was no longer any room in Mrs Plant's mind for additional emotions, and all at once, her brow furrowed, her bottom lip quivered, and her eyes filled with tears.

"I'm sorry," she whimpered. "I'm sorry. I'm so, so, sorry."

Jackie moved closer and placed an arm around her.

"You have nothing to apologise for," she said. "Nothing at all. She'll pull through. You'll see."

"It's not that," Mrs Plant said. "It's just that—"

She stopped there as if there was no going back from verbalising her thoughts.

"What is it?" Jackie asked, squeezing her shoulder.

"It's just..." she began again, breathing heavily between sobs. "This isn't the first time Tammy has done this."

"Done what? Stolen things?"

"I thought that when she started her business, maybe she'd leave it all behind," she said, and she peered up through her fingers in shame. "The truth is that if Maxim was burgling that house, then it's very likely that my Tammy had something to do with it, and I very much doubt if that was the first."

CHAPTER FORTY

Despite it being late summer, a cold chill seemed to be trapped inside Ben's old house. There had been a time when he would come home to find Michaela cooking dinner or sitting outside on the patio with a glass of wine.

But those days were gone, leaving a void in the old building like all the life had been sucked from it. There had also been a time when he would get home from work, dump his bag on the table, and cook himself something quick, easy, and from a can, before putting his feet up for the night.

But those days had finished when Freya arrived in Lincolnshire, bringing with her a whirlwind of chaos, fine wines, and foods suitable for a more mature and appreciative palette.

He closed the front door behind him, and before he'd even kicked off his shoes, he made his way upstairs and into the second bedroom. For the life of him, he couldn't remember the last time he'd been in there.

But today the room gained a purpose. A dark secret. Somewhere he could get all of his deepest thoughts down to somehow make sense of them.

It began with a single photo, which he pinned pride of place in

the centre of the largest wall, and from there, a mind map of embryonic theories, facts, and ideas took shape. He pinned photo after photo onto the wall, some of them, those he had found on his phone, were still wet with printer ink when he pushed the pins through.

A pack of yellow post-it notes provided the medium to narrate the theories, on which he scrawled dates and facts he'd gleaned during his time with Freya, until finally, he sat back and took the whole scene in. It was, in his mind, a venerable shrine to the person who had made the most impact on his life. Yet, despite everything he had ever learned about her being displayed in the most logical order he could find, a veil hung over the room, the wall, and most of all, that single photo in the centre of the largest wall.

But it was a beginning. It was the framework on which he could build an understanding of her, lifting that veil inch by inch, and maybe even learning a few things about himself along the way. Even though the end of that journey seemed so far off, in some distant and unknown future, he knew it would boil down to one question. A question that centred around him, not his ethereal subject.

Exactly what was it that he wanted?

The question tormented him, teasing him out of her mind and into his own so much so that when he heard those three familiar raps on his front door downstairs, he breathed a sigh of relief.

Today was not the day to answer that question. A whole lot of work lay ahead before he could answer that.

He closed the bedroom door behind him and was reminded by the click of his heels on the wooden floor that he still hadn't even removed his shoes. Beyond the frosted glass in the door, Freya's form took shape. It was like the wall in his spare room, a fragmented view of her. One he recognised but couldn't quite fathom until he opened the door, and it was like they had stepped back in time.

She too had yet to change from her work clothes, and she held up a familiar brown paper bag. Her face was a metaphor for her personality. It was as if nothing had changed and she still lived in a little labourer's cottage across the field.

"Hungry?" she asked.

Ben stepped to one side to let her pass, leaving a haze of perfume in her wake. He closed the front door and found his hand automatically reaching for the lock. He hesitated, then clicked the latch on, before following her through to the kitchen to the percussive tune of dinner plates and cutlery on the worktop. There was little in the way of refinement about the way she served the food. The rice was tipped onto each plate from the container and the masala was tipped on top of that. She tore open the little bag with the naan breads, took one, and then made her way through to the lounge, calling out as she made herself comfortable.

"It's been ages since we did this."

"I was thinking the same," he replied, opening the fridge and finding nothing but a tub of spreadable butter, some questionable cheese, two bottles of beer, and half a tomato. "Did you bring wine?"

"I'm driving," she said, her voice muffled by a mouthful of food, something she wouldn't dream of doing in public. "It was a close call though, I have to admit."

He grabbed his plate and cutlery and ventured into the lounge, where he found her sitting on one of the two armchairs with her feet up on the only pouffe and the plate of food on her lap. But it wasn't her familiarity with his home that startled him; it was the fact that she had rearranged the armchairs, drawing them side by side so they could share the pouffe.

"I hope you don't mind," she said. "I thought we could go over the investigation."

"Not at all," he replied, taking his seat. He kicked off his shoes and put his feet up beside hers, then took the first bite of his

food. There was no need to question what she had bought as she rarely bought any other curry than chicken tikka masala. "So, where should we begin?"

"At the beginning of course," she replied.

"Okay. Alice Glass goes for her morning walk in the hope of finding her husband. Or at least joining him in death? That's a lovely topic to discuss over a meal."

"No, before then," she said. "And don't pretend you find it vulgar, Ben. I know you better than that."

He grinned.

"Before then? How about when whoever it was lay in the ditch that Gillespie found, watching her?"

She took a mouthful of food, then set her plate down on the floor beside her.

"No, before that," she said. "I want to talk about when Alex Glass died."

"Okay," he said, forking another mouthful of food. "He goes for a morning walk and is attacked. Are you trying to say the two incidents are related?"

"Are you trying to tell me you think otherwise?" she countered.

"I haven't even given it a thought. Maxim Baftiroski was either caught robbing Alice Glass's house or stopping somebody else from robbing the place. We've got his prints on the drain pipe and the window ledge–"

"Yet none of her belongings in her bedroom were touched. What's the easiest thing to steal if, say, a burglar is on foot?"

"Cash," he said, then relented when he saw where she was driving her point. "And jewellery."

"Precisely. None of her drawers were open, cupboards were shut. Aside from the blood spatter on the wall, the place was immaculate."

"So, what are you saying?"

"I don't know what I'm saying," she admitted. "I just know

that he wasn't robbing the place, not in the conventional sense, anyway, and if what Nillson said about him being outcast by his colleagues is true, then I certainly doubt he was working with anybody else."

"In which case, he must have been there to *stop* somebody else like Nillson suggested." Ben scraped the remains of his meal into a neat pile on his plate while he chewed. "If he really cared for Tammy, then maybe he heard this Vlad chap discussing it, and was doing it for her?"

"Maybe?" Freya said. "Maybe not."

"I wish you'd just come out and say what you're thinking."

"No," she said, with a laugh. "No, you most certainly wouldn't want to know what I'm thinking. But I don't buy that a man murders another man in a field and isn't caught. Not in this day and age."

"You're from London," he said. "I thought that happened every day."

"There are no fields in the city, Ben," she told him. "I think we need to know more about Alex Glass. All we have so far is that he was younger than Alice by ten years, with whom he had a son called Henry, that he owned a refrigeration business, and that he wasn't faithful."

"Where are you going with this, Freya?" he said, sensing she was building up to something.

"Nobody was convicted for his murder," she said. "Why is that?"

"Stranger murder," he replied. "They're the hardest ones, right?"

"And how did he die?"

"According to Gillespie's report from his chat with George Benson, the attack was brutal. Severe head injuries."

"We need to look at that investigation," she said.

"Alright, I'll make a note and ask Chapman in the morning," he said, taking the last mouthful. But she had a look in her eye

that he didn't like. "What is it? Just say what you need to say, Freya."

She winced a little, then slipped her shoes off and tucked her feet underneath her.

"Freya?" he said.

She reached down and slipped a hand into her tote bag, retrieving a new blue file.

"What's that?" he asked, and she waited for him to set his plate down beside hers, then handed it to him.

He flicked open the cover to find a small stack of printed papers, the first of which bore the name *Alex Glass.*

"Why do I feel like I've been steered into this?" Ben said, scanning the summary of Alex Glass's murder.

"Because you have," she replied, unashamed. "I had Chapman print it for me while we were at Henry Glass's house."

"And I suppose you're about to hit me with some kind of revelation?"

"Look at the photos, Ben," she said, and there was a sincerity in the way in which she looked at him.

He flicked through the pages until he came to the images. The printer hadn't done them justice, and they weren't as clear as they could have been. But there was enough detail for him to get the gist.

"Head wounds," he said.

"Look closer."

He held the file up to the light, but even then, the images were far too blurry.

"Perhaps you should read the pathology report," Freya suggested, and she reached down to collect the plates, before leaving him to read through the paragraphs of findings.

Experience had taught him how to read the reports, how to cut through the medical jargon to reach the layman facts, and he found what she had referred to within the third paragraph, where the man's injuries were explained in detail.

The slap of her feet on the wooden floor betrayed any stealth she may have been attempting, or perhaps she was just giving him time, as they were slow and ponderous, and he looked up at her to find her staring back knowingly, holding a bottle of beer in each hand.

"The injuries were caused by a hammer," he said. "How have we only just found this out?"

"Because we weren't looking for it," she told him, as she re-entered the room, her hips rocking from side to side. She stepped over his legs, and then, catlike, she curled into the armchair.

"It doesn't prove anything, though," he said. "It just makes it even more bloody confusing. I mean, how do we link a five-year-old unsolved murder to what, until now, we thought was a robbery?"

She stared dead ahead at the unlit fireplace, and Ben was reminded of the previous winter when he'd admired the way the orange glow of the fire had accentuated those features he adored.

"Henry said his mother wanted to be buried with his dad," she said, passing him one of the beers. "In the same grave."

"Oh God, Freya," he said. "You want to exhume Alex Glass's body?"

"Oh, don't pretend you're appalled, Ben," she said, stretching her legs out from beneath her and taking a very ladylike swig of beer. "Now, how about one of those famous foot rubs of yours? Just like old times."

CHAPTER FORTY-ONE

"Good god," Nillson said, as she moved forward into the bedroom adjacent to the one Vlad had previously claimed to be used by Maxim Baftiroski. The room was almost identical to the first, but in place of an old armchair, there was an old, battered desk on which several photos and documents had been laid out. She turned back to Vlad who stood beside Anderson. "What is this?"

He took a breath, and for the first time since she had met him, his confidence waned.

"This is Maxim's room, isn't it?" Nillson said, filling the space where his words had failed him.

He nodded his fat head and forced himself to look her in the eye. Despite his arrogance and lies, he was by no means a coward.

"And his father's room," he said eventually. "Mr Venables told you he worked here."

"He did," Nillson said. She studied the various photos and documents, and her eyes were drawn to one image in particular. It was of the three cottages at either dusk or dawn, given the low light. "This is Alice Glass's house."

Anderson came to stand beside her and then flicked through a

small pile of papers. She held up a burgundy passport with what Nillson presumed to be the Moldovan coat of arms on the front.

"It's his passport," she said, then she too questioned Vlad. "I thought you said that Mr Venables kept your passports?"

"He does," he replied. "I think that maybe you should open it."

"Viktor Baftiroski," she said, reading aloud. "This is his father's."

"It was with his belongings," Vlad told them. "We gave them to Maxim in case Viktor ever returned."

Nillson scanned through all of the papers.

"These are all his father's. This is his visa application."

"What are these?" Anderson asked, reaching for a small stack of envelopes. "Letters."

"Who from?"

"I don't know. It's all in Moldovan, I suppose," Anderson replied, at which Vlad simply clicked his tongue.

"What?" Nillson said, and he gave her a look to convey that he thought her incompetent.

"It is Romanian," he said. "Moldovan language, it's Romanian."

"And what about Albanians?" she asked. "What language do Albanians speak?"

Pride swelled his chest and arrogance filled his eyes.

"We have our own language," he replied. "Albanians speak Albanian."

"But surely the languages are similar?" Anderson said. "Surely there's a crossover of words and phrases, like the romantic languages."

She walked over to him, presenting him with the letters.

"Read it," she said.

"I cannot—"

"Read it," she said, and reluctantly, he took one of the letters from her and briefly studied the contents.

"It is..." he began. "Private letter."

"Not anymore," Nillson said. "Who is it addressed to and who is it from?"

"It is to Viktor," he began. "And it is from Sofia."

"Sofia who?" Anderson asked, and he inhaled.

"Sofia Baftiroski. His wife," he said. "Like I said. It is private letter. I cannot read this."

He handed her the letter back with clear distaste thinning his lips, just as footsteps entered the hallway outside. They lingered there for a moment, the two women staring at the indignant man until one of his team came to the doorway.

"There is some people," he said, and the large man turned to face the door as the crime scene investigators joined him in the doorway.

"Ah, Sergeant Nillson," Katy said. "I'm sorry to bother you, but we've done all we can in the container."

"Any luck?" she asked.

"If it's DNA you're looking for, then I'm afraid you should prepare yourself to be disappointed."

"I live in a state of perpetual disappointment," Nillson replied, finishing her statement with a glare in Vlad's direction.

"But if fingerprints can help," Katy continued, "then we have an abundance of them. We'll run them through the database, of course, unless you have any specific examples, in which case we'll process them manually."

"I do, as it happens," Nillson said. "Vlad, I'd like you to round up your team."

"My team?" he said, buying himself time to think of a more suitable delay.

"All of them," she said, and stepped over to him, revelling in his sudden anxiety. "We have a saying here in the UK."

"A saying? What is this saying?"

"You scratch my back, and I'll scratch yours," she said, and she stepped even closer, bringing her face just inches from his, then lowered her voice to a whisper. "In other words, I know you are

responsible for the contents of that container, and with Katy's help, I can prove it. Help me, and I'll see what I can do to lighten the sentence."

"This is blackmail," he grumbled.

"No," she replied. "This is a murder investigation, and like it or not, you and the rest of your team are now involved. Have them assemble in the lobby. And make sure they have clean hands."

CHAPTER FORTY-TWO

The morning was bright and warm, and clouds loomed on the horizon. His father would have said something about them belonging to autumn, just biding their time for summer to wane, but Ben thought otherwise. To him, they were simply a threat of some much-needed rain, some damp to green the yellowed grass, and to soften the hard ground ready for the winter crop to be sown.

It was earlier than usual when he arrived at the station, and he was pleased to see only Nillson's car parked among the throng of liveried ones, along with a transporter and various other vehicles that belonged to the other staff.

The car park was more of a courtyard, and he remembered with some trepidation the time Michaela had handed him a particular file under Freya's scrutinising glare from the incident room above. He also remembered a few minutes before the moment he'd unceremoniously helped the shamed and hand-cuffed Detective Chief Inspector Standing into the back of a transporter.

There were hundreds of memories in that station, most of which were positive, others not so, and a few questionable.

He entered through the fire escape door and made his way up the stairs, only to be greeted once more by a wave of memories. Detective Superintendent Granger's office had once belonged to Harper, or Arthur as they had affectionately named him, on behalf of his ability to carry out half a job and then assign it to somebody else to finish.

But of all the memories, both good and bad, the incident room held the most. There was a time when the room had been informally divided to host two teams. Standing's team, who included Gillespie, Cruz, Nillson, and a few others, and Ben's team, which had been managed by Ben's old friend DI Foster until cancer had taken him far too early.

He pushed through the doors into near silence, except for the rustling of papers coming from Nillson's desk.

She glanced up, saw it was him, and then returned to her work.

"Morning, Ben," she said.

"Morning, Anna," he replied, setting his bag down.

He had planned on arriving early and making sense of the facts they had gleaned so far before the team arrived and chaos ensued. But now that he was here...

"Anna, do you ever remember the old times?" he said, and although her head remained bent over her work, her eyes rolled up to meet his.

"The old times?"

"You know? When Dave was alive and Standing was here. The first time around, I mean. Before he left."

"I do," she said, finally giving in to the fact that he wasn't going to let her work in peace. He could have apologised and let her carry on, but he valued her input. "Why?"

"Oh, no reason," he said. "For some reason, I just remembered things when I walked in this morning. I couldn't tell you why."

"Because the place is empty?" she suggested. "I get that some-

times. Without all the noise and the rabble, I find my mind often wanders."

"Do you miss them?" he asked. "The old times, I mean."

"Sometimes," she replied. "Sometimes I do, yes. But then I'm a sergeant now, and Anderson wasn't here. I don't honestly know what I'd do without her now."

She swivelled the seat to face him, crossing her legs and folding her hands in her lap.

"Talk to me," she said. "Has something happened?"

"No, not at all–"

"Well, if you're not going to tell me," she said, as she started to turn back to her desk.

"Can you keep a secret?" he asked, then heard himself laugh a little when she raised her brow. "Sorry, I know you can."

"Is it juicy?" she asked. "The gossip. Is it juicy?"

"Not juicy, as such. It's just that..." he began.

"It's Freya, isn't it?"

"What?"

"It is. It's Freya. Anderson said she thought there was something up between you."

"There's nothing up."

"Oh, come on, Ben. You've been pining after her ever since she arrived here."

"Is it that obvious?"

"Have you?" she asked, then nodded at him.

"Have I what?" he asked, as female voices grew loud in the corridor outside.

"You know," she said, making a lewd suggestion with her right index finger and her circled left hand.

Ben laughed and shook his head, refusing to answer the question.

"Listen, do you think you could come to my place?"

The voices outside were growing near, and he hoped his tense

body language and his furtive glances at the door suggested his cause was worthy.

"I'll have to check my diary," she said, as the doors opened and Gold entered with Anderson and Chapman in tow.

"Check your diary for what?" Gold asked. "He hasn't asked you out, has he?"

Ben straightened and looked at Nillson, hoping she would respect his request for discretion.

"Oh, Ben just needs some help with some decorating."

Gold hung her bag on the back of her chair and gave them both a quizzical and disbelieving look.

"I would have thought your brothers could help you," she told him.

"Oh, it's not really decorating," he said, averting his eyes. "More of an opinion, that's all. You know? Colour schemes and all that."

"And you asked Anna?" she said.

"Oy, I happen to be good at that sort of thing. I nearly went to art school."

"Nearly."

"Yeah."

"I didn't have you down as the arty type."

"Who's the arty type?" Freya said, as she too entered the room as if she'd just stepped into a palace ballroom, sauntering across the room to her desk.

"Nillson," Gold said. "She's giving Ben some interior design advice."

"Oh," Freya said, clearly not believing a word of it. She looked at Ben questioningly. "Well, I suppose there's a lot we still have to learn about each other, isn't there?"

Ben listened, processed, and thought of a response, but kept it to himself.

"Right then, no prizes for guessing who we're waiting for,"

Freya said. "I suggest we get some coffee before the two grace us with their presence, and then we can get straight down to it."

The room cleared in a minute or so, and the sound of female voices trailed up the corridor as most of the team went in search of their morning caffeine, leaving Freya and Ben alone.

"Thanks for last night," Freya said as if it was a passing comment while she emptied her bag of files and prepared to host the debrief. But it was far from a passing comment, she knew it, and he knew it.

"Thanks for the curry," he replied. "I'm sure you noticed how bare my cupboards are."

"I did, and it reminded me of the old you."

"Did it? That's funny."

"What's funny?" she asked.

"Oh, nothing. I'm just a little melancholy this morning," he said, then searched for a new topic. "I've been thinking about what you said last night."

"About a foot rub?"

"About..." he started, then checked the doors and lowered his voice. "About exhuming Alex Glass's body."

"Okay," she said. "And what did you come up with?"

"Well, nothing. But I think we should wait to hear what the others have to say before we go down that road. It's a bloody awful thing to have to do, and if you think Granger is just going to roll over and sign the..."

"Sign the what?"

"Sign whatever it is that needs to be signed. I don't even know what it is, but I can tell you he won't like it. You're going to need a bloody good reason if you want to go ahead with it."

"Well then, I'll find a reason," she said as if the answer was simple and the problem rudimentary. "He'll put forward a request for a Home Office licence from the Ministry of Justice. After that, all we need to do is seek Henry Glass's approval."

He watched her as she worked, setting files out on her desk in some kind of chaotic order.

"You've got it all worked out, haven't you?" he said.

"Of course. Haven't I always?"

"Yes, yes, I suppose you have."

The doors opened and the girls returned with Gold in mid-flow telling them about the previous day's events with Doctor Bell.

"How did it go?" Freya said, and Ben was pleased to have changed the conversation. "With the girl's mother. How did she do?"

"She did great," Gold replied, taking her seat. "Positive ID."

"So, it is Maxim Baftiroski?" Freya said. "Well done, you."

"Not only that," Gold said, clearly pleased with herself. "It seems that Tammy isn't a stranger to taking what doesn't belong to her. In fact, her mother truly believes that if Maxim Baftiroski was robbing the house, she had something to do with it."

CHAPTER FORTY-THREE

"Fear not," Gillespie said, as he burst through the door like a rock star, oblivious to the fact that the door swung back and slammed into Cruz's shoulder, who walked in behind him. He slung his bag onto a spare chair and plopped down beside it before looking around at everyone. "What?"

Freya shook her head but found it hard to refrain from smiling a little at the man's character.

"Have you ever thought about a career in show business?" she said.

"Ah, I know," he replied. "You're not the first person to say that. Move over Marvin Brando."

"Marvin who?" Nillson said.

"Brando. You know? The Godfather? An offer you can't refuse?"

"Oh, you mean..." Gold began, and Freya shook her head behind his back. It simply wasn't a conversation worth pursuing. "Marvin Brando. I know who you mean."

"Anyway, shall we begin, before Gillespie has to dash off to the Oscars?" Freya said. "I'd hate to miss out on what I imagine is going to be a thrilling debrief from his and Cruz's findings."

She perched herself on the edge of her desk and waited patiently for Gillespie to finish his daydream, which seemed to unsettle him.

"Me first, you mean?" he said, to which Freya nodded. He straightened in his seat. "Aye, well, we paid a visit to the old man–"

"George Benson," Freya added. "Let's keep the dialogue clear and concise, shall we? And hopefully, we won't offend anybody in the process."

"Right. George Benson," he said, shaking his head. "Found absolutely nothing. No blood-stained hammers, no bloody clothing, and, well, no blood anywhere. We bagged his dirty clothing up, of course. Took it to exhibits this morning. Aside from that, we trawled through his rubbish like vagrants and left him to it."

"And you found nothing?"

"Aye, boss. Nothing at all," he said. "Had a wee look about his place, like. Nothing out of the ordinary at all. It's exactly as you would imagine an old... I mean, an elderly gentleman's house to be. Clean kitchen, cupboards full of Bovril and soups, a bathroom that stinks of lavender, and two bedrooms both resembling a cheap Skegness bed and breakfast from nineteen thirty-five."

"Wow," Nillson said. "I can't wait to read your report."

"And where was he when the incidents took place?" Freya asked, disappointed at the result.

"Oh, he was at home, boss."

"And can we prove that?" she asked. "Can we at least remove him from our lines of enquiry?"

"Oh, aye, I think so," he said. "Him and the neighbour too."

"What makes you say that?"

"Because, boss, Henry Glass bought his old uncle a camera doorbell so he could keep track of his mother," Gillespie said with a beaming smile. "I can confirm that neither Mrs Blake, George Benson, or Debbie Blake left or entered any of the houses

between four a.m. and seven a.m. that morning. But the footage does show somebody running from the field at around ten minutes past five."

"You've seen the footage?"

"Aye, I have," he said as if he'd just solved the case single-handedly. "Other than that, there's nothing to see apart from at five a.m. when Alice goes for her morning walk. Thankfully, she was wearing her dressing gown on this occasion. She came back about thirty minutes later and walked up her garden path."

"So, Alice went for her morning walk at five a.m. and this somebody, presumably Maxim Baftiroski, runs from the field into the property."

"That's about the size of it," Gillespie replied. "He must have been waiting for her to leave."

"Then what?"

"Then there's a whole lot of nothing until Debbie Blake pays her mother her morning visit at around seven a.m., and then the next person we see is Tammy Blake going into Alice Glass's house at nine-twenty. She comes out a few moments later, visibly distressed."

"Is that it?"

"Other than Henry Glass leaving his Uncle's house later in the morning, nothing," Gillespie said. "It's a quiet road."

"His uncle's house. Not his mother's?"

"Nope. The camera shows him leaving with a bag, so presumably, he stayed the night. But he definitely didn't visit his mother, or we'd have seen him."

"My God," Freya said. "Are you saying we had access to a camera all this time and you two have only just found it?"

"Eh?"

"You paid George Benson a visit the morning we found her, Gillespie," she said. "How on earth didn't you see the camera?"

"Well, I, erm..."

"He actually came out to meet us," Cruz said. "That's when he took us into the fields. So, we didn't actually walk up to the house until yesterday."

It was a smart answer that had credibility, but Gillespie should have known better.

"And what about Maxim Baftiroski?" she said. "Do we see him approaching the house?"

"Afraid not, boss," Gillespie said. "But if he entered through the back bedroom window, then he must have come from the side of the house."

"Especially if he knew there was a camera," Nillson said, which caught Freya's attention.

"And how would he have known about the camera?" she asked, knowing the answer already but wanting to see who was switched on.

"From Tammy," Gold said. "Whose mother, as I mentioned earlier, clearly stated has a history of thieving."

Freya sat back down on her desk, smoothing a broken thumbnail on the pen lid.

"What?" Nillson said. "What's wrong?"

"She doesn't believe Maxim was in the house to rob it," Ben told them all on Freya's behalf.

"Neither do I," Nillson said, which again caught Freya's attention, and she sat up straight.

"You don't?"

Nillson shook her head and adopted Gillespie's smug grin, but managed to pull it off in a far more convincing manner.

"Do you remember the container full of stolen goods?"

"Yes, of course."

"Vlad and his team, or some of them at least, had access to a pickup, they could work in numbers, and they had somewhere to store it all."

"How do we know that?"

"Well, Katy, the new CSI, was there," Nillson explained. "And

I had her and Pat go through it all checking for DNA and fingerprints."

"And?" Freya said.

"That's not all," Nillson explained, still grinning from ear to ear. "Vlad obviously realised the game was up and decided to play ball."

"Play ball?"

"He showed us Maxim's actual room."

"I thought you'd seen that already?" Ben said, to which Nillson shook her head.

"He showed us somebody else's room and planted Maxim's phone there to make it convincing," she said. "It turns out that Maxim isn't actually here to earn a few quid. He has a far more compelling reason to be here, at Locks Wood Farm in particular."

"He's looking for his father," Freya said, piecing the facts together as Nillson spoke. "I'm right, aren't I?"

Nillson nodded.

"We found Viktor Baftiroski's passport, for a start."

"Which means he's still in the country," Anderson added, then looked to Nillson for her to continue.

"Plus, we found his visa application, letters to and from his wife, and interestingly, photos of Alice Glass's house."

"Why does Maxim have photos of Alice Glass's house?" Ben said, clearly thinking aloud.

Nobody answered as each of them gave the question some thought.

"The letters," Freya said. "What do they say?"

"Ah, this is where it gets interesting," Nillson explained. "I had to use a bit of creative licence, boss. I hope you don't mind."

"Go on," Freya said tentatively.

"Vlad the foreman is going to translate them for us," she said. Then she sheepishly added, "In exchange for some leniency with regards to the stolen goods."

Freya stared at her, and it was no surprise that Nillson stared back, unafraid of the consequences.

But it was Gillespie who spoke first, breaking the silence with his Glaswegian grumble.

"Bloody hell," he said. "And I thought we were in bother for not spotting the camera."

"You are in bother for missing the camera," Freya said. "But I see no reason to reprimand Sergeant Nillson."

"Eh?" he said. "That's not fair."

"As part of this team, you have my full support in making on-the-spot decisions," Freya told him, and the wider team. "If you make a decision, I'll stand behind you no matter what. But if you miss something as obvious as CCTV, then I'm afraid you'll pay the price, and hopefully, you won't make that mistake again."

"Ah, for God's sake," he said, slumping into his seat like a schoolboy.

"So, it was okay?" Nillson asked.

"We could get a translator anywhere," Freya told her. "What does this Vlad have to offer that a translator can't?"

"He knew Viktor Baftiroski and he knew Maxim," Nillson replied. "If he helps us bring the investigation to a close, then maybe we can help him out. He's going to prison either way. It's just a question of how long his sentence is."

"We don't get to play judge and jury, Nillson," Freya said.

"I know. But we can do something, can't we? I mean, we've got an investigation here with no clear end in sight, and if you factor in Viktor Baftiroski, we've got a missing person too."

"It might help us wrap this up, Freya," Ben said. "I can't see what harm it would do to see what kind of deal could be made."

Freya eyed him from the far side of the room, pleased to have his backing. Then she turned to Nillson and took a deep breath.

"Get him in to translate the letters," she said. "We'll go from there."

"He won't do it for nothing," Nillson said. "He's smarter than he looks."

"He will," Freya said. "It's your job to make sure of that, and I have every confidence in you to make that happen."

CHAPTER FORTY-FOUR

"Right, so where does that leave us?" Freya said. "We've got a positive ID on Maxim Baftiroski. We've got the stolen goods taken care of. And we have Gillespie's camera proving that nobody entered Alice's house through the front door. Now, unless I'm quite mistaken, that only leaves the rear access points as viable solutions."

"There were fingerprints on the back bedroom window ledge but not on the drainpipe," Ben said. "Is it too high for someone to jump, do you think?"

"Plausible, but that doesn't explain how they got in."

"The back door?" Cruz suggested.

"Locked from the inside," Ben said. "No broken windows, no sign of forced entry. So whoever killed Maxim Baftiroski either entered through the back door, locked it behind them, and then jumped from the bedroom window, or..."

"Or what?" Freya said, and Ben hesitated for a moment.

"Or she lived there."

"We've been through this," Freya said. "Alice Glass, A, was incapable of swinging a hammer, and B, had a distinct lack of blood on her clothing. Not to mention there is absolutely no sign

of the murder weapon, and the fact that Maxim Baftiroski fell to the floor in the front of the bedroom door preventing anybody from entering or leaving."

"So, option A then," Ben said. "They had to have entered through the back door or Gillespie's camera would have picked them up, and they had to have jumped from the rear bedroom window, or they would have left fingerprints on the drain pipe."

"Which means that the prints that CSI found on the window ledge belong to the killer," Freya replied. "Halle-bloody-lujah. Now all we need to do is match those prints to an individual. I want this done properly. Ben, I want those prints analysed against every individual involved in this investigation, that includes Tammy Plant, Vlad the foreman, or whatever his full name is. I presume we do have his full name, Nillson?"

"We do, boss," she replied, then added rather sheepishly, "I just can't pronounce it."

"Vlad will do then. Just make sure the paperwork reflects his true identity," she said, feeling the investigation shift up a gear. She returned her attention to Ben to continue her list, using the whiteboard as a guide. "Henry Glass, Debbie Blake and her mother—"

"She's blind and nearly deaf, boss," Gillespie said. "And she's older than electricity so I doubt she could leap from a first-floor window."

"George Benson," Freya continued, ignoring his comment. "And lastly, every one of the police, CSI, and ambulance staff that attended the scene. If that doesn't flag somebody, then at least we can eliminate most, if not all, of our suspects."

Nillson raised her pen, by way of getting Freya's attention, and Freya, happy with where they were, sat back down on the edge of her desk.

"Nillson?"

"Sorry, boss, but I don't think we can pin an entire investigation on one set of fingerprints, can we?"

"Quite right," Freya replied. "The fingerprints will provide us with the opportunity only. What we really need to concern ourselves with is the motive. And that's why it's important that we know what is in those letters and why Maxim Baftiroski had photos of Alice Glass's house. Was it research? Was he watching her to learn her movements? And what does the house have to do with Maxim's father? There's a link there, and until we learn what it is, we haven't got a case."

"Should we focus on Vlad?" Nillson asked. "He's coming to the station this morning."

"Yes. Book yourselves an interview room. Give him a few ideas of what he can expect should he decide not to help."

"Yes, boss," Nillson said.

"And the photos," Freya added. "Can you put them up somewhere? Clear a space on the wall so we can all see them."

Nillson glanced across at Anderson, silently giving her the task, and the two of them entered into a huddle around Nillson's desk to get started on a plan.

"Can I stick with Tammy, ma'am?" Gold said. "I'd like to see if there's been any progress."

Freya nodded, then addressed the room.

"Do we all agree that thanks to Nillson and Anderson's work at the farm, we can rule out burglary?"

Ben nodded, while the others looked at each other like sheep.

"Aye, boss. I mean, Maxim Baftiroski could have been robbing the place, but the whole business with his missing dad is a bit of a curve ball."

"A curve ball indeed," she replied. "But if we are to leverage Vlad the foreman's position, then we're going to need to build a case against him. We have to hold something we can threaten to drop."

"Right," Gillespie said, with obvious trepidation.

"Nillson, did you take an inventory of the stolen goods in the container?"

"I did, boss," Anderson said. "I got most of it down anyway."

"Good. Give it to Gillespie," Freya replied, turning back to the scruffy Scotsman. "Match the contents of the inventory to the items listed as stolen in the report we ran at the beginning of this investigation."

"Eh? Desk work?"

"Yes, Gillespie, desk work," she said. "We need the ability to demonstrate that Vlad and his band of merry men carried out the burglaries. I imagine some of the items will have been sold on already, but most of it will be there. If he's smart as Nillson says he is, then he'll know to hold on to the items for a few months before trying to sell them."

"Aye, boss," he said, sounding less than impressed. "So, we're basically CID now?"

"We all have our parts to play," she said. "Without the camera you found, we wouldn't be this far along, and without a case against Vlad the foreman, we'll have nothing to bargain with. I don't know about you, Gillespie, but I prefer to leave a casino with more than I walk in with."

She left him pondering the analogy, then moved on to Ben.

"As soon as you've asked CSI to run the fingerprint analyses, you and I will pay a visit to Henry Glass," she said. "Chapman, can you dig out the address for his firm, A.G Glass Cooling and Refrigeration?"

"Yes, ma'am," she said quietly, as she answered a phone call.

"Why Henry Glass?" Ben said.

"I don't know," she replied. "But something is niggling me. He bought a camera for his uncle's house to keep an eye on his mother's house, and he paid a visit to his uncle on the morning of her death, but didn't pop in to see her."

"He did say that he found talking to her difficult. I mean, she was suffering from some kind of mental illness. That's not an easy thing to witness."

"Even so," she said. "Let's pay him a visit."

"Ma'am," Chapman said, replacing her desk phone handset.

"Yes, Chapman," Freya said, as she gathered her belongings.

"That was the British Embassy in Chisinau," she said. "They've only just got back to me."

"And what did they have to say?" Freya asked.

"They received my emails and had meant to reply sooner, but then a name flagged up on their system."

"What name?" Ben asked.

"Sofia Baftiroski," Chapman replied. "She's on her way to the UK. She'll be landing at Manchester Airport this afternoon."

"Sofia Baftiroski?" Ben said. "Is that–"

"Viktor Baftiroski's wife," Nillson said. "But why would she be coming here?"

"Because her son has just died," Freya said. "The question is, who told her?"

CHAPTER FORTY-FIVE

"Thank you for coming in," Nillson said, as she entered the incident room, where Sergeant Priest had assigned a uniformed officer to accompany Vlad. She discharged the officer with a nod and let Anderson close the door behind him, leaving the three of them alone. "I hope you've been made to feel welcome and comfortable?"

"Comfortable?" he said and nearly laughed. "This is interrogation, no?"

Nillson kept a straight face while she took her seat. She waited for Anderson to sit and for the scrape of chairs on the painted concrete floor to cease.

"If this were an interrogation, Vlad, then my colleague would be preparing the recording, your legal representative would be sitting beside you, and you'd be wearing handcuffs. Now, would you care for some water?"

"No," he replied. "I want to finish. I have work. Mr Venables won't like me to be away for long."

"I doubt he'd be too thrilled if you were away for a year then," Anderson remarked, to which he said nothing and let his thousand-yard stare do the talking.

"Shall we begin?" Nillson said, sliding the packet of envelopes from her file. They were neatly bundled with an elastic band around them, which she undid before spreading them out before her. "I've been through them and put them in date order. All that remains is for you to explain the contents of each letter, Vlad. Detective Constable Anderson here will transcribe as we go. How does that sound?"

"How it sounds?" he said, in what Nillson felt like exaggerated broken English. "It sounds like good bargain for you. Not so good for me."

"Oh," Nillson replied. "Then perhaps we should pursue another route?"

He cocked his huge head to one side and narrowed his eyes.

"Other route?"

"The burglary charges," she explained. "My colleagues are, as we speak, linking the stolen items with your fingerprints to items reported stolen in recent burglaries. But I'm afraid if we're to venture down that route, Vlad, then perhaps I should request some free legal advice for you."

It was a stand-off, and to add weight to her point, Nillson began sliding the envelopes into a pile. It only took a few seconds before he raised his hand for her to stop.

"What guarantee do I have that this will help me? Will I walk free?" he asked.

"Well, that all depends on how much you can help," she told him. "If what you tell us helps us identify the man who murdered Maxim Baftiroski, then my boss will happily see what can be done to help your case."

"But if what I tell you doesn't help you catch this man..." he said, gesticulating wildly.

"Then that's where your guarantee comes in," she said with a smile. "You see, if what you tell us doesn't help us at all, or if we feel you aren't telling us everything, then I can guarantee that we will take the stolen items with your fingerprints on, and we will

build a case for the prosecution that will see you and your friends serve the maximum sentence possible."

"I see," he said, after a short pause for thought.

"And if you need any further convincing, Vlad," she continued. "You can also be quite sure that your friends, those men that work beneath you, are all made aware of your role in this."

"You will tell them I am informer?" he said.

"Not an informer," she said. "It's not within my powers to tell lies, sadly, but I will make sure they know you had every chance to help them, and you refused."

He nodded, clearly understanding the gist, if not every word, she had spoken.

Then he flicked his head at the envelopes and licked his lips.

"Show me," he said. "First letter."

CHAPTER FORTY-SIX

There was something familiar and relaxing about being a passenger in Freya's car again. The ride was far more comfortable, and when they spoke, Freya had a distraction that prevented her from staring at him until he answered. Instead, he could enjoy the views of the fields they passed, and the kites that hung effortlessly in the sky.

And they did speak – brief and fragmented conversations regarding Gillespie's attitude and the performance of the team as a whole, deducing collectively that whatever misgivings they had to work with, the best course of action was to let things be, for the time being at least.

It wasn't until they pulled into a parking space outside of A.G Glass Cooling and Refrigeration that Freya pulled the joker from her sleeve, landing him in a difficult situation and scrutinising gaze he couldn't avoid.

"I wanted to thank you for last night," she said.

"It was just a foot rub, Freya," he replied. "It's not like..."

He stopped there before he said too much. But the seed had been sown.

"It's not like what?"

He sighed a little but tried not to appear disinterested; that would just be plain rude.

"It's not like we did anything else, is it?"

"Not this time," she said. "But you never know."

He peered through the passenger window at the industrial unit. They were in a business park just outside of Metheringham, but they could have been anywhere in the UK. The units were not built of local stone, and there was barely a sign they were even in Lincolnshire, save for the various sign-written vans and lorries that filled the parking spaces of the other buildings.

Notably, Henry Glass's estate car was nowhere to be seen.

"I wanted to repay the favour," she said, breaking his chain of thought.

"A foot rub?" he said, to which she shook her head.

"Dinner," she replied. "My place. Tonight. What's your favourite?"

"Favourite what?"

"Favourite food, Ben. What should I cook you?"

"I haven't agreed to come yet."

"But you will," she said. "What should I do?"

He shrugged, and the only thing he could think of was, "Mashed potato?"

Her expression sank like a melting ice cube until a frown creased her forehead.

"Mashed potato?"

"And sausages," he said. "With beans."

"Sausage, mashed potatoes, and beans," she said. "Am I to assume you mean baked beans?"

"Of course. What other beans are there?" Ben said. "I suppose there's always runner beans, but with sausage and mash? I don't think so."

Of all the expressions Freya adopted throughout the day, perplexed was perhaps the most underused, Ben thought. Although, she did it so well.

"For a farmer's son, Benjamin Savage, your culinary knowledge is severely lacking."

He winked at her, so that she didn't think him a complete moron, then pushed open the door. She met him across the bonnet, a place they often fought for the last word.

"So?" she said.

"So what?"

"Dinner?"

"Can I take a raincheck?" he said.

"No, but you can just say no if you so wish."

"It's not a no," he replied. "It's a raincheck."

To have displayed disappointment would have been a slant on Freya's sense of pride. Instead, she chose to simply change the subject.

"Let's talk about Henry Glass," she said.

"His car isn't here," he said before she could push the dinner topic further. His watch read twelve-thirty, and just as he pulled his sleeve back over his wrist, a sandwich van pulled into the business park, and the driver honked the horn to let the workers of nearby businesses know they had arrived. "You don't suppose he's going to lunch?"

"Where?" she replied. "I can't imagine Henry Glass would eat from a sandwich van, and there's not much else around here."

"There's a good tea shop in the village," Ben suggested. "I'd eat there every day if I worked around here."

"Do they do sausage and mash?" she countered, then shoved off the bonnet. "Come on. Let's get this done."

They entered the building, where a small but functional reception had been built with very little effort given for comfort. The woman behind the desk seemed surprised to see them and stopped what she was doing when they came in as if visitors were a rarity.

"Help you?" she said, and from her expression, she most likely thought they were going to ask for directions.

"We're looking for Henry Glass," Freya said, and Ben saw her warrant card in her hand, held firmly below the desk.

"Oh, I'm afraid Henry's out, love," she said. "Is he expecting you?"

"No," Freya replied. "No, he wasn't. But I was hoping to catch him. Do you know if he'll be back today? Perhaps he's just popped out for lunch?"

"No," she said sadly. "He was here this morning, but he left a while back. Said he had to meet someone."

"Did he say who?"

"I didn't like to ask," the woman said, then leaned forward conspiratorially. "He's had a bit of bad news. His mother."

"Yes, Alice," Freya replied. "We heard about that. Oh, well, that's a shame. I wonder if you could give him a call?"

The woman, who Ben guessed to be in her mid-forties, shook her head.

"He said I wasn't to call him. But you could try," she said. "He can't fire *you,* can he? He's probably local. He did say he'd be arranging the funeral at some point."

Freya gave her an empathetic smile.

"We'll try again tomorrow," she said. "I wouldn't want to add to his woes. Thank you, anyway."

The woman watched on as they left the building, and Ben had a feeling she was still watching them when they stopped in the middle of the car park. A queue had formed at the sandwich van, consisting of a few men wearing greasy coveralls, young girls in smart clothing, and a man wearing shorts who looked as if he should probably have bought his lunch from a salad bar, rather than a sandwich van.

"Where to next?" he asked, as his phone buzzed in his pocket. Freya heard the vibration and although she ignored his question, she paid close attention to the call.

"Nillson," he told her, as he pressed the button to answer the call. "Anna, what's happening?"

"Ben, are you with the boss?"

"I am," he said. "For my sins. Hold on, I'll put you on loud-speaker."

He held the phone out for Freya to hear and hit the speaker button, feeling her eyes boring into him as if she were trying to read his thoughts.

"Anna? Can you hear me?"

"Loud and clear," she said. "Listen, I've just come out of the first sessions with Vlad."

"Ah, Vlad the interpreter? Did you manage to break him?"

"How long have you known me, Ben?" she asked. "And when have you ever known me to lose to a man?"

"Now that I think of it," he said, unable to stop himself from smiling. Freya nodded for them to take a slow walk to the car while Nillson spoke.

"The letters are mostly what you'd expect a man to say to his wife when working aboard. I won't go into the detail, but from what Vlad was saying, they were quite delicate."

"We'll save them for the pub then, shall we? I'm sure Gillespie will want to know all the sordid detail."

"But there are a few sentences that didn't make sense," Nillson continued. "They didn't seem to fit with the lovey-dovey stuff at all."

"Such as?" Freya said as she unlocked her car. But instead of climbing in, they leaned on the bonnet, far enough from the sandwich queue for anybody to overhear.

"He said that that man can't get away with it."

"Get away with what?"

"I don't know," Nillson said. "It was all a bit vague. He went on to talk about something being a matter of pride, and that a real man fights for his family."

"Fights for his family?" Ben said, as if that him repeating the statement might somehow make more sense. "Did Vlad say anything else?"

"He said lots, but aside from the romance not much made sense. Anderson transcribed the conversation so we can pick through it all and see if something jumps out."

"We might need to," Ben said gravely. "What do you think, Freya?"

He turned to where Freya had been standing only to find the space empty, and he spun around, seeing her march back towards the building.

"Freya?" he called out.

"What's happening, Ben?" Nillson asked.

"I don't know. I'll call you back."

He sprinted after Freya and just caught the door as it closed behind her.

"His office," she said to the woman behind the desk. "Where is it?"

"Freya?" said Ben, but she ignored him, and in the absence of a response from the woman, she pushed through a set of doors and began climbing the stairs.

"You can't go up there," the woman said, standing up from her seat. She looked at Ben. "She can't go up there."

"Are you going to stop her?" he replied, taking a moment to flash his warrant card. "I think perhaps it might be time to call Henry."

He followed Freya up the stairs and into a hallway, where they were presented with just three doors. The first was open, and was quite clearly a meeting room, though sparsely furnished with just a cheap table and a few chairs in various states of repair. She shoved open the second door, which appeared to be an office with several desks holding even more piles of paperwork than Gillespie's. But Freya clearly wasn't convinced any of the desks belonged to Glass. So she shoved her way through the final door, which opened into a large office with a single desk, an old bookcase, and various photos of men standing beside large refrigeration units.

"Freya, will you bloody well talk to me?" Ben said.

"Vlad mentioned a matter of pride," she replied with very little emotion or urgency in her tone. "She said he couldn't get away with it."

"Who couldn't get away with what?" he replied, and she searched the images on the wall, stopping beside an old, monochrome image to point at one of the men.

"Him," she said. "Alex Glass."

"Alex Glass? What did he get away with?"

But she didn't reply.

They were interrupted by the receptionist, who came storming into the room behind them.

"I'm afraid I'm going to have to ask you to–"

"You," Freya said, cutting her off and surprising her into silence. "Where does this firm operate from?"

"Operate?" she replied.

"Is this the only office, or are there more?"

"This is it," she said. "We don't need any more offices. We can barely afford this one."

"So, there are no international offices?"

"Freya?" Ben said, hoping to stop her from creating something from nothing.

But the receptionist shook her head.

"Why would we need an international office?" she asked, and the momentum faded, taking with it Freya's hopes. "Our remote engineers work from port-a-cabins on client sites, usually, so we have no need for permanent offices."

Freya was studying the photos on the wall as she spoke, but she tensed visibly once she'd processed what the receptionist said.

She turned slowly, a move Ben had seen a hundred times before, and one which she only did when her mind was moving at lightning speeds.

"Where?" she said. "Where are these international clients?"

The receptionist shrugged as if she couldn't see the importance.

"France mostly, a few in the Middle East, and some more dotted about Europe."

"Europe? Where precisely?"

"We used to have some clients in Ukraine, but we had to pull out of there for obvious reasons," she began, then looked up and to the right in deep thought. "Athens, Belgium, and a few in Romania, or thereabouts."

"Thereabouts?"

"I don't know exactly," she said. "One of those countries. I just know that we have to get them work visas now, since Brexit, you know?"

"Moldova?" Freya asked, and the woman's face lit up.

"Yes, that's one," she said. "How did you know that?"

Finally, Ben could see what Freya had worked herself into such a tizzy about. He turned away to prevent having to see her glory face but doubted he would be able to avoid it forever.

Men's voices and their heavy footfall came from the stairwell at the end of the corridor, most likely the staff returning after visiting the sandwich van. But it wasn't the approaching men that caught Ben's attention. It was a small, brass bucket-like container that had been positioned near the door for the purpose of keeping wet umbrellas. His father had one similar. But his father's rarely stored anything but his old umbrella, and not a walking stick made from gnarled beechwood, which Ben reached down and picked up carefully with two fingers.

He held it up to the light to examine the wood from top to bottom.

"Ben?" Freya said. "What have you got there?"

He was nearing the end of the stick when he saw the traces of red so deep it was almost black. He turned it in his hands, being careful to touch it as little as possible, and then studied the base of the stick.

"Ben, talk to me," Freya said, and he pointed it at her.

"What do you notice about this?" he asked and flicked his eyes at the receptionist to suggest she use the appropriate level of discretion.

"It's round, It's approximately an inch and a half in diameter," Freya said, and she tore her eyes from the end of the stick. "And it has what looks like dried blood on it."

CHAPTER FORTY-SEVEN

The evidence bags that Freya carried habitually were far too small for the walking stick, so instead, she and Ben had carefully placed one over each end. She slid it behind the front seats of her car, climbed in, and fired up the engine. She had dialled Chapman's desk phone before Ben had even closed his door, but he knew what was happening instinctively.

"DC Chapman," the polite young officer answered.

"Chapman, it's me," Freya said. "Is everyone there?"

There was a pause as she glanced around the room, and then she confirmed with a timid, "Yes, ma'am."

"Good, put me on loudspeaker and ask them to huddle around."

There were a few clicks as she prepared the phone and then the usual muffled and distant scrapes of chairs as the team all encircled Chapman.

"We're all here," Chapman said after less than a minute had passed.

"Okay, so we have our suspect," Freya began. "Henry Glass."

"Henry Glass?" Gillespie said, just as Freya thought he would,

and a low hum ensued as the team shared opinions, just as she thought they might.

"We're outside his office now," Freya continued, to bring the hum to a finish. "It turns out the murder weapon is not a hammer but a walking stick."

"A walking—"

"Yes, Gillespie," she said. "A walking stick, covered in dried blood, and most importantly, the end appears to be exactly the same size as the injuries that caused Maxim Baftiroski's death."

"Bloody hell," Gillespie said. "And he hid it in his office?"

"I wouldn't say he hid it," Ben said. "It looks like he gave it a wipe and dumped it in an umbrella stand. He probably thought we'd never suspect him or search his office, which is pretty poor form for a man who claims to enjoy Kevin Banner novels."

"Boss, it's Nillson," she said. "Can I ask something?"

"Not yet," Freya said. "Chapman, while we're talking, I want you to get on to ANPR and find Henry Glass's car. He can't have got far."

"Yes, ma'am," she replied.

"Nillson, what were you going to ask?"

"Only that if the blood on this walking stick turns out to be Maxim Baftiroski's, we have a means, but why would he do it?"

"He was in his mother's house," Gillespie said. "An intruder in her bedroom. What would you do if you caught a man in your mother's bedroom?"

"Pat him on the back," she replied. "He's a better man than I am, Gunga Din," she said.

"You'd clobber him and you know you would," Gillespie said.

"I might clobber him but I wouldn't bloody kill him. It's not like he hit Maxim once and he died, he hit him several times."

"Nillson is right," Freya said. "His motive wasn't simply blind rage. It was far more calculated than that. Far more calculated than any of us gave him credit for, in fact."

"You have a theory, then?" Nillson said.

"I do," she said. "I believe that twenty-five years ago, Alex Glass had an affair whilst working abroad in Moldova."

"Moldova?" Gillespie said. "Sorry, boss, but how the bloody hell did he manage that?"

"His business has clients across the Middle East and Europe," Freya explained. "Specifically, Moldova. I believe Maxim Baftiroski was the result of this affair."

"Holy crap," Gillespie said. "It's always a bloody affair."

"And I believe that approximately five years ago, Viktor Baftiroski learned the truth about his son."

"Oh my God," Anderson said. "What Vlad said in the interview, about pride and not letting him get away with it."

"Exactly," Freya said. It was tiring to be interrupted so often, but she'd learned to expect and manage it with a few well-placed, deep breaths. "It's not a coincidence that Viktor Baftiroski managed to land a job at Locks Wood Farm. He knew Alex was nearby because of the business address. All he had to do was follow him home and wait for the opportunity to get his revenge."

"Hang on, what does this have to do with Henry Glass?" Cruz said, and Freya could picture the bemused expression he often wore at times like this.

"Yesterday I asked Chapman to get me the file on Alex Glass's death," Freya explained. "I didn't make it known as I didn't want to add to the confusion. But, as it turns out, it was the right thing to do. Alex Glass died from several blows to the head."

"Don't tell me, his injuries were round?" Nillson said.

"And about an inch and a half in diameter," Freya finished. "It's the same weapon."

"But how did this Viktor Baftiroski get the walking stick?" Cruz asked. "Or was it his in the first place?"

"The walking stick wasn't Viktor's," Freya said. "It was Alex Glass's."

A silence followed, during which, presumably, Cruz was trying to make sense of it all.

"What's the two things we know about Henry Glass and his mother?"

"He found it hard to see her, due to her condition," Nillson said. "But he obviously still cared for her, or he wouldn't have installed the camera."

"Thank you, Nillson," Freya said, and saw Ben in her peripheral nodding his approval. "So, what if Henry Glass knew about the affair? And what if he knew about Maxim?"

"How?" Gillespie asked. "How would he know about that?"

"Because Henry Glass has worked for A.G Glass Cooling and Refrigeration since he was a boy, and his father ran the firm. That must be at least twenty years. He would have had access to everything – contracts, correspondence, letters. He would have seen the lot and he would have known what his dad was up to. Besides, people talk. You know what it's like. If he didn't read something he shouldn't have, he would have overheard it."

"Are you saying that Henry Glass killed his father?" Nillson asked. "For what? To save his mother from being heartbroken? That will never hold up in court."

"I'm saying that Viktor Baftiroski had the motive, but Henry Glass might very well have had the murder weapon. That means there's a potential link between the two that we have to find," Freya said. "And before you ask for further details, I don't have any. But we're going to find it. This is just the bones of a theory."

"Right, hold on a minute," Gillespie called out. "Let's say for a moment that Henry Glass killed his old man. How did he come to know about Maxim?"

"Gillespie, you of all people should know the answers to that," Freya replied. "Your parents gave you up as a child, didn't they?"

"Aye well, they did, but I don't think this is the right time to bring that up, boss."

"Bear with me," she said. "You told me once how you went to find your real parents. How you followed your dad and your

brother to a pub and sat nearby listening to what they were talking about."

"Aye, I did," he said after a moment.

"Don't you think Maxim would do the same?"

"Well, he might. But Alex Glass had been dead for five years."

"Maxim didn't know that Alex was his father. As far as he was concerned, Viktor was, and he hadn't been in contact for five years."

"So, he followed in his footsteps," Nillson said. "He followed in his footsteps, got a job in the same place, most likely through the same contacts, and when he arrived, Vlad and Venables gave him his father's belongings—"

"With the photos of Alice Glass's house," Freya said.

"No, the photos were Maxim's," Nillson said.

"Really?"

"I think so," Nillson said. "Hold on."

They heard her walk over to the wall where Anderson had pinned the images, and then they heard her calling out as she ran back.

"You're bloody right," she said. "The climbing rose is only halfway up the wall in one image, and in the other, it's all the way up to the window. The photos were taken years apart."

She felt Ben stare at her, presumably wondering why she hadn't told him what she'd seen.

"As far as Maxim was concerned, his father was missing, and this house had something to do with it. Yet the only person he ever saw coming and going was a little old lady."

"So how did Henry Glass know Maxim was in Navenby?" Nillson asked. "And how did he know he was at his mother's house?"

"Because Sofia told him he was in the UK looking for his father," Freya said. "She's on her way to the UK now. Who do you think told her that her son was dead?"

"Henry was in contact with Sofia?"

"He wanted to protect his mother. Even after his dad's death," Freya explained. "Making contact with Sofia Baftiroski was the only way he could maintain control and given that he took over the business when his father died, he would have had plenty of opportunity to pay her a visit. It wouldn't surprise me if he even sent money to keep her quiet about the affair."

"Jesus," Gillespie said. "He stayed at George's house that night. That's why there were two beds made up. He would have seen his mum go for her morning walk, and then he would have seen Maxim running across the road from the field."

"Very good, Gillespie," Freya told him. "Maxim Baftiroski *was* robbing the place, but not in the conventional sense. He was looking for answers to find his dad."

"But Glass got to him first," Gillespie said, on a roll. "Hit him a few times, probably heard his mum come home and jumped out of the window."

"We're getting there," Freya said. "But it's not very neat. We're missing something. More importantly, Gillespie's camera does very little for us except prove that Henry Glass did not enter his mother's house to murder Maxim Baftiroski. The fingerprints found on the window ledge and the drainpipe prove that Maxim climbed in through the window. The back door was locked from the inside and nobody entered through the front. So how did the killer get in and out?"

"Maybe Maxim was attacked outside the house before he climbed up the drainpipe?" Ben suggested.

"No, there was blood spatter on the bedroom wall," Freya replied dismissively. "Besides, how was he supposed to climb a drainpipe with a bloody great hole in his head?"

"Well, then maybe the murderer was already inside the house?" Ben said. "Maybe Henry somehow tampered with the footage to–"

He stopped talking and closed his eyes while in thought.

"Gillespie, how far back does the footage go?"

"Ah, I've been through it, Ben. All the way back to the previous day. Nobody goes in or out."

"Well, that's going to be our showstopper," Freya said. "CPS won't give us the go-ahead until we have an MMO, and without proof of somebody entering the house, we have no opportunity."

"So where does Tammy come in?" Gold asked. "She went inside."

"Tammy has been used and abused," Freya said. "Henry Glass enlisted her to keep an eye on his mum. Think about it. There was no envelope with Tammy's name on. Gillespie, do you have her journal?"

"Aye, boss. It's, erm, right here somewhere."

"Find the entry. You said there's a circle with the letter P."

"That's right," he said.

"P is for paid," she told him. "The appointment was prepaid. I used to do the same with my stylist when she was short of cash. And Debbie the neighbour? Why would an old lady who is capable of walking to the hairdressers and who can walk through the fields in all weathers need somebody to do her shopping for her? She's another of Henry's spies. He was just making sure she was okay without having to go and actually see her."

"Ma'am," Chapman said. "We've got him on ANPR. He's heading out of town, out near Nottingham."

"He's going to the airport," Freya said. "I think he's going to meet Sofia."

"Eh? Why the bloody hell would he do that when he's just killed her son?" Gillespie said.

"Why do you think?" Freya said. "Because he knows she won't find him. Because she'll ask difficult questions and maybe even go to the police."

"Because he's guilty of something," Ben said, nodding, to which Freya nodded.

"Chapman, get onto the local police. Let's bring him in. The rest of you, start filling in those blanks. Ben and I will drop the

walking stick at the lab. In the meantime, have CSI check Henry Glass's fingerprints against the window ledge."

She ended the call before anybody could raise anything else and sat back.

"You okay?" Ben asked. "It's going to take a lot of work to put all that together. It's quite the theory, Freya. And if I'm honest, I don't think he has a strong enough motive."

"But you agree that he's guilty of something?" she said.

"Yeah, he's guilty of something. I mean he's involved somehow. I just need some convincing, that's all."

"So do I, but he's all we have."

"You're going to lean on him?"

"I'll get a custody extension," she said. "That'll give us thirty-six hours to get him to talk. Are you up for the challenge, Ben?"

CHAPTER FORTY-EIGHT

A traffic unit pulled into the station car park and the driver performed a wide U-turn so that he came to a stop outside the custody suite. The two officers donned their hats as they climbed from the car and nodded a greeting.

"DS Nillson?" one of them asked, the older of the two, the driver.

"That's me," she replied. "You have a delivery for me, I believe?"

"Sensitive package," he replied. "Sharp edges, if you know what I mean."

"Then, I'll make sure we wear gloves when we're handling it."

He laughed a little then opened the rear door to allow Henry Glass to swing his legs out, then he grabbed the suspect's cuffed hands and pulled him up.

"Through here," Nillson said, leading them to the custody suite for the handover. Once inside, the traffic officer positioned Glass in front of the custody desk, where Sergeant Priest prepared a new custody record.

"Name?" he grumbled in his thick Yorkshire accent that seemed to fill the room like a double bass.

"Henry Glass," the traffic officer said, placing a clear bag containing the suspect's possessions on the desk.

"And for what do we owe this pleasure?" Priest asked, to which the officer turned to invite Nillson to contribute.

"Murder, Sarge," she said, which caused Glass obvious pain, and he gritted his teeth but held his tongue.

"Does he need a room, Sergeant Nillson?" he replied.

"He will, but I'd like to get him into an interview room as soon as we can if it's all the same to you."

"Fine by me. We'll process him and bring him through to interview room two," he said, then looked at Glass. "We'll just need your fingerprints, photographs, and then a DNA swab. Do you have any objection, Mr Glass?"

"Will it make a difference if I do?"

"Not to me, it won't. You're not obliged to provide a DNA sample, but of course, you might find that decision won't be in your favour later down the line."

Glass glanced at them all in turn as each of the officers waited for his response. Henry Glass eventually shook his head and gave a sigh.

"Just do what you have to do," he said.

"Very good," Priest replied, and he turned the form to face the suspect, then slid him a pen.

"Sign there, if you will," Priest said. "Then we'll get started on your portrait. How does that sound?"

Glass saw little amusement in the Custody Sergeant's rhetoric, but after his cuffs had been removed, he signed his name and then allowed himself to be led through into the processing room.

"Mr Glass, will you be requiring legal representation at this point?" Nillson asked. "Free or otherwise."

"At this point?" he said. "You make it sound like I'm going to be here for days."

"Thirty-six hours if we need to," she replied, and his expression dropped at the prospect.

He shook his head.

"No," he said. "No, not at this stage."

"Give us five minutes, Sergeant," Priest said, collecting the forms and sliding them into a tray. "Just enough time for you to grab yourself a coffee."

"I'd better be off," the traffic officer said. "As much as I'd love to stay and chat."

Despite the boyish dimples in his cheeks when he smiled and the deep laughter lines around his eyes, there was a maturity to him, a confidence that only came with age, which Anderson gauged to be around mid-to-late thirties.

To Anderson's surprise, he tipped his hat just as a gentleman might have done a century before, then exited the office.

Nillson glanced at Anderson, and for the first time since she had known the sergeant, her femininity shone.

Anderson flicked her head at the door, telling her to go after him. Then, when Nillson remained fixed to the spot, she widened her eyes to convey urgency without alerting Priest to the interaction.

With a quick look, suggesting Anderson wish her luck, Nillson followed him cautiously, leaving Anderson alone with Priest. He looked up from his desk, his expression as impassive as ever.

"Oh, to be young again," he said, then cocked his eyebrows once and slipped into the processing room, where his deep voice rumbled to a mumble.

She barely had time to contemplate her next move when Ben and Freya walked in, both of them looking over their shoulders into the car park.

"Who's that Nillson is talking to?" Ben said, looking around the room, presumably for Priest.

"Oh, he's the officer who brought Henry Glass in," she said. "Sergeant Priest is just processing him now. He said he'd take him through to interview room two when he's done."

"Well," Freya said, "I'm glad to see a thorough job of the handover."

She passed Anderson with a knowing smile and walked straight out into the corridor, leaving Ben a little perplexed. Anderson simply shook her head at him to tell him not to concern himself, and Freya called out from the corridor.

"Perhaps you'd care to join me in the interview, Anderson?" she said.

"Me, boss?"

"It'll be good experience for you," she replied, checking her watch. "Ben, I wonder if you could save Nillson from the clutches of a romance destined for failure, then go and crack the whip upstairs. The clock is now ticking, so I want those gaps in the theory filled as best we can."

Freya walked away towards the interview rooms.

"Romance?" Ben said, as Nillson re-entered the custody suite, blushing ever so slightly.

"What was that?" she said.

Ben's eyes roamed from Nillson to Anderson, and then back again.

"Nothing," he said suspiciously. "Freya wants us to light a fire upstairs."

"Aren't you doing the interview?"

"No, Anderson is," he replied, waving his arm to invite Nillson to lead the way.

"She said it'd be good experience for me," Anderson said. "You don't mind, do you?"

"It's a shame. I'd have loved the opportunity to watch the bastard squirm," Nillson replied. "But you knock yourself out. Enjoy it."

Then she and Ben disappeared into the fire escape, their voices trailing off, and Anderson pushed into the interview room where Freya was busy scrawling on a notepad.

"Come in," she said, without looking up. "I'm just getting my

thoughts down before they bring him in. Did you ask if he wanted a legal rep?"

"Anna did, boss," she said. "Sergeant Nillson, I mean. She did, but he declined."

"Then we can assume the interview will be extremely short," Freya replied, as Anderson took her seat beside her. "He knows what he's in for, but he doesn't know what we have on him yet. So he'll no doubt begin with a no comment stance until he realises the seriousness of his situation, then he'll request his solicitor."

"You sound very sure, boss."

Freya finished what she was writing and gave her a knowing look and a wink.

They were interrupted by a uniformed officer pushing the door open with one hand and leading Glass in with the other.

"Henry Glass, ma'am," he said.

"Thank you," she replied, then waited patiently for Glass to take the seat opposite her. She gave the signal for Anderson to begin the recording but said nothing until the prolonged buzz had finished, indicating the recording was in process.

Freya announced the date and the time, and then introduced herself and Anderson, before gesturing for Glass to reciprocate.

"Henry Glass," he said.

"Thank you," she replied. "And for the record, Mr Glass, can you please confirm that you understand why you are here?"

"I know what the officer said," he replied. "As for understanding, I'm afraid that's a bit of a leap."

"Well, for the benefit of the recording, you are under arrest on suspicion of murder," Freya began. "You do not have to say anything, but it may harm your defence if you do not mention when questioned something which you later rely on in court. Anything you do say may be given in evidence. Do you understand now?"

His chest rose and fell heavily, and he licked his lips nervously.

"No comment," he said, with very little conviction.

"Mr Glass, can you confirm that you stayed at your uncle's house, a George Benson, the night before your mother died?"

"No comment," he said, with a frown that suggested he had realised that it wasn't going to be a quick affair.

"Did you enlist the help of Tammy Plant and Deborah Blake to help you keep an eye on your mother?"

He looked utterly bemused at the line of questioning but maintained consistency in his reply.

"No comment."

"On the morning of your mother's death, did you enter your mother's house at all?"

It was a pleasure to watch Freya work. She asked the questions as she had written them, with no emotion and in an objective tone, as if she was simply ticking boxes, asking the questions to provide him with the opportunity to come clean, which would later serve him in court.

"No comment," he said.

"Did you kill Maxim Baftiroski?" she said.

"No comment."

"Did you strike anybody with a walking stick?" she said, and he hesitated, then placed his hands on the table before him.

"No comment," he replied, his tone much more thoughtful than it had previously been.

Freya read from the notes, then leaned forward to stare him in the eye.

"Mr Glass, are you responsible for the death of your father?"

"Eh?"

"Did you murder your father?"

He looked aghast, eyes wide and mouth hanging open. He swallowed again and inhaled through his nose to calm his nerves.

"No comment," he said.

"Finally," Freya said, "are you aware of the requirements to perform a post-burial exhumation?"

"A what?" he said. "No?"

"Well, for the record, Mr Glass, I am obliged to be in possession of a licence from the Home Office issued by the Ministry of Justice, and I am obliged to have written permission from a very close relative."

His brow furrowed in confusion, and he began picking at a loose piece of skin on his thumb, but he said nothing.

"The licence isn't an issue. I can obtain that in a heartbeat," she said, which Anderson thought was stretching the truth a little. "And as for the permission from close relatives, you are the only remaining blood relative."

"And suppose I say no?" he replied. "He's been dead five years for God's sake."

"That's the thing," she told him, closing her file. "That little requirement doesn't count if the only blood relative is, in fact, the murder suspect, and of course, the process is made far simpler seeing as you've already arranged for the burial proceedings to begin. Much less digging on our part."

"You can't—"

"I can because I have reason to believe you killed your father, Mr Glass," she told him. "Now, let's take a break, shall we? If I were you, I'd take the opportunity to call your solicitor, because maintaining a no-comment stance in your situation is a one-way ticket to prison."

CHAPTER FORTY-NINE

To Ben's surprise, the incident room was humming with activity and not the usual banter being tossed back and forth. Gillespie and Cruz were working on linking the stolen goods inventory to the burglaries, and Chapman was absorbed in typing what Gold was reading out, presumably collaborating on reports.

"Afternoon all," he said, letting Nillson enter before him. "Are we making progress?"

Gillespie glanced up from the spreadsheet he had printed with a fluorescent marker in his hand.

"In our careers or the investigation?" he said.

"The investigation, Jim," Ben replied.

"Oh, well, in that case, yes. It looks like the Navenby branch of the Albanian mafia is responsible for seventy per cent of the local burglaries, and we haven't even looked further afield."

"Good," Ben said, chuckling to himself. "When you're done there, can you pay Deborah Blake a visit? We just need to know if Henry Glass did in fact ask her to keep an eye on his mother."

"Eh?"

"I know, it's far below your pay grade, Jim. But the fact

remains that Freya's theory is good, but it has holes, and we need to patch them up."

"Can't we just give her a call?" he asked.

"Do you have her number?"

"Cruz does," he said, then grinned like a schoolboy. "I'm sure he won't mind an excuse to call her."

"Oy," Cruz said.

"Call her,' Ben said before the conversation turned into something he hadn't intended. "If you can't get through, then go and see her."

"Aye," Gillespie said, nodding at Cruz by way of delegation.

"Should I see if Tammy's mother knows anything?" Gold asked, and Ben contemplated a response carefully.

"It's probably best if we don't. Not yet at least. She's done enough for us. The last thing we need is for her to start telling people we can't do our jobs. No, perhaps Chapman can look into Glass's bank records?"

"Shouldn't be an issue now he's in custody," Chapman said.

"Good. See if there were any payments to Tammy or her business. The theory is based on the fact that Henry Glass wants to keep close tabs on his mother. It seems insignificant, but I get the feeling this whole case is going to be filled with insignificant details that have a collective significance," he said and then caught sight of the wall where the photos had been pinned. "So, these are the images, are they?"

"Here," Nillson said, showing him the two photos of Alice Glass's house taken years apart. "It's obvious they're different photos from the same angle from the colouring, but I just thought it was the variation in light."

"I see what you mean," he replied, leaning in close to see the climbing rose in both images. "I did have a quick look when you emailed the images through, but if I'm honest, I didn't pay that much attention."

He took a step back to look at the exhibits on the wall as a whole, and he was reminded of the wall in his study.

"What's wrong?" she said, and he snapped out of his trance.

"Oh, nothing. I was just trying to take it all in," he replied. "Are you still okay to pop round one night? When all this is over, I mean."

"You're being very opaque, Ben," she told him.

"Am I? I don't mean to be," he said. "I just..."

He faltered a little, unsure of how to phrase what he wanted to say.

"You just what?"

He lowered his voice and leaned in close to whisper.

"I just need someone with a level head to run something by."

"A level head?" she replied. "I'll try not to have a drink before I come then, shall I?"

But he didn't smile, and he felt her amusement wane as speedily as it had arrived.

"All right," she said. "When this is over and we've got him bang to rights."

"Cheers," he said. "And I'd appreciate your discretion. You'll understand why when you hear what I have to say. I'll do you a dinner, so maybe we can do it straight after the shift?"

"Wow, two dinner invitations from two different men in a single day," she said. "And both of them told me to keep it under wraps. I must be giving off some kind of signal."

"Sorry?" Ben said. "Two dinner invites?"

"Don't worry," she said, as Anderson entered the room alone.

"How did it go with Glass?" Gillespie called out.

"Oh," she replied, sinking into her seat. "No comment."

"Oh, so it's a secret, is it?" he said, winking at Ben. "And here's me thinking we were working on this investigation together."

"No, I mean, he gave a no-comment response," she replied and then saw that he was just winding her up and smiled at her own naivety.

"Where's Freya?" Ben asked, letting Gillespie enjoy his little victory in silence.

"She said she'd be in in a moment," Anderson replied. "She just popped in to see Granger."

"Granger?" he said, and she gave a little flick of her eyebrows and inhaled as if to convey it wasn't good news. "Is it what I think it is?"

"What's that?" Nillson said, and he tried to brush it off, seeing as the burden of delivering the news wasn't his to bear.

"Let's just see what she has to say," he said dismissively. "I'm sure she has some kind of motivational speech prepared."

"Now I really am intrigued," she said.

But they didn't have to wait long, as Freya pushed through the doors and made her way to her desk without even glancing up at any of them. She placed her files down, grabbed the marker pen, and then began striking lines through every name on the board save for Henry Glass's, which she circled, and then stabbed the pen into the board for a dramatic finish.

All eyes were on her. Chapman and Gold remained motionless, watching with clear trepidation, Gillespie and Cruz seemed to shrink in their seats, perhaps sensing an undesirable task heading their way. Nillson, however, as Ben was pleased to see, seemed to take a small step forward, eager to learn what was in store for them.

"Right then," Freya said as if her behaviour hadn't already gained their attention. "Who has plans for tonight?"

"Well, as it happens," Gillespie began, "I'm supposed to be seeing this wee lass from Wragby. Had to blow her off last night—"

"Cancel it," Freya told him.

"Anybody else?"

Ben looked around the room and saw that Gold wanted to speak up, but didn't.

"Good," Freya continued. "It's not often I ask you to work late—"

"Not this week, anyway," Gillespie mumbled.

"But tonight, we have something important to do," she said, glaring at him. "I'll fill you in on the details later. In the meantime, how are we getting on with adding some meat to the theory?"

Cruz raised his hand like a small child needing the bathroom, and Freya gestured for him to speak.

"I've spoken to Deborah Blake, boss," he said. "She confirmed Henry Glass didn't ask her to do his mum's shopping."

"Oh," Freya said.

"But he did call her every now and again to ask how his mum was doing."

"He did?" Freya asked, suddenly re-enthused. "Well, that is good news. Anybody else?"

"Me," Chapman said, raising her pen to get her attention. "Ben asked me to see if there had been any payments from Henry Glass's bank accounts to Tammy Plant's."

"And?" she said, nodding a thanks in Ben's direction.

"It's confirmed," she replied. "One payment this week of forty-five pounds, the same last week, and the same two weeks before that."

Freya sat down in her usual position on the edge of her desk and seemed to suddenly believe her own theory as if she had been harbouring doubts before then.

"Add both of those facts to the camera he installed in his uncle's property and I think we can prove without doubt that Henry Glass was indeed keeping an eye on his mother, however distant that may be."

"There is more, ma'am," Chapman said, her expression a far cry from Freya's newfound glee. "I've just had an email from the lab."

The laughter lines around Freya's eyes smoothed as she sensed the positivity wane.

"They ran the fingerprints from the walking stick against the

fingerprints Henry Glass gave during his father's murder investigation. They're a match."

"But?" Freya said.

"But the fingerprints on the window ledge aren't a match. In fact, they don't match any on the database or any of the suspects."

"Well, that is a shame," she said. "But it's not a show stopper. That doesn't mean he didn't climb from the window."

"But they do match another set on the window at the front of the house, and the coffee machine," Chapman added. "Whoever left those prints spent some time in the house and not just the bedroom."

Freya stood, averting her eyes from everyone while she thought. Then she took a few paces back to the centre of the room.

"We'll meet at eight o'clock this evening at St Peter's Church in Navenby," she said, by way of a closing statement.

"Ah Christ, we're not praying, are we, boss?" Gillespie said. "I'm not really into all that vigil stuff. I mean, I've nothing against other people doing it if that makes them happy, but—"

"We will not be attending a vigil and neither will we be praying, Gillespie, unless you wish to," she told him. "But I do have some advice for you."

"Oh aye?" he said, waiting for her to put him out of his misery.

"Tonight will provide you all with a rarely gleaned experience," she said, with a brief glance around them all and finishing on Gillespie. "I suggest you wear your boots."

CHAPTER FIFTY

The evening was peaceful and the air was still, the way it often is in late summer, when nature prepares itself for the onslaught of winter and seems to hold its breath.

Cruz closed his car door, noting the other vehicles parked nearby. The boss's Range Rover was there, as was Gillespie's old rust bucket, which was parked behind an unmarked van, and then Nillson's little hatchback. They were all parked on Cat Walk, a name that, at first, amused Cruz, until he gazed up at the church and his eyes fell on the little, white tent that seemed to dominate the churchyard.

The rest of the team were all standing nearby, positioned close, on hand but far enough away not to be a nuisance to the grave diggers and pathologists.

Gillespie caught his attention and waved him over.

"Come and join the fun," he said, when Cruz drew closer, which did little except turn a few heads in the team and cause a few eyes to roll, including the boss's. "I'm glad you're here, Gabby. We need someone to run around to the shop and grab some hot chocolates."

He made a show of doing a headcount but was interrupted by Doctor Bell, who leaned out from the tent flap.

"We're ready," she said, her tone deadly serious. "Not long now."

"No time for that, Gillespie," Freya said. "Look sharp everyone."

The pathologist re-entered the tent, closing the flap behind her, and the team seemed to wait with bated breath.

Cruz joined the team, who seemed to be huddled in a tight group, each of them watching for the flaps to open, and listening intently.

"Am I the only one who doesn't know what we're doing here?" Cruz said quietly.

"Yes," Freya told him.

"Shhh," Anderson hissed and gave him a stern look.

Cruz felt a little out of place. He looked around the churchyard, noting two men who were standing a way off, closer to the old building.

"Who are those fellas?" he asked, nudging Gillespie with his elbow.

"That's the environmental officer and the cemeteries officer," Ben whispered, then shook his head to suggest they were of no concern. "It's a legal requirement."

"Shhh," Anderson hissed again.

"Jesus, I could have stayed home and watched *I'm A Celebrity* with Hermione if I wanted to be shushed all bloody night."

"You're here because I want you to see what happens, Cruz," Freya said. "Contrary to the movies, exhuming a body doesn't happen very often. You may never get to see this again."

"See what?" he said. "It's a tent. I could see that at Glastonbury, except I imagine what's going on inside this one is wildly different to the ones at the festival."

"Shhh," Anderson hissed again.

"And why is the Welsh woman here? She's not digging the body up, is she?"

"Grave diggers dig the hole, Gabby, you numb nut," Gillespie whispered. "She's just here to oversee the removal."

"You mean, they're going to take the body out of the coffin *here*?" Cruz said, appalled at the prospect. "Won't it be all–"

"No, Cruz," Freya said. "There is a process to follow that ensures respect and decency."

"Oh, right," he replied, as Doctor Bell once more opened the tent flaps and leaned out to talk to Freya. She nodded once.

"It's him," she said. "The nameplate on the coffin lid is a match."

"Well, that's a bonus," Cruz said. "I mean, surely we checked to make sure we're digging up the right body?"

"Of course we checked," Freya replied. "It's part of the process. The cemeteries officer confirms the correct grave is being opened, and then, as surety, the nameplate must then be confirmed."

"Right," Cruz said. "I suppose it's better to be safe than sorry. We don't want to dig up an old lady's body, do we?"

Nobody replied, and he sighed to himself, finding the whole process incredibly dull. So much so that he checked his phone. He entered the passcode and the screen lit up to reveal a missed call from Hermione, but a sideways glance from Freya suggested that now was neither the time nor the place to be on his phone, so he stuffed it back into his pocket.

"So, they take the whole coffin out, do they?" he asked.

"No, Gabby," Gillespie said. "One of them will hop down into the hole and give him a wee piggyback out."

His comment raised a few smiles – and a few irritated glares.

"Won't it have rotted?" he asked, much to the agitation of Anderson.

"Yes, it will," Freya said, doing her best to keep Cruz abreast of the process while maintaining calm among the team members,

who were all straining to hear what was going on inside the tent. Cruz leaned in, wondering what they were listening to, as the whine of a power drill broke the silence.

"What the bloody hell is that?" he whispered as loudly as he dared.

"When the coffin has been in the ground as long as this one has, they can't pick it up without it breaking," Ben said, demonstrating far more patience than the others. "So, they're building a wooden frame around it, and then they'll lift that out along with the soil, which should hold everything together."

"Should?" Cruz said.

"Should," Ben repeated.

"I bloody hope so," Cruz replied.

"Oh, for heaven's sake," Anderson said as quietly as she could. "Will you just shut up? I'm trying to hear what's going on. Didn't you hear what the boss said? We might never see another one, but if we do, I want to know how it works."

Cruz was a little taken aback, and the team seemed to huddle closer as Doctor Bell leaned out once more.

"This is it," she said. "They're bringing him out."

Cruz took a step back to see if anybody would notice, but they seemed even more enthralled than ever. He took another step, and another, until he was sure nobody had noticed, and then he slipped in amongst the gravestones where the air, for some reason, seemed to be cooler and fresher.

He dug his phone from his pocket and hit the button to call Hermione, then as he waited for the call to connect, he wandered among the graves. He'd always had a grim fascination with headstones, enjoying the process of finding the oldest one and wondering what life was like when they were buried.

The call went unanswered, and he pocketed the phone again, just as he discovered a headstone from 1902. The trick, he found, was to find the most beautiful spot in the graveyard, where the most prominent members of society were likely to have been

buried. But as he searched the grounds, he saw a lone figure standing on the road close to the cars. It was a woman, and she seemed to be captivated by the events happening in the churchyard.

He cut through the gravestones, being mindful not to tread directly on the grass above the graves. Although he'd always taken care, he'd also always wondered why he bothered. He was unlikely to hurt the occupants.

He emerged from the gravestones near the gate.

"Hello," he said, approaching the figure. "Can I help you at all?"

The woman, who was in her late fifties, seemed to startle, and she gave a little yelp when she saw him.

"Sorry, I didn't mean to make you jump," he said. "Are you waiting to come inside? We won't be much longer."

The woman stared at Cruz like he was some kind of apparition, and she took several steps away from him.

"It's okay," he said, tapping his pockets for his warrant card. "I'm a police officer."

But she was not to be convinced, and she turned away from him in a hurry, sped along the lane, and didn't look back.

He looked after her, hoping that she didn't think he was some kind of predator.

"You okay, Gabby?" Gillespie said from behind him. "Who was that?"

"I don't know. Just somebody wondering what's going on, I suppose," he said. "It's not often you get anybody camping in the churchyard, is it?"

"I suppose not," he said.

"She probably thought I was some kind of predator," Cruz said, and from the corner of his eye, he saw Gillespie's head turn towards him slowly.

"A predator?"

"Yeah, you know?" he said. "Some kind of sex pest or something. A menacing beast just waiting to attack."

Gillespie was silent for a moment.

"Right," he said eventually, and slowly.

"What? I can be menacing if I want," Cruz said defensively. "Anyway, what are you doing? I thought you were keen to see the body?"

"We're not going to see the body, Gabby. It won't be opened until Pip gets it on her bench," he replied. "Anyway, they're nearly done."

"Is that it?" Cruz said. "It's over? It didn't take long, did it?"

"What do you mean? You missed most of it. And anyway, I've seen enough."

A rattle of steel castors caught their attention and they saw two men pushing a gurney, on which was a heavy sheet draped over a long, square box. The team walked in front, with Freya bringing up the rear.

"Right then," she said. "I hope that was all useful for you?"

"Aye, boss," Gillespie said, on behalf of the others.

"I'll take it from here," she said. "I'll go with the body. I want to be there when we get the evidence we need."

"I'll come with you," Ben said.

"No, you go home," she told him. "All of you get some rest. We've got a lot of work to do tomorrow and I want you all switched on. We might have our man, but we have a hell of a case to put forward to CPS, so it needs to be infallible. Every detail needs substance, every question needs an answer."

They parted to allow the men to push the gurney through the gate and out onto the roadside, and each of them watched in silence as it was loaded with care into the unmarked van.

One of the men closed the doors far more delicately than any white van man that Cruz had ever seen, and then they waited patiently for Doctor Bell.

"Right, that's my cue. Keep your phones switched on. With

any luck, by the morning, the end will be in sight," Freya said as she made her way towards her car. She stopped halfway there and turned to face them. "Oh, and Cruz?"

"Yes, boss?"

"I want you to do what Gillespie asked when you come to the office in the morning," she said, and Gillespie's face lit up briefly. "Except, in place of hot chocolates, it might be better if you bring coffees, and strong ones at that."

She climbed into her car, and then, as the van pulled away, she followed, her mind too occupied to even look their way.

"So that's it then, is it?" Cruz said. "I'm nothing more than a coffee boy."

"Not just a coffee boy," Gillespie said. "You're the most menacing coffee boy I know, Gabby."

Cruz chose to ignore him.

"Menacing?" Nillson said after each of them had looked to each other for answers for long enough. "I've seen more menacing hamsters."

Gillespie's laugh seemed to fill the quiet lane like thunder from above.

"Some lass was watching the exhumation," he said. "She ran off when Cruz popped out of the bushes."

"You jumped out on her?" Nillson said.

"I didn't jump out on anybody. I was walking through the headstones, that's all. She didn't see me coming."

"Aye," Gillespie replied. "You're a menace, Gabby. A bona fide menace."

"So," Ben said. "Shall we reconvene in the morning? I don't know about you, but I fancy getting an early night."

He addressed the team, but Cruz thought he saw something in the way he looked at Nillson while he spoke.

"Yeah," she said. "I'm looking forward to that coffee in the morning, Gabby. Can you make mine strong and black?"

"Aye," Gillespie said, checking his watch. "I've missed my date

now anyway. Might as well head home. With any luck, the Chinese will still be open."

From where he stood, Cruz continued to watch the discreet exchange of nods between Ben and Nillson, which nobody else seemed to be picking up on.

"I'll see you tomorrow," he said eventually before anybody else could get a coffee order in.

Cruz left them there and made his way towards his car, and he was just about to climb in when Gillespie called out.

"I think I'll have a hazelnut latte, Gabby," he said.

"Flat white for me," Chapman said.

"Me too," Anderson said.

He closed the door as more orders were shouted at him and then quickly checked his phone as he started his car, wondering how on earth his life could get any worse.

But it could, and it did, and it came in the form of a text message from Hermione.

CHAPTER FIFTY-ONE

"Thanks for coming," Ben said, unable to offer her any kind of warmer greeting.

"The way you've been talking, Ben, you couldn't have stopped me if you tried," she replied. He held his front door open for her to come in and then led her through to the kitchen, where the dinner he had prepared came in the form of yet another paper bag.

She smelled the air and eyed the bag.

"Chinese?'

"It was either that or Indian," he replied. "And we had that last night."

"We?"

He ignored her question and pulled two plates from the cupboard, and then unceremoniously tossed a couple of forks onto the counter beside them.

"Help yourself," he said, and she grinned broadly at how he'd avoided the question.

She took the hint and fished the cartons from the bag, and as he had hoped she would, she distributed the rice and plum duck across both plates with a friendly, "I'll be mother then, shall I?"

"Are you okay about what we saw earlier?" he asked, leading her through to the lounge, where he took a place at the small dining table.

She waited, perhaps to see if he would tell her where to sit and if he used a table mat, which he didn't, and it was only when he began to eat that she took the seat opposite him, but she didn't eat, not at first. Instead, she moved the food around with her fork, as if deciding how she should respond.

"I think it was a good move for the boss to get us all there," she said. "It was a bit boring, but if we ever have to do another, we'll know what the process is. Was it your first one as well?"

"It was," he replied. "And if I'm honest, I found it a bit morbid. Interesting, but morbid. I didn't know they built a frame around the coffin."

"How did you think they would do it?"

"I don't know. I'd never really given it thought," he said. "But I did at least know that one of them wouldn't be hopping down into the hole and giving the remains a piggyback."

She laughed, and eventually began tucking into her food.

"It's good," she said after a few mouthfuls.

"Gillespie gave me the idea," he replied. "I don't often take advice from him, but when it comes to takeaways, he has enough experience to know a good one from a bad one."

"Mrs Changs?" she asked.

"She said he's one of her best customers."

"Ben, you're procrastinating," Nillson said, dropping the friendly tone, and Ben suddenly saw what she would be like in an interview. "Just tell me what you want to say."

"No comment?" he said hopefully.

"That won't wash, I'm afraid. Not this time. And before you say it, I am not obliged to arrange legal representation either."

"Damn it," he said and set his fork down on the plate before wiping his mouth with a piece of kitchen roll. "There is some-

thing I want to discuss with you, well, not with you specifically, but I couldn't think of anybody else with a level head."

"Well, you know how to make a girl feel special, Ben, I'll give you that."

"I mean," he said, feeling himself floundering, "I trust you, and what I have to say needs discretion. No, more than that. It needs complete confidentiality. What I'm going to tell you cannot be disclosed–"

"Okay, okay," she said. "I get it. You're procrastinating again."

"Am I?" he said.

"Are you dying, Ben?" she asked as if she was asking about the weather.

"What? No–"

"Is anybody else dying? Jackie? Chapman? Don't tell me it's Gillespie."

"No, no–"

"Oh God, not the boss? Is Freya ill?"

"No, but you're getting warmer," he said, and she gave the comment some thought, saying nothing to reveal what those thoughts were. He stood and moved the chair out of his way, tossing the piece of kitchen roll onto the table. "Come with me."

If he'd waited for her, he might have changed his mind. If he had said anything else, that element of doubt might have construed some kind of delay. So, he left her there and made his way up the stairs, not looking back until he was standing outside the spare bedroom with his hand on the handle.

Curiously, she climbed the stairs but stopped just a few steps from the top.

"Ben, look, I like you and everything, and God knows when we first met I might have had some feelings for you, but–"

"The bedroom is that one," he said, pointing to the door behind him. "You can keep your clothes on."

"Thank God for that," she replied, trying to lighten the mood with a laugh. Then she must have seen hurt in his expression,

although he tried not to show it. He shoved open the door and stood to one side to let her pass.

"Don't take it personally, Ben. It's just that I can't remember what underwear I put on this morning," she said as she passed him, and he waited for her reaction. "Bloody hell."

He followed her in and found her gazing up at the wall he had spent an evening putting together.

"I thought there was something between you two, but I didn't realise you were infatuated," she said, gazing up at the various images of Freya he'd managed to find. "Ben, this is creepy. In fact, it's borderline bloody stalking."

"Read the file," he said and then dropped onto the little, wooden stool in the corner of the room.

She picked up the file that Michaela had given to him the last time he had seen her, when they'd parted company for the last time and ended what had been Ben's only true relationship for years. She opened the file and began to read, but after just a few seconds, she stopped and looked at him in amusement.

"This is years old. Look at the headed paper. Blimey, I doubt Surrey Police still use forms like this."

He said nothing but watched her expression morph from mild amusement to one of confusion.

"Archibald Bloom?" she said. "Is this the boss's dad?"

"Her uncle," he replied.

"But this is a murder investigation, from what I can see anyway."

"No, you're right. It's a murder investigation. The paperwork might have altered, but the content is the same."

"But why?" she said. "What is all this?"

He didn't need to reply, thankfully. Her mind was as sharp as his, if not sharper.

"You're not saying..." she began, unable to verbalise the dreadful thought.

"Do you remember Freya and I worked on a case in Mablethorpe a while back?"

"Of course," she replied. "The lunatic who framed the vicar for murder? How could I forget?"

"He may have been a lunatic," Ben agreed. "But he was smart. Too smart, for my liking."

"So?"

He took a breath, wondering where to start, but there was only one obvious place that would frame his motive adequately.

"He was smart enough to do his research on the two people hunting him down," he said, then explained. "Me and Freya."

"What do you mean by research?"

"I mean, he looked into us."

"So? What do you have to hide?"

"Me? Nothing. I don't think so anyway," he said. "But when Freya arrested him, they shared a moment. We were in an old, abandoned church – St Botolph's, remember? The one over by Saltfleet. Anyway, I was holding back the uniformed officers at the door while Freya dealt with him. They were close. It was as if Freya was daring him to kill her. She wasn't scared, I'll give her that much. But he said something, like he was analysing her, you know, like a psychiatrist might, as if he was trying to see inside her mind to understand why she is who she is."

"Ben, you're not making sense."

"He spoke about her as a young girl," Ben continued. "He spoke about somebody, you know, touching her."

"What? Abusing her? The boss?"

"At first the man was talking about her father, but that couldn't have been true. I've heard her talk about him, and it's clear she loved him very much."

Nillson held the file up.

"But her uncle?"

Ben nodded.

"I wouldn't have given it much credence, but there was some-

thing in the way Freya reacted, or rather, the way she *didn't* react. It was as if there was some truth in what he was saying."

"In what?" Nillson asked, and again, he mentally prepared himself to deliver the punchline. "Truth in what, Ben?"

He nodded at the file, gesturing for her to read on, which she did, scanning the summary with a practised eye.

"Bludgeoned to death," she said quietly. "Blows to the side of his head. Brain trauma."

She closed the file and let it drop to her side.

"Why are you telling me this?" she said. "Why me? I don't want to be involved in this–"

"Because I love her," Ben said, and let those words hang in the air with pungency. "There, I said it."

She put the file on the desk and took a few steps away from him to consider what she might say.

"If you read on, you'll discover that the murder weapon was believed to be a lamp or a heavy ornament or something."

"The type one might reach for when pinned to a bed, you mean?" she said, to which he gave a grave grin.

"You've answered your own question," he said. "That's why I told you. I need help, Anna. I need help to understand this. I need…"

He paused and found himself short of breath.

"Go on, Ben. There'll be no judgement from me."

"I need to know it wasn't her," he said. "I want to be with her, and I think she wants it too, but how can I when part of me thinks she bloody well killed someone?"

Nillson perched on the edge of the desk, the way Freya did so often.

"You are in a pickle," she said. "Can't you just be with her? I mean, for God's sake, don't let Granger find out, but what you do outside of work is your business."

"Can you help me?" he asked. "Even if it's just to help me carry the secret, can you help me?"

She nodded as if there was no question of her not doing so.

"Do you want my advice?" she said, to which he nodded.

"That's why you're here."

"Be with her. Enjoy life and enjoy her. You can't let the ramblings of a convicted murderer cast a shadow over what you have with her. I mean, how would he have known?"

"I don't know. Internet research I suppose."

"Have you done the same? Have you looked online?"

"Of course, I have."

"And what did you find?"

"Enough to find a few newspaper stories citing her uncle's crimes. Plus one that stated he was missing."

"How do you know it was her uncle?"

"Bloom isn't exactly a common name, and her father's family were wealthy enough to have useful allies who would be prepared to provide character references."

"And how do you suppose she managed to make DCI without somebody in the force learning of any of this?" she said. "Come on, Ben. This is madness. This is just an excuse your mind is using to avoid getting hurt."

"An excuse?"

"You're well matched, you know that? Ask anyone," she said.

"What do you mean?"

"Oh, come on, the entire station suspects it. Granger probably does too, but as long as you don't flaunt it, you'll be okay. Stay professional."

"And all this?" he said.

"Well, it's obvious you're not going to be able to let it go," she said, staring up at the wall. "So, carry on. Do your research. I'll help where I can if I can, although I don't know how. But whatever you do, do not let her see any of his."

"Yeah, I suppose it's kind of a relationship ender, isn't it?"

"Not just that, Ben," she said with a laugh. "If she is guilty, who knows what she's capable of."

He stared at her, feeling the muscles in his face tense.

"I'm kidding," she said. "She's not a bloody killer, Ben. Far from it. But if you need to prove it to yourself, then do so. But do it only for yourself. You're not doing this for anybody else, and whatever you do, don't throw away the best chance of happiness you've had for years for the sake of what that man said."

"Right," he said. "Yeah, you're right."

It felt good to have shared his secret with somebody, and he trusted Nillson with the loathsome burden. The air in the room felt cleaner, and somehow the guilt that had seemed to cling to the walls had dispersed, leaving just a room with four walls. It was not for Ben to find Freya guilty of murder, but for him to love her with no question of doubt.

"How did you get all this, anyway?" Nillson said. "Did you have to sign for this file? Because if you did, then you know Freya will get a report from the archives."

"I'm not that silly," he said. "Michaela gave it to me when we split up. A parting gift, if you will."

"Michaela? As in the crime scene investigator you were dating? You told her?"

"I was in a relationship with her. We told each other everything."

"Well, let's hope she doesn't feel the need to tell her next boyfriend everything."

"No, I don't think she'd do that. I think she's turned the page on that particular chapter forever," he said, pushing himself up and walking over to the wall. "This reminds me of the wall in the incident room."

"Speaking of which, I could have bloody kicked myself for not spotting that climbing rose. How the hell did the boss see that and I didn't?"

"Maybe because she's got the advantage over us?" Ben said, nodding at the wall.

"Oh, give over," she said, pulling the photos of the house up

on her phone and coming to stand beside him. "Maybe it's because she was looking at them on her phone, and I was looking at a couple of six-by-four photos."

"How does that make a difference?" Ben asked.

"Well, look," she said, holding the phone up for him to see. "You can zoom in on your phone."

Using her index finger and thumb on the screen, she zoomed into the older of the two images, taken by Viktor Baftiroski.

"Look, you can see the climbing rose clearly," she said, then flicked to the newer image, taken by Maxim Baftiroski, and zoomed in again. "Climbing rose is bigger."

She flicked back to the original.

"Smaller," she said. But just as she was about to flick to the newer image again to make her point, Ben saw something.

"Hold on," he said. "Show me that again."

He held the phone up closer and zoomed in as much as the phone would allow.

"There's someone in the window at the top of the house," he said, pointing out the vague shape of a man behind the glass, barely discernible in the low light.

"I wonder if that's Alex Glass," Nillson said. "Or Henry."

"That would explain why he took a photo of the house," Ben said. "He was proving that Alex Glass lived there."

Once more, Nillson flicked through to the newer image and zoomed in again.

"That doesn't make sense," she said.

"What doesn't?" Ben asked, replacing the file neatly where he had left it.

"This is Maxim's photo," she said, and he glanced up at her as she held the phone out for him to see. "If that was Alex Glass in the old photo, who's the man at the window of the newer photo?"

CHAPTER FIFTY-TWO

For somebody who seemed to spend every waking moment making the living feel awkward, selfish, or as if they have offended her, Doctor Bell gave great respect to the dead. In near silence, she watched the two men unload the van, wheel the coffin into the mortuary, and carefully heave it onto one of the stainless-steel benches. It was only when they were done, and the two men were preparing to leave, that she raised her voice enough for Freya to hear.

"Thank you, gentlemen," she said, her strong Welsh accent loud in the large open space. "Be seeing you in a day or so, I will. No doubt you'll receive instructions from our friends in blue."

She gestured at Freya, who was leaning on a nearby bench, nodding her agreement.

"That's correct," she said. "Just as soon as we have what we need. I see no need to keep him above ground for any longer."

"We have to make preparations for his wife, I believe," one of the men said, a broad individual with dark hair on the backs of his hands.

"That's right. Her body is due to be released," Freya told him and then handed the conversation back to Doctor Bell.

"She's in here?" the man said, to which the pathologist remained impassive, and then guided them towards the huge shutter doors.

"We'll be in touch," she told them, and then hit the button to close the shutters.

An electric motor kicked in somewhere high up and the shutters slowly rattled into place, coming to a stop when they were closed, leaving both Freya and Pippa in comparative silence.

They stared at each other for a moment, and then at the plywood frame that contained the soil, in which was the remains of a five-year old casket and a human body in an unknown state of decomposition.

"It might be for the best if I did this alone," Pip said, as she prepared herself a new set of PPE.

"No, I'll stay," Freya told her. "I can handle it."

"I'm sure you can. But rules are rules," Pip said, and she reached into a high-level cupboard and retrieved a mask not too dissimilar to those used in the Second World War. "And we wouldn't want to break any of those now, would we?"

Freya gestured to the empty space and overemphasised the cold drawers where only Pippa Bell knew how many bodies were stored.

"There's nobody here," she said. "And I doubt they'll tell on us."

But Doctor Bell was unmoving. Her expression didn't even crack with the faintest of grins.

"Rules," she said, rolling her R and somehow making the word sound as if it comprised two syllables. "Are rules."

"I see," Freya said, and Pip made a point of not even beginning the delicate task of opening the coffin lid while Freya was present. "I'll wait outside."

"As soon as I've got the lid off, I'll be extracting a DNA sample. You can take it to the lab if you wish. There's a new girl

there. Katy, her name is. She's agreed to process the sample overnight. Why is it you need the DNA anyway?"

"I believe I've managed to find the weapon used to kill him," Freya said. "The injuries are extremely similar in appearance. I just need to prove it's his blood."

"Very good," Pip said. "Well, like I said, you can deliver the sample yourself."

"Well, I'm glad to be useful, of course," Freya replied. "Even if it is just as a delivery driver."

"By the time you get back, I'll have exposed the skull and the injuries," Pip replied, with a long exhale. "You can join me then."

"Thank you," Freya said, and she made her way to the little door to the reception, from which she could access the rest of the hospital and the cafeteria. She stopped at the door and peered back at the doctor, who, true to form, was waiting for her to leave before she began.

The doors closed with a swish behind her, sealing in the cool air, and although the reception wasn't exactly a warm place to be, it felt almost tropical in comparison.

She took a seat and checked her phone for emails and messages, finding none, not even one from Ben. So instead, she took a moment to savour the peace and quiet, which was proving to be a rarity. The reception chairs were surprisingly comfortable. In fact, she couldn't remember ever having sat in them before. There was something quite calming about being in such close proximity to the dead, something reassuring, so that she may enjoy her thoughts with little threat of disturbance.

She found herself thinking about Ben and his recent behaviour, and she concluded, as she kicked off her shoes for comfort, that she may benefit from adopting a different approach. Maybe by simply working with him, and not trying to force his hand, the process of getting to know each other might begin again.

And it was with those thoughts that she closed her eyes.

It seemed like only seconds later that a gentle knocking disturbed her peace, and habitually, she checked her watch, finding that an hour and a half had passed.

Somebody knocked again on the doors that led out to the hospital corridor, and she stood to see who could be knocking at so late an hour.

An interruption to Pippa's work would only delay her progress, so Freya took it upon herself to open the door, after a brief check of her hair and makeup in the little mirror on the wall.

She peered through the narrow window to find a woman standing there, who Freya gauged to be in her mid to late fifties. She wore her brown hair in a tight bun, and the long coat she wore over her jeans seemed far too heavy for the season.

Freya opened the door cautiously.

"Good evening," she said, but the woman seemed to stare at her, a little wide-eyed and afraid. "Can I help you? Are you looking for something or somebody in particular?"

Again, the woman said nothing but tried to see past Freya into the reception.

"I'm afraid this area is out of bounds without an appointment," Freya told her, then pointed back up the corridor. "But you can access the hospital that way. There are signs."

"My son," she said, and Freya caught an unfamiliar accent in those two syllables. "I am here for my son."

"Your son?" Freya said, sensing she knew who the lady was but disbelieving that she could be there at that time. "I'm afraid there are no men here."

"Maxim Baftiroski," she said. "I am told he is here. Alex's son, Henry, he tell me on telephone. He tell me my son is dead."

"Sofia?" Freya said. "Sofia Baftiroski?"

At the mention of her name, the woman seemed to startle. Her eyes widened even further and she stepped back as Freya opened her warrant card for her to see, hoping to reassure her.

"I'm Detective Chief Inspector Bloom," she said. "It's okay."

"No," she replied, backing away.

"Just stay where you are," Freya said, wishing she hadn't kicked her shoes off to nap.

But whatever Sofia Baftiroski's reason for being there, it was not to speak to a detective, and when she saw Freya's bare feet, she turned and ran before Freya had a chance to stop her.

She heard the doors at the far end of the corridor slam against the walls and then bang closed, and all Freya could was look after her, wondering where she might go.

"Freya?" a voice said from inside the reception, and she turned to find Pip standing there. Pip glanced down at her bare feet. "What are you doing out there? And where are your shoes?"

"It's a long story," Freya replied, walking back into the reception and slipping into her shoes. "Do you have the sample?"

Pip held out a small glass tube with a blue, plastic lid. It was labelled and had been placed inside a clear, plastic bag.

"Right," Freya said, taking it off of her. "I'll be back as soon as I can."

"There's something you should know," Pip said, stopping Freya in her tracks.

"Go on," she said.

"I've exposed part of the skull. Not much, but enough to see a strong similarity to Maxim Baftiroski's."

"Good," Freya said. "But I'll still need the DNA to make the case—"

"There's something else," Pip said, clearly unwilling to let Freya leave just yet. "Do you remember how I knew that Maxim was not English?"

"Yes," Freya said. "The dentistry work was different, wasn't it?"

Pip nodded gravely.

"What are you saying, Pip? Please, come on. I'm on the clock here."

"I'm saying that there is a similarity between the dentistry work on Maxim Baftiroski and the teeth in the skull I have just

looked at," Pip said. "In fact, not a similarity. I'm not a dentistry expert, but from what I can see, the tooling is almost identical, as is the evidence of gum disease treatment."

"What are you saying, Pip?" Freya asked.

"I'm saying that not only do both sets of teeth share the same disease and treatment, but the manner in which the tools were used is identical. It's almost barbaric and not a practice a British dentist would carry out. I believe the victims shared the same diet, same hygiene habits, and..." she said, looking up at Freya. "I believe they shared the same dentist."

CHAPTER FIFTY-THREE

"Where are you, Ben?"

Freya's voice came through loud and clear, along with the sound of her engine being put to the test and the accompanying road noise. Ben held his breath for a moment before putting the call on to loud speaker, and signalling for Nillson to keep quiet.

"I'm just out and about," he lied, as he sat down on the bench just two hundred yards from the three cottages.

"Well, get yourself to Navenby," she said. "I'm five minutes away. I'll meet you there."

"I'm already here," he said, finding himself unable to lie.

"You are? Why?"

"I found something," he said, hoping that Nillson saw the apology in the look he gave her. "The photos from Maxim's room. There's a man in the upstairs window at the front of the house."

"In Viktor Baftiroski's photo?" she asked.

"In both," he replied. "It's too far away to see who it is, but it's definitely a man looking out. I just thought I'd come and see if I could find the spot where the photo was taken from. It might tell us something."

"Good idea," she said, not sounding one hundred per cent

convinced of his explanation. "Listen, I've got uniformed support on their way. I need you inside George Benson's house."

"What for?"

"Just get inside, will you? I can't explain while I'm driving. I don't even know if I'm right. But if I am, then we've made a huge mistake, and I just hope we're not too late."

"Right, we're on it," Ben said.

"We?" Freya said.

"I'll explain later," he said, and he ended the call, running the few steps to catch up with Nillson, who was already on her way. They jogged a little, then walked fast.

"What do you think it is?" Nillson asked. "Pippa must have found something on the body. It sounded like she had her foot down." Then she paused. "What are you going to tell her? I mean, you don't suppose she'll think that we're, you know?"

"Does it matter?" he said, as they reached the road, where they stopped to view the three cottages.

The night sky had drawn a blanket of stars over the village, and if it hadn't been for the gentle breeze swaying the black trees, they could have been staring at a painting, with the terrace of cottages in deep shadow and the moonlight reflecting off the windows.

Until an upstairs window in George Benson's house suddenly illuminated, and a figure ran past.

"What was that?" Nillson said. "Did you see that?"

"I did," Ben replied, and he started into a run with Nillson following close behind.

The roses in the front garden appeared to reach from the shadow into the light from the window as if every petal was a stroke from Rembrandt's brush, and the pruned box hedges formed an impenetrable border around the property. The gate had been left open, and they ran through it to find the front door closed and locked.

"The back," Nillson said, already moving before she had even finished speaking.

Ben took a few steps up, hoping to see some movement, but there was none, and not a sound could be heard from inside until the front door was wrenched open and Nillson was framed in the hallway light.

"You need to see this," she said, then ran back into the house.

He followed with caution and she led him into the small lounge, where he found her crouched over George Benson, who lay on the floor, unconscious, with a trickle of blood oozing from his brow.

She looked up at him, appearing as confused as he was until they heard a thud from upstairs.

"Call it in," he told her, as he ran to the stairs. "And get an ambulance."

He bolted up the stairs and stopped on the landing, which was the source of the light, and he listened for movement. But there was none to be heard. Carefully, Ben pushed open the bathroom door and peered inside, finding nothing but a dark space that smelled not too dissimilar to his father's – disinfectant masked by lavender.

The next door was a bedroom, and he flicked the light on. The room was empty, but the bedsheets had been thrown back and a small clock had been knocked from the bedside table.

One door remained, which Ben approached with caution. He pressed his ear against the wood. He heard nothing and slowly opened the door expecting to be greeted with either a flurry of movement or an open window.

Again, he flicked the light on, then sighed at what he saw.

"Nillson," he said, just loud enough that she might hear. "Nillson, I need you here."

It took only a few moments for her to climb the stairs, passing each open door with caution until she came to stand beside Ben and peered inside the room.

"Oh, for God's sake," she said, as through the window, they saw a pair of headlights come to a stop outside on the lane.

Ben found the torch on his phone and took three steps into the room until he stood at the foot of the loft ladder. He glanced at Nillson for some kind of support, and she nodded once, indicating that she was ready. Slowly he climbed, shining the torch into the darkness above as he did, praying that whoever was up there wasn't waiting, poised to strike.

But there was nobody there, and if he had been surprised by the sight of the ladder, then the sight that greeted him in the loft was truly breathtaking. He dropped down a few steps and opened his mouth to explain to Nillson when he heard a familiar voice call out from downstairs.

"Ben?" Freya said, and he heard her heels on the wooden floor. "Ben, are you here?"

Nillson stared at him, waiting for an instruction.

"Alice Glass's house," he shouted, then spoke to Nillson. "Go with her."

Without waiting for her to move, he climbed up into the loft, shining his torch across the beams to light up the wall that divided the properties, where a hole had been knocked through and the old Victorian bricks had been piled neatly to one side. He shone the light into the central property and was reminded of something Gillespie had said about the old blind woman hearing people in the house, despite being hard of hearing.

As expected, the central loft was void of people and movement, and the next wall had been knocked through in a similar fashion to the first. He leaned through into the loft belonging to Alice Glass's house, seeing dust particles dancing in the light from the open hatch. Carefully, he made his way across the beams, opened the floor hatch, and then leaned into the room below. It was exactly as he and Freya had left it, and the only item out of place was the spatter on the wall where Maxim had slumped to the floor blocking the door from opening.

He lowered the steps and climbed down. He'd just stepped onto the landing when he heard a commotion from downstairs. As fast as he could, he ran down the stairs as the front door burst open and Nillson ran into the house, followed by Freya. The three of them ran through the hallway and into the kitchen just as the back door swung closed.

"What the hell is going on?" Ben said as he shoved the door open and peered out into the night, shining his light onto the neatly pruned rose shrubs.

Freya turned and ran back through the house, calling out over her shoulder. "He's gone around the side of the house. He's heading for the field."

"Who is?" Ben said, sharing bemused expressions with Nillson before following her.

They caught up with Freya on the lane and together they ran towards the shouting and commotion. Ben shone his light on the rough ground so they wouldn't stumble, and soon it became clear where they were headed.

They slowed as they drew near to the noise, listening to the raised voices, one of which was angry, female, and most definitely Eastern European. The other was male, English, and clearly elderly.

"Sofia Baftiroski?" Ben said as they drew closer to the struggling pair. She looked up at them from where she kneeled astride a breathless man, who had reached the bench and then all but given up. A glint of light caught the kitchen knife in her hand which she held against the man's neck.

"Don't come any closer," she said, the venom in her voice accentuated by her accent. "This is not your fight."

"Who is he?" Nillson said calmly. But her body was tensed and ready to launch herself at the woman on the ground at the next safe opportunity.

"He's the man who killed her son," Freya said, casually pacing around the pair on the ground to the bench, where she sat and

crossed her legs as if she might enjoy the starlit sky above. "And he's the man who murdered her husband."

She sighed a breath of relief, loud and exaggerated for them all to understand that she was going to make no effort to stop Sofia from doing what she had come to do.

"The man who killed her husband?" Ben said, looking to see if it made any sense to Nillson and seeing only an equal amount of confusion. "Unless you mean–"

"That Alex Glass is back from the dead?" Freya said, finishing the statement for him. She stared down at the man on the ground with the knife to his throat. "Or rather, you were never really dead in the first place."

CHAPTER FIFTY-FOUR

"Are you trying to tell me…" Ben began but hesitated the way he always did when he couldn't quite articulate his thoughts in a logical order. "He faked his own death? But we exhumed his body."

He spoke as if the idea was beyond comprehension, but to Freya, it made sense. Not perfect sense, but sense enough to be the only logical solution.

"It wasn't the body of Alex Glass that we exhumed," Freya said, and Sofia slowly turned to stare at her, still clutching the blade to his throat, hard enough that a tiny trickle of blood shimmered in the moonlight. "Your husband is dead, Sofia. I'm sorry."

Even in the dim light, Freya could see the woman's chest rising and falling, and the strength of her grip waned at the affirmation of what she likely already knew but had, until now, disbelieved.

"Sofia, let him go," Ben said. "Don't make this hard on yourself."

"No," Freya said, meeting Ben's look of horror with an expression that she hoped conveyed that he should trust her instincts. "No, stay there, Sofia."

"Freya–" Ben began.

"Stay there and hear what I have to say," she continued. "And when I'm done, if you feel the need to press down on that knife, then you're free to do so."

"Freya, what the bloody hell–"

"This woman has lost her husband and her only child," Freya told him. "I don't know about you, but if I were in that position, I'd want to decide for myself if I spend the rest of my life in mourning or behind bars."

Alex Glass squirmed beneath her, and for a moment, Freya thought Sofia might release him. But instead, she tightened her grip on him and the knife, conveying to Freya with a thousand-yard stare that she'd better start talking.

Freya linked her hands behind her back and then paced a few metres until she had put the facts in order and found a suitable starting point to recount her theory.

"Mr Glass," she began, "if at any point in this, I am wrong, please feel free to correct me. I'm sure Sofia will allow you the freedom of speech while you're still able."

"Just get her off me," he hissed. "I can barely bloody breathe."

"Ah, breathing," Freya replied, as casually as she could. "Something that everybody thought you had stopped doing five years ago."

He closed his eyes and swallowed hard, causing the blade to rise and fall with the movement of his gullet.

"She's a lunatic," he said eventually. "She's going to kill me."

"The only thing Sofia is guilty of, Alex, is having an affair with you. All those years ago in Moldova," Freya said. "Tell me, Alex, was it a one-off night of romance and excitement? Or was it an ongoing thing? Did you make promises you couldn't keep?"

Sofia's face loomed over him, and when he opened his eyes, they revealed no look of lost love or regret.

"It was one night," Sofia said quietly. Her voice was almost masculine. "A night of mistakes."

"Mistakes that would not only change the courses of your lives

and those around you," Freya said, to which Sofia nodded gently
as if she knew what Freya was about to say, "but create lives. It
would create a life."

"My Maxim," Sofia whispered, her voice trailing away into the
night.

"When did Viktor learn that Maxim wasn't his child, Sofia?"
Freya asked, softly, as if she was speaking to a grieving widow
instead of a woman with a knife to a man's throat.

"Before he left," she replied, her voice faint and distant like
she was remembering the moment her dark secret had been
unearthed. "I did everything I could to keep it from him. He
didn't need to know. He was still Maxim's father. At least, he
raised him like a father. He was a good man."

"A man with pride," Freya suggested.

Sofia nodded. "Enough pride he spent every waking hour
finding the identity of the man who had wronged him."

"You didn't help him?" Freya asked. "He didn't force the information from you?"

"No," she replied. "No, Viktor was good man. He never raised
his hands to me. But he was smart man. It didn't take him long to
work out that Maxim had been conceived during the summer we
had hosted A.G Glass Refrigeration and Cooling in our home.
Alex was installing some systems for us. Good systems. British
systems. We had a cooling business in Moldova, but some of our
English customers didn't trust local suppliers, so we agreed on a
partnership."

"You had a refrigeration business?" Freya said, to which Sophia
nodded.

"Viktor sold it when he moved to the UK."

"And Alex stayed with you during this period?"

"It is not uncommon. We saw it as a way to reduce the cost
and maximise profits from the deal."

"But you paid the price for it in the end," Freya said. "And
Viktor traced Alex all the way back here. He used his connections

to land himself a labouring job nearby, from where he could devise a plan to enact his revenge."

"No," Sofia said. "No, it wasn't this way. Viktor was kind man. He was not violent man."

"So why come all this way? Why go to all the trouble of moving here?"

"He just wanted to see Alex," Sofia said, talking to Alex now as if over a cup of coffee. "He just wanted to talk to him, to tell him he knew."

"But he forced the door on Alex's house," Freya said. "That suggests he had something in mind other than a simple chat."

"Or maybe he didn't force the door," Nillson said, stepping into the circle from the shadows she had dwelled in until now. "Maybe the door was forced afterwards, to make it look like a break-in?"

"He was not violent man," Sofia said, and all eyes fell on Alex, who wet his lips with a stroke of his tongue, and sighed in defeat.

"I'd been out here in the fields," he said eventually. "There were some owlets in that oak tree. I came home and found Viktor on my doorstep. He recognised me and I recognised him. He started shouting—"

"But you couldn't let Alice hear him," Freya said. "So, you brought him here."

"Here?" Sofia said, and Freya nodded.

"To this very spot."

"I didn't know where else to go," Alex said, and his voice had taken on a helpless whine. "I didn't mean to do what I did. But I was frightened. I thought he was..."

He stopped mid-sentence to regain control over his emotions.

"It was me or him," he said softly. "I don't know why I did it. But he turned away from me. If I was going to do it then it had to be then."

The moment of thought that followed was broken by Sofia's masculine tone carrying a weighty tone.

"Tell me," she muttered. "Tell me what you did."

"I hit him," Alex said, and his chest rose as if a great burden had been lifted from his soul. "I raised my stick and I hit him, again and again. Once I had started, I couldn't stop, at least, until I couldn't hit him anymore. Until I was breathless with the effort."

Slowly, the blade slipped from his throat, and Sofia slid to the ground to kneel beside him, the knife hanging loosely in her hand.

Nillson looked up at Ben and then to Freya as if silently asking if she should remove the weapon, but with a subtle raised hand, Freya stopped her, to maintain momentum.

"I was going to turn myself in," he said. "I was ready to go straight to the police."

"But George stopped you," Freya said. "He was the only one you could talk to."

"He was the only one who knew," Alex said, making no effort to stand despite his freedom. "He was like me, you see? We were brothers-in-law. Outsiders to Alice's family. We had a bond."

"So you brought him here," Freya said. "You brought George here to show him what you had done."

"I was terrified," he said. "I didn't plan any of it."

"I don't doubt that for a minute," Freya replied. "Rarely are these crimes intentional, and yet it is these moments that define the rest of time. Whose idea was it, Alex?"

"I don't recall," Alex said. "Mine, I think. He was, that is Viktor, unrecognisable. It was only when I returned with George that I saw how much damage I had done. It was George who said that nobody would know who he was and that we should leave him there. But I couldn't. I couldn't risk it. If Alice found out about the affair, it would have killed her."

"So, you disappeared," Freya said. "George identified the body and claimed it was you, and you've spent the past five years in hiding, passing through the lofts of the cottages to visit your wife."

"We didn't think it would work. We didn't think it would go on for so long. We didn't think that–"

"Maxim would come looking for his father?" Freya suggested. "Or that Sophia would contact the business to warn you, and that Henry would see it?"

"Both," he said dryly. "Of course, she wasn't to know that I had died, and she wasn't to know that Henry would see my emails."

"So, you let him into the secret," Freya said. "And from that moment on, he was as guilty as you. The only person who didn't know was Alice."

"Oh, no," he said. "Alice knew where I was and why I couldn't come home."

"Sorry, what?" Ben said. He clearly felt that he had been a mere spectator for too long and now had a grasp on Freya's theory. "Your wife knew that you were hiding in George's house all this time? Why then would she go out in all weathers to speak to you?"

"Because the news had sent her over the edge," Freya replied for him. "She could no longer differentiate between what she was seeing and what she was imagining. You would appear in her bedroom via the loft hatch, and then you would be gone. And when she spoke about you to people, like Tammy Plant or the other villagers..." Freya said, shaking her head in disbelief.

"Say it," he hissed at her. "Say it. It's my most heinous crime."

"They didn't believe her," Freya said. "You created Mad Alice."

CHAPTER FIFTY-FIVE

"I didn't plan it," Alex Glass whined, as Sophia dragged herself to her feet, taking with her the kitchen knife. He held his hands up in defence. "I didn't plan for any of this to happen. It just sort of snowballed."

Ben kept his distance but positioned himself where he could intervene, if necessary, as did Nillson, who, from what Ben could tell, seemed to be almost willing Sophia into action.

"What, you did not think that Maxim would come looking for his father?" Sophia asked.

"I was his father," Alex said.

"Viktor was his father. It was Viktor who raised Maxim. Viktor who picked him up when he fell. Not you. It was Viktor who taught him to ride his bike, taught him to drive, to be a man. Of course he would come looking for his father one day. He was proud man. Like Viktor."

"And you helped him on his way," Freya said. "You gave him the details of the farm where Viktor worked, and most likely even helped him gain a position as a labourer. I'm right, aren't I? You gave him the head start he needed. Once he was here, all it took

was for his foreman to give him his father's belongings and Maxim could start the hunt."

"He forced it from me," Sophia said softly, then appeared ashamed. "He did not have his father's kindness or soft approach."

"He was violent against you?"

Sophia looked down at the knife in her hand, as if it held answers that she couldn't quite find for herself.

"Maxim spent some time in prison," she said, and Ben remembered the scar Pip had found on his stomach. Judging by the told-you-so look Freya was giving him, so too had she. "Nothing serious. But it changed him. It hardened him somehow. When he got out, he asked questions about his father."

"And so, you told him the truth?" Freya said, and she nodded.

"I told him about the affair. I told him Viktor was most probably dead," she said softly. "I had to. He was going to look for Viktor. I didn't want him to spend the rest of his life chasing a ghost."

"So, he knew Alex was his father and he knew Viktor was dead?" Freya said. "But how would he know Alex had anything to do with Viktor's death?"

"The photographs," Ben said, glancing at Nillson for support in what they had found while in his spare bedroom. "A photograph of the cottages showing a man in the window, which Maxim recreated, only to find the same man standing in the same window."

Freya cocked her head, as if she was reading something into that look Ben had given Nillson.

"What man?" she asked.

"Alex Glass," Ben said. "It's faint, but you can make him out in both images. We never saw it before because we were focusing on the climbing rose. So what does a man like Maxim do when he thinks he's found his father's killer?"

"He plans his revenge," Sophia said, shaking her head softly. "Which is why I contacted Alex. To warn him."

"But it was Henry who received the email," Freya said, and Ben saw in her eyes the moment a few pieces of the jigsaw clicked into place. "And that motivated him to install the doorbell camera in his uncle's house. So, he could keep an eye on who came and went."

"And no doubt gave him a reason to enlist the help of Tammy Plant and Deborah Blake," Ben added. "Unbeknownst to him, Tammy was in a relationship with Maxim. Bloody hell."

"It wasn't a coincidence," Freya said. "All Maxim had was a photo of the house. It wouldn't have been too difficult to follow Alice to Tammy's salon, and for a man like Maxim to work his way into Tammy's life, from whom he could learn everything he needed to know – how Alice enjoyed her morning walks in the field, how she lived alone. Maxim was planning this all along. He knew there was a man inside that house. He just had to get inside."

"And when he did,' Ben said, "Henry's camera picked him up, enabling you, Alex, to enter Alice's house via the loft and meet him as he climbed through the window."

"Giving you the perfect opportunity to bring the whole dark secret to a finish," Freya said. "All that remained was for Henry to take the walking stick away and for you to go back into hiding. After all, nobody could suspect a dead man of murder, however strong the motive."

Alex looked away – a silent admission of his guilt – and in the distance, the three cottages were lit by flashing blue ambulance lights. Freya gestured for Nillson to meet the paramedics and lead them to George Benson, and the spritely young DS disappeared into the dark field.

"What happens now?" Alex said.

Freya stepped forward and Ben noted the faint blue wash

across her face every second or so. She seemed to wait for Nillson to be out of earshot, then spoke quietly but clearly.

"That all depends," she said, turning to Sophia and glancing down briefly at the knife in her hand. "It depends on how Sophia wants to spend the rest of her life. God knows she has every right to kill you right here and now, and if I'm honest, I don't think I could bring myself to stop her."

"Freya?" Ben said, but she silenced him with a wave of her hand.

"But if Sophia wants to spend the rest of her life with the knowledge that everybody who had a part to play in this whole sordid affair is either dead or rotting in prison, then that's what will happen."

"Everyone?" he said.

"Everyone," Freya repeated. "You, George, and Henry."

"Henry?"

"Tell me, Alex," she said. "Who was the one person, outside of the Glass family, who knew you were still alive? Who did Alice confide in?"

"Tammy," he said dryly, his eyes wide open to the night. "She knew I was still alive, and she knew why Maxim was here."

"And tell me, Alex, if I was to send a forensics team to A.G Glass Cooling and Refrigeration, with a warrant to inspect every one of the firm's vehicles, what would I find?"

He said nothing but stared at each of them, finishing on Sophia, as if daring her to finish him.

"Your son is responsible for Tammy Plant's injuries, Alex," Freya said. "He was driving the truck that took her down. That's attempted murder in addition to the conspiracy to murder charges."

"No—"

"He'll do nearly as much time as you," Freya told him. "And as for George, harbouring a murderer for five years, plus the

conspiracy to murder charges, he'll spend the last of his days in a prison cell, just like you."

The life seemed to have been sucked from him, and Alex Glass fell back onto his elbows.

"What happens next, Sophia," Freya began, stepping away to stand beside Ben, giving the Moldovan widow room to decide, "is entirely down to you."

Sophia looked down at the knife one more time, holding it up to the moonlight, and then she peered past the blade to Alex, who lay on the ground at her mercy, his eyes wide, fear smeared across his face.

"Come on, Ben," Freya said, tugging his shirt sleeve and leading him away.

"What? Freya, we can't just leave her there with him. She's got a bloody knife."

"Sometimes, Ben..." she said, turning to him so that her face was just inches from his, her gaze fixed on his eyes as if reading his thoughts. She lowered her voice so that only he could hear her. "You have to trust in your sense of right and wrong."

"I've been under a cloud for twenty-five years," Sophia called out, and Freya gave Ben a knowing smile before looking back at Sophia, who tossed the knife to the ground. "It's time I lived my life."

CHAPTER FIFTY-SIX

The sun was a giant, orange bubble clinging to the three towers atop Lincoln Cathedral when Jackie Gold passed through the city centre, making her way along Eastgate and emerging onto Greetwell Road, where HMP Lincoln stood forebodingly opposite the sprawling hospital grounds.

There was an irony there, she had always thought, that a place filled with the hope of life and recovery, the joys of childbirth, even the easing of death, could sit beside a place where hope was a distant memory, joy was a distant memory, and life had become something entirely different.

She parked in the hospital car park, glad to have found a place close to the main entrance, and while she walked, she found herself studying the row of parked ambulances in the hope of spotting the paramedic she had ridden with when Tammy had been hit.

She imagined what it might be like to be with him. Her thoughts carried her from the casual moments in coffee shops to fancy restaurants, and then even further into the realms of intimacy.

The shape of his face was clear in her mind yet the details

were blurred by the occasion, and she hoped that, should he ever actually call her, her moment of vulnerability hadn't let her down and placed her in an awkward situation.

In just a few minutes, she was being let into the ICU where Tammy was being cared for. The little room Tammy occupied felt stuffy and warm. It was only when the nurse pulled open a tatty curtain that Jackie saw Tammy's mother asleep in the armchair, her shoes kicked off and a tartan blanket hanging from her shoulders. The sunlight roused the mother, who reached for a bottle of water before even acknowledging Jackie. She took a sip, clipped the lid back onto the bottle, and then sat up in the chair, feeling her hair in the absence of a mirror.

It was only when she had done all she could for her appearance that she spoke. Her raspy tones indicated a rough night.

"Morning."

"Can I get you a coffee?" Jackie asked. "The shop is just opening. I don't mind—"

"She woke up," she said.

Three words. Three slaps to the face that dragged Jackie from her teenage daydream.

"Sorry, what?"

"Tammy," the woman said. "She woke up. In the night, she was awake. She was talking."

"She's okay, you mean?"

"She's resting now," the nurse said. "We've given her a sedative to ease the process."

"But she's going to be okay, isn't she?"

"It's early days," the nurse said. "We'll be running tests as soon as the sedatives wear off, but until then, I suggest we let her rest."

"That's great news," Jackie said, studying Tammy's peaceful face. She turned back to the nurse who placed a hand on Jackie's arm, smiled warmly, and spoke quietly.

"Get her mother out of here, will you?" she whispered. "I have a feeling she'll come around faster if you know what I mean."

Jackie looked over at Tammy's mother, who was clinging to her daughter's hand.

"Leave it to me," she told the nurse

Then she stepped over to Mrs Plant. Gently, she took her hand from Tammy's, having to nearly pry her fingers open, and helped her to her feet.

"You need to sleep, Mrs Plant," Jackie told her, as she dropped to a crouch to help the lady with her shoes. She pulled them towards her, ready for Mrs Plant to step into, and was about to pick up her bag when she saw Tammy's belongings tucked neatly down the side of the bed – a small holdall for her clothes and the trainers she had been wearing when she had been knocked down.

"Are those Tammy's?" Jackie asked, reaching for them and holding them up.

"I did try to bring her up like a lady," she replied. "But she's always insisted on wearing trainers. Why's that?"

"No reason," Jackie said, feeling a sense of dread for the poor girl. She held the trainers up to see them in the light and the size six Reeboks woke a new smile on her face. "No reason at all."

"Is she in trouble?" her mother asked. "For stealing the envelopes, I mean. I knew it would get her into trouble again one day."

"Oh, I don't think we'll be taking it any further," a voice said, and Jackie looked up to find Freya standing there, leaning against the doorframe.

"Ma'am," she said.

"We made a few arrests last night," Freya told Jackie, being careful not to divulge details to Tammy's mother. "We covered every detail, answered nearly every question, but there were a few things I just couldn't work out." She entered the room slowly, her heels clacking on the hard floor. "It's the little details that always keep me awake at night."

"Little details like these?" Jackie said, holding the trainers up again, and Freya nodded.

"I think the only crime Tammy is guilty of is trying to make her business work by booking extra appointments for vulnerable old ladies who were just happy for the conversation, as well as keeping an eye on somebody's mother," Freya said. "And as for the envelopes, I think that, yes, she took them when she found Alice's body. But she tried to put them back. She wasn't lying in that ditch for any other reason than waiting for an opportunity to right her wrong."

"So, she's not in trouble?" Tammy's mother said.

"Far from it," Freya replied. "In fact, I'd go as far as to say that if Tammy hadn't taken those envelopes, we would never have found them in her bag, and we'd still be scratching our heads wondering who could have possibly had a motive to murder Maxim Baftiroski."

Tammy's mother looked between them, clearly confused and trying hard to conceal her hope.

"There was no envelope for Tammy, Mrs Plant," Freya said, reaching forward to touch the end of Tammy's bed. "The truth is that I believe that she's no more guilty of a crime than you or I."

"She woke up," Jackie said, mirroring those three words Tammy's mother had uttered. "She's resting, but she's going to be okay."

The news broke Freya's hardened and solemn expression, and she beamed for a moment.

"Well, that is good news," she said, letting her hand slide from the bed. She nodded at Jackie, and then Tammy's mother, before turning to walk towards the door where she stopped and held the doorframe to speak directly to Tammy. "I do so enjoy a happy ending."

CHAPTER FIFTY-SEVEN

Hitting the button to upload a final report at the end of an investigation incited a blend of emotions for Freya, rather like a fine wine containing subtle undertones.

Foremost was elation. The tiny details had all been filled in. Questions had been answered and those gremlins that played on her mind throughout the investigation had all been quieted.

Then there was the dread. The unnerving dread of what was to come. Each murder, as horrific as it may be, she knew, would not be the last. It was a fact of life. People harboured emotions, and emotions caused people to do things that they wouldn't ordinarily do. Another fact, Freya knew, most murders were not planned, and to add to that, most murders were carried out by a family member or close friend. Some would obey their conscience and hand themselves in, unable to live with themselves. Others, however, attempted to conceal their behaviour, creating complex murder enquiries and a web of lies.

There would be another, and another, and another. A sad fact of life and one which encouraged many detectives to pursue hobbies with no foreseeable end. Rebuilding a classic car was a favourite

among male detectives. She had endured many a dreary conversation with a colleague on the progress they were making on an old Triumph TR6, or an MGB, listening with feigned excitement as they discussed the trials and tribulations of restoring the carburettors or the fuel pump. The truth of the matter was that there was no end in sight. Sure, they might one day step back to enjoy the sight of a shiny classic car, but there was no doubt in anybody's mind that they would spend each weekend fettling, repairing, or tweaking something or other. And there was even more certainty they would corner some poor colleague over a drink one evening and provide minute details on how the repair was carried out.

Classic cars weren't really Freya's thing. The hobby she found most alluring was far less tangible – perfection. Perfecting her home, her life, and herself. There was no doubt in her mind that, should she reach retirement age, she would still be fettling, repairing, or tweaking some component of herself, whether that be physical or psychological. It was inevitable.

She closed the lid of her laptop, setting aside the thoughts of that unattainable goal long enough for the aroma of a far shorter achievement to tickle her senses.

And he would be arriving shortly.

She padded through to the kitchen, barefoot, and lazily stirred the contents of her new Le Creuset pan. She tasted it with a teaspoon, added a pinch of salt, and then stirred it again, reducing the heat to its lowest setting. A quick check on the tray in the oven released a cloud of steam that wafted through to the living room. The bait of her trap.

There was just time to tuck her laptop into her tote bag, rub a little French perfume on her wrists, and then light the candle she had placed in the centre of her new dining table before he rapped on the front door – his trademark three knocks.

He filled the doorway, not just with his broad shoulders and height, but with a confidence Freya hadn't seen for a while.

"I wasn't sure you'd come," she told him, a statement he chose to ignore as he followed her invitation inside.

"Something smells good," he said, wandering to peer into the kitchen.

"Good enough to eat?" she replied, and he leaned against the kitchen doorframe as a teenage boy might linger around his fancy.

"That all depends," he replied cryptically. "What is it?"

"Something French," she replied, ushering him away from the kitchen. "And it's rude to get a sneak peek."

"Manners have never been my forte."

"Take a seat, Ben," she told him, and he glanced at the table, nodding his approval at her efforts. "Wine?"

He opened his mouth to speak but Freya knew what was coming.

"And no," she said before he had the chance. "The bottle does not have a little sailing boat on it."

"I get the feeling you're growing tired of my humour."

She reached for two wine glasses, both of them bulbous in shape and thin-stemmed, then poured a polite amount in each before stepping out of the kitchen and handing him a glass. She raised her own in a toast and Ben stopped himself from clinking glasses. Instead, he looked her in the eye, lifted his glass slightly, and then took a sip.

"You're learning," she said. "There was a time when you would clink glasses and gulp down a mouthful."

"I still do," he said. "Just not when I'm in the company of the etiquette police." He took a seat from where he could view her and crossed his legs, toying with the stem of the glass as he did. "You didn't come in today."

"Very observant," she said. "You'll make a good detective – one day."

He grinned but knew better than to engage in a battle of wits and sharp tongues.

"You were missed," he said finally.

"By whom?"

"All of us," he said flatly and without hesitation. "The team has been through a lot in recent months, but I think it's fair to say you've won their hearts."

"All of them?" she replied, stepping back into the kitchen to add a quick blast of heat before removing the sauce from the hob.

"All of them," he called out. "You also missed out on gossip."

"Oh, Ben. You know me. I'm not one for gossip. I have enough trauma in my own life to be concerned with the lives of others."

"Hermione has left Cruz," he said. "The poor bloke was in pieces today."

"Did you send him home?"

"I did," Ben said. "I also put him forward for a defensive driving course to cheer him up. I hope you don't mind."

"But he doesn't drive anywhere. He works with Gillespie."

"Precisely," he said, and she leaned out of the kitchen to find him grinning from ear to ear.

"Gillespie has always wanted to go on that course," she said.

"Precisely," he said again, which Freya gave a moment's thought, then joined in his success.

"Well then, I approve. It's about time that lad had something to look forward to. Can you imagine having to work with Gillespie every day? We only see him for a few hours which, for me, is plenty."

"Nillson has a new man too," he said.

"Oh? I always thought she was gay."

"Why would you think that?"

"I'm not sure," Freya said. "Who is he?"

"It's a secret," Ben told her. "If I know her like I think I do, she'll keep it under wraps until the morning she walks down the aisle."

"Oh," she said, slipping back into the kitchen. "Well, if that's

her prerogative. He's a lucky man, that's all I have to say. Brave, but lucky."

"And Gold has a date with the paramedic who attended Tammy Plant's accident," he said. "She sounds quite keen on him."

Freya plated up the dishes she had prepared, then added two tablespoons of the gravy across the meat, finishing with a wipe of the plate edges and a sprinkle of parsley as a garnish.

She placed the two plates down on the table, then fetched her wine and took the seat opposite Ben.

"Love is in the air," she said, and once more she raised her glass in toast. "To romance. Long may it keep us young."

"To romance," he said, joining her in raising his glass before taking a sip and then admiring the dish. "Sausage and mash?"

Her grin revealed fresh, white teeth, and the tip of her tongue emerged to moisten parted lips.

"I couldn't quite lower myself to your standards, Ben," she told him. "This is chicken fricassee with pomme purée topped with a rich, red wine gravy."

"So, chicken and mash then?"

"I suppose it is," she said. "In some odd way. It is what you asked for, after all."

"And you aim to please, do you?" he said. "And am I to be on guard for some kind of favour request in return?"

"My generosity does not come at a price, Ben. You know that better than anybody," she replied. "But as it happens, I would like to ask for your help in something."

"I see," he said, mixing the gravy into his puree. "Don't tell me, you need your shackles fixing to the dungeon wall?"

"It's an investigation," she said, rising above his childish wit. "Something personal."

"An investigation? Does the force not supply you with enough investigations to keep that busy little mind of yours occupied?"

"Somebody is out to get me. To damage my career, I think,"

she said, taking a moment to sip at her wine. "I don't have the details yet, but if you're game, I'd like to enlist your help. If I may? I know you do so enjoy gathering dirt on people."

"What does that mean?" he said, rather defensively. "What dirt have I gathered?"

"Cruz, Nillson, and Gold," she replied. "You've been in my house for ten minutes, during which time you've gossiped on all three of them."

"Oh," he said. "Oh, I see. Well, it's not really gossip, is it? It was an open discussion, which you would have been involved in if you'd graced us with your presence today."

"So?" she said, savouring the flavours of the chicken.

"So what?" he replied.

"So, will you help me?" she said, setting down her cutlery for a moment and leaning forward to read whatever thoughts his eyes revealed. "Will you be my partner in crime and help me?"

"You're referring to the thing with the car the other day?"

"And a formal complaint made against me by a uniformed officer," she replied.

"Partners in crime?" he said thoughtfully.

"Partners in crime," she repeated, and he collected his glass by the bowl instead of the stem, a habit she would have to correct at a later date.

"I have one condition," he said, leaning forward so their faces were mere inches apart.

"Which is?" she said, studying those parts of him she so enjoyed – the Roman nose, the square jaw, and even the rough, unshaved stubble that accentuated his dark features.

"It's more of a perk of the job than a condition if I'm honest," he said, his gaze flitting from her lips to her eyes and back again.

"You've been working on your powers of intrigue," she said, and somehow, they closed the gap between them. "You'll be pleased to know that I accept your conditions, Mr Savage. You've got the job. That is, if you accept?"

"Oh, I accept," he said. "When can I start?"

They lingered there for a few seconds, both savouring the moment that they had been on the edge of for far too long.

Freya turned her head to one side slightly, holding his gaze while she blew out the candle.

"Immediately," she replied. "You can start this very second."

The End.

INTO DEATH'S ARMS - PROLOGUE

The early morning walk was the bane of Kyle's existence. It wasn't even his dog he had to walk, yet whether by Faye's skilled manipulation or his desire to avoid an argument he went along every morning, trudging through through the village, into trees, down the hill, and then along a little way so that when they climbed the hill they emerged on the far side of the village.

It was a pointless exercise, made even more laborious by having to go down the hill only to climb it fifteen minutes later, and to top it off, the dog didn't care if they went near the hill. He had usually done his business within five minutes of being outside, which Kyle then had to carry for the remainder of the walk.

"You're quiet," Faye said, as they passed the last of the houses in the village and entered the woods that lined what the locals referred to as the Lincoln Edge; a steep escarpment that runs south from Scunthorpe through Boothby Grafoe, like a scar on the otherwise flat and fertile farmland.

"Am I?" He replied, making little effort to sound enthused.

"Have I upset you?"

"I've been awake for ten minutes," he replied. "I haven't had a coffee, I haven't cleaned my teeth, and in fact I think these are

the first words to leave my mouth today, so how on earth could you have upset me?

"I don't know," she said. "You just seem quiet."

"Should I sing?" He said. "And if so, what would you have me sing?"

She smiled at his rhetoric, her eyes tracking Bramble the overweight and undertrained Labrador as he burst from the bushes and into the trees as if he'd never been there before. Surely the poor sod shared Kyle's sentiment and was bored of the same old walk every morning.

The evening walks were a little better for two reasons. The first reason was that Faye was rarely back from work in time to join them, so he could avoid the ridiculous hill, walking a slightly longer but flatter route that happened to take them past the second reason; The Tempest Arms. It was, of course, rude not to pop in and support the local businesses, which was all the excuse Kyle needed.

"Beyond the Sea," she replied. "I always enjoy it when you sing that one. You do a good Bobby Darin."

"Well, I might need a coffee before I attempt that," he grumbled, then found her watching after Bramble again and saw the reason he came on the bloody walks; the love and kindness in her eyes as she watched Bramble barking at a squirrel in a tree.

Regardless of how much he loathed the morning walks, she adored them. It was their time together, she had told him on numerous occasions. Time for them to discuss things if his mood allowed, or just to be out together if, like today, it should not.

"I've been things about this cost of living crisis," she started, which he recognised as both a tease into a conversation he didn't want to have and the premise of one of her ideas. It was, in his own words, a marital trap. Should he ignore her, she would only fall into silence for the remainder of the day, finding some other means with which to ruin his empty day. Should he enter into the conversation and agree to go ahead with whatever deranged plan

she had constructed then he would likely be setting himself up for either endless phone calls and correspondence to facilitate her plan, or endless phone calls and correspondence to reverse the failed idea, or both. But should he enter into the conversation yet decide to oppose the idea, he would risk being ignored and berated for an indefinite period of time.

"Ah, I wouldn't pay too much attention to all that," he said. "We've plenty to live off."

"It's all over the news, Kyle. I don't think we can just ignore it."

"Listen, love, there may be a cot of living crisis for the youngsters who are struggling to get by, but we've had our day. The house is paid for, my pension is enough for both of us and we still have your little job at the library for anything extra."

"I know but I was thinking-"

"We're okay, Faye," he told her. "Blimey, if I thought we were in trouble I'd have said something wouldn't I?"

"Well yes, but-"

"And I wouldn't have let you book that bloody cruise either, would I?"

"I suppose," she said, a little deflated.

"Well then, let it go," he said. "Leave the worrying to the youngsters, God knows we've had our fair share."

"I just thought that we could shop around for our electricity and internet. You know, shave a few pounds off here and there. Gloria does it and she managed to bring her monthly bills down by fifty pounds."

"Darling, you spend fifty pounds on having your hair done every month, plus whatever it is you pay for your nails. If you want to save a few quid, why you start shopping around for a new hairdresser?"

"That's not fair," she said, apparently taking the comment to heart far more than Kyle had intended. "I've been using Janice for years. I can't change now. What if she found out?"

"Well, we've been with our electricity company for years," he replied, as he stepped over a fallen branch and began his descent a few yards behind her. "I dread to think what they would say if we told them we were going elsewhere."

"It's not the same and you know it," she said. "Janice has two kids to feed, not to mention a husband who-"

She stopped mid-sentence, which Kyle took as a sign she was about to say more about Janice's husband, Steve, than she had intended.

It took a few seconds for Kyle to catch her up, and he came to stand beside her as she peered out into the trees.

"Go on?" he said. "What about Steve? What's he done now?

But Faye said nothing, her eyes were wide, and before Kyle could find what had caught her attention in amongst the trees, she let out an almighty scream that sent the birds scattering from the canopy above.

ALSO BY JACK CARTWRIGHT

Secrets In Blood

One For Sorrow

In Cold Blood

Suffer In Silence

Dying To Tell

Never To Return

Lie Beside Me

Dance With Death

In Dead Water

One Deadly Night

Her Dying Mind

Into Death's Arms

Join my VIP reader group to be among the first to hear about new release dates, discounts, and get a free Wild Fens Novella.

Visit www.jackcartwrightbooks.com for details.

VIP READER CLUB

Your FREE ebook is waiting for you now.

Get your FREE copy of the prequel story to the Wild Fens Murder Mystery series, and learn how DI Freya Bloom came to give up everything she had, to start a new life in Lincolnshire.

Visit www.jackcartwrightbooks.com to join the VIP Reader Club.

I'll see you there.

Jack Cartwright

A NOTE FROM THE AUTHOR

Locations are as important to the story as the characters are; sometimes even more so. It's for this reason that I visit the settings and places used within my stories to see with open eyes, breath in the air, and to listen to the sounds.

I have heard it said that each page should feature at least one sensory description, which in the age of the internet anybody can glean from somebody else's photos, maps, or even blog posts.

But, I disagree.

I believe that by visiting locations in person, a writer can experience a true sense of place which should then colour the language used in the story in a far more natural manner than by simply providing a banal description which can often stall the pace of the story.

However, there are times when I am compelled to create a fictional place within a real environment. For example, in the story you have just read, any resident of the village will know that no such lane exists (at the time of writing), at least, with three terraced cottages overlooking a field with a bench.

The reason for this, is so that I can be sure not to cast any real location, setting, business, street, or feature in a negative light;

nobody wants to see their beloved home described as a scene for a murder, or any business portrayed as anything but excellent.

If any names of bonafide locations appear in my books, I ensure they bask in a positive light because I truly believe that Lincolnshire has so much to offer and that these locations should be celebrated with vehemence.

I hope you agree.

Jack Cartwright.

AFTERWORD

Because reviews are critical to an author's career, if you have enjoyed this novel, you could do me a huge favour by leaving a review on Amazon.

Reviews allow other readers to find my books. Your help in leaving one would make a big difference to this author.

Thank you for taking the time to read *Her Dying Mind*.

COPYRIGHT

Printed in Great Britain
by Amazon

46422912R00223